SALVATION

Book 7 of the One True Child Series

Liminal Books is an imprint of Between the Lines Publishing. The Liminal Books name and logo are trademarks of Between the Lines Publishing.

Cover design by Cherie Fox

Between the Lines Publishing
9 North River Road, Ste 248
Auburn ME 04210
btwnthelines.com

First Published: April 2020

Original ISBN (Paperback) 978-1-950502-23-3

Second edition:
ISBN: (Paperback) 978-1-950502-93-6
ISBN: (Ebook) 978-1-950502-95-0
ISBN: (Hardcover) 978-1-950502-94-3

SALVATION

Book 7 of the One True Child Series

L.C. Conn

Other Books by L.C. Conn

The One True Child Series
Sentinels (Book 1)
Domination (Book 2)
Awakenings (Book 3)
Guardians (Book 4)
Redemption (Book 5)
Watcher (book 6)
Salvation (Book 7)

See what they are saying about....

Sentinels:

"An excellent beginning to a fantasy epic. From page one, you'll be swept up into this battle of good and evil with all of creation at stake."

         – San Francisco Book Review

"…we are committed to following this exceptional opening to a world that seduces our imagination and provides sensitivity to that state of awakening. An excellent overture!" - Grady Harp, The San Francisco Review of Books

Domination:

"Once more, Conn weaves her spell and we are immersed in Carling's spectacular world. Adventure, magic, and romance leave us hungry for more!"

         – San Francisco Book Review

"Fantasy is alive and well and exerting its power to enchant and beguile in this novel of foretold destiny." – US Review of Books

Awakenings:

"Once more, Conn gives the modern young female reader a heroine to look up to. Her prose is accessible, and her storytelling skills shine brightly, leaving us waiting for more in books to come." — Manhattan Book Review

"…a sensitive examination of the coming of age time of each of our lives but takes that discovery/recognition sequence into the realm of

philosophy, a survey of good versus evil/chaos versus order and the permutations those poles have on each of us."

- Grady Harp, The San Francisco Review of Books

Guardians:

"Friendship, family, and fate all play a part once more in book four of Conn's engrossing One True Child series. The best thing about this book? The fact that it isn't the last!"

— Manhattan Book Review

"…this exceptional world that seduces our imagination …a very fine series."

- Grady Harp, The San Francisco Review of Books

Redemption:

"A wonderful continuation of the gripping fantasy saga begun in Sentinels. I've loved seeing the expansion of this world and can hardly wait to see what the sixth book brings."

-- Seattle Book Review

Dedicated in memory of my mother

"Aroha"

Aroha is a word and name found in New Zealand Māori culture and is most commonly translated as 'love.' But the word holds more meaning than just that one idea.

It is a word that encompasses all five senses, the ego, and the intellect.

It means the breath of life and creative force of the spirit.

It assumes that the universe is abundant and that there are limitless possibilities.

It seeks to draw out the best in people and reject greed, aggression, and ignorance.

Aroha encourages and nurtures actions that are kind and full of love.

Go with Aroha and may your lives be blessed.

Chapter One

As she stared out of the kitchen window, drinking her coffee, Claire Drummond was feeling a little pensive. There was something happening up at the stones that sat on the hill behind the cottage, hidden away in a valley in the highlands of Scotland—her adoptive home. For days now she had felt the changes slowly emerging and spreading out to encompass its surroundings, including the old house in which she now stood. If she were asked how to describe it, Claire honestly did not think she could give a coherent answer that anyone would be able to understand. It was just a feeling.

Claire and her husband, Matt, now lived in the house that had been the home of his mother and grandmother. They split their time between Glasgow—where they both worked at the university—and the small hidden valley. But the cottage always felt more like home to her. Having been born and raised in New Zealand—which Claire still loved fondly—Scotland was where she felt she belonged and needed to be. There was a connection to the land, especially the valley, that she had never felt anywhere else.

Looking back over her life, she was in awe at how much it had changed since she discovered the beginnings of her Abilities at the age of seventeen. The many Talents that were once buried deep inside had grown from the initial two: Hide and Flight. Claire had been born into a very special group of people; so too her husband and their children. Her studies in the library in the outbuildings of the farm had revealed a rich history and insight into this group, more than she could ever have hoped.

Claire and her family were descended from an ancient race of people, the first to live in these lands, and created by the Guardians. These people had openly used their Abilities until it was necessary to hide them away, as the rest of the world came to their shores. Claire had read with fascination the references to the Guardians of the lands, the creators of this world and now, three new names she had discovered: Coimheadair, Ancient Ones, and more importantly the name they called themselves, Sentinels. She had just finished reading an account of an old creation story that had fascinated her and was still wondering if it were true or just some fanciful way of explaining how things had come to be. The Guardians were real—of that she was certain; she had seen and spoken to them herself.

Claire had emerged from the library with new wonder, and as always, she looked up to where the two hills joined behind the house. The large upthrust of rock was clearly visible and standing guard as it hid the stones, marking where the brook started with the spring at the top and tumbling down the rocks into the length of the valley.

She placed the still warm, empty mug down on the bench and looked at the brook once more. It sparkled under the weak winter sun that had managed to push its way through the clouds. According to the story, the spring at the top had been opened by an Ancient One to give water and life to the family of People who would guard the stones. Before she knew what she was doing, Claire was out of the house and flying through the air, finding herself already halfway up the hill. She rose up and landed carefully beside the spring. It burbled and bubbled up from the depths under the hill, tumbling down the first few rocks and disappearing over the edge.

Kneeling down, she plunged her hand under the cold water and lifted it to her lips. It tasted sweet and crisp. Claire stood and slowly, almost hesitantly, made her way around the guarding rock. They stood as they had done since the beginning of time, tall and straight; they were dark pillars, with only the clinging lichen giving any hint as to how old they really were. The standing stones still called strongly to her; she could feel their vibrations and the anticipation of her touch. She felt the energy swirling around and inside them as they reached out for her, pulling her closer. They had always healed and calmed Claire in her times of need.

Now she reached out her hands that had aged since the first time she had touched the stones. The energy immediately raced through her fingers and into her body; it filled her up and she felt revitalized. The energy surged and Claire felt the stones searching, seeking more of her. It was a frightening feeling. With great effort she pulled her hands away from the dark stone. Always she was wary of touching them for too long, afraid of being lost to them. She walked around the outside of the circle, touching each one briefly as she went.

This time as she walked it was different. The peace she normally felt was interrupted by voices. Faintly the murmuring came to her as if carried on a breeze from far away, She frowned as she tried to hear them, only for it to slip away each time, just as she thought she could make out what they were saying. Reaching the entrance stones, she stopped in the gap. Very rarely did she step inside the circle. The last time had been with her family when Aroha, her niece, had been given the blessing of the Guardians of the north and south. It was also when Claire had pulled the evil from Aroha that had lain hidden away in the depths of her soul, something she had inherited from her great-grandfather.

Stepping through the entrance, Claire made her way to the centre of the circle. She stood and looked around her. The change she had felt grew and increased in intensity. It was urgent now. So much so that she wanted to turn and leave. It felt expectant and weighed heavily on her, holding her in place.

From around the rocks a procession came, seven beings. All were dressed in dark hooded cloaks that covered them from head to toe, concealing their faces, hands, and feet in the dark shadows of the heavy robes. They entered the circle in single file and arranged themselves around her, standing in the gaps between the large stones. Claire did not fear them; she knew they were the Guardians.

"Greetings to the One True Child," they called in unison.

"My greetings to the Guardians of these lands," she replied.

"Carling." One of the figures stepped forward, greeting her with the name she had been told was hers. "You once asked that we give you an explanation of what has happened to you."

"I remember. It was shortly before I disposed of Marcus's remains," Claire said, nodding.

"It is now time that you know everything. That you were made aware of who and what you truly are. The many lives you have lived down the ages have been hidden from you, your actions and deeds only hinted at and drawn on when those skills were needed. You are so much more than just a wife, mother, and scholar. You are the Protector, the Staff and Sword of Order. Your spirit born from two who stand here and sent out into the world to guard against the darkness."

"I don't understand. What do you mean, 'born from two who stand here'? I knew my parents. Part of them is still with me in my mind."

"We know. We helped them be there so that they could guide and continue to love you," the figure said gently. "The time for your education to begin is now, Carling. It is time for you to come into your full potential in order for you to act as Guide and Protector to the Ultimate One, to help her achieve her goal. It has been written in the Book of Destiny and cannot be erased."

"The Ultimate One is Aroha, my god-daughter?" Claire asked, seeking confirmation to what she already suspected about her niece.

"Yes, it is she that the world has been waiting for. The Universe has sent her daughter to us."

"What is the task that lies ahead of her?" Claire asked, feeling anxious for her niece.

"That will be part of your education," another cloaked figure said in a deep male voice.

Claire looked at each of the Guardians present; they all stood upright, taller than her. Never once had she glimpsed what was hidden in the depths of those cowls.

"When does my education start?" she asked them.

"When Galen arrives." A third figure stepped forward, referring to Matt's true first name. "He will need to be with you. You need to draw on his strength and his love as it has always been between you. That is the reason my son was born."

"That is tonight," Claire said quietly, biting her lip a little.

Yet another figure spoke now, in a woman's voice this time. "It is the reason we called you up to the stones. There is so much you must learn, so much you must understand and not one piece can you doubt or reject. The writings in the library are all true, Carling. They were made so that you could read them now, to prepare for tonight. We cannot lie; it will be hard on you, and maybe a little painful. But the time is coming when you need to use everything you have learned over all your lives to survive and protect Aroha."

"You have told me in the past that you are the Guardians. But you are so much more, aren't you?" she asked them.

"We are, Carling, and so are you," the first figure said. "We must leave now and will meet you here tonight. You will know when it is time. Galen is not far away."

Slowly the host of beings began to file out of the entrance to the stones and Claire was left in the middle as she watched them disappear around the rocks. All she could hear was the wind as it wound around the stones and the lonely, haunting cry of an eagle on the wing, high up in the cloud-strewn sky above.

Claire made her way back down the hill, taking her time as she pondered on the Guardians' mysterious words. She recalled the texts she had been deciphering and flicked through the pages in her mind. It was part of the Abilities she had acquired—understanding their ancient language. It was knowledge that she had shared with her father-in-law, and with his help she had made great inroads into the myriad of volumes in the family library.

Walking around the house to the front, she saw a car making its way up over the rise in the track that led to the ford and the main road beyond. She waited by the door of the cottage for it to arrive and smiled broadly as her husband got out. Claire ran to him and flung her arms around his neck. Matt Drummond was tall; his dark hair now showing traces of grey and the beard he had grown was now almost completely white. He was still the most handsome man to her, still so full of life and love. Claire clung to him.

"Hey, what's up?" he asked, pulling away. He placed his hands on the side of her face, leaned down and kissed her gently. He could always tell when something had happened.

"Just when I thought I was free to live my life, they called me back," she told him.

"They said… They told you that you were free."

She could see the agitation growing in him. His hands dropped from her face and he stepped back from her embrace.

"We have to be at the stones tonight. Apparently, I have to finish my education and I get to learn who I am."

"But we know who you are. They told you that your tasks were done!" Matt said, a little forcefully.

He reached out and took her hand. They walked together into the house and headed to the kitchen, which always felt warm and comforting. The traces of Matt's grandmother were still there, and Claire had never tried to erase them.

"They want me to guide and protect Aroha as she faces her own tasks," Claire informed him.

"This is not fair, Claire," Matt growled. "You have already done so much for them. You have done everything they asked, and it almost destroyed you. They ask too much!"

The deaths of Jack and his father Marcus had affected her greatly, as had the ordeals that Marcus had put Claire and their family through. They were things that they had not spoken of for years; the memories were still too painful, and they had actively sought to suppress them.

She leaned up against the bench and looked out of the window up to the hill. Matt came up behind her, slipping his arms around her waist, his lips seeking the spot between her neck and shoulder.

"They want so much from you," he whispered to her. "I fear they want your life, that you will leave me behind. I can't live without you, Claire. I love you."

Claire turned in his arms and wrapped her own around him. "I love you, too. I couldn't have done what I did back then without you, without knowing how much you love me and feeling it within my heart. I still feel the rose that you created for me; it still surrounds my heart and protects me. It fills me with love and hope every day."

"That is not just my love, but everyone's."

"But the rose and dewdrop from your tear is from you. It is the source of my strength and my love."

"I guess we must go, then, and find out what they want," Matt said, seeming resigned to the fact. "I'm pleased that they want me there too. In the past they have kept me in the dark and I've been floundering around trying to help you."

"I know they have. I will make sure they include you in this; you have every right to know. Our lives are shared. We are one," she told him and kissed him again.

Standing in the centre of the circle, the couple waited. Beyond the stones the wind and rain that blustered in the darkness did not affect them. Inside it was calm and warm. Matt clasped her hand in his and was growing impatient. Claire turned to face him, her arms going about his waist as she drew him into her. He looked down at his wife and smiled, his bright blue eyes sparkling in the fleeting moonlight and showing the love he felt for her. He reached up and pushed her blond hair away from her face and kissed her.

There was no need for words, they had been together for twenty-eight years and knew each other too well. The connection between them ran deep inside their minds and was unbreakable. Claire rested her head on his chest and closed her eyes, taking comfort from his arms and his presence. Memories of their times at the stones came floating up and she smiled at the ones that meant the most to her.

"Claire," Matt said, softly bringing her out of her memories.

Pulling away from the warmth of his body reluctantly, she watched the Guardians enter the circle. Each figure took their place once more in the gaps between the large stones and faced the couple. With increasing nervousness Claire waited for the Guardians to begin.

"Greetings to the One True Child, daughter and sister of the Sentinels, Staff and Sword of Order, Guardian of the Stones and wife of Galen the Protector," one of the hosts proclaimed, as he stepped forward from his place.

"My greetings to the Guardians of the lands," Claire said.

"Greetings to Galen of the Boar, Protector and husband of the One True Child," another said, moving forward.

"Greetings to the Guardians of these lands," Matt said, his voice showing how unsure he felt in his response.

"That is a lot of titles and some I have never heard before," Claire spoke to the first.

"The time for all knowledge is now. What once was hidden and kept from you will now be laid out and revealed, Carling," he replied.

"Before we begin, there is something I must ask," Claire interjected quickly, her hand still clasping that of Matt's.

"If it is within our Abilities to grant it to you, Carling, then we shall," the first Guardian told her.

"I ask that the knowledge is also passed on to Galen," she requested, using her husband's real name. "He has a right to know what I do. We share everything, and we are one."

"My son shall know what you do as far as your joined history together. But there is still knowledge that my son will not be able to comprehend or understand. I do not intend to insult you, Galen, but some of the knowledge is specific for Carling to do with her Abilities," the first Guardian replied.

"I understand, Guardian," Matt inclined his head.

"I thank you, Guardians." Claire bowed her head to them.

"Carling and Galen, it may pay that you sit. I fear that the knowledge will be weighty and hard for you," spoke yet another figure with a gentle feminine voice.

The couple sat facing each other, legs crossed, and hands held together. Their knees were touching, and Claire couldn't tell if it were her hands that were shaking or Matt's. She gave him a small smile of encouragement and closed her eyes.

The Guardians' chanting started slowly and quietly, rising in tempo and volume. Some of the words Claire understood and recognised as a blessing. The words then formed a request from a higher being than the host gathered, to grant knowledge to the couple. The pressure inside her mind increased as she saw her beginnings here in the stones. Claire witnessed her birth from a great being clothed in sunshine yellow, surrounded by others in multiple hues. Lights under their skin swirled as a storm raged overhead and around the stones. The scene shifted before her, showing Carling as a child with golden hair, her small hand clasped in that of a tall boy with bright blue eyes. Claire recognised the spirit of her husband. They had been destined for each other from the moment of her conception.

Deeds played out before her, travels and people. Marveling as she recognised the spirits of so many, linking them with those she knew in this life. They had followed her down through the ages to be at her side, to support and love her. So many were there her mind began to rebel at the enormity of it and a flash of pain seared through her.

"Peace, Carling. Accept it," a gentle voice called to her. It was familiar and she relaxed under its smooth tones.

The imprisonment of Chaos was before her. The crystal cave and its bright light she understood. Order was still standing guard over her brother, who was bound to two large pillars of pure clear crystal that pushed their way up through the floor of the cave.

The scene changed quickly. She saw the lives of her children and that of her husband, the love she felt for her ultimate parents, and the Guardians. She saw them once more transform into the seven great trees to stand guard around the sacred lands.

Another life rose to meet Claire. Another called Carling. The same in every single way. The house which sat over the water, flames leaping from the thatched roof and the roar that frightened the small child, the fire that claimed her family. The scene changed and once again she saw the spear as it pierced her grandmother, the blood and the sound of her cries. The man who had taken her and who wanted to possess her. The hazel eyes, the face the same as the Marcus Claire had known, only younger. She saw the evil begin to take hold of his soul, to forever hold him captive.

She saw the great fire she had caused at the Roman fort and the final battle. Galen killing the man, the first Marcus, as he cried out for him to do so. The darkness had not fully possessed his soul; there was a part that was still human and capable of love. Claire also understood where that love had come from: the Guardians.

The aftermath of the great fire and the life as she lived it with Galen and their children on the side of the mountain. The broch she recognised, the little village she knew and had helped to rediscover, and had dug the stones from the earth with her own hands. The pendant Matt had found, with the image of a boar, the one she had once worn at her throat, the work of her husband Galen. It all came to her and she smiled at the memories.

Other lives she had lived: in the area around Loch Tay; some later on, further afield in America. She saw the lines of their children who had travelled far and wide across the world, so many now. One she recognised and she stood before her spirit—that of Maddison, her chosen brother Tony's first wife.

She saw her own home. The small settlement in the valley in New Zealand. The stones as they had once stood at the head of the gully, green stones from the ground, polished and gleaming in the southern sun. She felt the Sentinels of the south as they gathered there, joining their energy to that of the north as they imparted all their knowledge.

With the memories finished, it was now time for the truth. In the darkness of her mind, in a small corner, where the glow from the crystal that was the facilitator for her Abilities could not reach, she found herself. It was there that Claire tried to centre herself and accept the new memories.

From the shadows of that corner came another to stand in front of her. Identical to herself in every way except for golden points of light which danced and swirled under her skin. Her hair was the same, her eyes the same shade of blue. Dressed like one of the Sentinels she smiled at Claire.

"We are one," the woman said.

"I take it you are the one I call Crystal?"

"I am. It was necessary for the Sentinel side of us to manifest itself in such a way. It was too early for us to understand and accept it. Our first life showed us that the human side would take a little convincing."

"This is what the Sentinels look like?"

"It is. They were born of the light of Order, although for ourselves we were born from the bodies of Yellow and Blue."

"This is a lot for us to take on, Carling," Claire said to her twin.

"It is, Claire, and there is more. All the Abilities must now be released. It will be painful as our mind grows to accept them. To do this, Claire, we must wake from here and open ourselves up to the Stones. Do not be afraid of losing ourselves to them, they will not absorb us. The energy we have felt inside the stones is that which has been stored for us, to draw on at this moment."

"We shall trust in the knowledge that is stored in your side of our spirit," Claire told her glittering twin.

"Are we ready?"

"We are ready," Claire nodded and opened her eyes.

Matt was sitting watching her, still clasping her hands in his own. His bright blue eyes widened as he came to terms with his own history and that of his wife.

"The time is now, Carling," one of the male Sentinels intoned. "Open yourself to the stones and take the knowledge that is yours. Use it well and protect the world and the Ultimate One. The task is yours to take on and once more we ask you to be the Staff and Sword of Order."

"I accept the task," she told them and turned to Matt. "I must do this, Galen, it is the reason I was created."

"I understand, Claire. And where you go, so do I, as your support, love, and protector."

"We cannot touch you, Carling, while you are communing with the Stones. This task is for Galen to support you. You must hold her onto the stones, my son, and do not let her release until it is time."

"I understand, my Ancestor," he nodded to the Sentinel.

"I'm ready," Claire told him, and he walked with her to the largest of the stones.

Standing in front of it and feeling very small in comparison, Claire could sense the knowledge already reaching out to her. She raised her hands and placed them on the flat, hard surface and found it warm to the touch. It vibrated with energy as it started to impart knowledge, releasing all the Abilities and so much more. In her mind a bell began to toll; it was a sound she had heard before at the stones and the understanding of where it came from washed over her. The Universe herself was giving Claire her blessing.

When Claire was first granted access to some of her Abilities, she had trouble controlling the influx of information. It was the same feeling she was now experiencing. Everything around her was blocked out, including the feeling of Matt holding her.

"Let it in and do not try to control it. Accept it," the calming voice told her.

"We are trying to," Claire replied, gritting her teeth. She forced herself to relax, and the pressure eased some.

Beads of sweat appeared on her brow as she concentrated on the knowledge. Her body shook with the force and weight of it. Matt held his wife tightly and was amazed at the capacity she had. He noticed small points of lights flickering to life just under the skin of her hands. They spun and swirled as they made their way slowly up her arms. Looking around at the Sentinels who stood guard over them, he was concerned and sought their guidance.

"The side that has been hidden from her, she is now accepting, my son. Keep her there, the time is not right to release her," the Guardian reassured him.

"What are they?"

"They are the Lights of the Universe. When Order created us, she took the light from her own body, the light that was created from the explosion of the old world and split it into its many facets. We are those facets. A rainbow of colours to stand guard over this world and protect it from the darkness. Carling's light is purer than ours; her light is greater. It burns brighter and the Abilities she has been granted by our Mother Universe far exceeds our own. She is a gift from the Universe to help bring back balance. Chaos was never meant to be only darkness, the Universe created Order from Chaos's destruction to bring balance. But unfortunately, it never came to pass. The great plan of Carling was only the beginning. She was always meant to be a tool to be honed and used to prepare and protect the Ultimate One. Aroha is meant to replace both Chaos and Order. The balance shall be returned when she has banished them."

"And what is to become of Claire when it is over?" Matt asked with a great fear beginning to grow inside him.

"It will be decided on the day of the banishment. We cannot see the outcome. Carling, when she does pass, will join us and take her rightful place with the Sentinels, at our side to continue our work. This has been seen."

"So, I will lose her…?" He looked at Claire. The love he had for her was written clearly on his face, and the pain of knowing they would be separated from one another.

"We cannot see that," another spoke gently.

"But you said…"

"Yes, it is written in the Book of Destiny, but we cannot see what becomes of either of you," she told him.

The lights that had started underneath the skin on Claire's hands were now spreading faster up her arms. They pushed their way with a surging force, advancing and then retreating a little until Matt saw them reach under the pushed-up sleeves of her jacket. They emerged at her throat and he could see them seeking out the rest of her body. The moment they reached her face she grimaced in pain and he almost pulled her off the stone.

"A little longer, my son." A thin, bony hand was raised over Claire's head and a spark of light jumped from the hand to Claire, like a little piece of golden lightening. The Guardian pulled back and held the hand under its robe.

The others stood their ground, waiting for the moment when all knowledge had been passed onto Claire. Matt could feel her tremble under the pressure, and she began to weaken. He held onto her, keeping her in place. The weight of her body slightly pushing him off balance as he tried to adjust. The lights were now rushing through her body, streaking and pulsating like a meteor shower in the heavens. Under his hands he could feel her racing heartbeat as she absorbed all that she should be, and it became a part of her.

"Now, Galen." One of the gathered hosts placed a hand on his shoulder and gently pulled him back.

Claire's hands released their hold on the stone, and she collapsed into his arms. Matt gently lowered her to the ground and cradled her, smoothing the damp hair from her face. Claire's eyes flickered open, showing the lights had even invaded the soft blue of her iris. They flashed for a moment before disappearing and she focused on his face.

"Claire," he said softly to her.

"Galen, my Galen. So long have we loved," she said in wonder as her golden laced hand reached up to his face.

"And we shall continue forever more," he promised as he bent and kissed her lips.

Chapter Two

At odd moments during the day Matt caught his wife glowing. The lights that had appeared under her skin that night up at the stones had diminished within hours of coming back to the house. But they played and flickered brightly when she was concentrating on something or lost in her thoughts. He would take her hand and draw her gaze to him, then they would settle back down.

"I don't know how you are going to control them when we go back to Glasgow," he told her over breakfast two mornings later.

"I'll be able to. There is just so much to explore and understand. Here I can be me, I can let them shine." Claire turned her eyes to him with sudden concern. "Galen, tell me truthfully, do you not—"

"They are part of you. I knew who I was falling in love with; I knew who I married and committed myself to. It seems I never had a choice," Matt told her, taking her hand.

"I was afraid, that the—"

"They don't scare me, Claire," he said. "I love to watch them; they tell me your moods. When you're angry, they race." He reached up with his other hand and traced one of the lights on the back of her hand with a finger. "When you're happy, they shine brighter. And when we make love, they…" He grinned.

"They what?" she asked him, with a smile of her own.

"They flutter. It's like there are a thousand glittering butterflies under your skin, and it's so beautiful to watch."

"There have been many changes in the last few days. I was worried that it may be all too much for you to accept and take on."

"I was given instruction and my own memories to help me deal with it. Do you know when this great event is to take place?" It was a question that had been clearly playing on his mind.

For a moment her eyes closed, and she looked into the future. It was one of the Abilities she didn't like to use: Foresight. But now she felt the need to confirm things.

"Not until summer. Aroha will come to us in the middle of spring to start preparing. I think we may have to organise a family reunion to get her to come, though. I still feel a great reluctance in her to accept who she is."

"Your birthday is in the spring. We should organise it for then, we didn't do anything for your fiftieth last year."

"We did. It was what I wanted, just you and me."

"But the kids were disappointed. Bree told me at Christmas."

"Did she? Well we shall celebrate my fifty-first, then."

"Do you want to do it here or in New Zealand?" he asked her.

"Here, of course. This is our home."

"It seems that it has been the family home since the dawn of time."

"There is a lot of history in the area." She smiled with a faraway look as she saw them all down the ages, starting from the very first family.

"So how do you intend to start preparing her?" Matt asked, trying to get her back to focus as the lights began to shine once more.

"Aroha? I don't know. I guess I need a little more guidance before I can guide her."

"After the other night, I would have thought you had had enough," Matt told her smiling.

The date was set for the celebration and invitations sent out. Neither Claire nor Matt had told anyone what had happened up at the stones, nor the real reason behind the gathering. They had discussed it, so there was no need for the other members of the family to know. The only one it really affected was Aroha, and Claire decided to tell her only after her niece had arrived.

The trip back to Glasgow was long and Claire usually slept through the drive. This time, however, she did not. She tried to keep a tight control on her feelings and the lights that played under her skin. Her hands firmly balled into fists on her knees as she fought them down, but she found her mind wandering. Matt would nudge her when he could see her glowing out of the corner of his eye and laughed when she jumped.

Claire felt the pressure of the normal life hit her as soon as she went through the front door. While she had been tucked away up in the valley, the world had continued without her and she had been lost in her studies in the library. Now she had to get back to her real job, which was the study of the Pictish stones and their symbols. This was the work that Matt's father, Gerry, had started, and she had continued when he had died two years previously.

They had slowly published their findings, along with the translations and keys to the Pict language. When Gerry had first released his initial findings there had been great excitement and he had wanted to go full steam ahead with the rest. Claire had to pull him up and ease back the release, so as to not throw suspicion on the process of discovery they had outlined. Now the only information that she had held back was that of the Abilities of The People and the fact that they had existed at all.

Another of her side projects had been tracking down those with Abilities from around the world. With the mass emigration of Scots over a three-to-four-hundred-year period, she found that they had spread themselves wide across the globe. Initially the idea had been to first discover where her own family had come from and how they had made their way to New Zealand. This search was advanced a great deal with the help of her brother, Tony, and the resources he had made available to her.

Tony was not related to her in the conventional way. She now recognised his spirit as that of her brother from her second life. The brother that had been taken from her too soon. He had been there from the moment she was born in this one, watching over her and caring for her, and was Aroha's father. Tony and his son, John, had introduced Claire and Matt to his first wife's family in the States. They had welcomed the contact and had shared with Claire their own secrets. They had flown over eagerly and visited the stones. She had taken to them warmly and they fast became part of their own family. The information Eliza and Tom had gathered about their own community had led them to the name of a whaling ship that had set sail from Virginia. When Tony had finally tracked down the logs for the boat, it had been an exciting moment for Claire. They had shown that a group of twelve families had left Virginia and been dropped off on the shores around where the city of Napier now sat, on the east coast of the North Island of New Zealand.

The last question of their lineage had been answered. Claire used this information to trace the names of the twelve families. This new information threw up fresh surprises. When she traced the genealogic lines, Claire found that they were all connected, both to her own family, that of Matt's and the Buchannan's in the States. Now, with the new awakening of her collective memories and Abilities, it seemed to make sense, and all fitted into the marvelous jigsaw that was the story of her lives.

The beauty of living in two houses was the fact they didn't need to worry about luggage, except for their work. Claire trudged up the stairs to the spare room, which had been converted to an office. Two walls were dedicated to bookcases with volumes jammed into every available space, and sitting under the window side by side, were two desks. Piles of papers, books, magazines, photos, and files were stacked up on one of the desks; the other was neat and tidy. Claire placed her bag full of her new findings from the valley on the tidier one and tried to ignore her husband's organized mess.

The room had once been the domain of their children, Bree and Callum. Both had now moved out; Bree to live with her husband, John, in New Zealand, and Callum into student accommodations with friends in Edinburgh. Their daughter was trying to pursue a career as an artist but was finding she was actually doing more to help John set up his fledgling advertising company. It was starting to become successful. Callum had broken away from the family field of archaeology and was currently attending law school in Edinburgh. Claire found her son was becoming more and more like her Great-Uncle Geoff, the man who had raised her from the age of ten. He had been a very respected lawyer and she was so proud that her son was following in his footsteps.

As Claire started down the stairs, the events of the weekend hit her. She stopped and landed heavily on a step half-way down, staring into space. The fact that she was essentially two people made her mind whirl with different emotions and thoughts. A normal human descended from The People and also a Sentinel.

"Claire, are you okay?" Matt asked from the bottom of the stairs. He climbed up to sit with his wife after she didn't respond. "Claire?"

"I can never be normal, can I?" she asked without looking at him.

"I don't think you have ever been normal, sweetheart." His arm went around her shoulders and pulled her close.

"But I can never just be me. My whole life was created to be used by the Sentinels, by Order. You heard what they called me, the Staff and Sword of Order. I was created to be used as a weapon."

"Yes, you were. I did hear and I saw too, how in your past lives you were used. I felt the pride the first Galen had for you, the way you handled yourself in battle. It's the same pride that I have for you now. I know it's not fair, that you've done your part already and to ask more of you is too much. But, Claire, could you really trust this task to anyone else?"

"No. I couldn't. Matt, I just want to be with you and enjoy our time together. I was looking forward to growing old with each other, surrounded by our children and grandchildren. I'm getting too old to go racing off everywhere."

"As I understand it, you will only be supporting and helping in the task, not doing the actual deed. Your job is to prepare Aroha for her challenge."

"From what I've seen of the ancient enemy, I don't think he likes to play fair. I have an uneasy feeling about it. Before, when I faced Marcus, I knew what had to be done, how to act, and the steps that needed to be taken. But now I have no clue how to face him."

"Look back into your other lives. See how the other Carlings dealt with him. At least you have this tool to steel yourself with."

"I need guidance, and I am going to need your strength again."

"And you have it. Always. That is what I was created for." He pulled her to him and kissed her gently.

The door to the outside world suddenly burst open, bringing with it the freezing cold winter wind. A young man filled the yawning space of the doorway. His blond, shaggy hair was blowing across his face and he pushed it back out of the way. His soft blue eyes opened wide as they took in the scene and he shut the door behind him. He did not move or make a noise as he stared at Claire.

"Callum, what are you doing here?" Claire asked him.

"Mum, is there something you need to tell me?" he asked, staring at her.

"They're shining again, Claire," Matt gently explained, smiling beside her.

"Bugger." With the small exclamation she pushed the lights away.

"What's going on?" Callum asked, still standing at the bottom of the stairs.

"We have a lot to talk about, son." Matt stood and pulled his wife up with him. "But first, why are you home?"

As they took the stairs down and joined him at the bottom, he looked a little sheepish.

"Callum, there is no point hiding anything," Claire told him.

"Just like you're hiding something from me?" he good naturedly retorted.

"Out with it."

"How about some lunch first and then I can tell you while we're eating," he countered.

With the food prepared, they sat at the small round table and watched as their son devoured his sandwich. Callum ate like he had not had a decent meal in a long time. Claire sat back waiting for him to begin.

"So, the reason I'm here," Callum started around the last mouthful. "I got your invitation for your birthday bash and I wanted to know what you wanted for a present."

"That is not the reason, and I don't want anything." Claire saw right through his lie.

"I actually didn't know you were going to be home," he relented, going slightly red with embarrassment as he leaned back in his seat.

"So why come here when you thought we would be out?" Matt asked him.

"I need a place to stay. There's a guy who has been after me for a bit."

"What guy, and what have you done?" Matt demanded.

"I haven't done anything, Dad, I promise. This guy is in school with me. At first, I thought he was just being friendly. We did in fact become friends. Then he started asking me questions about our family and where I came from."

"What sort of questions?" Claire asked.

"The type that seemed like he was digging into my past and trying to confirm some information type of questions."

"So, why come home if all he's asking is questions? Which I assume you haven't answered."

"Only in general terms like I was born here, my sister was born in New Zealand, and that you two work here. Nothing of the family secrets," he assured them quickly.

"So, why come home?" Claire repeated.

"I think he's following me. I keep seeing him everywhere and my digs have been gone through. I'm sure of it."

"I think we could use Tony's help on this." Matt looked between Claire and Callum.

"He could help getting a background check on this guy. Have you done anything to him, gone inside his head?" Claire sat forward and leaned on the table.

"No. When he started to ask really specific questions, I knew it wouldn't be a good idea. I can tell when people are hiding things from me, Mum. You taught me well. But this guy takes masking to the next level. I'm sure he has some Ability. I just don't know what."

Claire checked her watch for the time difference between Scotland and New Zealand. "Tony will still be up, it's nearly eight o'clock over there now." She closed her eyes and called out to her brother, reaching out across the great expanse with ease to connect with his mind.

"Claire, I was just thinking of you. How are you?" Tony's deep, rich voice answered her call and she drew his consciousness into her mind, to stand before her. At the age of sixty-five he was still healthy and strong, standing so tall and upright, his dark brown eyes still so bright.

"I'm good. And you?"

"Good. I take it this isn't a social call, otherwise you would have asked how Bree and John were doing by now."

"We have a little problem. Callum is being followed. Someone he got to know at uni is asking a lot of questions. I was hoping that we could get you to do your snooping and find out some things for us."

"I don't snoop, Claire; I investigate."

"Whatever you want to call it to help you sleep at night, Tony. I'm just worried about Callum at the moment."

"There's something else, isn't there?" he asked, looking deeply into her eyes. Even though they weren't biologically brother and sister, they still had a connection and he knew her so well.

"There is, but that doesn't matter at the moment and can wait until later," she told him.

"Mmm. I will wait with bated breath then," he smirked. "Get Callum to call me with the details and I'll get on it."

"Thank you, Tony. Now, really, how are you? Are you looking after yourself properly?" Her concern was real. His wife Tia had passed away the previous year from a sudden illness. Claire had spent some months with him afterwards as he fell to pieces over her death.

"I'm fine, doing a lot better now that I'm back at work," he told her sadly.

"Which means you're living at your office."

"No, I'm back at the apartment. I'm selling the house," he told her.

"Is Aroha coping?"

"She's doing better than I am, and Bree is being our rock at the moment."

"Is she still interrupting your thoughts?"

"She never did learn the boundaries." Tony smiled. "And I'd like to say, I would be delighted to come to your birthday party. I had a big speech all prepared for the last one, which didn't happen."

"You can't use it this time. It's my fifty-first."

"I can modify it."

"I better go. Matt and Callum are waiting. I'll get Callum to call to you."

"Give Matt my best. And Claire..." He took her into his arms and hugged her. "When we talk next, you are going to have to explain the beautiful display of lights that have been playing under your skin."

"Oh, shit." Claire pulled back and looked at her hands. "I really need to concentrate on keeping them down. I promise I will explain everything when I know how."

Gently she pushed away the connection with his mind and came back to the table. Matt and Callum were sitting waiting patiently for her.

"Tony says hi, and that he is coming over for the celebration," Claire told Matt.

"Good. What else?"

"Callum, go talk to your uncle. He's waiting for you," Claire spoke to her son. He got up and moved to the lounge and made himself comfortable on the couch. Claire stood and started to clean up the dishes. Matt reached out and took her hand, a finger tracing the light that played on her skin.

"Callum asked me what the lights were." He looked up into her face with such love that Claire sat back down and held his hands, losing herself in his bright blue eyes.

"What did you tell him?"

"I told him that something happened at the stones and that you would tell him when you're ready. That there was nothing to be worried about. He asked if it had something to do with Aroha; apparently, he has been having a lot of dreams about her lately."

"I know they've kept in contact." She watched as Matt's eyes returned to her hands and she concentrated on subduing the lights. They faded slowly from sight and Matt sighed.

"They are beautiful," he mused.

"But a nuisance. I think I should stay home until I can get a handle on them. I probably should have stayed in the valley."

"We can work on it together later, if you like," Matt offered as he stood and picked up the dishes.

"There is a problem there, Professor Drummond. Every time we work on something together, we get distracted." She smiled shyly up at him.

"I know." He grinned back and took the dishes to the kitchen.

Claire was still smiling as she joined her son in the lounge. His breathing was even and deep, and she could sense that his conversation with Tony was an involved one. As she studied his face, she could see both her Great-Uncle Geoff and Uncle David in his features. He was just as tall with their broad shoulders. He could be serious like Geoff, but also ready to laugh and have fun, just like his father and David.

It was while Claire was waiting for him to come back to her that she had a flash of insight. It was so strong that it pushed through the normal barriers she had up for the Foresight Ability. He was being used and was going to be in danger. A darkness was looming up behind him. It was gone as soon as it came, and Claire gasped.

"Mum, you okay?" Callum asked from the couch across from her.

"I'm fine," she said, trying to hide the feeling that came with what she had seen. "What did Tony say?"

"He'll get on it straight away. He has the picture of the guy and his name. I didn't tell you it, did I? It's Finn MacLean. Uncle Tony was surprised by the name, but he wouldn't tell me why."

"I know his first wife's grandfather's name was MacLean. That could have something to do with it. I wouldn't worry about it, Callum. Tony will find out what there is to know about him."

"What your uncle can't find out about a person is not worth knowing," Matt said coming to join them.

"Are you going to tell me what those things are now, Mum?" Callum asked pointing at the lights that were once more shining brightly.

"Ah, yes. Well, that's a long story."

"I'm not going anywhere." He leaned back and spread out over the back of the couch. The posture was a mirror image of his father, who sat beside Claire.

"It seems your mother is more than just blessed by the Guardians," Matt started. "It seems she is part Guardian."

"Except now we know that the correct term is Sentinel," Claire added.

"Growing up I used to love hearing the stories that you would tell us. Now I just wish you would get on with this story and tell me what I want to know." He smiled at his parents.

The old familiar feeling of being interrogated by her Great-Uncle came over her and Claire smiled. "All right. But it's a long story and it starts with the creation of the world."

The telling took all afternoon. Callum sat back and listened but at some points he clearly had a hard time believing it. Occasionally his eyes would flit to his father, who would nod, confirming the story. When Claire had finished, he sat in silence. If this had been told to someone outside the family, he thought, even if they did have an Ability, they wouldn't believe a word. But being who he was, he believed his mother and father. He had heard enough stories not only from them, but also his sister and other family members.

"So, you are a Sentinel, a Guardian?" he asked her.

"A part of me is. For some reason we have been separated, the human and the Guardian. Crystal is the Sentinel, Carling. And I am me, Claire."

"But you have all the Abilities of the Sentinels?"

"Yes, I do."

"So, does that mean Bree and I are part Sentinel?" he asked, still trying to grasp the concept.

"No. There is only ever One True Child. What I have passed on to you and Bree is from myself. The fact that you two have more Abilities than anyone else is a mystery to me."

"The lights, what are they?" he asked, staring at them again.

"Part of the Universe. The explosion Chaos caused when he destroyed the old world created the great light of Order. Order was born to bring a balance to Chaos' actions. But she understood she could not do so alone. So when Order created the Sentinels some of her light was passed onto them."

"But their lights don't shine anymore. You told me they hide themselves away under cloaks and hoods, that their hands are bony and white. Why won't they let theirs shine anymore?"

"I don't know, Callum. It could be that they have hidden themselves away from the world for so long that maybe they have diminished."

"So, the lights are back. Why now?"

"That has to do with the next part of the story. And I cannot tell you that, because it's not written yet. Some is already in the Book of Destiny, but not all. I can tell you that it's another task that has been laid at my feet."

"I asked Dad before if it has something to do with Aroha." He leaned forward, elbows on his knees, concern and worry clouding his features.

"It does. You have always known that Aroha was special, haven't you?"

"Yes, but that it was a taboo subject that no one talked about."

"It was never taboo, just not forced on anyone or her," Claire told him.

"So, what is it that makes her so special?"

"She has your heart, doesn't she?" Matt asked. Callum blushed.

"I like her. I always have," he told them.

Claire smiled, but the news made her a little sad as well. She was afraid that Aroha might not share the same sentiment.

"Aroha is a very special person. I'm not sure that telling you who she really is will help you if you're in love with her."

"Can't you see for me, Mum? Can't you look into the future and find if we are meant to be together?" he pleaded.

"You know I don't like using that Ability, and you know the reasons why."

"You have that Ability yourself, Callum, why don't you look?" Matt asked.

"I have and I can't see anything," he exclaimed, throwing himself back into the couch in frustration. "It's all hidden behind a cloud of darkness."

"Darkness?" Claire asked him suddenly. "You see darkness in your future?"

"Yes, it surrounds me." He looked at his mother. "Why, what does it mean?"

"I don't know. It probably means nothing. As I said, some things are not written yet." She tried to hide the sudden fear that gripped her.

Chapter Three

Claire spent the next few days sequestered away in the little terrace house in Glasgow, trying to control the lights that glowed under her skin. Each afternoon she eagerly showed her progress to Matt as he returned from work. By the third day, she had finally managed to control the lights without too much concentration. Callum had spent a few days with his parents and had continued to grill his mother about the story, wanting her to go into greater and greater detail. There was something that had been bothering him, she could see that, and suspected he was trying to figure out where Aroha fitted into things.

Callum had left early that morning to return to Edinburgh by train. Claire loved her son, but he had grown into a large man and took up a lot of room in the small house. He was also noisy. Callum had never learned to do anything quietly; his voice was naturally loud and when he moved about it seemed like there was a herd of elephants playing in the small house. When the door shut on him and the house descended into quiet, Claire breathed in deeply and enjoyed it.

That same afternoon Tony called out to her. When she joined him in his mind, she found Callum there as well.

"Well, this can't be good. Shall we get Matt here as well?" she asked them.

"I've already sent the call. He said he will be here directly. He just has to find somewhere safe to talk," Tony told her.

"You called out to him first? Now I *know* the news is bad."

"I'm here," Matt said, finally joining them. "So, who is this mysterious person?"

"Finn MacLean is who I thought he was. He is the son of one of Maddison's cousins. His father is Old Tom's great-nephew. Finn's mother left his father and the country when he was still quite young."

"So how did he turn up at the law school in Edinburgh?" Callum asked.

"She remarried a Welshman and they moved to a small village in the north of Wales. Finn was packed off to boarding school as soon as he was old enough."

"What else are you not telling us, Tony?" Claire asked him.

"I rang Mike and Sarah. They asked around and apparently Finn recently got in contact with his family back in the States and learned about the Abilities. He does have an Ability, but thought he was the only one to have it. When he found out about the communities in America, Scotland, and New Zealand, he became bitter about it."

"So, is he a danger?" Claire asked, becoming worried.

"I wouldn't say that, but he is hungry for knowledge. He discovered about your little family via the Buchannans and MacLeans, and when he met you, Callum, I believe he wanted to find out more."

"He is one of The People then; we can share our knowledge with him if he wants it," Matt said, clearly relieved.

"As far as I can tell he is no threat to the communities and only wants to know more about his heritage. I can't find any police records or even a hint of danger around him," Tony told them.

"He's sort-of family, then?" Callum asked. "I mean, through you."

"Callum, we are all related in one way or another," Matt told his son. "The People are a fast-dwindling population now. Within another hundred years or so we will have died out altogether."

"That's a depressing and scary thought," Callum mumbled.

"We were placed on this earth to carry out a great plan. That plan is coming to fruition, and as a result the Abilities will no longer be required," Claire said.

"What do you mean?" Tony asked her.

"When you come to see us for my birthday, I will explain it all then, Tony."

"Is this to do with the lights?" he asked her.

Claire looked down at her hands quickly; there were no pinpoints of light swirling and she breathed a sigh of relief.

"Yes, it is. But I'm not going into that story now. You'll just have to wait."

"Keeping secrets from me again, Claire. I don't know what you're becoming over there in Scotland," Tony chuckled.

"It's not a secret. I'm just still trying to understand it myself."

"How's Aroha?" Matt asked and looked quickly at his son.

"She's doing well. I've convinced her to come with us for your birthday, Claire. She wasn't going to at first, but Bree had a talk with her."

"We're looking forward to seeing her again. It has been such a long time, hasn't it, Callum?" Matt asked, keeping a close eye on him.

"Yeah. I mean, we talk sometimes, but I haven't seen her in a while." He went bright red.

"Right, I think I might need to keep an eye on you, young man," Tony said, teasing him.

"I think I'd better go. I've got a lecture to get ready for," Callum said and made his goodbyes then left.

"Will the pair of you please leave them alone," Claire demanded sternly.

"Who, us?" Matt chuckled along with Tony.

Work and the usual day-to-day responsibilities took over Claire's life. She was sitting at her desk in the university when she started to yawn, long and loud. She stretched, working out the kinks in her back and leg muscles. It had been weeks since she last went for a run and she could feel it as she glanced at her watch. It was only mid-afternoon. She looked longingly out of the window at the blue sky that peeked through the gaps between the university buildings.

She tidied up her desk, shut her laptop and placed it in her bag. She headed out of her broom-cupboard-sized office and went to find Matt. Outside his office a group of students were camped, waiting to be admitted for a tutorial. The young men and women barely looked up from the phones in their hands as Claire passed them and knocked on the door, then let herself in.

"Hi, sweetheart. What can I do for you?" he asked, looking up from his overcrowded desk, his eyes taking in her body.

"Nothing with that lot outside," she said indicating the door behind her as she made her way around his desk. "I'm going to take the rest of the day off and get some fresh air. What time are you going to be home tonight?"

"The usual. Do you want me to pick something up on the way home?"

"Yes, please. You choose. I could always delay the run and you could join me," she suggested, with an eyebrow raised.

"When was the last time I went running with you? I'll stick to the gym thanks," he said with a chuckle.

"Never hurts to ask. I'll see you later." She leaned down and kissed him quickly, then danced out of his grasp with a giggle.

After a quick change at home, she grabbed her keys and phone, plugged in the ear buds, and started up the playlist. Matt had often complained about her taste in music, but these songs all reminded her of people in her life and the places she had been.

The front door closed behind her with a thud and she made her way to the gate to head out onto the street and down the road to Kelvingrove Park. She ran through the streets, skirting around the pedestrians and tourists, enjoying the freedom of an afternoon off. Anyone looking at her would not believe that she was about to turn fifty-one.

She entered the park, keeping to the paths, and quickly crossed over the river and made her way around the large grounds. Some of the trees were still in winter hibernation, but a few were evergreen against the blue of the sky. The remains of discarded leaves lay piled up against the hedges, fences, and benches as she passed them. The park was one of her favourite places to run while she was in Glasgow.

She reached the other side and began to make her way back, lost in the rhythmic music. Her running steps began to slow and Claire found herself walking. The winter sun dimmed around her, almost as if it were trying to push through a dense fog. Claire glanced about, pulling her earbuds out as she realised there was no one else around her, which was unusual for that time of the day. She could hear nothing, only silence; not even the sound of a bird. The rushing sound of cars on the roads that surrounded the park had become muted and seemed more like the sighing of water as it tumbled over small rocks in a riverbed.

Out on the expanse of grass to her left, an immense old ash tree, with a massive, gnarled trunk stood by itself. It was clearer than all the others in the misty haze, its bare branches reaching out wide and high, clawing at the blue sky. Claire's curiosity urged her on and she was soon leaving the path. Large roots reached across the bare earth at its base, before they plunged into the ground. Claire sank down to sit on one as she looked up into the branches above.

"I welcome my sister," a woman's voice called out behind her, "and I am pleased she has come to visit me at last. I have seen you many times pass by as you run."

Claire twisted around and found a tall figure of a Sentinel, cowled and hands clasped before her.

"Other people will see you," Claire said, standing quickly and looking about to see who was around.

"No one but you can see me, Carling. It has been such a long time since we have had the chance to talk. I have missed you."

From the reaches of Claire's mind, a memory of the Sentinels leaving her to take up their mission of guarding the sacred lands came to her. The name of the one stood before her rose and she just about speak it. Indigo.

"Please, do not say my name. Not yet. The time will come shortly, Sister, when you will be able to say our names out loud once more. It is time, Carling, to go out and find us. Find all the trees in which we, the Sentinels, have been sleeping. Time also to use another of your Abilities that have lain dormant for too long. It is a useful Ability and will take you far."

"Which one is it, Guardian?" Claire asked, unsure of which one Indigo could mean.

"You will find it when you search for it. There are seven of us. Use your memories—they will point you in the right direction. I must go now and return to my magnificent tree. She has protected and guarded me so well for so long."

"What if I can't find the trees? What if they are gone from the world?" Claire asked, suddenly afraid for the Sentinels.

"Our trees are all still standing. We chose the sites with great care when we went into hibernation. Now I am looking forward to reawakening."

"But you are here now."

"Not on the same plane as your body. Where we are talking is more like a dream. It is complicated, but if you study it, you will find how it is done. You can appear to people this way if you wish. Though, I would not recommend it until the lights are fully contained."

"How? Can you help me with them?" Claire looked down at her glittering hands.

"Go inside yourself, Carling, the answers are all there. Remember your Abilities are far greater than our own," Indigo said, her voice trailing off as she began to fade. "Until we meet again, dear Sister."

Claire looked up and found the Guardian had left her. The day seemed darker and she looked at her watch. The hours had marched on without her as she had sat under the ash tree and she still didn't want to move. The familiar feeling she received from the tree was like that of the oak that guarded the entrance to the little valley and she saw a face as it disappeared into the bark. The eyes that bored into her were full of love and sadness. She shook her head at the vision. Claire knew the location of another Sentinel but was reluctant to go there just yet.

She leaned back on the rough bark, then did as she had been instructed and went into her mind. The memories were tucked away and ordered; Carling had done her work and brought them out ready for her use. At her side the glowing being stood as she thought of her.

"These are the memories we are looking for, Claire. Our first life is when they left us," she said sadly.

"We can feel the pain of separation from them. They meant a great deal to us."

"They did; they were our family. Our brothers and sisters, who were also our aunts and uncles, and then there is our Mother and Father. Claire, they once meant the same to you."

"That was before our spirit was separated."

"But we are still entwined." Carling took her hand, holding it gently, imparting some comfort to Claire. "We are still one, and always will be. There is nothing that can separate our lives."

"There is one who could damage us still." Claire thought of Chaos still trapped in his prison.

"And one who is still watching over him. Any man he sends to hurt us has always been defeated. He is not strong enough with Order still protecting us and the world."

"But there will be no more coming, will there?" Claire asked.

"We cannot know that and must be on our guard. We must protect Aroha. Until she defeats Chaos there is still a chance he will prevail. He will use everything he can against us, and he will still try to sway us over to him."

"Charm does not work on us."

"But he will not be using Charm only. Shall we begin now, or should we go home and be surrounded by the love and comfort of Galen?" Carling asked Claire with a smile.

"We think that is a much preferable idea, Carling. After all, as he keeps reminding us, that is why he was born."

"It is indeed."

Claire came back to herself and shivered in the cool air, noticing the shadows had lengthened even more. Spring was only just around the corner, and now with the event before her—and more certain than before—Claire was not looking forward to it. Heading back onto the path, she continued her run, the music in her ears and her stride matching the beat.

She stopped at the edge of a main road with only a couple of streets to home and waited for a gap in the increasing late afternoon traffic to cross the road. The cars were whizzing past, the noise from their engines drowned out by the music still playing. Spotting a gap, she took her chance and stepped off the curb. Concentrating on making it to the other side safely, she was not aware of the little blue car as it came hurtling out of nowhere. The edge of the bumper clipped her leg and spun her around. Her arms came out to protect herself and she landed heavily on the curb and lay in the gutter. Strangely, her first thought was, "*Not again*," as she tried to suck in enough air to satisfy her expelled lungs. Kind hands pulled her off the road and onto the safety of the footpath.

"Are you okay? Stay down," a voice told her. Claire looked about her and saw someone calling for an ambulance. A young man was holding onto her shoulder to keep her in place. "Ambulance and police. There's been an accident on University Ave, a hit and run."

"I'm fine. There's nothing broken," Claire insisted and tried to rise.

"You should wait. They'll be here soon," the man told her. His accent was not that of a Scottish native.

"I didn't see anything. I couldn't even say what colour it was."

A siren cried out from a distance, gradually coming closer. The man stood and waved them down. Claire was flanked by two police officers in yellow hi-vis jackets, both insisting that she wait for an ambulance.

"It was my own silly fault. I ran across the road when I thought I could get over. I didn't even see the car." Quickly she brushed off their hands and wondered if all they saw was an older woman. "I'm not hurt. It was only a glancing blow," Claire declared, ignoring her stinging palms which had scraped the asphalt road.

"Are you sure?" the younger of the two officers asked.

"I'm sure. Thank you for your concern and for getting here so quickly but, truly, I'm fine." She turned to her rescuer. "Thank you, also. It's not very often people stop to help these days."

"It's not a problem. But I saw the whole thing. I can tell the type of car and the colour. Also, the license plate," he added.

"And you are?" the older officer asked.

"Finn MacLean. I'm visiting Glasgow from Edinburgh. I go to law school there."

"Can we get your details then, ma'am, just in case we can track down the car?" the younger officer requested, pulling out a notepad.

"I'm Claire Drummond." She saw the young man look her way. *So, this is Finn*, she thought, wondering why he was there. Claire gave her address and phone number to the young officer and started to walk away.

The sound of running steps from behind made Claire send out a searching thought, and she slipped easily into his mind with the intent on only giving it a quick once-over. There was nothing there that she could see to indicate his intentions. There was no shadow around him that she could find, either. Claire stopped and turned to face him.

"Mrs. Drummond," he said, coming to a stop in front of her.

"I know who you are, Mr. MacLean. I know the connection with the family and where you come from. What I don't know is why you have befriended our son and why I now find myself face to face with you."

"Can we go somewhere where we can talk? I have a lot of questions for you. Callum gave me some answers, but he suggested that I come and speak to you about the rest." He seemed very eager and Claire pondered it a moment.

"Talking about those kinds of things in public is not a good idea. There are too many people who can eavesdrop," she told him as she watched the increasing pedestrian traffic around them. "You had better come to our home."

"Thank you, I really appreciate the opportunity to talk to you."

"It is the duty of The People to help each other." Claire continued to walk, and Finn kept pace with her. They remained silent and she sent a quick message to Matt to let him know they were going to have company for dinner and to get more food.

As they walked in the door, she sensed Matt wasn't home yet and she felt a moment of hesitation in letting this stranger into her home. But as she had told him, the sense of duty was powerful, and she stood back as he walked over the threshold at her invitation.

"Would you like something to drink? A glass of wine or beer?" she offered, placing her phone and keys down on the table.

"A beer would be great, thanks." He stood in the dining area while she opened the fridge and pulled out a bottle. They moved to the lounge.

"Do you mind if we wait until my husband is home before we go into your questions?" she asked as she settled herself.

"That's fine with me. But I don't know what we're going to talk about until he gets here." Finn opened the bottle and Claire studied him.

The young man she now found herself confronted by was taller than she was, but not as tall as Matt. His brown hair was almost in the same style as Callum's, shaggy and covering part of his face. His grey eyes reflected the ready smile that he was now giving her, and he sat on the couch looking already at ease with his surroundings.

"Well, I have had a full report on you already, so I know where you come from and which family," Claire told him.

"Am I allowed to know the same information about you? Seeing as you have me at a disadvantage," he countered.

"I was born in New Zealand, in the capital, Wellington. I left there when I was seventeen and became aware of my heritage. From there I came to Scotland and met my husband and we married shortly after. We moved here just before Callum was born. How much of our history has he told you?"

"Not much. He was actually very cagey. Mrs. Drummond, all I want is answers to questions my mother cannot help me with."

"What about your father's family? Couldn't they help you?"

"They did to some extent, but my father never had a power."

"You wouldn't have inherited it from your father. The Abilities—as they are called—are handed down through the female line."

The back door opened, and Matt called out as he entered. "I'm home. Who is this mystery guest?" he asked, placing bags of food down on the counter.

"Matt, come and meet Finn MacLean," Claire said as she watched his face.

"Well, this is a surprise," Matt said, dumping his keys on the table beside his wife's belongings.

Finn stood and shook Matt's hand. "I am very pleased to meet you, Mr. Drummond."

"So, to what do we owe the honour of this visit?" Matt went to the cabinet and poured himself a measure of Scotch, then sat by his wife.

"Information, sweetheart," Claire told him. "He wishes to know more about his heritage."

"In that case then, we should talk over dinner. It's going cold on the counter."

"What did you bring home?" Claire asked him.

"Thai," he said, getting up.

With dinner laid out on the table in front of them, Claire started dishing up the food, wincing at the grazes that were on her hands that she had been stubbornly ignoring along with the other aches and pains that now were starting to become pronounced. For some reason Claire didn't want to seem weak to this young man.

"Looks like you had a fun afternoon. What happened?" Matt took the serving spoon from her hand and looked at her red, raw palms.

"I was silly and took a little tumble," Claire told him and passed her other hand over the wounds. As her palm emerged from under the other there was no sign of any injury from either.

"How did you do that?" Finn asked her with wide eyes, still staring at her hands.

"What is your Ability?" Claire asked him, taking the spoon back from her husband.

"Flight," he told her.

"Only the one? Do you have a minor?" Matt asked him.

"Minor?"

"Art or music perhaps?" Claire passed him a container and he began to dish it up himself.

"I play guitar," he offered.

"Music then."

"And you are a Healer?" he asked Claire, quickly scooping rice onto his plate.

"Among other things. My Abilities are—"

"Not for discussion at the moment," Matt cut across her, "and neither are mine."

"But—"

"What are you looking for, Finn?" Matt interrupted him, placing his fork down on the plate and leaning on the table. "Because I don't think this is just about information on where you came from. Your family should have been able to provide you with that."

"I understand. You don't trust me," Finn said with a disarming smile.

"No, I don't," Matt told him honestly.

"Matt, he is one of The People." Claire placed a hand on his arm.

"Yes, and it was one of The People who tried to kill you remember. Twice."

"He didn't want to kill me, he wanted to use me. Marcus and Jack were themselves being used."

"Be that as it may, sweetheart, we don't know anything about this boy."

"I think you're taking your title of Protector of the One True Child a little seriously, Matt." Claire took her hand off his arm and picked up her fork to start eating.

"And I don't think you're taking your role seriously enough, Claire," he chided her.

"Who…? What…? I don't understand." Finn sat back in his chair and was looking between the husband and wife. "I just came to find out where I come from. Who are The People and who or what is the One True Child?"

"The People are the original occupants of this land, the sacred lands of the—" Claire began.

"Claire, he doesn't need to know that part yet."

"Galen Matthew Drummond." Claire shot him a look then turned back to Finn. "The People have descended down through the ages, with each successive race that has conquered the land."

"And the other?" Finn prompted her.

"That can wait until we are sure of what your intentions are," Matt told him.

"So, we are descended from the Picts?" he asked Claire

"No, the Picts—as the Romans so wonderfully named them—are descended from us. From the moment people have occupied the sacred lands we have been here. Our people were the first, created specifically for one purpose."

"What is that purpose? And why isn't this common knowledge?"

"It was at one point. The knowledge has been lost as the millennia have passed."

"So how come you know?"

"We know because we have been told, and because my wife is one hell of a researcher." Matt looked proudly at her.

"I had help, sweetheart, and you know it. We know because of the writings that have been left to us, from..." She looked at Matt and smiled. "Well, from us. Our past lives left us clues in the form of a rather large library that we have been adding to over the years as we find more and more of the old texts."

"Callum said you were archaeologists," Finn told them.

"Yes, and we are always looking. It is amazing where these writings come up. Some are just innocuous signposts and place names. But others tell a different story and have actually been written down for me to find," Claire told him.

"What was the purpose?"

"That I will not tell you, as it has nothing to do with you."

"But it must do as I have a power."

"Ability, or Talent if you prefer, but never a power. Power suggests that we are greater than those who don't have Abilities, and we are never greater than our fellow man. They should never be used for own personal gain, but only to make the world a better place."

"What use is Flight, or any of them, to our fellow man? Why should they be kept hidden and away from the world?" Finn demanded.

"Have you never been taught anything?" Matt asked him.

"There's been no one to teach me anything. My mother had Charm; she didn't know anything about Flight or any of the others. That is why she eventually gave me the information on my father and sent me to the States to meet his family there."

"And we know they call them powers. I'm sorry I raised my voice at you. The American branch do things a little differently."

"As does the New Zealand and I suspect the Australian as well. The only ones who still practice the old ways are here in Scotland," Claire said to them both.

"Can you teach me, tell me what I need to know?" Finn begged, placing his fork down on his plate.

"I can if that is what you wish." Claire stood from the table and went to a bookshelf. She ran her hands over the spines feeling them shiver at her touch until she came to the book she was looking for. Pulling it out carefully she headed back to the table and handed it to the young man. "This should give you a start. We have already worked through the history of where your family comes from, when we met Tom and Eliza

MacLean. Your clan is the Eagle, they originate from the west and north of Scotland. All the details are in there, including a map."

Finn took the book from her hands and opened it reverently. He flicked through the pages. Claire watched as he read through the description and studied the map that was laid out. This was a new addition for this book, one Claire had made after discovering where the boundaries of each Sentinel's land lay. Her own and her husband's were the same: the Boar, in the central lands, encompassing many of the highlands and hidden glens, including that of the special valley.

"Thank you for this. Can I borrow it?" he asked eagerly.

"It's yours, you may keep it. I have other documents as well that can help with the history of the journey of the MacLeans. I can send it to you by email if you wish."

"Please. I would be very grateful."

"So what prompted this sudden push for knowledge?" Matt asked him, as he tucked into his meal.

"It will sound very stupid, but I had a dream. In my dream I was visited by a man in a cloak, who told me to go find where I came from. He told me it was important."

"This cloak … was it dark and of the deeply cowled variety, not showing any part of the person?" The knowing grin that tugged at Matt's mouth suggested he had guessed it was no normal dream.

"Yes, it was," Finn confirmed, and he resumed eating, the book now laying on the table beside him.

"He was no man. You were visited by a Guardian. They have many other names, but that one will suffice for now and will be less confusing." Claire gave Matt a brief look before continuing. "There are seven Guardians in total. Each presides over a different part of the sacred lands."

"What are these Guardians?" he asked, taking the last mouthful of green curry.

"That can wait for another time, when you have taken in all that is in that book." Claire ran a hand over her forehead, the beginnings of a headache were starting to push its way through.

"Are you all right, Claire?" Matt asked concerned.

"I'm fine."

"It might have something to do with your accident. You should have waited for the ambulance," Finn said, from across the table.

"Accident? What accident? You said you only tripped. Claire, what happened?" Matt took her hand in his and was searching her eyes.

"It was my own silly fault. I ran across the road and didn't see a car. It clipped me, but not very hard. I fell into the gutter and Finn was there to pick me up. That is how we met," she told him. "I wasn't hurt, there's not even a scratch apart from my hands. Really, it's nothing."

"She landed pretty hard," Finn told Matt. He picked up the book and stood. "Thank you for dinner and answering some of my questions, but I think I should go and let you get some rest, Mrs. Drummond. May I come back and talk to you again?"

"Yes, and bring Callum with you next time," Claire said from her seat. Matt held her in place and got up to see Finn out.

After the door was shut, Matt came back to his wife and sat beside her. "Where did the car hit?"

"It was just a nudge."

"Where?"

"My left leg," she told him and watched as her husband lifted her leg and began to run his hand along it.

"What type of car?"

"I can't remember, because I didn't see it. It was gone by the time I realised what had happened."

"Go to your memory and do a Recall on it." He looked up as his hand hit her ankle and saw the small wince she made.

"There is no point," she told him.

Matt slowly undid her running shoe and slipped it off gently and pushed the leg of her training pants up. A large bruise was already forming just above the ankle and spreading down. His hand pressed gently over the contusion for a moment and when he released her it was healed.

"Thank you," she told him, leaning forward to kiss him.

"There is always a point to Recall. What if this was a deliberate act?"

"All right, I'll do it. Do you want to join me?" she asked him pulling back.

"Yes, but not to make sure you do it. I want to see for myself."

"What are you worried about?"

"Finn shows up just as you are hit by a car, and then there are all these visitations from the Sentinels and the forthcoming event."

"Speaking of Sentinels, I was visited on my run today. Did you know there is a very ancient ash tree in the park, which is just as special as the oak by the ford?"

"Really? And what did this Sentinel want?" Matt indulged his wife, knowing she was delaying the Recall.

"She wants me to search out the other trees. There is one for each Sentinel and I have to know where they are. But I already do."

"Looks like you might be taking a road trip."

"Not necessarily. There's an Ability she suggested I try and now seems like a good time to begin," she said with a grin.

"What is it?"

"Transportation," Claire told him brightly.

"You can look at it after you have done the Recall. Stop delaying." He grinned back at her.

"All right. You're no fun sometimes. You'd better join me, then." Claire slipped into her mind and found Matt there already and shook her head.

Finding the memory was easy enough as it had only just happened. She hastily went through it and started to place it back.

"See, I told you."

"Slower please, Claire. Why are you so adamant that it was nothing?"

"Because it was nothing," she insisted.

"Please, just indulge me, sweetheart," he asked, placing an arm around her waist.

"Fine." She pulled it back up and started to play it again, slower. It was as she had said: she had not seen the car, and there was not even an image of the offending vehicle. But Matt had not been looking at the car; he had already seen that in the first playback.

"Claire, did you notice Finn?" he asked slowly.

"No. why?"

"Look again." Matt directed her and played it without her permission. She looked at him sharply for touching her memory. "Sorry."

"So you should be. That was rude." Claire turned back to the image and this time watched what Finn on the other side of the road was doing.

At first it looked like Finn was just walking down the footpath towards their home. But on closer inspection Claire could see him watching her. As the image carried on and the road was being crossed, she saw him stop and seemingly wait for her. When she was hit there was an immediate reaction from him.

"He told the police officer that he had seen it all, he even gave them a description of the car and the license. But how could he see that or even have time to take note of the license when all his attention was on me, even after I was hit. He didn't once even glance at the car."

"I don't think he was telling us the full truth tonight. I have a feeling there is more than meets the eye with that one."

"I'm pleased we were circumspect about the information we gave him. Well done for not letting me blurt it all out."

"You're welcome," Matt placed his other arm around her as Claire banished the memory back to where it belonged. "How about a shower and bed?" his eye arched.

"Anything for you, my darling." She reached up and kissed him.

Chapter Four

The headache that had started the previous night at dinner, continued into the morning of the next day. It was a continual throb that invaded Claire's concentration at work and finally she gave up, heading home to try and get rid of it. The painkillers she had taken were not working, so she headed upstairs to bed. As soon as her head hit the pillow her eyes closed against the light.

"Claire!" A shout from somewhere inside her mind came to her and Claire soon found herself at the side of Carling.

"You needed me, Carling?" she asked wearily, the fog of the headache making it hard for Claire to even see her.

"Yes, we do. We have found something, and we need to work together to rid it from us." Carling pointed to an area that seemed to be turning black and dark.

"What is it?" Claire asked, stumbling slightly towards the infected area.

"It feels very much like the memory dream that our brother inserted into our minds," Carling told her.

As Claire neared the dark shadow, pain began to sear through her head, pulsating and thumping. Wave after wave crashed over her, driving her onto her knees.

"I can't. It hurts so much," Claire gasped, her head dropping into her open hands. Carling rushed to her side and held her up.

"Tony, our brother, help! We need you!" Carling called out to Tony so insistently and loudly that he joined them straight away.

"Claire?" Tony asked when he saw two women before him.

"There is no time to explain. We are being hurt," Carling told him. The points of light under her skin were now moving rapidly with her agitation. "We need your help to get rid of this," she begged, lowering Claire gently to the ground.

Tony turned from the glowing image of Carling and inspected the darkness that was spreading. His hand came up and went to touch, then he pulled back quickly.

"This is not good. I'm going to need Matt's help. Call him, Claire," he ordered.

He turned to the crumpled form beside him and pulled Claire into his arms, carrying her to her subconscious and the couple who had had become like parents to him. John and Jess were there waiting to take their daughter from him. As soon as he was sure she was safe with them he returned to the infected area and found Matt waiting.

"We are going to need to have a very long conversation when this is over, Matt," Tony told him.

"Yes, we are, but first... what are we dealing with here?" Matt asked.

"It's like something I found that can infect dreams. But it's been changed. It's attacking Claire's mind."

"She complained of a headache last night after Finn left, and again this morning."

"Finn? That friend of Callum's?"

"Yeah."

"Okay, here's what I want you to do. You work from that side and I'll work from this. Claire," he turned to her, "though I don't think you are Claire, I want you to encase the darkness with light as we gather it up. We need the strongest that you can produce."

"It shall be as you ask of us, Brother," she told him nodding.

The three got into position and started to contain the growing darkness. As they pushed on it, trying to gather it up, they heard a snarl and felt it resist them. The strain of trying to dislodge the mass played out on all their faces.

"Bree, help!" Matt called out to his daughter.

A tall, slender figure emerged from the darkness and saw what they were trying to do. Bree spotted the problem straight away and lent her Abilities to the matter. With her help, and after one final push and burst of energy, the grey shadowy matter was shoved into the small bubble of light Carling had produced.

Matt and Tony stepped back breathing deeply, sweat glistening on their faces and reflecting the light that Carling now held in her hands. Bree went to her father's side and checked to make sure he was all right before turning her attention to Tony. When she was satisfied that they had not exhausted themselves, she stood in front of Carling. The tiny points of light now moving slowly and holding out the darkness contained within the light.

"Mum?" she queried, looking at Carling closely then shook her head. "No. You are not my mother."

"At one point I was but we can discuss that later. This needs to be dealt with first," Carling said, looking down at the shimmering orb in her hands.

"That is nothing," Bree told Carling, taking the ball of light and shrinking it down into a tiny speck of light and handing it back to her. "I think you know what needs to be done with it."

"We do, Daughter." Carling disappeared for a moment and then was back, minus the infected darkness.

"Who are you?" Tony asked her.

"What a question for your sister?" Matt said, coming to Claire's side.

"This is not my sister, nor your wife for that matter, Matt. Can't you see that?" Tony said, turning to him.

"This is Carling. She and Claire are one. Carling is the Sentinel side and Claire is the human side."

"The *what*? Have you gone mad, Dad?" Bree asked him, shaking her head, sending her mess of dark curls to tremble.

"Surely you of all people should understand, Bree. Having part of my sister reincarnated in you."

"But that's... It's not..." she spluttered.

"Shall we go find the Claire side? I would very much like to make sure my wife is recovering." He took Carling's hand and they moved to the subconscious.

Claire was sitting up on the blanket when they arrived. She arched an eyebrow at the sight of her husband and the glittering Sentinel hand in hand. "Don't get any ideas, Matt," she told him cheekily.

"How are you? And why didn't you tell me something was wrong?" Matt left Carling to go to Claire's side, taking her into his arms.

"I'm fine. What was that?" she asked, looking around at who had followed them. "And why are you all here?"

"They are here because we called them," Carling replied.

"And now we would like some sort of explanation," Tony demanded, still looking at Carling, and crossing his arms over his chest.

"You had better get yourselves comfortable. There is one person missing and we need him here as well." Claire closed her eyes for a moment and sent out the search. "He is dozing in a lecture at the moment, so he should be here soon."

Callum came striding into the family group and did a double take at the two visages of his mother.

"Okay, we are here now. What is going on, Claire, Matt?" Tony asked the pair.

Claire held out a hand to her other self and Carling took it, sitting down on the rug next to Claire. "This is Carling. Carling is the Sentinel side and I am the human."

"Dad told us, but how…? Why…? How?" Bree said, sitting down in front of them.

"We are still one person. Only our spirit has been separated for some reason."

"If it would help you understand more, we can join back together into one being," Carling offered.

"Not just yet," John, Claire's father, said, looking hard between them.

"It has to do with being the One True Child. Our spirit was born from two Sentinels. We were not conceived the normal way," Claire carried on the explanation.

"Um, excuse me. I think I know how you were conceived, Claire," Jess, her mother, spoke up.

"No, Mum. I'm not talking about this current incarnation, but the original. We are a necessity and because of the manner of our spirits' birth we are both Sentinel and human." Claire tried to make it clearer. "The making of us comes from a forbidden union. The joining of two Sentinels to produce a child was deemed necessary by Order, to fight the evil darkness of Chaos who has tried to take our home from us. We have seen so many lives, have protected and defended our homeland so many times. We were created to be the Staff and Sword of Order."

"Who—or what—is Order?" John asked her.

"Order was sent to this world to be a balance to Chaos. They are both the children of the universe." Claire looked up at Tony at that point. "So is Aroha."

"My daughter?" he asked, disbelieving.

"Yes, Tony. That's why she is so special. That is why she has come to this world. The beginning of her task is coming soon, and she needs to prepare for it. Chaos is once more sending out his men, if what I am judging happened to me today is right."

"What is her task, Mum?" The worry and concern for Aroha was clearly evident in Callum's tone.

"It is her job to defeat Chaos. Ours was to imprison him and fight off his agents. So far, we have done that. But Aroha is the one who will hopefully dispel him, and his sibling, Order."

"You keep mentioning these Sentinels. What is a Sentinel, Mum?" Bree asked.

"The Seven Sentinels were created by Order to protect the sacred lands. They themselves sent out others to different parts of the world. They created our world, shaped it."

"And you are one of them?" Bree asked Carling.

"Not yet. At some stage this part of us will be joining them and then we shall depart. The seven shall become eight," Carling replied.

"This is doing my head in, seeing two of you," Tony said, looking between them.

"So you are both my daughters?" Jess asked, trying to quantify it.

"Yes, Mum, we are. But at the same time, we aren't. We know this is confusing for everyone." Claire looked at Carling and the other nodded. Slowly they merged until only one person sat before the gathered group. So very faintly the lights swirled under her skin and Matt placed an arm around her.

"So, now you know what is happening with Claire. Can anyone tell me what that thing was and who placed it there?" he asked.

"It was similar to the dream suggestion I placed in Claire all those years ago, just after Geoff passed away. But this one seemed darker somehow, more menacing," Tony said.

"That is because the one you implanted into Mum was only meant to plague her dreams and give her a sense of what you were feeling. I agree, this was very menacing and I feel it was meant to destroy," Bree said, looking up at her uncle.

"It was dark and the only being who could have created such a thing would be Chaos. Somehow he managed to get to me." Claire looked down at her hands.

"Finn," Matt stated then carried on when his wife looked up. "He is the only stranger you've met lately."

"I don't think it was him. It takes a while for something like that to do its work. This was placed on me some time ago."

"Finn came to see you?" Callum asked, kneeling down by his parents.

"Yes. He seemed very eager to learn. I don't think he is a threat. I went inside his mind and found no deceit or hidden agendas."

"I think we need to talk to him further," Tony said, a menacing tone to his voice.

"No, that won't be necessary," Claire protested. "Finn is more like a lost soul looking for direction. He needs our help in finding his way with the Abilities."

"But he turns up out of the blue, and then this happens to you," Matt continued. "You saw the way he was watching you in that recall. He already knew who you were."

The weeks passed with no more unusual instances occurring. Claire put the meeting of Finn out of her thoughts and refused to search for who might have placed the damaging, dreamlike infection in her mind. She could sense Matt becoming more and more frustrated with her apparent lack of worry or action over the matter. But she did worry. It was always there, the awareness of what had happened, and Claire was now very careful of how close she came to people while she was out in public spaces.

More and more often she found herself drawn to the tree in the park. It stood alone in a large grassed area, tall and resplendent as the leaves began to bud and burst forth as the spring season began in earnest. The life force she felt within was so close to the surface now. It would not be long until the Being hidden inside would send out the call to come back to the world. While she sat at the base amongst the massive roots, she concentrated and found the brothers and sisters that were spread out in the lands. Their names came to her, and she smiled as she remembered each.

That call Claire had been waiting for came early one evening, as she and Matt were cleaning up after dinner at the cottage in the valley. She stood with a clean dish in her hands as she wiped it dry, while staring out into the darkness. Outside and from far away, Claire felt the soft tug at her subconscious. She went to see who was calling so gently, unlike the normally urgent and familiar pull of her family she was so used to.

"Carling, it is time to find us. It is time we came back to the world," a familiar voice called, and she knew it was the being from the tree.

"You okay?" Matt asked her as she came back to herself.

"Yes. I have to go do something. It's time to bring the Sentinels back and it has to be done tonight," Claire said, placing the plate down on the bench and leaving the cloth on top of it. She turned to her husband.

"Go. I'll finish up here." He placed a hand on the side of her head. "I'll be here waiting for you."

"I won't be long. Matt, I'm nervous." Claire gathered his hand from her face, kissed his palm and placed it close to her heart.

"Let the Sentinel side guide you. You have met them all before. There is nothing to be nervous of," he told her and kissed her gently.

Claire felt his fears and nerves increasing and knew the reason for it. She had seen the memories, remembered the kiss and the look from one in particular.

"I'll be back soon, I promise," she told him, trying to allay her fears. With one last kiss she left him, vanishing from his arms, and leaving a hole into which Matt's own fear hastily spilled, filling it to the brim.

"Please come back to me," he whispered to the sudden emptiness and quiet.

Thick rolling clouds scudded across the face of the full moon, which hung heavy in the inky sky, sending fleeting eerie shadows over the expanse of darkened green lawn. Claire walked slowly up to the tree in the park and placed a hand gently on the rough bark. The energy and life force that she felt under her touch was great and pushing out to greet her. She heard the voice calling to her. A sister and aunt. Closing her eyes, Claire returned the call, uttering the being's name for the first time in over a millennium.

"I release you, Indigo. Join me, Sister. The time is almost upon us and you are once more needed in this world." Claire's voice was loud in the darkness of the park, but there was no one about to hear, except for some sleeping birds and squirrels which had made their home in the spreading branches above.

Slowly, through her fingers and palm of her hand, the energy was released. Drawn up from the earth at her feet, from the very centre of the world, it came and passed into the large ash. It fed the soul that was caught up and bound by the mighty tree, slowly drawing it forth and freeing forever the ethereal being of Indigo.

Standing at her side now, the Sentinel glowed, her deep blue-purple lights swirling under her skin. Indigo drew a deep breath of the night air that was quickly becoming frostier under the silvery orb that hung in the sky.

"My Sister," Indigo said, placing arms around Claire and drawing her near. "I am free once more to aid you."

"Welcome back, Sister. The time for the Sentinels to return is now." Claire took Indigo's hands in her own.

"It is, and now we must go release our brothers and sisters. Do you know the way?" Indigo asked her.

"I do. I know where each and every Sentinel is waiting, and we have only a little time before the moon sets. Are you ready?"

"I am, Carling. Lead the way."

Claire closed her eyes and a large twisted weeping willow came to mind. It sat where once a stream had run beside it, the trailing branches no longer caught up in the rushing waters. Now a dry valley bed, but the willow was still strong, the roots plunged down into the ground where the forgotten stream still flowed. The great draping branches starting to bud into life and turn green, encircled the gnarled trunk.

Claire and Indigo moved through the night. The park and the miles slipped past them to their next destination, and she stood waiting for the lurching sensation to leave. The willow was everything she had envisioned and more. It trailed the ground and left a hidden space in the centre. Stepping through the curtain, the two beings made their way to the trunk.

There was a sense of impatience there and expectation. The Sentinel was bursting with life, trying to break free and join her sisters on the outside world. Claire fed her the necessary energy to pull herself free from her self-imposed bonds, felt her rushing towards them both with love overflowing her heart. She stood before them and let her lights shine once more. They burst forth brightly the soft violet shade that was her name.

"My sisters," she greeted them both with an arm around each.

"Violet," Indigo said softly.

"Who is next, Carling?" Violet asked, taking Claire's hand.

"It shall be as you left me. The next is my ultimate father, Blue." She grasped a hand in each of hers and she guided them to the next location.

The great Scots pine now stood in the heart of a mighty and ancient estate. Claire stood on the hill looking down on the castle that was the summer home of the current monarch of the land, but it was not enough to hold her interest. Her nerves were building at seeing him again, and she turned to the large tree with reverence. Reaching out her hand she touched the bark gently.

"Father," Claire called softly with a slight catch in her voice.

The return answer brought tears to her eyes. The soft whisper of a solitary word, "Daughter."

Blue was there. Tall and with the love of a father in his eyes, Blue gathered her into his arms and held her close. His glittering hands cradling her head close to him.

"Daughter, I am so proud of you." He dropped a loving kiss on the top of her head.

"Father." Claire's golden lights now flared under her skin to match the brilliance of his, bright blue.

"We hate to interrupt your reunion, Sister and Brother, but the others are waiting," Violet said, her own eyes glistening.

"You are right, Sister," Claire said, releasing her ultimate father and turned to Violet with a small smile. "Green is next."

"I believe you are right, Sister." Violet returned the smile a little shyly.

With a quick change of location, the elm which held the spirit of Green in its depths was now before them. Indigo held Violet's hand as Claire called forth Green. When the Sentinel stepped forward, he briefly kissed Claire on the forehead and then went to meet Violet. They stood holding hands and staring into each other's eyes for such a long time.

"It is time to move on," Claire said, impatient to release her Sentinel Mother.

"Of course, Sister," Green said, finally dragging his eyes from his love.

This time when they shifted it was into a small cemetery. Once there had stood a great forest in this location, and Claire remembered meeting the hooded being under the heavy spreading branches of the same great yew tree. Now the ancient forest was long gone, and it stood in a walled church yard. The tree had at some point split under its own weight, but the internal presence within was still strong.

"Mother, please join us," Claire called softly.

"I never left you," Yellow said, as she stepped through the boundary that had held her for so long. "My daughter, you are as beautiful and gentle as ever." Her hand cupped Claire's face and she felt the warmth of it.

Blue was at their side and joined them in the reunion. Claire felt the connection rebuilding and held both of her ultimate parents close.

"The night is marching on, Daughter," Blue told her.

"Orange is next," Claire told them and pulled away from the loving embrace. Closing her eyes, she found the spot she needed and pulled them along with her.

The rowan was perched on the side of a fast-moving stream. It appeared to be teetering as if the next good storm would plunge it off its precarious perch, to be swept away in the rapid water. The dark grey bark felt smooth under Claire's touch and she felt the recognition from her brother Sentinel. He was eager to leave his seclusion and rejoin the family, and she had to slow him down. When Orange joined them, he picked Claire up in a large hug and kissed her soundly on the cheek.

"Welcome back, Brother," Claire told him as he put her down. "There is one here who has been particularly keen to see you once more."

Taking his hand, she led him to Indigo and saw her sister blush as they approached. Claire picked up her sister's hand and joined it with her brother. They stood together shyly.

"I am waiting, Sister," a voice called eagerly and with some mirth through the ether. Claire tilted her head and smiled a little.

"Are we ready?" she asked the gathered group, who all nodded their assent.

The giant oak sat beside the track. Its large branches spread out, shading an enormous area. The buds were only just starting to release their new, bright-green leaves on the twisted branches, which clawed up into the starry sky that stretched above it. Claire moved under the canopy and reached out a hand. Once more she sensed in the depths of the tree the awareness she had felt the first time she had approached it. She could feel the warmth and love coming from the being inside, a flash of a smile and love-laden eyes, a brief kiss that held so much meaning. And then he was there. Red.

"My Sister. I believe this belongs to you." In his hands he held a wooden sword. Moving towards her he held it out, hilt first for her to take.

"I don't wish to hold it," she told him, shaking her head and stepping back from him.

"It is yours, and you need to remember how to use it." He stood so tall above her and his voice was gentle.

With a hesitant hand Claire reached out and wrapped her fingers around the grip. Slowly she drew it out of his hands and felt the weight of it. Flashes of memory came back to her. The practice sessions with Galen near that very spot; fighting in the hills and mountains of Wales; the battles with Chaos. Pain caught her off guard as it sliced through her shoulder where he had used her own sword against her the first time they had met. But worse was the excruciating agony from her arm, the same jagged cut Chaos had caused with his own shadow sword. Her fingers went numb and the tip of the sword in her hand dipped towards the earth as the strength left her.

Driven to her knees, Claire cried out with the pain and her other hand went to where the shadowy sword had cut her flesh open. In the pale moonlight she pulled it away and saw dark blood over her hand. It dripped down her hanging and useless arm and onto the dirt at the base of the large tree.

"We must get her to the stones," Yellow said, going to her daughter's side.

The Sentinels acted as one. Linking hands, they transported Claire to the large stones hidden on the hill, her hand still clutching the old wooden practice sword.

"Up against the largest," Red ordered, his arms going around her now to hold her against the cold stone.

"No," Claire called out. "That won't work this time."

Transferring the sword to her other hand she concentrated, and it changed. Gone was the old polished and beaten wood and in its place a golden glittering sword was now held in her left hand. The light that shone from it was bright in the dark and illuminated those around it, dimming the lights of the Sentinels.

"Please hold me up and don't let go." She looked up to her father and Red who were both standing before her.

A lick of flame suddenly flared along the edge of the shimmering sword. Claire took a deep breath and swallowed hard. The golden metal moved before her as she raised it up and held it over the still seeping wound. With another couple of quick, heavy breaths Claire took one last gulp of air and held it, pressing the hot metal against the dark festering gash and screamed out into the night in the agony necessary to rid herself of the ancient injury.

The golden flames cauterized and cleansed the wound, forever banishing the darkness of Chaos from the ragged edges and pushing it back to the being that had created it. From far away she could hear him rile against her actions, cursing and crying as the light burned all presence of him away from her. When she felt the last of his cries die away, she pulled the sword from her arm and it fell to the ground by her knees. The flames now extinguished, it lay there shimmering, the lights echoing those in her own hands, winking out slowly and soon it was gone, drifting off in the wind until it was needed again.

"Carling, are you all right?" Yellow's hands were stroking the bloodied mess of her arm. When Claire pulled away Yellow's hand only a silvery scar was left in its wake.

"I am fine, Mother. I am whole again," Claire whispered and stood shakily, stumbling to the largest of the stones. She reached out her hands and pressed them against the basalt rock, drawing the energy up and restoring all that had been lost with her efforts of that night.

"We are whole again, Carling," a voice said behind her. When she turned, she found shadowy forms of the Sentinels all in their places in the gaps of the circle. In the centre was one being. Clothed in white and with bright white lights swirling under its skin.

"Order," she greeted the being softly.

"Our Child. You have come so far, and your journey is nearly at an end. Are you truly prepared for what is to come?" The Great Light stepped towards her.

"I believe I am, Order. I have accepted who and what I am. I am Carling, the One True Child of the Sentinels, Staff and Sword of Order. I am the Guardian of the Stones and Teacher to the Ultimate."

"It is this last name that you have to live up to now, Carling. Aroha is the way of the future. My Sister shall be all that our brother and I were supposed to be. You have my blessings and my love. I wish you well in your journey. There is a place to where you need to take Aroha. You know where that is. Your brothers and sisters will assist you in teaching her, just as they taught you."

"The island is well known now. Many people visit it on a daily basis," Claire said with a worried frown.

"I am aware of this. The family that was put in place to guard it is still there, and the cave is still protected and hidden. You have the skills to change the time," Order reminded her gently.

"Messing with time does not sit well with me, Order. There are so many other factors that could change the course of history."

"There are. But there are also things that have been written in the Book of Destiny and cannot be changed."

"Am I allowed to read this book, Order?" she asked with a half-smile, taking her hands off the stone and facing the Great Light.

"It has always been available to you if you wished it. But being the type of spirit who does not like to use the Foresight Ability, I would think that you would not wish to know what is to come," Order countered back with an equal smile.

"I shall be guided by your wisdom then, Order."

"My time is short; I cannot leave him for long. When you come to the island you will need to go to his prison. I would not ask if it were not necessary. The crystal you placed so long ago needs to be fed more energy. Time is moving quickly."

"I shall do as you ask, Order," she said and bent her head to the Great Being.

"My blessings and my love are with you, Carling, for always," Order told her.

Lifting her head, she found that Order had left. She felt the loss of her presence and the Sentinels all moved from their places. Not once during the visitation had they moved or even spoken. She understood that it had taken their combined energy to project the image of Order into the circle.

"We will go to the island to prepare for you and Aroha," Green told her.

"It is so good to have you all back in the world with me. All of this life I have felt that there was something missing. I thought it was the loss of my natural parents, but it was much more." Claire looked around them.

"We will see you soon, Carling." Yellow came and kissed her forehead in farewell, to be quickly followed by Blue. They took each other's hands and faded from her view. The others all bid their goodbyes and left as well, until there was only one standing before her.

"So, Carling, you are yourself once more," Red said walking towards her.

"No, Red, I am not. I am currently still two. Claire and Carling." The voice came from Claire, but she felt like it was not quite her own.

"When I felt you near that first time you came back, I was so happy. You have always brought me joy, Carling."

"I know I have," she told him simply and sadly.

"I have looked after this valley for so long. I have watched over your family and kept them safe. I have waited for you to come back to us." He reached up his hand and laid it gently on her cheek.

"Of all the Sentinels, you were always the closest to me. But you know that my heart belongs too fully to someone else. Your son, Galen," she reminded him.

"That is why I created him. I could regret my decision to do so, but I choose not to. He is waiting for you," Red said with a tinge of sadness.

"I know. I can feel him in my heart. I can hear his thoughts. He remembers too."

"Go back to your husband then, Claire, with my blessings and my love. And to Carling… I shall wait until it is time." Red leaned forward and kissed her forehead in a brotherly way and left.

His words puzzled Claire a little. Red had spoken to the two parts of herself, the human and Sentinel. She moved to the entrance of the stones and trailed a hand over the largest, gathering more energy to her. The golden lights flashed under her skin, swirling brightly in the darkness.

Lifting off the ground after she had made her way to the spring, Claire gently lowered herself down to the cottage with its glowing windows, and her husband, who was still awake and waiting for her. She went in, pushed off her shoes, and closed the door behind her quietly. The stairs seemed to take an eternity to climb and she pushed open their bedroom door, creaking a little in protest of moving.

Matt was sitting up in bed, a book held loosely and unread in his hands. His face expectant and a slight worry frown creased his forehead. The smile he gave Claire brightened her heart and she rushed to his side and his arms. They folded around her and she kissed him deeply and long.

"I was worried," he admitted to her.

"I could feel it," she responded, her hand stroking his hair and face. "I love only you."

"But his life force is so strong, so is the love he feels for you. I felt it through you," Matt whispered.

"I know. I didn't follow him then, and I won't go to him now. You are my one and only, Galen. Our spirits have been together since the moment I was born. We were destined for each other. You were my first love and my only."

"It feels strange having the memories of my past life to draw on. I remember so much. It was Red who showed me images of you growing up in our first lives."

"He created your spirit to be with me, to love me."

"But you are part Sentinel. One day I will die and you will go on." Matt's fears gave themselves a voice as he asked, "What then? You wait for my spirit to be reborn and you find me?"

"I can't tell you that, Galen. But my past lives have all died. It may be that we grow old together and we pass on once more. We can choose this time to come back or to stay with the Sentinels in the afterlife."

"I only wish to be with you and share our life together." His hand came up and held her shoulders. Immediately he pulled one away and found the wet blood that had been transferred from the sleeve of her shirt. "Claire, you're hurt!"

"No, I was. Do you remember the wound I suffered from our battle with Chaos? You pressed it up against the stones, but it never truly healed."

"Yes, it always had a dark tinge to it and it used to give you trouble."

"I dealt with it tonight, once I had brought them all back to the stones." Claire pulled her shirt off and showed him the silvery scar. "See, it's all healed."

"But how did it come back?"

"I don't know. Red handed me the wooden practice sword and it erupted into fire. That and the previous one." She lifted her fingers to trace the other scar.

"I remember that one; I didn't recognise you." He placed his hand over hers and pulled them away so he could see it. "You have changed, Claire. You have completed the change back to Carling."

"Does that frighten you?" She was worried herself now that he might reject her.

"No. You are you, the Claire or Carling that I have always known and loved. That will never change. Come to bed, my love. Let me show you how much I love you." He pulled her to him and kissed her again.

Chapter Five

All morning Claire kept her mind focused on many things. The whereabouts of her children and extended family, the feeling of where the Sentinels were in the world, and the work that lay on the table in front of her as she sat in the small library. Although she had already absorbed all the information many years before, she loved to bring out the actual pages and tablets to study the writings. The translation of texts within this special library was nearing completion; when it was done, she had a feeling her work and time on the earth would be finished. But to whom could she hand it over?

The role of Guardian of the Stones had always been passed down the female line, except twice. Initially, it had been handed to her first incarnation, a foster daughter married to a natural son, and now her present self, again through marriage to a grandson of the previous Guardian. Claire had not felt the time when the mantle had been passed on to her, and there was only one who could take it on now. But that meant that they would need to move to the valley.

Her daughter Bree and her husband John were building up their fledgling business in New Zealand. Claire could not see them wanting to move halfway around the world and be stuck out in the middle of nowhere to look after a stone circle. Bree's own connection to the place was strong, she knew that. It was her aunt, Matt's little sister, who had been supposed to take up the position of Guardian. Breena had died at the age of six in a freak and unexpected accident, upending all the carefully laid plans of Order and the Sentinels. Breena's spirit had come back in part in their daughter and helped her in the past when Claire had battled Jack and then Marcus.

Claire sat back in the chair and sent her thoughts out to see how far away Bree was. They were halfway there from Glasgow and she could see her. A smile played on her lips as she also saw the secret her daughter held. Bree had hoped to surprise her mother and father with some very special news, and Claire would need to be equally careful in how she reacted. She hated spoiling her children's fun in keeping secrets from her.

The other family members were also on their way, in the convoy of cars winding through the glens and hills of Scotland. They had all agreed to come and she was looking forward to seeing them all again. Tony and Aroha were with Bree and John, and Jasper and his wife Angela were in the same car as his parents, David and Beth. Hunter, who was still single, travelled with Ben and his cousins Owen and Oliver, both of whose partners were at home, too pregnant to make the trip.

Adam—her best friend from childhood and first sweetheart, now happily married to Matt's cousin Addy—and their twin boys Dominic and Cameron, brought up the rear of the convoy. The boys now had lives of their own and were fast growing into their roles in the flourishing family business.

She missed keenly those that had already left them. Charlie, her aunt and Ben's wife, had passed away only a few years ago, and Tia, Tony's wife, who had passed the previous year, leaving her brother and his children still grieving. She still missed her Great-Uncle Geoff, who had raised her from the age of ten. Her grandparents, who had all come to mean so much to Claire, and her Great Aunt Lilith who had become her teacher. Then there were her parents who had been ripped away from her far too soon. Also, Matt's mother and father, Leana and Gerry, and his grandmother Rowena, who had been there for him when his mother could not.

Their spirits were all there waiting to be reborn, waiting to come back to the world and play their parts in the story to come. In the life that hid under the heart of her daughter, Claire could recognise the spirit already bursting into being.

"It does you no good dwelling on the losses you have faced, Carling." Red appeared before her on the other side of the worktable.

"I miss them," she told the Sentinel.

Red pulled out the opposite chair and sat down facing her. "They will all come back. Eventually."

"Are they happy where they are?"

"Yes, they are happy."

"But some cannot come back, can they?"

"Some are too damaged or have been changed too much. Your brother Loc being one."

Claire smiled as she remembered his spirit, but found she only remembered him in his wolf form.

"Why are you torturing yourself with losses?" he asked her curiously.

"I don't know. With the family descending on the valley it feels like an appropriate time. Do you never think of those lives that meant so much to you?"

"Often. Your spirit and those of Breena and Anthony I have followed closely. I have watched over you all."

"Bree is going to sense a difference in the tree when she comes."

"I will make sure I am there for her. And I would not worry so much about who is to become Guardian of the Stones after you, Carling. It will not be Bree. Her life is her own to go out into the world, her spirit is far too restless to stay here."

"Then who?"

"It will come to you, in time." He gave her a small secretive smile.

"So, is that the reason you came here today, to allay my fears of the future and stop me thinking of the past?"

"In some respects, yes. Despite what you think, you have not yet completed the change. You are still two separate spirits. You may have taken on the physical changes to become Carling, but your actions and thoughts are still those of Claire."

"I know this. Carling has explained it to me. Our thoughts need to remain separate for now. And we are not separate. We are one. We inhabit the same body and remember the same memories. Together we are stronger, and we will need to be, to face what is coming."

"You have seen what must be done?" he asked, eagerly leaning on the table.

"We know what must be done."

"Carling, I am so frightened for you. To face him again, after he nearly killed you last time."

"Remember it is not us who must banish him. We are only the support for Aroha. With the cauterizing of the wound, we have the strength once more to be the Staff and Sword of Order. Red, there is something that you will need to do and you need to put your love of Galen as your son aside to do it," she told him carefully with a flash of insight.

"What is it?"

"You will know when the time comes. It will be hard for you to do. Think of it as your own task." She gave him a wink along with the sly upturn of her lips.

"You are being very cryptic today."

"Annoying, isn't it?" She grinned at him.

"Very well. I will think on it and start to steel my heart."

"No, you cannot block your love of your son. If you do that then Galen will fail."

"I cannot put that love aside, Carling. I have guided and watched his spirit from the moment it burst to life. Galen is very much my son as any human can be."

"In doing this you will be making him happy, and in doing it you will also be happy, Red."

"Can you not speak plainly and let me know?" Red asked with some frustration.

"No, I cannot. Now you must go. Galen is coming across the yard towards us. He still feels that human emotion of jealousy when you are around."

Red looked at her strangely for a moment. "I have a feeling our conversation is not over yet."

"It isn't." Another small smiled played on her lips as the lights flared for a moment under her skin.

"Until we meet again, Carling. My blessings and my love be on you."

"And mine on you, Red."

Claire watched as the Sentinel faded from view and then went into her mind as the lights diminished from her body.

"Carling, can you tell me what that was all about?" Claire asked her Sentinel side.

"Just as with our brother, Red, I cannot tell you. But it was a necessary conversation to help him do what he must later. Galen is opening the door; we should not be rude and ignore your husband."

With a gentle push, Carling brought them back to awareness as the door opened and the fresh spring air flooded the room. The heady scent of a rose in full bloom came with it and she looked up at Matt with the love that it always brought with it.

The line of dark coloured four-wheel-drive cars began to arrive at the ford that served as a border to the valley, the tires crunching on gravel as they moved off the hard, black bitumen of the road. The river was running far higher than usual, its banks under pressure from the spring snowmelt racing down from the hills and mountains. Added to that was the last couple of days of torrential rain, that was normal for the time of the year. The lead car—driven by John with Bree sitting beside him and Aroha and Tony in the back—paused briefly at the edge of the river. Claire watched in amusement as John made his way carefully through the fast-moving water as it spilled over the ford and smiled at the reason behind his care.

Standing under the great oak, she felt the presence once more in the area, but curiously not where it should be, in the depths of the tree. The car pulled up beside it, bringing the following vehicles to a slow halt. Bree hopped out and raced around to greet her old friend, the tree. Her surprise at seeing her mother there was great and she rushed to her arms.

"Welcome back, Bree," Claire said holding her close.

"Mum, what are you doing here?" the young woman asked, pulling out of the embrace.

"I knew you would stop and wanted to be here when you said your hellos." Claire stepped back and waited for Bree to approach the tree, watching her closely.

The look on her daughter's face said it all. Claire could see that Bree sensed the change and turned confused eyes to her mother.

"What's happened? He isn't here."

"He is here, but he's no longer part of the tree. The Sentinels have returned, Bree. But we have time to talk about it once we are back at the house."

"This is the real reason for your birthday party, isn't it? You don't really like celebrating your birthday and this big party is an excuse to get us all here. You have some explaining to do, Mum," Bree told her seriously.

"Yes, I do. You'd better return to the car. I'll see you at the house," Claire flashed a smile and started to steer her daughter back to the car and family which were waiting for her.

"But—"

"Not now. They are waiting for you and you are holding everyone up." She pushed her on and watched as Bree got back into the car and John drove off up the track.

"That wasn't fair. I wanted to surprise her," Red said from behind her.

"It was completely fair. I have to prepare them all for you." The lights once more glowed softly under her skin.

"I am getting very confused as to who I am talking to. Is this Claire or Carling?" he asked hesitantly, his suspicions clearly growing.

The smile she gave him was meant to confuse and she disappeared before she could give him a response.

"What games are you playing, Carling?" Red called out before shaking his head and disappearing himself.

Claire smiled to herself at Red's obvious confusion. She was enjoying putting the Sentinel on the back foot as they all had done with her at one time or another. She called into the house to let Matt know the cars were arriving and stood within the crook of his arm as they watched the cars come down the track. The line of vehicles trailed after each other and she had a momentary flashback of other visitors to the valley down the centuries.

Bree was first out and rushing to her parents. They collected her up and held her tight. Matt, as always, held her face in his hands and searched for the part of her that was his sister.

"Welcome home, my wee angel," he told her and kissed her forehead.

"I am no longer wee, Dad," she told him with a giggle.

"I know, but you will always be my angel." There was a slight tear in his eye, and she hugged him close.

John was next, so much like his father in looks, and very much growing in confidence. Now well and truly a part of the family and always happy to see them.

"This place never changes, does it?" John said, gathering Claire into a hug.

"No, it doesn't. How have you been?"

"Good," he said sheepishly. Claire could see him bursting with the news the couple had kept a secret. But there was no time to say anything as everyone else was soon making their way to them to say hello.

"Tony. It is so good to see you," Matt clasped his hand and pulled him into a hug.

"It is great to be here. I love this valley. You are so lucky you get to live here," Tony told him.

"I wish we could be here more often," Claire told him, holding him close. "Welcome back, Tony."

"You haven't changed. What's your secret?" he said, looking down into her face.

"No secret, just good living. You should try it for a change," she joked with him.

"I tried once—it didn't get me anywhere." Tony laughed.

The rest of the family were greeted and reconnections made. Claire was saddened by how old Beth, David, and Ben seemed to be getting. They were now the older generation.

They had replaced her grandparents and great-uncle and great-aunt. Claire made a mental note to spend a good amount of time with them; they were her connection to her parents.

The boys were men now. Hunter had the farm fully in hand and regaled her with how it was producing even better yields than during his father's time. Jasper was still teaching and enjoying it, never for one moment regretting the brief side-step into the world of espionage for Tony. Owen and Oliver were well-known and award-winning architects, having taken over from Ben in the family business, although he still liked to look in every now and then.

Addy sought out Claire in the kitchen as she was getting dinner ready. She was still slim and sporting a very vibrant ginger colour in her hair. She leaned against the door frame and watched as Claire went from bench to stove and back again.

"You need a hand?" Addy asked.

"No, not from you." Claire grinned at her. The fact that Addy still couldn't cook was well known in the family. "Unless you brought that housekeeper of yours?"

"No, we left Margret at home. She's probably relaxing without us there, and she deserves to." Addy laughed and stepped into the room. "For a moment I could see Gran working away."

"I still feel her watching over the house. I think she doesn't always approve of how I do things."

"She was so set in her ways, but they worked. How have you been, Claire?" Addy asked, leaning up against the bench and pinching a carrot.

"I'm good. Happy that nearly everyone could make it. How are you?" Claire opened the oven and started to baste the roast.

"I couldn't be happier. Do you remember that day when you helped Breena pass over?"

Claire closed the oven slowly and turned to her best friend. "Of course I do. Why?"

"You asked me what she said to me before she left."

"I did and you wouldn't tell me."

"Would you like to know?" Addy raised an enquiring eyebrow.

"If you think you can tell me now, of course I would."

"She said that Adam and I would be together forever. That we would have two boys and four grandchildren."

"I figured it was something like that." Claire smiled at her as she started to cut up more vegetables.

"But that was not all. She also said that you were special, that when we were older you were going to go through a big change and would need our help and love. I have been watching you since we arrived, Claire. You are going through a change, just as Bree said. What is it?"

Claire stopped what she was doing and turned to her. "I am, Addy. So much has happened in the last few months. And so much more is going to happen in the next few. If anything happens to me, I want you and Adam to be there for Matt." A tear formed in her eye.

"What is going to happen? Have you seen something?" Addy asked, taking up Claire's hand.

"No, but there is one final task that needs to be done, though it's not clear that I'll make it through. Matt is going to want to protect me, and I'm afraid he won't be able to." The tear slid down her cheek and Claire dashed it away with the back of her free hand.

"Why won't you use that Ability to see? Why do you refuse it?" Addy asked her.

"Because that particular Ability can bring a great deal of pain," a voice from behind them came. Beth was walking into the room, still very much upright but the years were now showing on her features.

"It can, Aunty Beth. That is why you chose not to use yours," Claire responded with a sniff.

Addy looked between her best friend and mother-in-law, clearly confused. "But I thought you didn't have an Ability?"

"I did once," Beth said as she reached the pair of them.

"I know the reason you pushed it away," Claire told her quietly.

"I had guessed that you did. Thank you for not pushing, unlike your brother and Adam."

"They knew? Why didn't they tell me?" Addy asked.

"Because it was not their place. Tony found out by entering my mind uninvited and then told Adam. Claire, I am guessing you found out a different way?" She stared at her niece.

"I did. It seems secrets still have their way of coming out around me." Claire grinned and sighed.

"Well, I have new one now for you that you cannot have guessed." Beth paused for a moment. "It has been awoken, Claire. Such vivid visions I have seen of you, Matt, Tony, and Aroha. I was also visited by a Being, one who glowed orange. He told me that it was time to put away the past pain, that my Talent was needed. He helped me understand how to control it. I know what it is you must do, Claire. I know who you are."

"I was going to tell everyone after dinner," Claire admitted.

"Then I will say no more on the subject. Now, can I give you a hand with anything?" Beth offered. Addy was still flicking her head between the two women.

"Yes, thank you. Can you check on the roast? I've been using your tip for roasting lamb, but it still seems to come out a bit dry," Claire said, resuming chopping vegetables.

"Um, excuse me! Would either of you like to let me in on what the hell was not said just now?" Addy's voice went up an octave.

"Shh, not so loud. I promise you that you will know when we're finished with dinner," Claire told her.

"And make sure you have a warm jacket handy, Addy, because we'll be making the trip up to the stones," Beth advised her.

Addy stood with her mouth open and stared at the pair of them.

After dinner, as the younger men were set the task of doing the dishes, a commotion at the door brought Claire out of her seat and to the front door. A bitter wind was blowing in and the large shape of her son stood in the open doorway.

"What time do you call this? We were expecting you hours ago," Claire told him as she pulled him into the house.

"Sorry, Mum. We got delayed," Callum told her, stepping forward and dropping a kiss on her cheek.

"We?" She was confused for a moment. Callum had not given them any warning of anyone joining him on the trip to the valley. "Who?"

"I'm sorry, Mrs. Drummond. I thought Callum had told you I was coming," Finn said at the doorway. Claire moved her son out of the way and faced the young man.

"Sorry, must have slipped my mind," Callum told her sheepishly.

"Slipped your mind? Never mind, you are here now. Come in. Are you two hungry?" she asked the pair of them and in unison they answered.

"Starving."

"There are leftovers in the kitchen, but before you go there, go see your aunts and uncles in the living room, Callum." As he went to move past his mother, she held onto his arm for a moment longer, halting his steps. "Aroha is here," she said gently.

"Thanks, Mum." He kissed the top of her head and led the way into the inner house.

Claire remained in the entrance waiting for Matt, who arrived shortly after. He gestured to the lounge as he walked towards her.

"Is that such a great idea?" he asked her with a whisper.

"What else are we to do? Turf him out and say no? This, of all places, is where The People have always been welcome, as long as they have no ill intent in their hearts."

"But what about your news?" he asked.

"There are things I can do, remember. I can put him to sleep, or I can transport him elsewhere and keep him in limbo for a while. Don't panic, Galen."

"I'm not happy he's here," Matt whispered, then turned as the two younger men came out of the room.

"Let's get you something to eat," Claire said, moving past her husband and heading to the kitchen.

The whole family was crammed into the front room. It was the same room Claire remembered Gran giving her the first hint that she belonged to something a lot larger than the Community. The floor space was soon taken up with the younger generation, as they settled in waiting for her to speak. Claire very carefully crept into the mind of Finn and found Tony already there. She shook her head at her brother's audacity and gently implanted the suggestion she had prepared for Finn. She took her brother's hand without a word having been spoken between them and pulled Tony out with her. The look she threw him from across the room had him smirking and looking forward to hearing her telling him off.

"If I can have everyone's attention," Claire called out from where she stood by the door. Slowly the conversations stopped, and she saw Callum try to rouse Finn. "Leave him. This does not concern him, and he won't wake for you anyway."

"Finally, we get some answers," Bree said over in the corner from her husband's knee.

"Yes, Bree. Please be patient," Claire told her. "Some of you already know that there have been certain changes to not only this special place, but also to me."

"Who knows already?" David asked, a little hurt he was not let in on the secret earlier.

"Only a few, Uncle David. Please, I am nervous enough as it is." She gathered herself together again and took a deep breath. "You all know the story, and how I came to possess these extraordinary Abilities, but it seems there are more. The Guardians have visited once more and charged me with another task. Not only that, but also allowed me to see who I really am. It seems that my spirit is not quite fully human."

"What are you talking about?" Ben asked, sitting forward. "How can that be possible? You are my brother's daughter. We know who your parents are."

"I know who they are, Uncle Ben. But when my spirit was first brought into this world, it was not born of human parents," she told him.

"Then, what?" Ben demanded.

"The Guardians, who were the original people of this world. They were first known as the Sentinels." She stopped and looked around the room, seeing the uncomprehending stares and began to feel a little irritated. "Didn't any of you read my email about the origin story I found in the library?"

"I thought that was just a children's tale," Jasper told her with a shrug.

"I didn't have time," Owen admitted.

"Sweetheart, why don't you just run over it now?" Matt told her gently.

"This world was created from a vast explosion, caused by the being called Chaos. From the explosion the being Order was born and from that being the Sentinels were created to protect this world from Chaos. There are seven of them, one for each colour of the rainbow."

"Technically there are only six colours in the rainbow," Jasper piped up. "Indigo is in dispute as being a tertiary colour rather than a primary or secondary."

"I wouldn't tell her that," Claire warned him with a small smile. "These Sentinels protected the world from Chaos, but it soon became evident that they would never defeat him. So, a plan was born. That plan was my spirit. Order decreed that one should be born from the Sentinels, to be the Staff and Sword, the Champion—hence why I was originally named Carling, it means 'little champion.' My first life was born up at the stones, in the centre, from the Sentinels called Yellow and Blue. I battled Chaos twice in that lifetime and managed to imprison him in a cave. He still remains captive there, under the watch of his sibling Order." She paused to take a breath and looked at her husband, taking his hand.

"At my side from the moment I was born, watching over and protecting me, has always been Galen. Whenever my spirit was reborn Galen has always been there and we have found each other. Our lives are intertwined, and so closely connected that there is nothing that can tear us apart. He was there again in my second life and helped me defeat the very first Marcus. The spirit of the man we faced more recently has haunted my lives. He has always been a creature of Chaos. And that is who he was trying to bring forth that night at the circle in New Zealand. If Chaos had been able to inhabit his body fully, I would not be standing here before you all."

"I still don't understand this, Claire," Ben said, confusion written all over his face. "Who are Chaos and Order?"

"They are the children of the Universe. Order was born to counter Chaos, but their contention has left the world unstable."

"So why didn't your previous spirit destroy this Chaos when she had the chance?" Oliver asked.

"Because it is not the job of my spirit to do that. That task belongs to another."

"Me," a small voice called out from beside her father. Tony placed a protective arm around Aroha as heads turned in her direction.

"What? You can't be serious?" David asked, looking between Tony and Aroha.

"It is true, David. My daughter is rather special," Tony said proudly.

"Mum?" Callum turned his blue eyes to his mother.

"Callum, later." She could see the questions already forming in his mind.

"So, what now?" David asked. "You go off again on another harebrained adventure? Because, my girl, I am getting too old to help you."

"I thank you, Uncle David, and you too, Uncle Ben, for the help you have given me in the past. I thank you all for your support." Claire paused for a moment. "But this time it has to be just Aroha and myself."

"And me, of course," Matt said from where he sat beside her. "You can't go without your protector and support."

"Can we talk about it later, sweetheart," she said quietly.

"Claire, you cannot leave me behind. You know what can happen when I am not there to help and support you," he said, referring to not only their own past, but the past lives of the other Galen and Carling.

"I'm not sure, Matt." She took up his hand and gave it a squeeze.

A loud call came from up on the hill, from the stones themselves. An energy burst so strong it shook Claire for a moment and Matt steadied her.

"Are you all right?" he asked, standing and taking her elbow.

"Yes, I'm fine. We have to go to the stones. There is someone there who wishes to talk to us all," Claire told them.

"Who?" Tony asked sitting forward.

"Someone very important for the Great Light to leave her post." She frowned a moment, before leading Matt out of the room, and to the back door.

Spring was all around the valley, but the wind that caught at the gathering as they ascended the hill was bitter, with just a hint of ice. Before leaving the confines of the house there had been a collective rush to don warm jackets, and Claire checked on Finn one last time to make sure he would not wake until they returned. Now in single file, the younger ones helping their elders, they walked up the track. Claire had not climbed the hill this way in some time but felt it was necessary. There were enough with the flight talent to take the party up, but the pull to walk the track was great.

As they reached the top, the moon was just rising above the horizon, over the rolling hills behind the protective rock. It was full and bright, sending its light out into the world. Claire approached the spring and cupped a hand to raise its sweet water to her mouth and drank. Slowly she approached the stones as the others made their way up to the great upthrust of rock that protected the circle from view.

As always, the great stones clawed their way into the sky, standing proudly as they had since the Sentinels first pulled them up from the earth. The power thrummed into the night. Claire could feel the vibrations coming from them as they pulled the energy from the centre of the earth, in anticipation of what was to come. Claire placed a hand on the first stone and began her ritualistic circuit of them. Each sang a slightly different song to her, in a slightly different note. Now she smiled in understanding, where once she had been just a bit afraid of their knowledge.

She waited at the entrance, impatient to enter the circle. Never before had she had that feeling at the stones. The others stood in the protection of the rocks, waiting and watching her. The wind whistled around the area, lifting her golden hair up and tossing it around. Then the sound she had been waiting for came. The sound of feet.

From the other side of the rocks it could be heard getting nearer. Then the figures appeared out of the darkness, their skin glowing with swirling points of light in the multi hues of the rainbow. They passed the family group and entered the circle, coming to stand in between each stone. Softly their voices began to chant and Claire recognised the language. The chanting became louder as they raised their arms to the centre and began to walk inwards. They met and each grasped the hand of the being beside them. In that moment a flash of the purest white light blinded the group. When the light dimmed, a single Being was standing in the middle of the circle and beckoned Claire and the others in.

Claire approached the Being with wonder. She watched as the points of light raced over her pale skin. Kind eyes crinkled at the corners as she held out a hand for Claire to take. Her small one slipped into the long-fingered hand of Order and her own lights blazed alight, sending out a soft golden glow.

"Our child, you have grown and finally come to your full potential. It is time to start preparing my sister for her hardest of tasks," the Being said to her.

"Order, we welcome you back to the sacred circle. You have been missed from this world, though The People do not know you anymore," she said.

"I thank you for your words, but that is what I wished. By diminishing ourselves, I gave less temptation for Chaos to spread his woe on the land and sought to protect your line. It has now come to fruition." Order turned her kind eyes to Aroha. "My sister, you are just starting your journey. Heed well the words of our child, as she has great knowledge to impart to you. Our Mother has brought forth a magnificent being and I look forward to passing this world into your hands for your protection."

Aroha looked about her shyly at being singled out, then stepped forward to meet Order. "I have much to learn, I know this. But you have been with me my whole life. I remember such vivid dreams of you being there, telling me stories."

"I have watched over your development, imparting what I could of our history. I have protected you as much as I could from the eyes and wrath of Chaos. It was me who made Claire aware of the spark of evil that lay dormant in you, so she could wrestle it away from you. Heed what she must tell you, learn from her. My blessings and love be on you, my beloved Sister."

The shyness that had been evident within Aroha only moments before slipped away and a look of calm confidence replaced it. She stood taller as she looked into Order's face. "We thank you, Order, and mine be with you as you face the end of the task which took you away from The People. You have worked long, and your rest will be well deserved. My blessing and love on you, also our strength." Aroha reached out and took Order's other hand.

Claire could feel the energy as it raced through Aroha, reaching up from the centre of the earth and fortifying Order for the final days she now faced. The lights under Order's skin flared brightly, and as the energy spilled over to Claire, so did her own golden ones. For a moment there were bright points of light, multi-hued sparks appearing under Aroha's skin. They were gone as soon as she let go of the Great Light's hand.

"My thanks, Sister. But you still need to visit the cave. The crystal is diminishing, and my child needs to boost the energy within. This will be the first time you face Chaos. You must steel yourself against what he will show you. You must be strong for the task ahead."

"It will be as you ask, Order." Aroha bowed her head and stepped back to stand with her father.

"Whether you know it or not, each of you will have your own tasks in the coming meeting. Even if it is just thinking of our child and my sister. You must all send your love to them. Your love will strengthen their spirits and help them face what must come." Order turned to Galen. "Our son, your love has been readily given to our child and I thank you for it. You must not worry. You will be at her side once more to aid her. You will be needed."

"I thank you, Order. It has always been my wish to love and support Carling. I shall not stop now," Matt spoke up, standing straighter at the task.

"Our child, there are some who wish to spend time with this group. They wish to get to know them once more. We shall see you soon in the cave." Order released Claire's hand and raised her arms to the sky. "Mother Universe, my time is almost upon me. Give me strength to carry out your wishes and charge those with your love who must perform your tasks. I give my life to you."

Off in the distance a bell rang a clear note. Some of the group gathered looked around, trying to figure out where it had come from. Carling understood. The Universe was accepting the pledge.

Before her eyes the Being flared into a bright light once more and then the other colours erupted from the centre. Where only moments before one stood, now seven had taken her place. As they coalesced into being, two stepped forward and greeted Claire.

"Our daughter," Yellow said placing a hand on the side of Claire's face.

"Time is fast running out," Blue told her. "We only have a little while here with you all."

"It is good to see you once more," Claire told them truthfully, feeling the connection coming down from the first Carling.

"We must go inside your mind for a moment, Carling," Yellow told her gently. "We need to visit with your earthbound parents."

"Why?" she asked them, confused.

"Their task has finished. It is time for the last of their spirit to rest. You already know that they are to be reborn into this world. And one is amongst this group already," Blue told her.

"Yes, though they do not know it." She nodded and closed her eyes. "I am ready when you are."

The slip into her subconscious was so easy it was like stepping through a doorway. With ease, she found the blanket that lay out on the grass in the autumn parklike surroundings and saw her parents walking towards her hand in hand. They smiled and greeted her with a warm embrace, one which Claire held onto.

"There is a change about you, Claire. What is happening?" Jess asked her as she tucked a stray lock of hair behind her daughter's ear.

"There are two who wish to meet you. I have told you how my spirit came to be." She saw them both give each other worried looks.

"You did. Who are they, Claire?" John asked.

"They are the Sentinels, Yellow and Blue," she said quietly.

"They are welcome here," Jess said, taking her husband's hand and holding on tightly.

From the darkness that surrounded the little scene came the two Beings. Their lights dimmed in the confines of Claire's subconscious. They were holding hands as always and their steps were cautious as they approached Claire's parents. The feeling of awkwardness emanated from both sides. Curiously she could see a resemblance between the two couples.

"Mum and Dad, this is Yellow and Blue."

"We have already met your mother, Claire," Blue said with a nod to her parents.

"Was it you who came to visit me in my dream, told me how to place this part of ourselves in our daughter?" Jess asked.

"It was. And it was a necessary thing to do. Claire needed your guidance and your love at that time, and you have both done your jobs very well," he told them.

"I feel there is a 'but' here," John said, placing a protective arm around Jess's shoulders.

"There is, John," Yellow said gently. "Your time for rebirth is near. We wish to send the part of you which remains here to join the part that is preparing to be reborn. It is time for you both to leave. Your part in your daughter's life is over."

"What if we don't want to?" Jess asked with hesitation, clinging to John.

"Then the small sparks of life that are hidden in the depths of their mothers' wombs will falter," Yellow said sadly.

"Mum, I have already sensed whose child you shall be. I don't want to visit that pain on my daughter," Claire stepped closer to her mother.

"And me? What about me, Claire?" John asked. "I don't want to be separated from your mother."

"You won't be. Just as Matt and I have always found each other, so have you. You have always been my earth parents. From the originals, Tarl'a and Mailcon, you have loved me. I have already seen that you will find one another, but to be together again, you must agree to leave now."

Jess looked up at her husband and then back to her daughter. "We will do as you ask, Claire. It has been our privilege to be here with you like this, even if we could not be physically in the real world. Will you watch over us?"

"Of course, I will." With tears in her eyes Claire placed her arms around her mother and hugged her tightly for the last time. John wrapped them both up together and kissed his daughter's head.

"Can you do one thing before we go?" John asked her.

"Anything, Dad."

"Can you bring Ben and David in so we can say goodbye properly," he asked, pulling away a little.

"They are on their way as we speak," Claire said as she looked out into the darkness that surrounded the park scene.

Wandering down a path as if they were out for a leisurely afternoon stroll, came David and Ben. Their figures no longer that of old men, but as Claire remembered from first meeting them when she was seventeen. Both tall and strong, with cheeky gleams in their eyes. They neared the little family group and John and Jess went to greet them. Their reunion was silent as they looked at each other. The love that bonded them was renewed and they embraced.

Claire sniffed back a tear and a hand was placed on her shoulder. She turned and found Blue's steady and understanding gaze on her.

"Go join them, Carling. Share the love that is there. It's you that is the true bond between them," he told her gently and then removed his hand.

Claire reached them and was immediately enfolded into the family reunion. The love flowed from the four people who meant the most to her. She sent them each her own love in return.

"It is time," Blue told the gathered group.

"Time for what?" David said, his arm still around his sister.

"For us to go, to pass on and be reborn," Jess told him.

"We can't stay here, our daughter already looks older than us," John teased Claire.

"So, this is it? This is really the last time we will see you?" Ben asked his older brother.

"It is, Ben. Keep an eye out for me out there. And thank you both for keeping an eye on our girl for us."

"You don't need to say it, John. It has been our pleasure, if not sometimes our anguish, to do so," David said holding out his hand for his brother-in-law to take.

They shook hands and embraced for the last time then Ben and David stepped back, leaving Claire with her parents once more.

"We are ready, Claire," Jess told her with a shaky voice and tears in her eyes.

"I don't know what to do," she told them.

"Yes, you do. It is there inside you. The Guardians cannot do it, and neither can I. It has to come from you," Jess said gently.

Centering herself, she found what she needed and called up Carling to help her. The Sentinel side manifested herself beside Claire and took her hand.

"We love you, Mum and Dad," Claire said to them.

Carling placed a glittering hand on Claire's shoulder as Claire took up a hand each of her parents.

"Go and be at peace until we meet again. Take my love with you and know that I will look out for you both. I thank you for your love and support and thank you for being here with me when I needed you most. I love you both," she said, her voice cracking and she sniffed.

Tears formed in their eyes as they nodded to her, their own words stuck in their throats. Gently Claire pushed out, finding the connection that held her parents there in her subconscious and took it up in her hands. "Go and be happy."

With a slight twist, the connection was broken, and the image of her parents slowly slipped away before her eyes. Her hands were left empty. A sob welled up inside and she released it to her mind, the bitterness of her action overcoming her, and she felt the loss of her parents all over again.

Warm gentle arms were with her, they supported and embraced her, holding her near and filling her with the love and support of family that were still present. Ben and David were both there to comfort and share her loss. Then another pair of arms was there to take over. Claire looked up and found Matt's loving eyes. He held her face in his hands and kissed her softly, then pulled her into his strong arms. He rocked and filled her with his love, with his strength and his comfort.

"It is time to go back now, Carling," Yellow told her as she stroked her golden hair.

Claire nodded and pulled away from Matt. Slowly her two uncles took a hand each and gave them a squeeze before they pulled away, heading back out into the real world. She looked around after they had left and found the park now a cold and empty place. Where once it held love and support and felt like a warm autumn afternoon, now it felt more like winter. Soft, white flakes slowly began to drift from the empty sky.

"Change it. Make it your own," Matt whispered to her, reading her thoughts and feelings.

"But it was their home. This is what they made it," she replied.

"No, it is what you made it, Carling. This was your happiest memory of them," Blue told her.

"I don't want to change it then. I want to keep it the same," she said adamantly.

"But it will bring you pain every time you come here," Blue told her.

"I'll think about it," she told them. She pulled away from her husband and took his hand. "We should get back."

When they returned to the circle, she found that her family were talking to the Sentinels. Each of the great beings had found their descendants and claimed them once more. As Claire looked, she could see the traits that made each of them tied to one of the Guardians and she smiled, though she still felt sad. Walking towards her now was Red and she felt Matt's hand tighten around hers as he approached.

"Relax, my son. I came to talk to you, not my sister Sentinel," Red said, trying to ease Matt's fears.

"I am sorry, Guardian. I don't mean to react this way."

"I know you don't. I have invested too much energy and time into your spirit, my son, into your whole family actually, to see it wasted by some careless word or look. But know that I love Carling. I have loved her and will continue to love her, and just as she needs your love to survive, she needs mine as well. You have no need to fear that I intend to take her from you. I thought we had sorted this out in your first life. I told you then that of all the Sentinels, I am destined to be alone, that the love I have for you, Carling, and your family line is too great and encompassing. That is my role in this task."

"I thank you for your honesty, Red. It means a great deal to me," Matt told him.

"Now, your daughter has some news and I am very much impatient to hear it. Although I think, Carling, you already know?" Red said.

"Yes, I do, Red." Claire looked over to her daughter and moved towards her. She took her hand and placed it on her daughter's still flat stomach. "I know, Bree. I couldn't help myself. I felt the first fluttering last month when I was checking in with you."

"I wanted to surprise you, Mum. I don't want to look, and I know you don't like to, but will you see for me, for us." Bree took John's hand and held it tightly.

"I see a beautiful child, a girl. One who has been on this earth before and one who has strong links to us. She will grow happy and strong, and she will have her father's Ability." Claire looked to John who looked down at the ground a little ashamed. "Why have you never told us you have an Ability, John?"

"It didn't seem to be as important as everyone else's. And there is only one," he admitted quietly, trying not to let his father hear.

"Tell him. Tony will be so proud of you. He already is." She looked to Tony and then back to his son. "Show him. Tonight is about revealing things that were hidden. It's time they all know."

John kissed Bree and then went to his father. Both men were the same height and the younger clapped his father on the shoulder in a good-natured gesture, before disappearing before everyone's eyes.

"He didn't want to tell anyone. I kept trying to make him, but he wouldn't," Bree told her mother.

"So, when he came into his Ability, did he come visiting?" Claire asked, trying to hide a small grin.

"No, it was too far away. He tried one night, but he couldn't," Bree said, blushing under the moonlight. "Does Dad know about the baby?"

"No, he doesn't. Why don't you go tell him? He's going to be so happy."

"Mum, the baby's spirit, is it…?" she trailed off, unsure how to ask.

"Yes, it is my mother. And the spirit of my father will find her. Don't try and keep them apart, they were always meant to be together. Now go to your father and let him know your news." She kissed Bree's cheek and watched her go.

Claire leaned against one of the stones and felt the energy release into her. The night was so calm and warm in the safe confines of the stones. The companionable chatter of her family washed over her and she closed her eyes and listened. There was the joyous cry of Matt at hearing Bree was pregnant, the sudden exclaim as John and Tony re-joined the group, and excited babble asking about his Ability. She felt so connected to each of them, feeling their thoughts.

"The lights are showing, my love," Matt said into her ear as he gently pulled her away from the stone.

"I want to let them shine. I can feel so much love here. I'm so happy and sad all at once," she told him.

"Why sad? I thought that knowing your parents will soon be reborn would make you happy." His hand caressed her cheek.

"It's not just the loss of my parents, it's also knowing that soon I will be heading out to finish my task." She looked up at him. "Galen, I'm scared. I'm scared I'm not going to survive this."

"You have in the past, and I will be at your side. I won't let anything happen to you, my love." He wrapped his arms protectively around her. "I promise I will be there to protect you."

Chapter Six

The party lasted for the whole week. It had been lovely to have them all visit, and when the time came for the family to leave, Claire felt saddened that they had to go. Although, with their special Abilities, they were never really far away. She stood on the drive, waving the last car goodbye, and sighed deeply. Around her, spring was taking a firm hold. The sheep that grazed in the meadow were now joined by their frolicsome lambs. She smiled at their antics.

Taking a look at the house and at the library, Claire knew she should be going to one or the other to either study or to start training Aroha, who had stayed behind. But she didn't feel like it. As she had done before, so many times, when she got into one of these moods, Claire started to walk towards the brook that ran the length of the valley, to join the river near the ford.

The water sparkled in the sunshine and she looked into the deep pools, the memory of her first life and the many fish that had once lived in the depths surfacing. Now only a few were seen each year. On she moved, towards the end of the valley and remembering the great towering trees that once guarded the way to the house, hiding it from casual passers-by. She wondered if she could start planting more trees to rejuvenate the old forest and decided to talk to Matt about it at some point.

She leapt over the brook to the other side and found the spot where a red tent had stood one summer night in the meadow surrounded by wildflowers. She remembered how that first Carling felt, the excitement and love she felt for her Galen. Claire smiled. There was so much history in this valley. She could feel it seeping up from the ground. The long line of women who had dedicated their lives to this valley, the Guardians of the Stones, had all known why they had to stay here, but as the years had passed and the Ancestors' knowledge had faded, so too had the Guardians' knowledge.

She thought of Gran, her predecessor, the last Guardian to protect the stones. Claire now realised that Gran had not been aware that she held such an important role among The People, nor that she had been the latest of such a long line of women to do so. Claire gave a little chuckle at how the old woman would have marveled at this news, then felt sad she was not there to share it.

On she wandered to the river and then followed it back to the ford, that well-worn track where many people crossed over at the shallowest point. The gateway to the valley was now bare, save the large old oak that still stood guard beside the track. Claire made her way under the large branches of the tree and patted the trunk. She hauled herself up to the spreading limbs and remembered the first time she had encountered Breena, her husband's sister. The thought of the ghost child made her smile, as she remembered her scampering in amongst the branches and her laugh.

"My sister is in a reflective mood this morning," a calm voice said from the ground. When Claire looked, she found Breena staring back up at her. The sight of her gladdened her heart and she leapt down from the branch on which she sat and into the arms of her sister-in-law.

"Breena!" she exclaimed.

"Claire. What is the matter with you?" Breena pulled away and smoothed the blonde hair away from her face.

"I don't know."

"This is not like before when we fought up at the stones. This reflection is from you." Breena linked her arm with Claire and they began to head back up the track that led to the house.

"No, it's not like that day. I'm unsure of my future and remembering my past lives. Breena, did you know about that—that I have lived before, that my spirit is who it is?"

"To some extent I knew you were special, that there was something amazing about you. The Guardians did not tell me much at all. I was only six, remember? I was given specific things to say to you, but they did not share that knowledge with me."

"But why are you here now? I thought you could not come back," Claire said.

"Red sent me. He told me that you were troubled and needed a sister to lean on. They are magnificent, aren't they?"

"In their natural form you mean? Yes, they are."

"And you? Your light, even though it does not shine now, is so beautiful. I am envious of you, Claire."

"Why? If you were in my place you would be the one to meet Chaos once more. It's not something I'm looking forward to."

"No, but once your life is over you will be joining the Sentinels. I am only doing their bidding and cannot be one of them."

"Why are you still with them then? Why don't you leave and be reborn?"

"I can't remember. A part of my spirit is still with Bree."

"I thought that was just a temporary thing, that you could withdraw it and be whole again."

"No, I can't. Bree's spirit is a new one and if I were to leave it now, she would stumble and with her carrying a child that would not be a good idea. No, I will remain with the Sentinels until she joins them and then I will be reborn. By the way Ma and Da send their love."

"Are they happy, Breena?" Claire stopped and turned to her.

"They are, Claire. They are happier now they are together. Da is very impressed with the work you have done, and Ma has sent you a gift." Breena held out her hand, and in the palm, appeared a seedling rose bush. "It is hardy and will grow here in the valley without a care to the weather or wind."

"Is this what I think it is?"

"It is. It's the only one in existence. Red said that it was significant to you and worked with Ma to make it perfect."

"I remember the very first one he made for me. It was just before I married Galen the first time; we were at the home of the Sentinels, and we were discussing Order leaving and facing Chaos. The one crafted by Matt and Tony still surrounds my heart."

"Plant it when you get back to the house. It will flower at the beginning of summer and the scent will fill the valley. Red said that it was important. I sometimes think he believes I am still only six."

"Was it Red who guided you the day you passed over?"

"It was. As my Ancestor it was his duty to help me. He protected and comforted me while I stayed in the tree." Bree paused for a moment before carrying on. "Be careful of him, Claire. I believe his feelings for you are more than he proclaims. He gets agitated when he gets questioned about it."

"Who questions him?" Claire asked as they walked on, the sapling in her hands now.

"The other Sentinels, Galen, Ma, Da, and me," Breena admitted.

"Please don't. There is no concern on that front. That is all in hand. There is a plan for him that Carling has seen. She has not let me in on the matter, but I know she has something in mind."

"It sounds so strange to hear you talk about yourself in such a way. You are both Carling and Claire."

"Yes and no. I am both but separate, and she cannot tell me why."

"There will be a reason. Oh, and I am also supposed to tell you—by way of Blue—that it is time to start Aroha's training."

"Do you have any more messages from the Sentinels for me, Breena?" They were nearing the top of the rise before the track dropped down into the valley.

"No, that's it. I must admit that I offered to be messenger so I could see you again."

"Matt would love to see you."

"No, I will not be joining you at the house. He still gets so sad that I am gone and it hurts us both."

"He won't like that I've seen you and you haven't gone to see him."

"I know, but I don't want to cause him any pain."

"Please come and see him. The pain that he feels comes from the love he still has for you. Please, Breena. It will also bring him joy."

They stopped at the top of the rise and Breena looked towards the house at the other end of the valley. Smoke curled from the chimney before it was caught by the soft wind that blew and spread out and dissipated. The sheep grazed lazily in the meadow while their lambs fed or leaped about playing a game. The few highland cows looked up curiously at the pair and one let out a mournful call.

"I will," Breena said quietly. "But not at the house. Please, Claire. Can you call him?"

Claire nodded and sent the call out to her husband. She watched as the front door opened and he pulled on a jacket as he headed out. Head down and hands pushed deeply into the pockets, Matt started to head up the track, until he raised his head and saw the two women walking to meet him and stopped. Now he walked with a faster stride. They met halfway and Matt gathered up his sister in his arms. Claire left them alone and headed back to the house. When she had nearly reached the door, it opened and Aroha stepped out.

"Who is that?" she asked her aunt.

"That's Breena, Matt's sister," Claire told her.

"I thought that Bree was Breena?"

"No, only a part. The other part remains with the Sentinels. They send her out to help them when it's necessary, except this time she asked to come to pass on some messages." Claire looked down at the sapling. "Can you help me plant this, Aroha?"

"Sure, what is it?" the younger woman asked, clearly confused with both the appearance of Breena and the sapling.

"A very special rose."

When Matt joined them later in the afternoon, Claire could see he was sad, but also happy at seeing his sister once more. She could also see he was not ready to talk about their meeting and felt that it was too personal for him to discuss. As the rose was planted, a bell sounded in the valley, and she watched how Aroha reacted to it. They spent the afternoon discussing what it meant, and also went into more detail about the creation story.

The pair found themselves in the library going over the records and finding all the clues that Claire had uncovered in her previous search. It was late when the door opened, and the cold night air came spilling into the hermetically sealed room. Matt came through the door juggling a tray in one hand, while trying to shut the outside air out as quickly as possible with the other.

"If you two won't come in for dinner, I thought I would bring it out to you," he said as he laid the tray down on the table and proceeded to place a plate of pasta down in front of each of them.

"What time is it?" Claire looked at her watch and found that it was late.

"Late enough that this has almost spoiled, so if it tastes like shite, it's all your fault." He gave them a little laugh, but Claire could see a certain tightness around his eyes.

"Thank you, sweetheart. It looks wonderful," Claire said, giving him a beaming smile, which he returned. She picked up her fork and began to eat as Matt sat opposite. He looked at the pages in front of them.

"So, what have you learned, Aroha?" he asked.

In that one question Claire could see that he was going to be as much a part of Aroha's training as she would, and she was relieved that the burden would be shared.

Aroha, between mouthfuls, related the story with Matt asking for more specific details. It amazed Claire that he had retained so much of the story; she had suspected that he had switched off when she relayed it to him the first time.

Matt glanced up and found her looking at him, a cheeky glint in his eye. When Aroha stopped for a breath and another mouthful of food, he turned to Claire.

"I remembered. You forget I have Recall as well, my love. And I was listening to you." He gave a little chuckle.

They spent a cozy few hours going over the history of The People in that special library. Imparting their own knowledge gleaned from the pages that lay in the bookshelves and drawers. At the end, Aroha leaned back in her chair and let out an explosive breath.

"Is there something you're unsure of, Aroha?" Claire asked her, concerned.

"I know who I am. I know *why* I came to be, but I don't understand *how*. I know your spirit was initially born of two Sentinels, but what about mine? How come I was conceived in the conventional way, so to speak?" she asked blushing a little.

"To be quite honest, I have no idea. Would you like me to call some of the Sentinels to help? They might know. After all, they know more of Order's plan than we do," Claire replied.

"Not tonight. I think I'll call it a night. Since coming here to the valley, I have slept amazingly well, and I think I'd like to make the most of that before I leave again."

"Don't you sleep peacefully normally?" Matt asked.

"Not really. I always feel like there's someone watching me. At first, I thought it was Dad being overprotective and sometimes that thought was a comfort. But I asked him one night and he told me that he has never done that. He has checked up on me, but never on the mental plane."

Matt looked at Claire. "Is the protection you placed on the valley still in effect?" he asked.

"It should be, but it wouldn't hurt to reinforce it."

"Why?" Aroha asked, looking between her godparents.

"A little extra protection doesn't hurt," Claire told her. "Would you allow me to enter your mind while you sleep and stand guard? I want to see if there is any outside force trying to find you."

"Of course you can, Aunty Claire. Who do you think it is?" She looked worried.

"I'm not sure, and I would rather not speculate at the moment. I just want you to go to sleep."

That night, Claire stood in the quiet and peaceful confines of her god-daughter's mind, concentrating on the outer layers, looking for tell-tale hints of someone searching for Aroha. It was late into the night when she found what she was looking for. A slight vibration on the mental plane, a tiny ripple as another mind was trying to penetrate the protection of the valley.

Latching onto it with the gentlest of touches, Claire followed it back. The search had been started so far away and she found it was a mind she knew well. Callum. So as not to frighten him, she sent out a call and joined him in his mind.

"What are you doing, son?" she asked him when he finally acknowledged her.

"Protecting her," he said sheepishly.

"Aroha is under protection already. But this is not the first time you have done this, is it?"

"No," he said, unable to meet his mother's eyes.

"For how long?"

"Since the night Bree and John announced their engagement. When they came over to visit." He replied a little sheepishly. Claire could see he had wanted to lie, to cover up his embarrassment at being caught, but she had always been able to ferret out the truth from him one way or another.

"I know you love Aroha, but there are better ways of protecting her."

"But I remember you telling me that Chaos can infect someone without them knowing."

"He does not know who she is. Yes, I took that seed of evil from her, but that was just a seed she had inherited from her great-grandfather. It was not a direct result of him interfering."

Claire tried to ease his fears. "She does not know how you feel, does she?"

"I've never had the courage to tell her, Mum. I'm sure she only sees me as one of the family."

"But something has changed, hasn't it?"

"While Finn was with us all at the house, I thought that they had…"

"You think she has feelings for Finn?"

"Yes. I saw her looking at him; she has never looked at me that way." He hung his head and she could feel the sadness and hurt that went with his perceived rejection.

"If she has feelings for Finn there is nothing you can do. I know it hurts, Callum. Would you like me to find out what her feelings are?" Her heart went out to her son as he struggled with the problem of his own.

"No." He looked her directly in the eye. "Please don't do that. I would be so embarrassed. I know she is staying there for a while as you train her. We are bound to meet up and I don't want her to feel awkward around me. Please, Mum," he begged.

"All right, I won't. But you'll have to deal with this somehow. You are either going to have to ask her yourself or accept that she doesn't feel the same way. You can't keep this up. It won't do you any good while you're studying."

"But I can't ask her. I know who she is and what she will mean to the world. How can I ever ask her to accept me?"

"There is a reason you were gifted with so many Abilities yourself. You shouldn't look down on yourself like that. You're a strong person. You remind me a lot of your father and your uncle. For now, leave the protection to me; that is my role. Get some rest yourself and concentrate on your studies. It will all work itself out, these things always do," she told him gently.

"All right, I will."

"I love you, son. Talk to you soon." She watched as he nodded, and she removed herself from his mind. When she returned to Aroha's mind, she found her there with a worried expression on her face.

"You were listening in?" Claire asked her.

"Yes. And I do know how Callum feels about me. I've always known," she told her.

"But you don't feel the same?"

"I don't know how I feel about him. I love him as one of the family, of course." Aroha sighed a little, then began to speak hesitantly. "There was a point when we were younger that I thought... maybe. But right now, with everything else going on, I really don't know."

"And Finn?"

"He's nice and I was attracted to him, but again I couldn't tell you. Aunty Claire, I really don't think that I'm meant to be with anyone. I've never had a boyfriend, never even been kissed. With what is in my future, how could I ever find the time to give to someone who is supposed to be so special to me."

"As I told Callum, these things have a way of working themselves out. I felt the same way in my first life. It took a long time before I accepted the love that I was supposed to have. You're still young, Aroha."

"I'm twenty years old. Don't you think that is a little old to not even have been kissed?"

"No, I don't. Don't rush into a relationship, or any sort of emotional tie. Especially at the moment. It will come for you, I'm sure. Get some sleep. You should have no more disturbed nights now. Callum promises that he won't watch over you anymore."

"Thank you."

Re-entering her own mind Claire sighed. Young love. She remembered her first foray into that world—the angst of it all, the painful pleasure of being in someone's company when they had no knowledge of how much they were adored. Of trying to let them know, but also trying hard not to. Looking over to her left she watched the silent form of her husband as he slept beside her and thanked her lucky stars they found each other.

But, she thought to herself, *it was always going to be that way*. Galen and her spirits were meant to find each other. Their bond had been cemented by the Sentinels and linked to each other forevermore. Until evil was banished from the land.

That phrase struck her. *Until evil was banished from the land*. It started to worry her mind as she turned it over. Did it mean that they would not be together in their next lives? Would the love they felt for each other be gone? The questions started to pile up inside her and she turned onto her side.

"Will you just be at peace, Claire?" Carling said inside her mind, while she yawned.

"How can I when the future is so uncertain?"

Carling took her hand and held it. "The future, beyond dealing with Chaos, is unwritten. We cannot know what it will be, and we have never worried over it before."

"We love Galen so very much, with all our soul and being," Claire stated, almost feeling the loss before it had even happened.

"And we will continue to love him. The love that we share can never be broken, just like that of our human parents, and in a strange way, of our Sentinel parents."

"But…"

"Claire, there is no point worrying about something we have no control over for now," Carling told her. "We need rest and peace. Sleep, Claire. Tomorrow is another day, one in which Galen will be at your side and loving you. Quiet our mind and sleep."

"All right. I will," Claire said, and dropped Carling's hand. She faded from the internal space and Carling could feel her start to slumber.

Carling stepped through the sleeping mind of her other self and made sure that the dream Claire would have that night would be a sweet and happy one. Making her way through to a darker space she stopped at the primeval part where Claire had once been held protectively. It pulsated and undulated before her. It reached out, seeking her before pulling away almost in fright.

Stepping forward, Carling entered the space confidently. The lights that swirled under her skin did nothing to invade the darkness which enveloped her. She hung suspended and closed her eyes, sending out a powerful thought.

"My child," the voice said in a whisper.

"Mother Universe, she is still unprepared. Surely the meeting can be postponed?"

"It is to be soon. It must be soon. The fate of so many hangs on it. This world depends on balance being restored."

"Does Order also need to go? Couldn't the Great Being stay and help your daughter?"

"My child, you know the answer. There cannot be one without the other. The world groans with the injustices that are building. Each day my son Chaos becomes stronger and his influence is growing. Soon the bonds that hold him will no longer be able to contain him. Order is fading fast. You must carry out our wishes."

"What of the Sentinels then? What will become of us?"

"My daughter will need to be guided still. When Order passes, you—her children—will continue for a while. You will help my daughter in her work."

"So we are to stay."

"For a little while yes. Then the Sentinels will have other work elsewhere. Many changes will happen to you, Carling. Some you have seen already. They will be necessary, and some are rewards."

"Thank you, Mother Universe. Your daughter will be prepared." Carling closed her eyes and found the link of Claire outside to pull herself out of the darkness. Standing with her back to the black mass she shook her head. She had gained some answers to her questions, but more were starting to grow.

Chapter Seven

The persistent ringing of a phone split through the darkness of Claire's mind, and she dragged herself out of bed. The dream had been wonderful, and she suspected Carling had interfered to give her some much-needed rest. The phone stopped as she heard movement in the house and a male voice downstairs. Rolling over, she found the space that should have been occupied by her husband was cold and empty. She pulled the blankets around her shoulders to shut out the biting morning air.

Footsteps on the landing alerted her to Matt's presence and the door opened with a protesting squeak he had promised to fix. She pulled the covers down and opened one eye, watching as he crept into the room, the phone still in his hand.

"Claire, are you awake?" he whispered.

"I am now. Who is it?" She sat up and pushed her hair from her face, then reached out to take the phone.

"The University. There's been a break-in."

"What? Where? Our offices?" She was suddenly alert.

"Your office. The door has been forced, but they don't know if anything has been taken. They want you back to have a look."

"I'll dress and go now. I can be there in ten minutes," she said, climbing out from under the warm covers into the cold air. She shivered a moment while goose bumps formed on her exposed skin.

"Ten minutes?" he asked inquiringly.

"Yeah. Remember, I can transport myself. No need for cars now." She grinned at him, trying to hide her concern about who would break into her office and what they could possibly want.

"They rang here looking for you. They know how long it will take to get there. If you want to use your Ability, do so, but you are going to have to make it look like you got there by normal means. So come downstairs and I'll make you a sumptuous breakfast, you can relax, talk to Aroha a little more, and then go."

Claire was pulling a jumper on, and as her head poked through the hole, she smiled. "What would I do without you? I'm back to being the impulsive reactionary I used to be."

"Yes, the woman I fell in love with." Matt tossed the phone onto the bedside table, placed his arms around her and kissed her long and slow.

"You promised me breakfast," she said when he finally broke the kiss.

"We have time." He grinned at her. "And Aroha isn't up yet."

Entering the kitchen sometime later to the smell of cooked breakfast, Claire remembered the first time she had entered this room. A small smile played on her lips as she saw the knowing look Gran had all those years ago. The old lady had already seen the love building between Claire and her grandson.

Aroha was at the stove carefully trying to flip the eggs, and the plates were already laid out on the old wooden kitchen table. A pot of tea sat to one side with steam curling out of the spout. The first of the spring wildflowers that Aroha had picked the previous day loosely filled a small vase in the centre, and their delicate perfume permeated the room.

"Good morning, Aunty Claire. Did you sleep well?" she asked, dishing up the breakfast.

"I did, and you?" Claire replied as she sat down at the table.

"Wonderful, as always when I'm here," she said, but made no mention of Callum.

"Speaking of which, did you find out what was causing your interrupted sleep?" Matt asked, coming into the room.

"I did and he has been spoken to. I don't think we need to talk about that now," Claire said as Aroha blushed.

"Later, then," he replied with a wink to his wife. He sat down and started to eat.

"It snowed last night," Aroha said looking out of the window, her knife and fork in hand.

"Did it? I suppose you want to go for a walk in it?" Claire asked, knowing how she had felt about the first snowfall she had experienced in the valley.

"Yes, please," the young woman replied eagerly. "I've been in snow before, but not here. It's always been summer when I've visited."

"Do you want to go up to the stones or just along the track?"

"I think down the valley for now. If I go up to the stones, I get the feeling that we would be interrupted."

"They do have their own work, you know." Claire smiled.

"I know, but I'm still not comfortable in their presence." Aroha looked down at her plate.

"They just want to get to know you. You will have to talk to them when we go to the home of the Sentinels."

"I know. But for now, can we just avoid them?" she asked quietly.

"For now." Claire smiled.

They ate in silence, the only sound the odd birdcall and the ticking of the old clock that hung on the wall. Matt picked up the empty dishes and started to take them to the bench as Claire finished off her cup of tea.

"You two leave the dishes and go for your walk," he said as he started to fill the sink with water.

"Thank you, sweetheart. Go and put on something warmer, Aroha," Claire said.

In no time the two women were rugged up and walking through the freshly fallen snow. It was not deep and was already becoming slushy on the track. Their breath was visible as they exhaled, and they didn't talk as they walked.

"What's on your mind, Aroha?" Claire asked, realizing that the younger woman wasn't going to speak first.

"Finn," Aroha said as she stopped for a moment.

"What about him?" Claire asked as she turned to her.

"I couldn't figure him out. He seemed to fit in well with everyone, but it was like he was holding something back."

"Did you go into his mind to see?"

"No, not without his permission. I would never do that, Aunty Claire."

They carried on walking. "I don't think there's anything really you need to worry about with him, Aroha. I have been in his mind, a couple of times now actually, and I couldn't see anything out of the ordinary."

"It's not like I'm attracted to him or anything," she said quickly.

"It would be okay if you were." Claire tried to hide her smile.

"It's just… I've never met anyone who doesn't belong to the family who has an Ability."

"But he is part of the family in a roundabout way, through your brother and father."

"Only distantly and he didn't know about them growing up." Aroha sighed deeply. "Callum is nice, but…"

"But he is family," Claire finished for her.

"Yes. He's Bree's little brother and your son, and Dad is like your brother. It's all too close and complicated," she said laughing.

"It is a little. You have heard about the story of Adam and I?" she asked her.

"Sort of. I didn't really pay much attention when Mum was trying to explain it all."

"Another relationship that was perhaps a bit too close." Claire gave a little laugh and began to explain the connection between herself and her first love. When she had finished, they had reached the start of the climb up the hill to the entrance of the valley.

"But you weren't meant to be together anyway," Aroha said after Claire had finished her tale.

"No, only for that period of time. I suppose you could call it a preparation for the ones we were supposed to be with."

They carried on walking and started down the track, heading to the old oak. Its branches were bare, and it stood as tall as it was wide, the last vestiges of the previous night's snowfall dripping from the newly formed leaves on the old wood. Ahead of them the sound of the river could be heard, already swelling with the snow melt. It cut a dark swathe through the blanket of white that covered everything.

Claire stepped under the branches of the tree and pulled the glove off her right hand. Stepping up to the old trunk she placed it gently on the rough bark of the tree. There was no sign of its previous occupant. It was only a tree and no more.

"It feels lonely now," Aroha said, coming to stand next to Claire. "The tree misses him."

"You can talk to the tree?" Claire asked, looking at her hard.

"Can't you?"

"I can speak to animals, but I've never tried to speak to a tree."

"They talk slowly. It has to do with how long they've lived. And this one has lived a very long time. It misses its companions, the ones that have been cut down and been lost. It also misses Red, and the conversations it would have with him. And it is telling me it misses Bree. Why would it miss Bree?"

"I think it means Breena, Matt's sister. Her spirit lived in the tree for a while until she could pass over. But it could also be Bree. When we would come here, she would spend so many hours climbing the branches, just as her aunt did." Claire sent out a search to the tree and found the spark of life that kept it rooted to the spot it was in. She felt the age of it and heard it sigh with the wind. "I have been thinking that we could plant a new forest here, put it back to the way it was and hide the valley once more."

As she spoke the words, she felt the tree almost tremble with delight at the thought of company. Claire smiled and resolved to do as she had said.

"Thank you, tree, for guarding the way to the valley. Long may you live and pass your wisdom onto the younger trees that will come." Claire patted the trunk once more and put her glove back on to ward off the chill.

The two women continued their walk and headed towards the river. They turned at the ford and made their way to where it joined the brook. The snow was still clinging to the grass and was a few inches deep here. Claire's thoughts were reflective as they made their way back into the valley. The history of the land was once more pushing into her conscience. It invaded her senses and almost blocked out the warning from the protection that hung over them. There was an intruder. Claire became alert very quickly for any danger that might come.

Within moments of sensing the shot being fired Claire reacted without thinking, raising her hand and stopping time. The crack of the gunshot was only just starting to be heard when the world hushed and became silent and still. Claire stood, shocked. Just a few short feet away from a startled Aroha a small grey object hung. So fast had it sped through the distance that the air around it rippled with shock waves. It glowed slightly red with the heat that it generated, and Claire approached it, once more pulling her glove off.

With her bare, nervous fingers she reached out and plucked it from the air. Juggling it slightly between her hands, she let it drop into the thin snow on the ground and heard it sizzle as it cooled. Bending down, she picked it up and held it between her thumb and forefinger and studied it. A piece of lead, now cold and grey. Small, but so deadly.

She looked in the direction from where it had come; she could see and feel the presence of the shooter. A man with some Ability, but weak. Stealth. Untrained and unaware that he had such a Talent. But behind it was another presence. She could feel the evil force invading his mind and body. It was an ancient foe she recognised.

"You will have to do so much better, Chaos," she called out. "Aroha shall have our protection and our strength until she banishes you once and for all."

A growl crept over the hills, echoing around Claire and the shaking figure of Aroha, who blinked and turned her head to her Aunt.

"Was that him?" she asked, her voice trembling slightly.

"It was."

"How did you stop the bullet?"

"We both have the Ability to stop time. It's not hard to do."

"What are we going to do with the man with the gun?" Aroha's eyes were trained on the spot where he still lay, in the midst of dealing with the recall of the rifle he had just used.

"What would you like to do?" Claire asked her.

"Well, it's not his fault that he tried to kill me. I would like to send him back to his home. I think I know how to protect him from Chaos so he can't be used again."

"Do you want to try? Because I know what you're thinking and you're more than capable of performing it. Actually, far better at it than I am."

"Can I run it past you first, so I don't make any mistakes?" Aroha asked her.

Claire nodded and entered the young woman's mind. Having been so used to sensing the difference between her own and others' spaces she was still surprised by the extreme vastness she found. The suggestion that Aroha was forming floated in front of her and she studied it and made a few suggestions to refine it a little more.

When she came back to herself, she looked at the girl carefully. Her potential was there on the surface and she encouraged her on. The suggestion left Aroha and snaked its way towards the figure on hill. She felt it wrap around him and invade his mind, searching out the spaces to implant and put it into action. Carefully the pair watched as the darkness that sought to hide itself from them was pulled from the man's mind and was driven from it. Their thoughts pulled back and returned to the meadow where they were standing.

"Can you please restart time again, Aunty Claire?" she asked politely.

"Of course, Aroha." With a wave of her hand, time restarted. The sounds of the valley blossomed once more, suddenly seeming so loud after the eerie silence.

After checking to make sure that the man was acting on the suggestion from Aroha, they continued walking. The bullet was now in Claire's pocket.

"I have to go back to Glasgow for a few hours. There's been a break-in at the University. But when I get back, I think it might be time for you and me to start our trip to the home of the Sentinels," Claire said.

"I think it is. It's time to face my fears and put them aside. Thank you, Aunty Claire, for saving my life."

"You're welcome," Claire told her.

Under the calm exterior, her insides were screaming in horror at what had almost happened.

After giving Matt a quick rundown of what had occurred out in the valley and leaving him with strict instructions about protecting Aroha, Claire centered herself and thought of their little house in Glasgow. Around her the world slipped away and she slid so easily, finding herself in the living room when she opened her eyes.

It was quiet in the house and the sound of the constant traffic outside was muffled. Claire took a deep breath and headed to the back door. Above her there was a thumping noise and she froze. She sent a search upstairs and found a presence.

She climbed the stairs quietly and stopped at the doorway to the office, watching as a man searched her husband's desk. A pile of papers and books lay on the floor where they had fallen in his hasty search.

"I hope you're going to pick those up, Callum," Claire demanded, her arms crossed over her chest.

Callum turned quickly to the sound of his mother's voice, upsetting another pile of his father's work. Quickly he grabbed them and held them in place before they could join the last lot on the floor. He looked guilty.

"Mum, what are you doing here? I thought you were still at the cottage," he said as he righted the pile, pulling his hands gingerly from the teetering mess and hoping that it wouldn't topple.

"I was, but I had to come back." Claire moved into the room.

"Is Dad with you, and Aroha?" he asked, his face brightening a little as he said her name.

"No, they are still back in the valley. What are you looking for?" She stooped to pick up the papers from the floor, placing them back on her husband's desk chair, the only place free from clutter.

"A book. I lent it to Dad a while back. I thought it would interest him. It belongs to a friend of mine and I need to get it back to him," he explained hastily.

"Why didn't you use your Seek Ability?" she asked.

"Sometimes it's easier to just look with my eyes than having to use my energy to send out a search," he told her sheepishly.

"You're lazy. Well, do it now, then you can be on your way back to Edinburgh." She waited for him to perform the search and he turned immediately and pulled out a book that had been crammed into an empty space.

"You have the Abilities; use them. Are you using Recall for your studies?"

"Yes, Mum. I am. But I can't get everything right, they'll become suspicious."

"I'm not expecting perfect marks, Callum. Do you want me to transport you back to your rooms or do you want to go the normal way?" she offered.

"I hitched a lift with a friend who had to come to Glasgow." He looked at his watch. "Shit. I better go. I'm supposed to be meeting him in five minutes."

Claire stepped out of his way and he headed for the door. Callum stopped and looked back at his mother. "Why did you have to come back?"

"Someone broke into my office at work. I have to go in and see if anything is missing." She told him.

"Bloody hell! So, I suppose finding me here going through your things was a bit of a nasty surprise." He grinned at her.

"Yes, it was, and they weren't my things, but your father's. You better get going or you'll be late." She grinned back and watched as he headed down the stairs and out the door, slamming it behind him. Claire shook her head and headed to the university.

Her office door had already been fixed and the administrator hovered nervously as Claire inspected the mess. He was of medium height with a receding blond hairline. His beard was slightly lighter than the hair on his head and his ice-blue eyes pierced his thin face.

"Without going through all the papers, I really can't tell what has and has not been touched or if anything is missing, Michael."

His full lips were pursed momentarily. "What are you working on at the moment?"

"Just the usual, the Pict carvings, and I was starting on the older cup and circle carvings, trying to see if there was a correlation." She began to put papers into a pile.

"So, nothing out of the ordinary? Your work has been so valuable to the university, Claire. We would hate for this incident to mar it in any way." He looked at her carefully.

"You mean, am I frightened of a little mess and someone going through my things? No, I'm not, Michael. I'm here for as long as the university will allow me to be." She sighed. "This mess is not going to clean itself. If you're staying, you can help."

"Ah no, I have my own work to get on with. Let me know if you find anything. I have a feeling this is the work of a disgruntled student, but why they would target your office I have no idea. I'll leave you to it," he said, and turned and walked out of the room.

Claire carefully closed the door behind him and leaned up against it. The solid wood at her back felt comforting somehow but she knew that there could be things hidden that were spying on her. She went and sat down at the desk, her hands held loosely clasped together before her. She closed her eyes and called out to Tony.

"Hello, Claire. How's Aroha doing?" he asked when he joined her mind.

"She's doing very well and learning fast. There are a few things I need to run past you, Tony, and you might get upset."

His dark eyes narrowed slightly as he waited for her to go on, and as Claire told him what had happened in the valley, he became agitated, just as she had feared.

"What? And you've left her there with Matt?" he demanded.

"Matt is more than capable of keeping her safe, you know that," Claire retorted.

"Yes, he is. Sorry. Do you know who did it?"

"I know who is behind it. And the man who actually fired the gun has been dealt with by Aroha. She has a very forgiving nature."

"And she's going to need it," he told her pointedly.

"Yes, she is. The second thing is that my office at work has been tossed," she told him.

"Tossed?" He chuckled at the term.

"Yes, gone through, messed up. Stop teasing me. I don't know what you call it in your business," she said, laughing.

"In my business we call it 'searched.' It was obviously done by amateurs if they left a mess. None of my guys would have left anything out of place."

"But now I'm worried about bugs and cameras. You see, I have a very long history of being spied upon," she told him with a smirk.

"I don't do that to you anymore. You're more than capable of looking after yourself now. Seriously, I have a couple of guys over there that can come and inspect it for you, but if someone is targeting you then you need to be careful. You know what to look out for."

"I do. Thanks, Tony. Oh, another thing. Can I give your guys the bullet that was fired at Aroha? I still have it. I'm sure that the gun did not actually belong to the man who fired it."

"By all means I'd be very interested to have it for examination. Claire, I hope you don't mind, but I think I might put these two on you and Aroha for a while to shadow you. I don't like what's happening over there."

"I don't need them, and anyway, Aroha and I will be going away for a bit while she trains."

"Where?" he asked.

"It's an island, but the part of the island we need is hidden from the public."

"The name of the island, Claire. Please," he insisted.

"It's now called Staffa Island."

"Thank you. Now, that wasn't so hard, was it?" he laughed at her.

"You won't be able to find where we are." Claire joined him.

"Leave it with me. I'll get those guys to you this afternoon," he told her as he prepared to leave.

"So, I just look for men in nice suits then?" She arched an eyebrow.

"No, we don't have a uniform in this organization. You're very old-fashioned, Claire."

She could still hear his chuckle even after he had left her mind and she shook her head.

The papers that had been strewn across the room were now in neat piles to be sorted. Claire looked around and felt the tug of Carling trying to get her attention.

"We can look into the past as well as the future to find out who did this, Claire," Carling told her as she approached.

"But what is that going to tell us? Just another person being used by Chaos. What we want to know is *why* he wanted our work searched. What was here that he was desperate to know?"

"That we cannot answer. But we are right, he seems to be getting stronger. The time is getting short now, Claire. We need to move Aroha along so she can face him."

"We've already decided that we need to go to the home of the Sentinels and start her training properly. While we're there, can we not go and strengthen the bonds that hold Chaos, keep him locked up a little longer?" Claire asked.

"Yes, we think that might be a very good idea. Before we go, we need to visit the stones and restore our energy, maybe even store a bit more for the task," Carling said, pondering.

From outside her mind Claire heard a knock at her door. "We must go. Those will be the men Tony has sent."

"Yes, we must. Be careful, Claire."

"Always, Carling." She smiled at her Sentinel self. As she came back to the room she called out, "Come in."

The door opened and two men dressed in jeans and polo shirts were standing on the other side. They both smiled broadly at Claire and she recognised the pair of them, even though it had been many years since she had seen them.

"Well, well," Claire slowly said as she smiled back and stood to greet them. "If it isn't Mr. James Boyle and Mr. Greg Carter."

"Hello, Claire. It's good to see you again," James said, hugging her and kissing her cheek. She received the same greeting from Greg.

"How are the kids?" Greg asked.

"You should know. You both work for Tony." She gave a short laugh.

"You got me there," he laughed with her.

Claire looked at the two men who had helped her many years before, while she was a prisoner of Marcus Ryder. "So, I take it you are the two that I am to expect?" She leaned against her desk and took in the backpack Greg was holding.

"When did the break-in happen?" James asked as Greg opened his bag, pulled out a device and started to scan the room.

"Last night. No one else's rooms were touched, only mine," Claire told them. "So far, nothing is missing, and I cannot find out what they were after. How much has Tony told you?" Her eyes tracked Greg as he moved around the bookshelves.

"He said that you would fill us in, and to keep an open mind. Now after what happened before, you know we are the right two to be here," James told her, obviously trying to be reassuring.

"It is so good to see you. I don't think I thanked either one of you for what you did back then," she said sincerely.

"There's no need, Claire. We did what we had to do," Greg told her and stopped as the needle on his device started to waver. He pulled out a couple of books and into his hand fell a little black object. "But I suggest that we keep any discussion about what is going on until we are a bit safer." He held it up and placed it on the desk for James to have a look at.

"I agree." James sat down on one of the chairs and waited for Greg to finish his work. Another of the devices was placed beside the first along with a tiny camera in short order.

Claire leaned down and inspected them without touching, then stood as Greg disabled the devices. "They're so small."

"Yes, but very effective. They have a long range, so pinpointing where the signal is being sent to will be a hard job. I might be able to find some markings inside to see where they were made." Greg placed them into a plastic bag before depositing them into his backpack.

"I understand that you have something else for us," James prompted her.

Claire dug into the pocket of her jeans and pulled out the lead bullet. She held it between her fingers before dropping it into another bag, held out by Greg.

"This was fired this morning and it was meant for Tony's daughter, Aroha."

"Shit! No wonder he wanted us here quickly. So, shall we start from the beginning?" James asked as he sat back in the chair.

Claire looked at her watch. "It's getting late. How about we go back to our place, I'll cook you two dinner and we can discuss it over a nice bottle of wine?"

"Sounds like a good plan to me," Greg said eagerly, hefting the bag onto his shoulder.

"After you, Claire," James stood and indicated the door.

The tale had been told and the two men were cleaning the dishes as they went over the story in more detail, making sure they had it right. Claire felt that old familiar feeling and smiled at the memories of reporting to her Uncle Geoff, missing him even more. With the kitchen spotless once more, they settled in the living room, each with a glass in their hands.

"So, now you know what has been happening in my life, what about yours?" Claire asked them.

"Not much, for me anyway," James said as he swirled the scotch in his glass. "I got out of the business for a while. Adam and Tony made sure we were paid out nicely, so I went travelling for a bit. When I came back, I was at a loss. I had no other skills. So, I looked Tony up, but it seems that he had kept an eye on me anyway and was waiting for me to rejoin them."

"That sounds like Tony. He doesn't like to let people go, especially if they could be useful to him," Claire told him. "And what about your personal life?"

"I've never found anyone that I could be happy with," he said a little regretfully, his eyes flicking to Claire and she let it go.

"And you, Greg?"

"Tony and Nik offered me a job there and then. I've been with them ever since that time. I was married for a while, but she wasn't happy that I was away all the time. This business can be a bit of a lonely one at times," he told her.

"I can imagine it would be. But surely there are other things you could do. Interests you could pursue?" she asked them.

"Not that I can think of. Our skillset doesn't lend itself to many other professions," James said as he swallowed the last of his drink.

"You should take some time off and come join us on a dig this summer," Claire offered half-jokingly.

"If this assignment lasts that long, we might have to." Greg raised his glass to her.

"It won't." Looking down into the depths of her own glass, Claire could sense the time rushing onwards, hurtling towards the confrontation.

"It's to be soon then?" James sat forward and placed his glass on the coffee table.

"Too soon. I don't know if Aroha is going to be ready for what she must face. For what *I* must face. This is not like what happened with Marcus. The evil that had invaded him will be there, standing in front of us this time. There will be no out, no other possibility. It needs to be done and we are the only two who can." She downed her drink and felt it burn down her throat.

"So, you are not truly human? It would explain a lot about how you acted when we were last together," James said quietly.

"Only a part of my soul is not human," Claire said.

"But it is our souls that make up who we are."

"I'm still me. Just the other half is separate in this life for some reason."

"You said that you glow. What did you mean by that?" James asked.

"First, before I give you any sort of demonstration, I need to check a few things. Do you two trust me to go into your minds?"

"I have no problems," Greg told her, putting his glass down.

"You already have, haven't you?" James asked.

"I would never go uninvited into someone's mind unless it was necessary to do so. That night, I had to find out what you still harbored for that woman and if it would affect the events that would happen later. What you did that night had to come from you, not me. I was not allowed to interfere or influence your decision."

"I still have some reservations about you going through my mind," he told her with a slight blush, trying to avoid her eyes.

"I will start with Greg, then." She turned her focus on the younger man. "Just relax and sit back. It won't hurt and I promise not to go through personal things."

Greg leaned back in the chair and closed his eyes. Claire crept into his mind and scanned it gently. When she had finished, she pulled away just as carefully.

"You can open your eyes now, Greg. I found nothing untoward," she told him.

"I didn't even feel you there!" he told her, opening his eyes.

"James?" She looked at the man who had once been placed on her to suppress her Talents. "Will you allow me?"

"Reluctantly, I will," he told her, and he sat back.

Claire could feel how tense he was and was becoming curious as to why he was so reserved in letting her in. She found herself in his mind and everything was ordered, just as it had been in Greg's. She put that down to the early training they had received from Marcus's organization.

James came striding towards her. "What is it you are looking for, Claire?" he demanded, his tone a little more urgent that it had been out in the room with Greg.

"The darkness that is evident on people who have been influenced by Chaos. You won't even know it's there. I hadn't even realised someone had implanted it in my own mind. James, please don't fight me on this. I have to ensure that

Aroha is safe. Tony wants you two to trail us, and I need to make sure that no one has gotten to you first."

"There are parts of my mind I don't want you in. And as for slipping in uninvited, I can't believe that you had the audacity to search my memories."

"I'm sorry for doing that, but at the time you were less than forthcoming about what happened, and I needed to know."

"What do we need to look for?" he asked her, clearly still unhappy.

"A darkness or a shadow that shouldn't be there," she told him.

"All right. You can check everywhere else, except my memories and my subconscious."

"What are you hiding, James? I thought we were friends." Claire was becoming concerned with how he was acting.

"Those places are private, and I don't want you to see what is there," he told her plainly. "And we are friends."

"All right, I'll do as you wish." She nodded to him.

The search didn't take long, and she came out just as smoothly as she went in. She watched as James came back to himself and waited for him to report what he had found.

"There was nothing in the parts that I searched," he told her as he moved uncomfortably in his seat.

"Good. Then I can move you to the house in the valley without any worries," she said, getting up and picking their glasses up to take to the kitchen.

"How long will it take to drive there?" Greg asked, also standing.

"We won't be driving, gentlemen." Claire rinsed the glasses out and turned them upside down on the draining board.

"How else are we getting there?" James was now standing also.

Coming out of the small kitchen to stand before them she smirked. "I have my ways. Shall we go collect your things first, or we can go back for them later?"

Chapter Eight

The bags were packed and ready by the door, which was standing open in the spring sunshine. A cool wind blew through the farmyard and Claire looked at the old cottage as she locked up the library, making sure all was secure before they headed out on their trip. When she had arrived back at the house with Greg and James in tow, Matt had not been happy. It had taken her a while to convince him that they would follow Aroha no matter what she said, as Tony would ensure that they did.

As Claire walked across the rutted, muddy yard, she spotted Matt heading out of the door of the house, the last of the bags in his hands and heading to the back of the "new" four-wheel-drive car. His old, blue, beat-up Land Rover had long since been scrapped after it finally started to fall apart. It had hurt him deeply to lose the old car and he was still getting used to the new one, even though it had been over ten years since they bought it.

He shut the boot and smiled as she walked towards him. His eyes crinkled at the corners, and the mischief behind the bright blue was still there. Claire smiled back, feeling like she had when she first met him all those years ago.

"You ready to go?" he asked, wrapping his comforting arms around her.

"Yep, the library is locked up and the house is ready. Where are the others?" she asked, looking around.

"Aroha is just finishing up the dishes and the two guys are sorting their own stuff out. I'm pleased we won't all be travelling in the same car. I still don't see the need for them."

"Talk to Tony, then. I'm not going to argue with him, and we've talked about this over and over. You don't even need to go with us if it comes to that. Aroha and I will be on the island all the time with the Sentinels. So, you're going to have to deal with them. They're nice enough and I am sure you will all get along fine. Teach them about archaeology. Speaking of which, the university … what did you tell them?"

"I said that we had just got a lead from a friend of ours about a possible site, and we needed to get out there right away to check it out. It's all covered. But I'll never be able to pass those two off as associates."

"Give them a metal detector each and send them out into a field." She laughed. "Actually, the way Greg goes on about gadgets he would probably have a great time."

"I wish I could go with you. I don't like leaving you alone anymore." He held her close.

"I know you don't, but it needs to be done," she whispered.

"Ahem, sorry to interrupt, but we are ready to go when you are," James said from the doorway.

Claire and Matt broke the embrace.

"Right. Then go get the other two and we'll head out," Matt told him.

The trip through the highlands was beautiful. The landscape still caught Claire's imagination and the further west and south they went the more she recognised from her first life. She told the story to Aroha and Matt as they travelled, showing them the places where she had driven the Romans off the cliff, and where she finally accepted who she was. In some ways it was almost as if history was repeating itself. Except this time, she was the one doing the guiding.

Although that very first trip had taken almost a month on foot, on this one they reached their destination later the same afternoon. The last rays of sun were dipping over the horizon as they pulled up into the hotel carpark, painting the white building red and orange like flames. The clouds were gathering to the south and the wind was starting to pick up, pushing in from the bay nearby. In the distance they could hear the surf pounding on the shore and pulling away with an elongated sigh. The hotel was set apart a little from the nearest village, isolated in amongst the rough landscape.

Claire breathed in the salty air and let it out in a long slow breath. The pull of the island was becoming urgent, insistent, and she felt the need to be there. Matt felt her hesitation and put his arm around her waist.

"Soon," he told her quietly and gently guided her into the hotel.

Matt led her upstairs to their room. He sat her down on the bed as he deposited their bags at the end of it.

"Okay, Claire, you need to snap out of it, now. We are going to get something to eat and everything needs to be as normal as possible," he told her as he took her chin in her hands.

"It's there and calling for us. This is so different from the other times," Claire said with a small frown.

"Is the call coming from the Sentinels or someone else?" he asked her as he sat beside his wife.

"I don't know. But I need to get Aroha there."

"What about Transportation, tonight after dinner. Or you could fly?"

"No, not Flight. The weather is turning anyway. No, it will have to be Transportation. I think there may be questions asked if we take a boat and decided to stay there." She looked around at him. "How are you going to explain our disappearance?"

"That's easy. James has organized a cottage for us to rent for a bit, while we do our 'archaeology.' We collect the keys tomorrow. Anyone who asks will be told that you went on ahead of us. Are you going to be all right for tonight? Will you be able to keep focused?"

"I'm sure I can." She smiled at him and stood. "We better not keep them waiting."

The night was a pleasant one. The lounge had beautiful dark wooden paneling with an ornate-looking bar, decorated with brass plaques. The room was crowded with locals and tourists alike, full of noise and chatter, and warmth thanks to a fire dancing merrily under a heavy, large roughly cut stone mantlepiece. Some locals were playing acoustic instruments in a corner, and the atmosphere was hearty with drinks flowing all round. Claire as usual stuck to her limit of two and left the others to the local tipple. She laughed and talked with them, but she was aware of the pull of the island in the back of her mind.

Part way through the night Claire began to become aware of someone watching her. The feel of strange eyes on her made her curious to discover who it was. When she saw no one acting suspiciously, she sent out a search. Letting it creep around the room, Claire touched the minds of many and found most were just ordinary people. Some had an Ability they were completely unaware of and a couple more she pulled away quickly from, as they began to feel her search.

Then she found it. The beacon that flared from this woman was strong and bright. An amazing vivid orange colour burst into her consciousness. Using both her sight and internal eye, Claire once more looked around the room and found who she was searching for. A young woman behind the bar was wiping up a spilt drink and smiling at the man who had done the deed. Her eyes flicked to Claire and she looked away again immediately, embarrassed to have been caught out.

"Who would like another?" Claire asked getting up from the table and picking up her empty glass.

"Are you having another one?" Matt asked his eyebrows rose in surprise.

"No, I'm going to get something a little more sedate to drink. Would you like another, my love?" she asked him.

"I wouldn't say no." He finished his glass and handed it to her.

"Not for me. Thanks, Aunty Claire," Aroha said as she pushed the still half-finished pint of beer from her.

"And you two gentlemen?" she turned to James and Greg.

"Not for us, Claire. We still have work to do tonight," Greg said, and he stretched.

"Speaking of which, are you taking first watch tonight or am I?" James asked him.

"I'll do first. I'll head out soon and do the rounds of the hotel. You need all the rest you can get, old man," Greg said jovially and ducked the subsequent backhander that James swung at him.

Claire laughed at them and headed to the bar. The woman who had caught her attention was just setting out clean and dry bar cloths and she greeted Claire with a large smile.

"What can I get for you?" she asked. The woman was young, in her early twenties, with dark ginger hair and sparkling grey green eyes.

"A lemonade and another of scotch please." Claire placed the glasses on the bar and the girl took them.

"I detect an accent. Where are you from?" she asked as she started to pour the drinks.

"New Zealand originally. But I've lived in Scotland for many years. I married one and we raised our children here," Claire told her as she watched the young woman carefully

"I've been to New Zealand. Such a wonderful and beautiful country." She placed the lemonade up on the bar and then busied herself pouring the scotch.

"What part of the country did you see?" Claire asked, trying to keep the conversation going.

"Mainly the South Island, but I got to see a bit of the North. Around Rotorua and Taupo way." The young woman shot another look at Claire.

"Did you get to go out to Napier?" Claire leaned against the bar.

"Yeah, but we didn't make it. We had car trouble and found ourselves in a quiet little town, a village you may call it really. The mechanic was such a nice old man. Oscar, I think his name was. He was talking of retiring." Again, she looked at Claire.

"I think I know the place you're talking about. One shop, a café, a garage, and a hall all on each corner of a crossroads?" Claire watched as the girl recognised her description.

"That sounds about right." She placed the scotch on the bar and gave her the price for the drinks. Claire paid for them and waited for her change.

"I spent quite a few years in that village," Claire told her.

"There is more that cannot be said now. Can you come back at closing?" the woman asked quietly.

"I can. I'm Claire by the way." She held out her hand for the woman to shake.

"Keelie."

The name rang a small bell in her mind as Claire picked the drinks up and headed back to the table, thinking about it. Greg got up, acting as if he were going to head for bed. Claire followed him in her mind as he wandered the grounds, checking for anything untoward. James turned in shortly after and Claire suggested to Aroha that she do the same.

As their niece bade them goodnight, Claire and Matt sat at the table, listening to the music as it began to wind down for the night. She slowly entered his mind so they could talk privately.

"Don't be alarmed, but I'm meeting the girl behind the bar after closing," Claire told him.

"Why?"

"There is something definitely different about her, Ability-wise. She has already picked that I'm the same."

"It could be dangerous. I'll stay with you."

"Good. Because I would like you there to hold my hand. This place is making me feel very nervous and unsettled and I don't know why." Not only in their minds but also in the physical world Matt took her hand and held it gently.

It seemed to take forever for the pub to empty the last of its patrons. Matt and Claire were still seated at their table and Keelie soon joined them, a drink of her own in her hands.

"Keelie, this is my husband Matt," Claire introduced them.

"It is nice to meet you. So where are you from?" she asked him.

"Glasgow mainly. But I grew up in the highlands," he told her.

Keelie looked nervous for a moment and seemed to hesitate in going on with what she wanted to say.

"I've already noticed you're like us." Claire said quietly, looking directly into her eyes.

"And I you, Claire. Though you go by another name, don't you? And so do you, Matt. Ancient names which are even older than my own." She sat back in her seat.

"For the moment can we leave those names unsaid?" Claire requested.

"For the moment." Keelie nodded in agreement. "I have already called my grandfather. He's very keen to meet you."

"It seems to be the way sometimes. It also seems that I have been coming across people my whole life who are interested in meeting me. Is there a specific reason your grandfather is eager?"

"He holds a lot of the old lore of the area. Our family has been living around here for generations. Back into the mists of time, some say."

For a moment Claire searched her memories of the area and the only inhabitants she could remember were Lucan's people.

"I am most interested in hearing from your grandfather. When will he be here?"

"In the morning. He likes his chair too much of an evening to leave it. Even for you. If you are back here, it means that things are moving along." Keelie lifted her drink and took a sip.

"Just like our names, it is best left unsaid. I would like to confirm a few things with your grandfather first before we speak of them." Claire stared her down.

"I know I'm young, but I've been hearing and learning the old stories from Granda since the moment I could walk," she started to protest.

Matt lifted his hand to stall her words. "It's not that you're young, Keelie. Our own children are as learned in The People's ways and history as we could teach them. It's that there are the other forces at play that we don't wish to expose ourselves to just yet."

"We understand what that force is. It is what our family has been guarding since we were charged with the task. You have no idea how excited we are that you're here."

"Your Ability burns about you so brightly. There were a few with some Ability in the bar tonight, but most were unaware that they possessed it. Yours is like a flare, a beacon for others." Claire narrowed her eyes.

"There are not many of us around now. I was raised by my grandfather, who taught me all I know."

"You're a Recaller?" Claire asked.

"I am. We're of the Eagle," Keelie said proudly.

"It was thought that the family had died out, like the other families. There has been no communication between The People of the Eagle and The People of the Boar for many, many years."

"We have been here, always here in this area. The town no longer exists, but we survived."

"Which town was that?" Matt said, becoming interested suddenly.

"The fishing village that originally stood near the shore. This hotel sits on the outskirts of where it once was. If you look when the tide is low, you can still see where the original jetty stood for the fishing boats," Keelie told him.

"Excuse my husband. He's an archaeologist through and through," Claire said, looking fondly at Matt.

"There's plenty of history and stones in the ground that you can investigate," Keelie said.

"It might give us the cover we need, my love," Matt said eagerly.

"You can put James and Greg to work, sure. But there are still things that need to be discussed, like how do we explain—" Claire stopped mid-sentence and looked at Keelie.

"We can work that out," Matt told her.

"I know why you're here on our shores once more," Keelie said.

"For now, I think we'll leave it until the morning and we can talk to your grandfather."

Keelie stood and held out her hand to Claire. "I'm so happy you're here."

Claire took the girl's hand and shook it. "I wish I could say the same," she said honestly.

Even before the sun rose behind the mountains in the morning, Claire was up and out of the doors of the hotel, leaving a slumbering Matt behind to enjoy more sleep. She walked down the road towards the sound of the surf and could feel the raw natural power of it, as it came crashing onto the stone and sand that made up the beach. Wrapped up firmly in a warm jacket to protect her against the wind that blew in off the water, Claire stood at the start of the track and watched the tempest that gripped the bay.

The whitecaps shone in the early morning light as they rolled towards the beach. The wind picked up her loose hair and whipped it around her face. She walked down the track and out onto the sand, footsteps echoed from her past life as she looked to where she could feel the island calling to her. But the call was different now, changed. There was a darker overtone. A menacing and angry presence that could feel her and was becoming excited that Claire was nearby.

"The sea is a dangerous place," a male voice said behind her.

Claire turned and found a tall man with a stick in hand and a cloth cap on his head. He was wearing a dark green padded jacket, and warm woolen trousers. His grey eyes had a distant look to them, and they crinkled in the corners as he turned them to her. With his gaze came the memory of the conversation between them, well over a thousand years previously.

"How long have you been in these lands?" she asked him.

"Ah, too many to count now. The memory of that day is with this body, as is the spirit of Lucan. I am getting too old now to go through the whole conversation again, Carling," he said with a small chuckle.

"It is you. How is it that your spirit remembers?" she asked him.

"A curse handed down the generations. Just as there has only ever been one of you, there has only ever been one of me. I am Guardian to the Island; it is my duty to make sure that its secret is kept, that the people who now explore its surface never know and can never be affected by it." He stepped closer to her. Claire noticed the limp in his left leg. The man saw her looking and chuckled. "Ah yes, but it is not a reminder of that life."

"So, what name do you go by now then?" she asked him.

"In this life it is a plaintive Harry. Though it would greatly gladden my heart to be called Lucan if it were to take your fancy."

"Would it seem strange to those that live here if I do?" She moved the hair once more from her face.

"No, it wouldn't. It is the name that I have come to be known by. When my spirit surfaces, it seems that the name is the first word spoken by the child. It was my first word. That is how it is known that I have been reborn. Order, I think, has meddled quite a bit with things. I was born with all my memories, all the stories and the old lore already intact. As I said, a curse." He gave her a wry smile.

"A gift. Order does not do these things without a purpose, Lucan. The purpose was so that you can keep the secret of the island." As she spoke, her eyes once more searched the horizon for where she knew it lay.

"It pulls at you. But so does the other." Lucan was now beside her, his own eyes looking out to sea.

"It does," she agreed.

"So, the time has come. Your time is here to banish him forever?" Lucan asked her.

"No, it is not time. And it is not my task. My task is to support, guide and teach the one who will. She will be the one to banish him. We must go to the island so she can complete her training."

"I'll organise a boat for you. My grandson can take you. Carling, our family line may have started with Lucan, but yours also joined it, through one of your daughters. We are family."

"I remember. The line stretches back to that child. I would appreciate your help, Lucan. It is so nice not to have to explain it all, to just know that the person I am speaking to is already aware of all there is to know."

"It is indeed. I'm feeling so grateful that this shall be the last time my spirit shall roam this earth. My granddaughter will carry on the stories, but there will be no Lucan to pick them up. I shall see the end and I will go to my rest, happy knowing that I have helped in the business of the Sentinels and Order."

"You have done a good job and we thank you," Claire told him sincerely.

Lucan sighed and sniffed a little. "Keelie is expecting us for breakfast. She wants to impress you with a large meal."

"She seems to be very eager. I like her a lot," Claire said as she turned her back to the surf with him.

They walked together in slow companionable silence back to the hotel. The white walls of the building stood stark against the morning sky. The clouds were scudding along on the wind that was blowing offshore, picking up the colours of the rising sun.

Lucan led the way through the back door of the hotel to the private family quarters. Seated already at the scrubbed kitchen table were Matt and James. Claire made the introductions to Lucan.

"I thought we should eat in here," Keelie said to Claire. "We have a couple of other guests at the moment and Granda thought it would be a bit more private."

"Has Aroha been called?" Claire asked Matt.

"No. Do you want me to go?"

"No. I will." She smiled and headed upstairs. As she reached the landing, Greg was emerging from his room, shutting and locking the door behind him. "All peaceful last night?"

"It was, Claire. Is it me or is there something about this place?" he asked curiously.

"It is very special." She smiled at him, knocked gently on her niece's door, then tried the handle after there was no response. Claire found it locked as she thought it would be. "Aroha?"

From inside she heard footsteps and the key turned in the lock. The door opened and the appearance of Aroha that greeted Claire had her worried. There were dark shadows under the girl's eyes and she looked pale.

"Are you all right?" Claire entered the room and closed the door behind her. Her eyes took in the room. The bed was unmade and the curtains wide open. The view from the window looked out towards the water.

"A voice has been talking to me all night." Aroha turned and sat on the crumpled bedclothes.

"What has it been saying?" Claire knelt down in front of her, taking her hands.

"All sorts of things. Making promises of love and devotion." She shook her head, clearly trying to dispel them.

Claire reached up and placed a hand on her temple. Carefully she slipped into Aroha's mind and found the problem. Pulling away she sent out a call to Matt. Within moments she could hear his quick footsteps thumping up the stairs. The door opened behind her and Claire turned.

"I need your help. We need to protect her mind," she told her husband and then carefully explained what she wanted him to do.

They held hands together, each standing on either side of Aroha. Together they touched her temples and entered gently and quietly. Inside they could hear echoes of a voice, soothing and flattering all at once. Full of hope and promise, and most disturbing of all for Claire, love. But there was a darkness which came with the voice and the promises it made. She shivered as she remembered the pleas it had once made to her.

In Claire's free hand she created a golden ball of light; it sparkled and shimmered in the dim light of Aroha's mind. Raising it up before her, Matt also created one of his own. Curiously his was blue, almost the same shade as his eyes. The pair of lights lifted and danced around one another, building up speed until it was impossible to determine one from the other. Their light joined together and expanded into the mind of Aroha.

From the depths came a growl as the voice was pushed from the deep reaches where it had gained a hold. The overwhelming force of the backlash from the evil entity made Matt stagger where he stood. Claire held on tightly to his hand, as she also felt Aroha flinch at the pain it caused her. The combined blue and golden light shimmered for a moment as the will of Chaos pushed at it. With a little more effort Claire bolstered the energy, finally evicting the voice from Aroha's mind.

As they came back to the room Claire staggered a little and Matt was there, supporting her, helping her to sit beside Aroha, who held Claire's hands and passed some of her own energy to her aunt. Claire looked into Aroha's eyes and gasped at the depths of the girl's hidden resources. Feeling better, she gently kissed Aroha's cheek.

"Thank you," she quietly said.

"No, thank you, Aunty Claire. I have so much to learn. You have shown me now. I understand more because of you. We need to go to the island and soon," Aroha told her simply.

Over breakfast, Lucan explained to Matt, Greg, and James the meaning of the island and his part in protecting it, with the help of Keelie. Lucan looked proudly at his granddaughter as she helped in the telling of the story. With the food finished and the table cleared, she left them to call her brother. The conversation then turned to other things, one being the history of the area.

"Our family has been here since the beginning of time. We merged with those that travelled from Ireland, and then again when the Norsemen came. Not once was the town ransacked, until the lands were taken from us by the English overlords. But still we remained, stubbornly hanging on. The direct line has always kept to this area. If it is archaeology you are wanting, Matt, you are welcome to open a pit or two. We have guarded it well, but now I think it is time that it was uncovered once more. I remember great piers which reached out into the bay and a large broch. The village at one time was quite big and everyone was protected and looked after," Lucan said, his hands resting on his stick and leaning back in his chair.

Matt looked over at Greg and James. "You'll not be able to go where Aroha and Claire are going, so this is what we'll be doing."

"We can at least travel to the island with them," James started to protest.

"No, you can't. I won't risk any of you," Claire told him. "I know you both have been taught well to put up walls and defend your minds. But the force that would be attacking you would be far greater than anything you would have come up against before. Please, it has to be this way."

"I don't like this, and Tony won't like it," James told her, sitting forward and leaning on the scrubbed wooden table.

"Tony will understand. He knows the force we are dealing with. It is the same one that took over Marcus," she told him.

"They will not be alone," Lucan told the two men. "I shall be there also. There are protections that need to be reinforced every now and then. With the help of my grandson, we shall wander the island and go about our work."

"But you cannot go where we need to be," Claire told him gently.

"I know, as much as I wish I could. It has been my honour to protect the island."

A noise at the door brought their heads up and a young man stepped through. He was tall and had the type of body which had been honed from years of hard work. He looked about the room as he flicked his ginger hair out of his grey eyes.

"This is Niall, my Grandson," Lucan said.

"So, what Keelie said was true then?" Niall asked. Claire noticed his searching eyes came to rest on Aroha.

"It is indeed, boy," Lucan told him.

"The boat is ready when you are, then. I'd be honoured to take you wherever you need to go," he said, bowing his head slightly to Aroha.

Aroha blushed under his gaze and looked down at her hands. Claire noticed immediately that the girl was attracted to the tall young man that stood before them, and a little worry line creased between her eyebrows.

The farewells that occurred a few hours later were short. Matt was still concerned that he could not be with his wife, to follow through with his role as her protector and support, but he understood. The drive to the wharf and the waiting boat was quick for Claire; she looked about them for any sign of danger or anything unusual. A few people in the nearby area had Abilities and used them, but most were ordinary people. The signs she received back were all normal and all strangers to her. She let out a long sigh of relief.

The boat sat tied up to the dock, rocking gently on the incoming swell of the tide. It was short and stocky looking, but well maintained with a high pointed prow and the wheel house situated at the front. Written on the side of the boat in gold lettering that stood out against the blue stripe which ran the full length, was the name Little Champion. Claire smiled to herself recognizing it as a nod to her ancient name, Carling.

They boarded the boat, Niall helping his grandfather aboard before starting the engine and casting off the lines. Lucan took the wheel, carefully maneuvering it away from the dock as Niall stowed the lines and then joined the rest in the wheelhouse, taking over from his grandfather.

The sea had calmed and the sky was blue; the clouds from earlier seemed to have departed and the sun shone down on them warmly. As they left the confines of the harbour, they were joined by dolphins and seals at play beside them.

"I have never seen that before," Niall said as he watched them. "Dolphins, yes. But to be joined by seals." He shook his head.

"I think they know that the boat contains something special," Lucan said with a mysterious smile on his lips. He watched his grandson steal a peek at Aroha and she returned the look.

They descended into quiet as the boat made its way up the Sound of Mull and started to head around the Isle of the same name. Claire left the wheelhouse and stood watching the island go by, dark and distant and hiding that which she and Aroha could feel pulling them.

"Some of our people live on Mull," Lucan said, coming to stand beside her, his hand resting on the railing in support. "They still practice the old ways there, in secret of course."

"The witch hunts did a great deal of damage to The People. But in some ways, it was also a blessing," she said and saw his eyebrow raise in surprise. "Don't get me wrong, the lives that were lost can never be reclaimed, but it forced The People to spread out into the world like they were supposed to do. Otherwise I would not be here now. This life was meant to be raised in New Zealand, was meant to be watched over by both north and south Sentinels."

"The Sentinels. They should not have hidden themselves away." Lucan shook his head.

"It was necessary. They could not do the work they needed to do if they were still in the light. Chaos had been confined. The line from the original Carling had to be protected, nurtured, and looked after. I look back at the ages and see all the branches that lead back to her."

"Back to you," he corrected her.

"No. Her," Claire insisted. "I may be the reincarnated spirit of the original Carling, but I am not her. My Abilities have been suppressed, until only recently. My spirit is still that of Claire. Carling is separate."

"But I recognised you. I saw Carling and not Claire," he insisted.

"Yes, she is there and when needed she comes forward. But for some reason our spirit has been split into two. Inside this one body are the spirits of both Carling and Claire."

"Have you talked to the Sentinels about this? I felt their return, by the way. And I was visited in my dreams by Orange," he told her.

"No, I have not. But it shall be a topic of discussion while we are on the island," Claire told him.

As they left the Sound, the waves coming in from the North Atlantic grew larger, great rolling waves that they gently motored through, making the boat toss back and forth. The two stood watching the horizon as the boat turned, keeping the coastline of the Isle of Mull to their left. Off in the distance other islands could be seen as dark smudges.

Laughter from the wheelhouse caught Claire's attention and she looked through one of the salt encrusted windows. She saw Aroha at the controls with Niall standing behind her. She saw the younger woman look up at him with a shy smile.

"They would make a lovely pair," Lucan said when he looked at what she was seeing. "But their destinies are vastly different."

"They are," Claire chewed on her lip for a minute, undecided as to whether or not to separate them.

"Let them be for a bit and enjoy each other's company. It is a pleasure of the young to be attracted to someone and to feel attraction in return," he advised her.

"It is." She remembered how she had felt about her first love. How before she and Adam had confessed their feelings for each other, it had been exciting and thrilling to catch the other's eye and just be in their presence. "I will. Things will change for Aroha on the island. She will see life so very differently when her training is over."

"I cannot see into the future, Carling; that is not one of my Abilities. But even I can see the immense energy and potential that surrounds the girl. So much greater than your own."

"Yes. I worry that it will be too much for her, sometimes, but then at other times I see her taking things in her stride, like it was nothing." Claire studied Aroha.

"Like what?" he asked.

"Chaos is at work. He has been using people to try and get to both of us. There was an incident in the valley. Someone shot at us. I am sure it was meant for Aroha. The way she reacted was calm and methodical and she dealt with it the same way. But this morning, she was under direct attack from Chaos and she was having difficulty with it."

"She is young. Maybe the direct attack took her by surprise, rather than the evil one using someone else. I wouldn't worry about her, Carling. She will grow as she learns."

"I am sure you are right, and I am worrying about nothing." She gave him a small smile and turned from the two young people and looked out once more at the island off the port side.

A little while later the dark and foreboding island of Staffa started to appear at the bow. It loomed larger in their sights as they neared it, and a shiver went up Claire's spine.

Home, Carling said from inside her mind with a sigh and a smile.

The great columns soon appeared in focus and they saw the waves crashing up against them from the ocean. The sound of the booming collision between the immovable dark rock and the power of the rolling water became louder and louder.

Seabirds flew overhead, riding the thermal updrafts from the meeting of rock and ocean, their cries carrying on the wind.

Aroha came and stood beside her aunt as they made a circuit of the island. She took up Claire's hand and held it.

"He's there. I can feel him. He is waiting for us," she said quietly, staring intently at the dark island.

"He is. But you shall not meet him now. You are not ready for that confrontation yet. I have to go meet with him by myself. I don't want you to worry, you will be in the care of the Sentinels and they will help you while I strengthen the bonds that hold him."

"Thank you, Aunty Claire." She gave her aunt a small but weak smile.

"It was necessary that he was bound on this island. The power of the home of Sentinels has helped Order to create his prison."

The fishing boat reached the southern tip and the entrance to the cave that had come to be called Fingal's Cave. They watched the surge of water as Niall expertly reached the small dock used by the tourists who came to visit the island. Once he had tied off the lines, he helped his grandfather to disembark and then made sure Aroha and Claire made it off without incident.

"I can't stay tied up here. I'll go out a bit and anchor, then use the small inflatable dingy to come back," he told the two women, as he climbed back on board.

"We'll wait for you here," Lucan told him, and Niall cast off and headed away.

The sound from the cave could be heard even from where they were standing, though it was some distance away. The pull was more urgent now they were standing on the island, its call so great that Claire was having to restrain herself from following the path that led to the cave and the secret entrance that it contained.

Niall was soon with them once more and they started up the path. It diverged into two and they stood at the parting together.

"Thank you, Lucan, Niall. We must go on alone from here," Claire said to them.

"And we must go to the top. We wish you well, both of you," Lucan said, holding out his hand for them to shake.

Claire looked at it and then shook her head. "As you said, we are family in a roundabout way." She placed her arms around him and kissed his weathered cheek. The old man smiled.

"That we are." He nodded and returned the embrace.

Aroha and Niall stared at each other, as if to etch each other's faces on their memories. She gave him a small smile and then followed Claire. She stopped for a moment, then turned, quickly ran back, and kissed Niall. Her hands held his face to hers and then just as quickly released him, searching his eyes before heading after her aunt.

Niall watched them until they were out of sight, a stunned look on his face. Lucan watched his grandson and gently placed a hand on his arm.

"Come on, boy. We have work to do," Lucan said with a bemused look on his face.

The path that led to the cave was even in most places, but soon dropped near the water. On one side was a metal handrail secured to the sheer rock face, and they followed it. Aroha kept close behind her aunt, while the giant hexagonal fingers of rock pushed up beside them, rugged and weathered. Claire, sure-footed and now feeling the urgency of their trek, carried on without hesitation on the uneven ground, never once needing to hold on.

The cliff suddenly rose beside them as the handrail stopped. Tall basalt columns held up the alluvial rock above. Flotation rings hung on the face of the cliff for anyone who found themselves in trouble in the water. The path was smoother now than it had once been and Claire remembered her first visit, finding her way into the mouth of the cave. Now she found stairs for the more difficult parts, where once she had had to climb to gain access.

They followed the new set of rails along the cliff base, while the water pushed itself against the rocks to their left. The white water receded only to once more be dashed against the blackness of the basalt. The sound was ringing in their ears and they stopped a moment to marvel at the deep blue ocean, watching it change to emerald green as it entered the cave. It sounded like the cave was breathing.

They continued along the path into the darker depths. It was narrow, and Claire carefully made her way over the man-made steps. They came to an abrupt end and the entrance was secured by a chain. She looked at her niece.

"We need to go to the very end. But I can't see the stone that once stood there," Claire said.

Aroha looked past her. "It's there, I can feel it. It will rise when we ask it to." She looked back to her aunt. "We can always go in the other way."

"No, we need to enter this way. That I am sure of." Claire took a deep breath and ducked under the chain and stepped down onto one of the columns.

With great care they made their way to the back of the cave, careful of the slick green moss that clung to the rock. The breathing sound continued around them, as if there was an expectation of their arrival. Now standing at the end, Aroha looked down into the depths of the water as it rose and fell. Just under the surface, and only visible when the water was at its lowest point, was a single finger of basalt rock, standing higher than those that surrounded it.

Reaching out a hand, Aroha closed her eyes and concentrated. It seemed to Claire that the girl used no effort whatsoever to call the rock up from the water. It was a large piece, larger than the rest and only a step away from them. The water streamed from the top of it down the sides of its uneven faces. The sound as it rose was rasping and deep. When it stopped, the air seemed to hold its breath. The cave gave another sigh.

Aroha looked at Claire and took her hand. The two women stepped onto the rock and turned to face the back of the cave.

"Call to them, Carling," Aroha said to her.

"Mother, Father, brothers and sisters, I have returned and seek entrance to the home of the Sentinels," Claire called out in a ringing voice that echoed off the rock around them.

"We welcome back our Sister Sentinel and the Ultimate One. Enter and join us." The voice was as soft as the sound of the waves.

The rock in front of them began to open and a light shone out into the cave. Together they stepped from the rock and into the entrance that had been created. Behind them the doors closed, and the cave went back to the way they had found it, just as the first tourists of the day came, chatting and laughing into the entrance of the cave.

"Carling." Yellow stood before them and embraced Claire.

"Mother," she said, returning the hug.

"The others will be here soon. They did not wish to overwhelm either of you. Welcome, Aroha," Yellow said, turning to the girl and bowing slightly.

"Thank you, Yellow," she replied.

160

"Come and sit. You will be tired after your journey. I have kept watch over you while you travelled." She led them into the common room and the large table that sat there. On its shining surface sat drink and fruit.

Claire looked around her and found that the room had not changed at all. It was just as she remembered it and she smiled.

Chapter Nine

Aroha's training began as soon as the rest of the Sentinels joined them. Claire watched as they were deferential to their young pupil and careful in how they addressed her, just as they were with Order. Her study of this interplay between them was overshadowed by an increasing anxiety of her own task: facing Chaos and securing his bonds.

Claire sat back in her chair and let her eyes close slowly. The image of a small enclosed cave formed in her mind. Even though this cave had no major opening to it, it was still brilliantly lit, with sunlight streaming through a crack in the roof. The single ray of light was refracted and bounced around the room as it hit a myriad of crystals that were imbedded in the floor, walls, and ceiling, illuminating everything inside. Within moments she transported herself from the main room to this small cave that lay elsewhere on the island.

Chaos was still bound to the two fingers of clear rock and he regarded her with a burning hatred in his eyes. He had not changed since the last time her spirit had seen him. His presence within his prison was overbearing and she could feel his strength was quickly returning.

"Carling. Welcome to my home. I would offer you something, but as you can see, I have been living very simply since my confinement," Chaos growled at her.

"I can see that, Chaos. Everything is as it should be. Well, not quite everything." Claire moved around the room and stood beside the plinth of crystal and looked into the smaller glittering stone that sat on top.

Her hand hovered over the white and golden glowing crystal, while concentrating on the diminishing energy within. Lights flared under her skin and rushed to her hand, then leapt to the stone, increasing the intensity of the glow. When she had pushed enough in, she closed her hand and pulled away.

"I hope this helps you, Order. It is only a small amount, but I give it willingly to help you," Claire addressed the crystal, and then she turned once more back to Chaos and studied the bonds that held him.

She produced a glowing golden rope to twine around his wrists, in addition to that which was already there, anchoring him deeper into the columns.

"Is that all you can think of to restrain me, Carling?" He laughed at her. Not once had he flinched at the light touch of the rope.

"It will do for now, until the Ultimate One is ready to meet you."

"How is my sister doing? Is she growing in skill and power?" he asked her with a grin.

"Yes, and with my protection you will not touch her. Stop trying to get into her head." Carling folded her arms over her chest.

"Such a pity you were around to force me from her. I just about had her."

"I don't think you did. She is far stronger than you, for a start. She will defeat you."

"But if she does, she will also take your beloved Order from you." He laughed menacingly.

"It is something we have accepted already, as has the Great Light. There cannot be one without the other; we know this. That is why the Ultimate One was created—to take the place of you both. Order sacrifices herself willingly to protect the world from you."

"There will always be evil in men's hearts; you cannot change that. The Sentinels gave the gift of free will to their people, including the ability to do harm to each other."

"Yes, they did. They saw that it was necessary, that it was needed. But when you are gone, the job of balancing out that evil will become easier."

"Ah, Carling. We could have been very good together." He sighed and looked her up and down. "But you are looking so old now."

"That is the way of humans, to age. And I haven't aged that much, Chaos. I am still healthy and strong. And I have a great love who supports me."

"Yes, the Protector of The One True Child. Is he with you on the island?" he asked curiously.

"I am not going to answer that." She smiled at him.

"It doesn't matter anyway. I shall be free of my bonds soon. I have been working hard lately on my own project. I think it will surprise you," he chuckled.

"You will not be getting free anytime soon, Chaos. Enjoy your last moments in this world. The next time I see you will be your last," Claire said, and transported herself back to the home of the Sentinels.

"You may be surprised," Chaos said after she had left, his laughter echoing off the walls of the small chamber.

With the Sentinels' guidance, Aroha did grow and learn, but their knowledge only took her so far. She had spent a great deal of time with each of the Beings, learning everything that they could teach her, but Claire could see her frustration growing. Taking the opportunity of a calm day, Claire bundled up some food and a blanket and transported them both up to the surface. They walked on the cliffs and listened to the booming of the waves below. They watched the sea birds flying on the thermal updrafts and calling out into the sky.

Finding a sheltered spot, far from where the tourists landed, Claire spread out the blanket and together they ate their lunch. She regarded her niece carefully before she spoke.

"What's bothering you?" Claire asked her.

Aroha looked out at the ocean and the other islands far in the distance. She sighed and turned to her aunt.

"The knowledge that the Sentinels have given me is everything I know already, thanks to you and Dad. I know there is more. I want to know more," she told her quietly, almost shyly.

"I can help you with all I know, which is more than the Sentinels and even more than Order. But if you wish to know everything, there is only one place you can turn. The Universe."

"Don't get me wrong, I am grateful for their help, and for your help," Aroha said quickly.

"Aroha you are going to have to face the Universe at some point. Our knowledge will not be enough to sustain you for what is to come. And I don't just mean the battle with Chaos. Once Order and Chaos have departed this world, it will be in your care."

"That frightens me," she whispered. "I will be responsible for every life on this planet."

"And you will get no thanks or devotion from anyone. They will not know who you are or what you do for them. Are you comfortable with that?"

"Yes. I don't think it would be a good idea to be worshipped. I don't think I would be comfortable with that at all." Aroha gave a little laugh.

Claire reached over and placed a hand over Aroha's hands clasped in her lap. "You will be fine—more than fine. You may bumble along to start with, but once you find your feet you will be amazing." She gave her a warm smile of encouragement. "I think it's time to meet your mother, the Universe."

Standing, Claire pulled the girl up to her feet and held both of her hands in her own. Aroha nodded and placed all her faith in her aunt.

Closing her eyes, Claire reached out over space and time. She called out to the Universe and felt the presence there. Mother of all. Slowly they rose up off the rock in the ocean, leaving it far behind as they ascended into the sky. The land below them sat like a jewel in the sea. The sky changed to the deepest of black, the light of a million and more suns shining back at them.

Higher still they rose until the world now stood small under their feet. Their bodies changed to survive the vacuum of space. The lights under Claire's skin flared, golden and swirling, just under the surface. For the first time Aroha saw her own lights, pin pricks in all the shades of the rainbow.

In Claire's mind, Carling now took over. Still holding onto Aroha's hands, she called out to the space that surrounded them.

"I bring before you your Daughter, the one on whom all our hopes rest. We, the Sentinels, children of Order, have taught her all we can. She seeks your guidance and knowledge. Help her now so she may be ready to perform the task she was born for. We leave her in your care."

Slowly Claire released Aroha's hands. The girl's eyes widened in panic at being let loose into the emptiness of space.

A bell tolled.

"Our child, Carling, we thank you for the care you have given our Daughter." The voice was soft and quiet but held so much weight that it wrapped itself around Claire's mind. "Go now and leave her with us, go with our blessings and love."

Claire slowly sank back down to the world far below, keeping her eyes on Aroha as she moved away. At first Aroha looked back, but then her head rose as if she were listening to something. Her arms were suddenly bound to her side and she sped away into the stars.

Landing back on earth, Claire bundled the blanket and basket up and transported herself back to the hidden home deep in the rock. She put away the things and headed to the table. The lights which had shone while she was high above the earth were still swirling now that she was back.

Lying on the ancient wooden surface was a leather-bound book and she placed a hand on it. Normally with books she could just be in their presence or touch them to know what the contents were, the knowledge that they held. But she got no sense whatsoever from this book.

"You actually need to open this one, Carling," Red said as he appeared at her side.

"I don't know if I want to learn what is written inside," she said, still looking down at the book.

"That has always been your decision. Your spirit has never wished to know the future, but on this occasion, I believe you should. There are things in there that you need to know beforehand." He moved and stood on the other side of the table.

She caught his eye and held it. This time she could actively feel Carling pushing her away and taking over once more. It felt strange and she was curious about it.

"Claire does not need to know now," Carling spoke through her lips.

"So, you are separate. The prophecy was not talking about Claire and Breena was it? *'Two as close as twins of the old shall come and be with the new. Abilities so great and untried. Those lives so precious must be protected and hidden. The Ancient Ones will claim the lives as their own,'*" he recited.

"We cannot speak of that just yet."

"You know what is to come already, Carling. What happens to you?" he asked eagerly.

"We cannot speak of that just yet," she repeated, shaking her head.

"Why not? Why can we not know what happens? What are you hiding?" He leaned on the table staring into her eyes.

Carling sighed. "It will all be revealed when it needs to be. The outcome must be decided by those that will be involved at the time. I know what I wish the result to be, but I cannot influence the decision. I am bound by the Universe, just as you, Galen, Aroha, Tony, and everyone else is."

"You have just given me a clue already, Carling. I will not press you more to say that which you are not allowed to." He pushed back off the table, his eyes still studying her, and gave a smirk. "The golden lights suit you."

"Thank you." Carling sat down at the table and pulled the book towards her.

"I will leave you to your study and we will talk some more later, Carling," he said softly before he disappeared, leaving her alone in the quiet of the room.

Inside her mind, Claire was waiting for Carling to join her. She was becoming impatient and made the call louder than necessary.

"What was all that about?" Claire demanded of her other self.

"Something *we* do not need to know just yet. Please believe me. If we were to know then we would act differently, speak, and react to certain people differently. And that cannot happen. Not yet. Red is becoming infuriating with his demands."

"He loves us. In more than just a sister-brother way. I have seen it down through the ages how he has spoken and been with us," Claire said.

"Yes, he does. He tries to keep it in check, but sometimes he does not realise it spills out and is obvious to others. This is why Galen has always been jealous of him."

Claire thought about Carling's words. Then she did something she did not take pleasure in, and before Carling could stop her. Foresight. Her eyes widened with what she saw, and she turned back to her other self.

"It is not certain yet, Claire. It may not come to pass," Carling said sadly.

"But if it did—if that vision is true then…"

"Let us not get ahead of ourselves. Please, there are other forces which can turn that vision aside."

Claire stepped forward and took Carling's hand in her own. "But it may, we can still hope," she said eagerly. "The prophecy was not meant to mean Breena and I, was it? Just as Red said? The prophecy is about us. Carling, we are not just two sides of one spirit, are we?"

Carling shook her head slowly. "No, we are not. We are just as it says, 'two as close as twins.' We share the same memories, the same Abilities; we are as twins. It is why there are so many twins down our line."

"So why were we born into the same body?"

"It was necessary; we needed to be so that our combined strength could work together for the task that lies ahead."

"Why did you not show yourself to me sooner? Why did you wait?" Claire asked her.

"Because it would have changed you, as the knowledge is already changing you now. It will affect how you will deal with certain people."

"The Book of Destiny. Is our fate written in it already?" she asked.

"No, it is not. Only part of our lives has ever been written in it. The main being our love for Galen."

Claire smiled. "Yes, I remember Yellow telling us on more than one occasion. I think we should read the book now, Carling."

"Yes, Claire, I think we should."

As Claire closed the cover of the book, she pushed it back to the center of the table and stretched. The room around her was silent and she sent out a search for Aroha. The girl was still up above somewhere, communing with the Universe. She looked at her watch, and realised it was now late evening.

Before her on the table, platters of food and a jug of water appeared. Yellow and Blue soon joined her. Claire stood and met them in an embrace. She knew these two were her ultimate parents and could feel how close the Carling side of her was to the pair, but she herself felt unsure how to deal with the situation.

Yellow placed her hands, with their sparkling yellow lights dancing, on each side of her head. "We understand, Claire," she smiled at her.

"It is a little bit unusual," Claire said.

"But one that is not fraught I hope?" Blue asked as he sat at the table.

"No, not fraught, just a little strange."

"You don't seem to have a problem with Red," Yellow said as she started to dish up the meal.

"No, Carling deals with him mostly." Claire took the plate and then began to pour the water.

"So, how is Aroha's training going? I remember your own was a little frustrating for you," Blue said, taking his plate.

"The memories I have of this place are all wonderful. But yes, I do remember my training from my first life and feeling frustrated that certain important things had been kept from me. But that wasn't really my fault, was it?" she smiled at Yellow.

"No, I suppose it wasn't. In my defense, though, it was necessary to keep your visions of Galen from you. Your spirit was not ready to see him. You still would have only seen Galen as your brother."

"I did anyway." Claire sighed. "It has been a very long journey."

"It has, Carling. We have watched over your lives with such pride and love. You have performed your tasks with great efficiency and strength," Blue said as he began to eat his meal.

"Can you tell me why it was necessary for the Sentinels to leave and go into seclusion?"

"Near the end of your first life, when you helped us go into our trees, we felt it was necessary. Our age had ended and your own had started. The People needed to lose knowledge of us, to stop depending on us being there for guidance. We were still here, whenever a Guardian had need of us, and to make sure the lines were kept intact. But our strength needed to be saved, to be put away for this final task," Yellow explained.

"Why do I get the feeling that the Sentinels will no longer be here when Chaos is banished?" she asked, laying down her fork.

Blue cleared his throat and leaned back in his chair. He lifted his goblet and took a sip of water. "Because that is what is supposed to happen," he told her gently. "When Chaos has left this world for good, we will no longer be required."

"But I don't understand. This world will still need the Sentinels. You created it, shaped it. And what about Aroha? Won't she need your support?"

"No, she won't. And this world will go on without us. We will have completed all our tasks." Blue placed his goblet back down on the table.

Claire sat for a moment, her hands clasped in her lap as she sat back in her seat and thought hard. A thought came to her.

"What about the Carling side of me? What will become of her if you leave? She is a Sentinel."

Blue nodded. "The Carling side of you is indeed one of us. We do not know what will happen to her. You have just finished reading the Book of Destiny. It is, as always, not fully written, your future still a mystery. Believe us when we say that it has Yellow and I worried. I cannot speak for the other Sentinels."

"Where will you go?" Claire's question came out sounding very childlike.

Yellow smiled at her. "We will still exist, but our lives will be elsewhere. The Universe is a vast place; there are many worlds like this one that are in need of our work."

"Of your protection?" Claire sat forward eager to hear more.

"No, not protection. There will be no need to protect it anymore from the likes of Chaos once he is gone. But there are other worlds that need to be developed and prepared. The People will live on, Carling. Not all will lose their Abilities; some will continue to carry them. In a far distant future they will become explorers and spread themselves out among the stars. We go ahead to prepare their way," Blue told her. He waved his hand and the table cleared, except for the goblets and jug of water.

"And those that do will be descended from you. The strongest of the Abilities have been passed to your children in preparation for this, which is why both have so many Abilities. Breena and Callum's children will become great thinkers and innovators." The pride that shone on Yellow's face made Claire smile, as she realised that the Being before her looked at her children as grandchildren.

Claire woke from a deep sleep the next morning, stretched, and slowly rose. After dressing, and with a hot cup of coffee in her hands, she transported herself to the top of the island. The sun was just starting to rise and the sea was calm as the wind had dropped. The water reflected the colours in the early morning sky. Oranges, purples, pinks, and golden hues glowed brightly as the sun rose higher, fading out until only the golden light was left, and the sky was now a blue that matched her eyes.

A gentle breeze blew now and lifted her hair from her shoulders as she sipped her coffee. She removed a stray lock from her face and stared out at the water. A pod of dolphins broke the surface briefly before ducking back down, taking pleasure in their play as they searched for a meal. Joining them, a few seals poked their heads up through the calm water, before diving back down.

It was quiet on the island. The tourist boats were still tied to their wharfs and jetties, the tourists still slumbering in their beds. Claire savoured the peace and closed her eyes a moment to listen.

The quiet lapping of water on the rocks below grew louder as the wind gathered pace. The call of the sea birds was high above her as they took to the air, their wings stretched out to make the most of the morning thermals. The wind sighed through the scrubby grass and clumps of small flowers that clung to the rocks. It had to be the most peaceful place in the world at that moment.

"It is peaceful, isn't it?" a quiet voice spoke beside her, and Claire heard someone sit at her side.

"Welcome back, Aroha." Claire smiled and opened her eyes to the girl. But she was no longer the girl she had watched over and instructed. In her place sat a woman with knowledge and determination behind her eyes. "You have grown."

"I have," Aroha said, hugging her knees to her. "I have learned so much from my Mother Universe."

"Are you prepared, then? Are we to go banish Chaos from this world?" Claire asked and held her breath, steeling herself for the confrontation.

"Yes. It should be soon and I can think of no better day than this." Aroha turned her eyes to Claire. "Are you prepared, Carling?"

The question cut deep into her soul and mind. Slowly Claire nodded. She pulled energy from the surrounding landscape with which to equip herself. She felt determined. "I am ready, Aroha."

"Then I suggest we go for a good breakfast before we begin." Aroha stood and held out a hand to help her aunt from the ground.

As they reappeared in the room below the rock, they found themselves joined by the Sentinels. The meal they shared was plentiful and good, but the mood was quiet and subdued. As they finished, Aroha and Claire found themselves surrounded by the Sentinels, their hands raised over their heads and bestowing blessings upon them. Soon they were saying their farewells before Aroha took Claire's hand.

"Take us to the spot, Carling," Aroha asked as she squeezed the hand.

Within moments the world was slipping from underneath them and they found themselves back in the small room of crystals. The pair were greeted by the dazzling light that glittered and refracted off the crystals and at first the two women were blinded. Blinking in the light, Claire looked at the two pillars that held their prisoner and gasped.

The space where he should have been was empty.

Chapter Ten

"I don't understand!" Claire exclaimed. "I tightened his bonds just a few days ago. I fed energy into the crystal that holds Order. Chaos should still be here!" She looked to where the small crystal still sat on the large plinth of clear shard.

The crystal was dim and the light within it almost extinguished. Claire picked up the small orb and held it in her hands, willing energy into it to feed the life she still felt there.

"Give it to me, Carling." Aroha was at her side and held out her hand to take it.

Reluctantly, Claire released the orb and watched as Aroha encased it in her own hands. She held it up to her chest to where her heart sat. The light between her fingers grew steadily, increasing until it was blinding, and Claire had to look away. She stepped back from the glow, watching with squinted eyes in fascination as the young woman poured so much life into the being within the crystal.

As the light began to fade another figure joined Aroha. A figure in white with startling pin pricks of light under her skin.

"My Sister, we thank you," Order said, bowing slightly to Aroha.

"My Sister, what happened, where is our brother Chaos?" Aroha demanded.

"He had help to escape. A man came in the hours of darkness before the dawn. He drew the life from us until we were too weak to act. He used that force to release the bonds on Chaos and they left. They thought they had defeated us," Order said to Aroha. As she spoke, the lights flared under Aroha's skin, a rainbow of colours.

"Who was it? Who was the man?" Aroha asked. Claire was watching her carefully and could see fear cross her face. She suspected Aroha already knew the answer.

Order looked between the two women and her pale eyes rested on Claire's face. "It was your son, Callum."

"No!" Claire shook her head. "No, it can't be. Callum wouldn't have. Couldn't." She stumbled back a moment and Aroha was at her side to support her.

"I am afraid it was, Carling," she told her. As Aroha held her up, she waved a hand in front of them both, and Claire watched in horror at the scene that now played out in front of her.

An image of Callum appeared in the darkness and he placed both hands over the crystal orb. She saw the energy flow from the gem into her son and she cried out, shaking her head. When the light had dimmed to only a small speck he turned, taking the rope bindings in his hands. The golden threads shattered into pieces, the light from their fragments flaring for a moment before winking out as they fell to the floor.

Chaos stood straight and tall, rubbing at where his bonds had been for thousands of years. His hand clamped onto the broad shoulder of Callum and he spoke a single word before they disappeared from the room.

"No! Callum, why?" Claire cried, a hand going over her mouth.

"I have felt our brother getting stronger for some time now. I had hoped that you would have been ready to banish him and take up our place. I did not see this," Order said, coming to lay a soothing hand on Claire's face. "To use your child in such a way."

"Callum," Claire said softly.

The world moved around them, and she found that Aroha had transported them all back to the common room of the Sentinels. The colourful Beings stood as one as they appeared, and they were in shock at the appearance of Order.

"What happened?" Blue asked first, stepping towards the trio.

"Father!" Claire called out and stumbled into his arms. Carefully he held her while he looked at Aroha and Order.

"Chaos has escaped," Aroha told the gathered host. Claire sobbed, the noise echoing in the stunned silence.

"No! He can't have. How?" Red demanded. The others were now stepping forward. Yellow was now at Blue and Claire's side.

"He used my son," Claire said, wiping the tears from her eyes and pulling away from Blue. Anger was swelling inside her at the thought that her boy, her sweet child, had been corrupted in such a way.

Red turned to her. "Callum?" As soon as Claire nodded, he disappeared.

"But, how? He has been protected just as Breena has," Yellow asked.

"Unfortunately, I think I am to blame," Aroha said. "I think Chaos used his love for me, his jealousy whenever I talked to another man, to manipulate him."

"You cannot blame yourself, Aroha," Claire said, her hands clenched in fists. She began to gather her energy to send out a search, but Red reappeared before she could release it.

"I can't find him. He is being hidden from me. Carling?" He turned his anguished eyes to her.

Claire closed her eyes and sent out the search. It spread out from the island in all directions and headed out into the world. It was a desperate act, trying to find her child. Further and further out she pushed as she searched. The others helped her, added their own energy to hers.

Finally, a glimmer of light caught her attention. A soft glowing red, so tiny and small, like it was trying to shine from under a blanket, and she focused all her thoughts on it. So tiny and bent in on itself, it gleamed weakly. Claire had found him, and she breathed a sigh of relief.

A darkness like a great storm cloud caught the spark up and moved it out of sight, but she had it. Claire followed the small glimmer until she recognised where it came to rest. Returning back to the Sentinels, she looked around her.

"I know where he is. I know where Chaos is keeping him," Claire exclaimed when she came back to them. A tugging on her mind let her know Matt was trying to contact her. She pushed him aside for a moment and concentrated on those before her.

"Where?" Red asked her quickly.

"It's a cave in the mountains to the east of Rome in Italy. I came across a reference to it in the library at home. Matt and I went to find it one summer," she said quickly, and as she mentioned her husband's name, his call to her strengthened.

Within moments she had transported herself to him and then brought him to the home of the Sentinels. He wobbled a little at the suddenness of the movement.

"What the—?" he started.

"Matt, he has Callum," Claire said, flinging her arms around his neck, seeking the comfort of him.

In stunned silence he took in the room with all its occupants and folded his arms around his wife. "Who?" he asked, dazed.

"Chaos. He has Callum," she said, pulling back and staring into his blue eyes.

"Chaos? I don't understand, Claire. What has happened?"

Explanations made and doubt ironed away, Claire and Matt now found themselves sitting on a chartered plane in the company of Aroha, James, and Greg. With the help of Tony, they were winging their way to Italy and the ancient city of Rome. She remembered their last trip, so full of sunshine and laughter as the family had travelled together to find the cave that she had needed to go see for herself.

The reference Claire had found was obscure and lacked detail. It listed a mountain range that one ancestor had noted during an early attempt at genealogy and the links of where The People had emigrated. As she looked back at that trip now, she remembered details in sharp focus. They had found it, almost exactly where the note had said it would be.

Claire remembered exploring it, listening to the children calling out, their voices echoing through the chambers. She smiled as she remembered the twelve-year-old Bree being almost as childlike as six-year-old Callum had been. They had played in and out of the smaller caverns, their parents always keeping an eye on them as they explored. There had been signs of habitation in the cave at some point and Claire had experienced a strange sensation while she was inside.

It was the sudden silence of the children that had scared her most, then Bree calling to Callum. She ran back to her parents saying she couldn't find him, the scared look in her eyes imprinted in Claire's memory. The hurried search for the boy before he was found, laughing at having hidden so well. It had been after that moment that he had discovered some of his Abilities coming in already. With hindsight, she wondered if there had perhaps been some external interference during that time. Almost as if he had read her thoughts, Matt took up her hand and held it tightly. Claire rested her head on his shoulder, and he kissed her gently.

There was no talking between any of the passengers on this flight and the interior was dim. Aroha was looking out of one of the windows at the tops of the clouds that sailed underneath the aircraft. Greg had headphones on, and his eyes were closed, his head leaning back. Claire thought he was asleep, until his eyes opened and looked at her. James was reading a book. Claire had not seen him turn a page for some time and it did not surprise her when he shut it and threw it on the table before him. He stood up, stretched, and moved back to Matt and Claire's seats.

"Just what are we walking into, Claire? I need to know how to prepare," he said as he sat down across the aisle from them.

"It is a deep cave system, from what I understood from the locals. It's not very well known; they know to stay away from it. There are the usual local legends. You know the sort of things, animals and children lost inside," she said, raising her head from Matt's shoulder.

"Okay. Are we going to need any specialist equipment? Ropes, harnesses, lights, that sort of thing?" he asked. He seemed to be on edge.

"All of that sounds like a good idea. Are you okay, James?" she asked.

"Not really. I don't like the idea of going into caves," he told her sheepishly.

"You can stay outside if you like, and keep in contact with us via radio," Matt offered.

"No, Tony is expecting me to go in with you. It's part of my job," James said stoically.

"We don't have to tell him. He won't be there to find out." Claire smiled at her old friend. "Anyway, I think Aroha, Matt, and I can handle whatever is down there."

"Is it true about Aroha?" James asked solemnly.

"It is. She has the knowledge of the Universe at her fingertips and has access to everything. Did you not believe me before when I brought you up to date with the history I have discovered?" she asked him.

"Sort of, it just seems so far-fetched. Every culture has a creation story. This just seems like another one. I have known Aroha since she was very small. I have seen her grow, have even been on her protection squad at one point. To know now that she is who she is—it just boggles the mind." James looked over at the young woman staring out of the window.

"Do you need me to show you, James?" Aroha asked, turning to look at him.

"I don't think that will be necessary," he replied, looking a bit sheepish again.

"I am still the girl you used to know. I haven't changed much." She stared at him with an intensity that made him avert his gaze.

"No, you're not. You are so much more now."

"Dad should have made you and Greg stay where you were and not involved you. We could have been there by now and Callum could have been safe," Aroha said, returning to her contemplation out of the window, then just as fast turned back to him. "And you can stop thinking that as well, James. You are needed and wanted."

James sat stunned for a moment until he realised she had read his thoughts. "How did you manage to get past my defenses?" he asked.

"Everyone's mind—every beast, bird, and fish's mind—is now open to me. I have been sitting here, plucking at the thoughts of all the people down on the ground. I can hear their wishes and deepest desires, their pain and heartache, their joys and triumphs. I can be here and in another place at one time."

If Claire had expected an exalted look as Aroha spoke, she would have been disappointed. Instead, she saw sadness creep over her face and it wrung at her heart.

"Aunty Claire, Uncle Matt, Callum knows we are coming for him. He can feel you holding onto the tenuous connection between you. He is grasping at it—trying to keep it hidden from Chaos. He has not given himself fully to the dark one," Aroha said. "I am trying to protect him. His mind is very fragile at the moment. He is scared. I'm there with him." She had a faraway look in her eye.

"Tell him we still love him. Tell him we will never give up on him," Matt said, still holding his wife's hand tightly.

"I will."

Aroha turned back to her window.

The plane touched down and they waited patiently for Greg to pick up the rental car. James was on alert, searching the crowd that surged around them in the drop off and pick up area outside the airport. Aroha stood close to him. Claire could see she was concentrating on something and hoped it was still Callum.

A large black SUV pulled up to the kerb beside them and James quickly bundled them inside. He climbed into the front seat and they headed out of the complex, trying to avoid the worst of the traffic.

Their first destination was on the other side of Rome. Greg made his way around the city and headed for the foothills and mountains that lay to the east. The drive was long, and Claire fell into an uneasy sleep. Her dreams were frantic and disturbed. Shadows so dark she couldn't see through them, clouding things and holding others back.

"Stop!" she yelled into the murkiness of the dream. She extracted herself from the dream space and found Carling there with waiting arms and comfort.

"He will be fine, Claire. Our son will be fine."

"But Chaos has a hold of him. Once he has someone, he will not let him go. We remember what must happen. We remember burning Marcus and Onnist."

"We know. We will sort it once we have him back. There is nothing we can do until that time, Claire."

Claire pushed herself away from Carling and a thought struck her. "What happened to Jack's body after we killed him?"

"We don't know. We never learned. We only know that he fell down the cliff after Tony threw him off."

"His bones. If he was buried, Chaos could use them to come back."

She cried and then called out to the only two people who might know what happened to the man who was once so obsessed with Claire.

They answered her and joined her in her mind. Adam, her first sweetheart and best friend, also half-brother to Jack, came walking towards her beside her brother in spirit, Tony.

"What's wrong, Claire, Carling?" Tony asked as they approached.

"What happened to Jack after he died?" she asked them quickly.

"I don't know, I didn't stick around to find out," Tony told her and looked to Adam.

"He was buried in the cemetery in the village, beside his mother. Why?" Adam asked.

"He wasn't cremated?" she asked.

"No. Marcus didn't want him to be. I remember the cost of getting his body back to New Zealand," he told her. "Why, what does it matter now?"

Claire sighed and turned away. Carling looked at the two men. "It matters because his bones are intact. They are a gateway for Chaos and have helped him escape."

"I don't understand," Adam said.

"Once Chaos has hold of someone he doesn't let go. His grasp invades even the smallest of a person's cells. That is why the Sentinels had me burn Marcus after he died. I didn't even think about Jack. Until now," Claire said, turning back to them.

"You're worried about Callum?" Tony asked suddenly.

"Callum? What's happening, Claire?" Adam asked her. She brought him up to date. "My god. Does that mean...?" He couldn't bring himself to say it in front of Claire.

"We hope not. We hope we can save him completely, that he has not been fully taken over, like Jack and Marcus were," Carling told him gently.

"What can I do? There must be something I can do?" Adam asked them both and turned to Tony. "We could dig Jack up and burn his body."

"Adam, think about what you just said. I think The Community back in New Zealand would have something to say on the matter of us arriving and digging a body up in their cemetery," Tony said calmly.

"But if it will help Claire and Aroha..." He turned back to Claire, hoping to see her agreement.

"I don't know," she said, shaking her head.

"Leave it with me. I'll talk to David and Jasper. We'll organise it and go through the Elders of The Community. It will be all right, Claire," Adam told her.

"Thank you. I just hope there's no one else he has managed to get his claws into. The Elders have all been sent my latest findings. They should be up to date with the history, and I only hope that they believe it," she told him.

"Don't worry. I'll go with Adam. Between us we can make them see sense. And if they don't then it will be shovels at midnight." Tony chuckled as he took her into his arms. "You just concentrate on keeping yourself, Matt, and my daughter safe." He dropped a kiss on the top of her head.

"I will. Once again you've come to my aid in an unusual way." Claire pulled away from him. "By the way, James and Greg did not need to come with us. There is nothing they can help us with."

"What are you talking about? I told them to get back home after organising your transport and accommodation." Tony looked puzzled.

"James told me that you said to stay with us and keep watch on Aroha."

"I didn't. I know you could have handled anything on your own. I'll give them a call and send them packing, they will only slow you down."

"No. Don't. Let me look into it first." She frowned at the thought. Doubts were starting to seep into her thoughts, along with a sinking feeling in her stomach.

"Claire, don't put yourself in any danger," Tony told her.

"I won't. I promise." She smiled at the pair, trying to hide her growing fear. "Thank you, for helping. Let me know how it all goes."

Gently she pushed them away before Tony could say another word, the uneasy feeling growing deeper as the different scenarios played through her mind as to why James and Greg were with them under false pretenses. She turned to Carling.

"Let me. You are too close to either one and I can slip in between their defenses where you will be discovered," Carling told her and Claire nodded.

To Claire it felt as though she was creeping into the minds of Greg and James but detached from the process. The action was smooth and careful, deliberate. She marveled at how Carling managed to sidestep the traps that James had set in his mind and glided through his thoughts and hidden secrets.

"It's all clear. We cannot find any sign of tampering in either one. We think they just simply disobeyed Tony because of the love they feel for us. Especially James. He wants to help, to be a part of what is happening. We got the sense that he wanted to make up for what happened."

"That is nonsense. He doesn't need to make up for anything. It was not his doing. We will talk to them tonight." She sighed.

"It is the way with our spirits, Claire. People give us their love and support even when we don't need it. But in some strange way we need their love to survive."

"As we have seen. We must wake now, Carling. Our journey is nearly at an end."

"We will be there when we find our son. We will join our spirits to wrestle Callum away from him."

"Thank you."

The old house Tony had booked for them stood proudly in an established garden, set back from the road. Large trees gnarled with age cast long shadows as the sun dipped on the horizon. Outside the freshly painted door sat a beat-up old car, and as Greg pulled up, a woman climbed out of the front seat carrying her shopping bags.

Claire went to meet her and shook her hand.

"Welcome. I'm Gemma." She was tall and willowy with long blond hair and big blue eyes and her smile was large. Her accent was decidedly from New Zealand. "Tony told me to give you all the courtesy I could afford, so I have stocked the pantry and fridge, and everything is at your disposal. If there is anything else you need, you are to let me know and I will add it to the bill."

"Thanks. How do you know Tony?" Claire asked her

"I used to work for him. Well, in some ways I still do," she said and started to blush when she saw James.

"Hello, Gemma. Long time…" he said.

"It has been, James. Too long," she said quietly, blushing as she eyed him up and down.

Claire smiled secretly to herself as she could sense the attraction between them. An unspoken and misjudged attraction from both sides. A little plan was starting to form in her mind. "Come inside. I'll show you around," Gemma said, opening the large door which swung wide on well-oiled hinges into the brightly lit interior of the entryway.

Inside, the old building had been renovated and updated to some extent but keeping a lot of the original features still intact. It was cool without being chilly and tastefully decorated in muted tones. The original large flagstone floor had been kept; the wear of so many feet over many decades, if not centuries, could be seen on them. The age of the house seemed to hang comfortably in the air, giving it that cozy feeling of being occupied by many people who had loved living there.

Gemma guided them around the house and showed them to their rooms. She met them again downstairs where her eyes fell on James. She poured them each a glass of wine then headed to the kitchen to make dinner.

"You don't need to wait on us, Gemma," Claire said, wandering into the kitchen with her glass in hand.

"It's all part of the service. I am being paid very well for it," Gemma grinned.

"So, you know James?" Claire sat on one of the large stools that was placed on the opposite side of the island in the centre of the room to her host and sipped her wine.

"Yes, we go back some way," Gemma said, trying to hide a smile.

"How far back?"

"He was one of my trainers when I first joined Tony's company." She chopped the carrots with great precision and speed.

"Did you two get along? Was he a good trainer?" Claire watched as Gemma's blush deepened.

"I think we did. But fraternization was, I think, frowned upon."

Claire watched her concentrate on the job at hand.

"Strange. I didn't think that was a problem in that company. Considering how Tony and his wife met." Gemma looked up and frowned. "Tia worked for Tony. I actually got them together." Claire smiled and took another sip.

"I never knew that. I mean, I knew Tia worked in the company, but I didn't know that she started there before they got together." Her knife hand stilled on the chopping board.

"Yes, she did."

"So, how did you get them together?" Her curiosity was rising.

"I took their hands and placed them in each other's. It didn't take much. They were very much in love to begin with." Claire was watching her carefully. "James is very nice."

Gemma looked up quickly, then back down at her work, and carried on chopping the vegetables. "Yes, he is," she said, almost breathless.

"I'll leave you to it. Let me know if there is anything I can do for you," Claire said, getting up off the stool. It seemed to

Claire as if Gemma was about to say something, then she smiled.

"Nothing at the moment."

"Okay, just call." Claire left the kitchen and wandered back into the living room where the others sat. She spotted James at the open French doors looking out into the garden as dusk settled on the property and she went to stand with him.

"Walk with me, James?" she asked as she stepped through the doors and felt him following her.

The night air was cooling down and the stars began to make an appearance. Birds were still calling out in the trees as they came in to roost and insects could still be heard making their own music. James walked at her side as they made their way under the large old trees away from the house so they couldn't be overheard.

"I spoke to Tony," she said quietly as she came to a bench and sat down.

"Ah," he said, taking a seat next to her.

"Why?"

"I was concerned. I thought that with Greg and me there we could give you extra protection." He shifted uncomfortably under her gaze.

"There is no need."

James hesitated a moment before he spoke again. "I know that. But I wanted to help. I felt that I owed you."

"You don't owe me anything. You helped me then, supported me and gave me the friendship and love that I needed at that time. There is no debt to be paid."

"You may think so, but in my mind, there is a great debt. One I mean to keep paying until I am satisfied that there is clean slate."

Claire thought about his words for a moment before she spoke again. "There is something you can do for me. And with that one thing the slate will be wiped clean. But you have to promise me that you will do exactly as I say, and there will be no more guilt."

"Anything. I promise, Claire. What is it you want me to do?" he asked.

"I will let you know when the time is right. And you had better not argue with me. It will set my mind at rest knowing that you will do this one thing." She smiled and hoped it didn't really show in the creeping darkness.

After their sumptuous dinner, Claire drafted James and Greg to do the dishes. Aroha had remained quiet throughout the meal and Carling went and sat beside her on the couch in the living room.

"He is still holding on. Callum is clinging to me, fighting the mind of Chaos," she said quietly and under some strain.

"Do you want me to take over?" Claire asked.

"No. I need to do this. We need to go to him soon, Aunty Claire. He is weakening."

"We'll go tonight." Claire looked up at Matt who was watching the pair of them and nodded. "I don't want Greg or James there; I won't risk their minds. I'll create a diversion for them so we can slip out. I can guide us to the cave."

"I'll try and get the keys from Greg," Matt said, heading to the kitchen.

"I can get us to the cave without the car," Claire said. "Just give me a few moments and meet us outside."

Matt nodded and went upstairs to change. Claire shifted her mind, copied what Carling had done earlier, and slipped into Greg's mind. She felt grubby and terrible for doing this to someone she knew, but it had to be done. She carefully placed the suggestion of a deep sleep into the younger man's mind and then left.

That only left James. Her idea for him was to carry out the plan that had formulated earlier while she had talked to Gemma. Claire stood and headed to the kitchen. In the room the two men were finishing up the dishes. Greg started to yawn loud and long. Soon he was handing a cloth over to James.

"Here, I'm dead on my feet. I have to go sleep," he said bursting yet again into a loud and protracted yawn.

"You can't leave all this to me," James protested, but Greg only waved away his concern.

"I'll help," Gemma said, coming into the room. From the doorway Claire watched the two working and grinned at the looks each gave while they thought the other wasn't watching.

As the last of the dishes were done and Gemma was wiping down the bench, Claire entered the room properly. She walked up behind the pair.

"You remember that thing I said I wanted you to do and to not argue with me when I told you?" Claire asked James.

"Yes, what is it?" he asked.

"It's only something very simple, and I promise it won't be difficult to achieve." She tried hard not to smile. Gently she took his hand and then turned to Gemma and took hers. Slowly she placed the two together. "Now, go be happy."

As Claire walked away towards the living room, she snuck a peek back at the couple and smiled broadly. James and Gemma were still standing before the sink, their hands clasped, and he leaned in and gently kissed her.

Matt had returned back to the living room, now dressed in his old jeans and a warm shirt. In his hands he held a jacket each for both Claire and Aroha. He looked at the grin spreading across her face and frowned.

"What have you been up to?" he asked.

"Nothing much. Just making sure Greg and James are occupied." She took a jacket placed it around Aroha's shoulders as her niece continued keeping their son sane.

"Claire?" he asked her, holding out the jacket.

"I sent Greg to bed because he is tired, and James… I was just finishing something he would have eventually done, but it suited my needs to do it now." She grinned at him.

"You can be very frustrating. Have I told you that?"

"I think you've said that a few times now."

"What did you do?" Matt demanded again.

"I just showed Gemma and James that they were supposed to be together. Now if you're ready, I think we had better go and save our son."

She reached up and kissed him on the lips, before helping Aroha stand and guiding her out the French doors and into the garden beyond.

Chapter Eleven

Around them the world coalesced into deep shadows under the tall trees of the forest that blanketed the mountainside. The evening noises were muted, and the wind sighed as it blew through the tops of the trees, sending their branches to quiver and creak in the stillness of the night. The barely visible narrow path underfoot was littered with fallen twigs and branches. A bright green moss clung to the rocks that jutted out from the ground, and drifts of still-rotting leaf litter were piled against their bases and in amongst the twisting roots of the trees. An ancient air surrounded them and there was a sense of time weighing heavy upon them.

Claire produced a light that hovered in the air, feeding it more energy to make it swell and grow brighter, illuminating the area. They set off to find the entrance to the cave, their shadows moving around them and merging with those of the trees as they passed. Matt had a protective arm around Aroha and guided her as they followed Claire. Her sure feet started to climb the gully, and she sensed the cave just ahead of them.

From out of the gloom an even darker shape formed. The entrance was tall and narrow, looming high above them. It seemed like some mason had deliberately carved a large vaulted archway into the ancient limestone. They went inside, the little light bobbing merrily along above them to show the way. Fallen stones almost blocked the path that led into the cave, leaving only just enough room for them to enter one at a time. Matt helped Aroha through the portal and into the main cavern.

The area opened wide before them, an enormous space with a flat and slightly sloped floor covered in a layer of dust and dirt that had blown in from outside. Large stalactites and stalagmites met in slender columns. The constant dripping of water created tinkling music that filled and echoed around the void. At the rear there were three jagged openings in the rock wall, all of which led further into the belly of the mountain. Claire, Matt, and Aroha came to stop in the center and looked at the three openings.

"The middle is the one we want," Aroha said quietly, nodding to the dark yawning space.

They headed down a long corridor. The work of ancient tools could be seen on the rock as they passed it. Some long-forgotten people bent on doing their master's work. Claire got a flash of the history and could feel the workers' fear.

The further they walked, the bigger the feeling of dread and fear that she felt. Claire sensed the first faltering steps of Matt before she could hear or see them. She stopped and turned to her husband who was still trying to guide Aroha. Taking his hands in hers and looking deeply into his eyes, Claire began to feed energy and love to him. Matt straightened visibly and gave her a small smile.

"I'm fine now," he whispered.

Deeper and deeper they went into the mountain. The weight of the rock above surrounded Claire. She recognised it for what it was: an illusion to frighten lesser and more susceptible minds. She sent out a large energy burst of Seek, finding all the small hints and suggestions that had been leeched into the walls of the corridor. With the touch of her forward vision, the obstacles burst with a popping sound and winked out of existence. The way was then clear for them to continue.

The tunnel then came to an abrupt end. Branching out were two other openings, both similarly dark. The sound of rushing water came from the right-hand entrance, while the smell of fresh air and spring flowers tempted them from the left. Claire looked between each branch. They had not reached this far the last time the children were with her and Matt.

"We need to take the right," Aroha told them and turned slowly towards that entrance.

"I was afraid you would say that," Matt muttered as he followed her.

The sound of water grew louder and louder with each footstep, the ground and walls surrounding them growing damp and glistening in the light. They rounded a bend and found themselves on a small ledge. The roar that greeted them was accompanied by a fine settling mist, making the stone at their feet slippery. Claire sent out her light and it burst to life as it rose into this new space, now surrounded by a nimbus in the floating mist.

A wall of sparkling white water flowed before them, cascading from an unseen opening far above, and dropping to the depths below. It crashed on the rocks behind it, filling the void with a sound louder than a roaring train. The light moved around them, searching for a way out. It came to a stop and hovered over a small crevice in the wall, just beside the waterfall.

"Be careful not to slip," Matt advised them, raising his voice so he could be heard over the waterfall. He headed out first, hugging the wall at his side.

The ledge was narrow, and the edge crumbled away if they shuffled their feet too close. The sound of the loosened stones and pebbles hitting the bottom of the enormous pit was lost in the sound of the water that was constantly booming in their ears. Inching along they made their way towards the crevice and the glowing ball of light, which suddenly hiccupped and winked out. The darkness was absolute and terrifying. The sound of the waterfall seemed to increase, and they froze.

Claire concentrated, pushing down the fear that flared inside her. She made another light, holding onto it for a moment before sending it out and directing it to where its predecessor had disappeared. Where the last seemed to dance and be almost playful, this one was sturdy and steady in its glow. It seemed to take on its responsibility for lighting their way seriously and it hung as a guide to the opening.

It was a tight squeeze getting through the crevice; the opening was jagged, and the rock seemed to grasp at their clothing. The sound of tearing material had Claire look back and she saw the jacket she wore had caught on a shard of sharp rock. Reaching behind, she unhooked herself and carried on, catching up with Aroha and Matt, trying to keep away from the sides of the narrow fissure.

Aroha reached out and stopped Matt from going on any further. She raised a finger to her mouth to warn them both to be quiet and she closed her eyes. Claire could sense Aroha searching and communing with Callum, feeding him the necessary energy he needed to keep that corner of his mind from Chaos. She wanted to add her own strength to that of her niece but knew it would only open her son's mind to their ancient adversary. Bringing her energy back under control Claire took a deep breath.

"It's not far now. The Dark One is also there, waiting for us," Aroha's voice said in their minds. The size of the task at hand came to them, along with a plan to help wrest their son from the clutches of Chaos.

On silent, stealthy feet the group moved forward. Ahead the fissure opened up and from around the corner came a dim light. Claire snuffed out the ball she had created, and they made do with the glow from ahead as it washed softly over the rocks. Claire went to stand with Matt, while Aroha brought up the rear. They rounded the corner and saw before them a large room, opulently decorated with gold and gems. The light that shone at the entrance did little to radiate into the rest of the room. But it was enough to see who was there.

Crumpled in the corner, curled up on himself, was the unconscious form of Callum. His blond hair covered his face and his arms were clasped tightly around him. Claire and Matt's first reaction was to run towards him, but Claire held her husband back as the dark presence made itself known.

The laugh that greeted them was deep and dreadful. There was no hint of humor in it at all, only malice. It echoed off the walls and emanated from the large golden throne set against the far wall.

"Welcome, Sister," the voice said, and Chaos materialised in front of them. He was sat back, and his muscular arms rested on the high sides of the chair. Chaos's dark hair was slicked back, and his face, which was in shadow, scowled at the intruders. He was breathing deeply, hands clenching the ends of the arm rests. The vest he was wearing was made of a dark leather, the same material as clad his legs. His presence filled the room, casting fear before him.

"Brother," Aroha said, moving to stand ahead of Claire and Matt, shielding them from him.

"Have you come to accept my offer? Or shall I crush the final remnants of this one's mind?" Chaos's hand moved towards Callum.

"I will not let you do that, Chaos, and I am not here to accept your offer," she told him.

There was a calmness to her voice that Claire and Matt did not share. Their eyes were still on their son and they were desperate to get to him but found that their feet were held where they stood.

"So, this is to be the meeting that was foretold? Do you come to banish me finally, Sister?" he asked eagerly, sitting forward in his seat.

"If necessary," Aroha told him almost flippantly.

"So, you will face me alone, with only the help of these two mortals?"

"I am not alone, Brother. I have never been, and I never will be. Our Mother is with me."

Chaos winced at the term and his eyes narrowed. "Our Mother?" he spat. "The Universe is not my mother. She seeks to banish her own son from this and every other world. That is not the act of a mother."

"You turned from your true path, Brother. The other world was placed in your hands to care and nurture, but you became twisted with power. The mistake must be corrected so that the Universe can continue."

His voice became low and suggestive. "We two are the same, Sister. Would you not like to see the worlds that we could create, the people we could birth together?"

"Not with you, Chaos. Your offers did not work on the One True Child and they will not work with me. Why do you always have such suggestions?" Aroha cocked her head to one side slightly and looked at him hard, trying to see what was going on inside the Dark One. Then her eyes grew wide and she nodded with a small smile. "I can see why, now. Is it that you do feel the loneliness of being on your own? Of not having the love of another to help and support you?" she asked softly.

"This is ridiculous. I need no one!" he roared, launching himself onto his feet. His fists were clenched and his knuckles white from the pressure. His biceps flexed and his face was going red.

"I believe it is, and I pity you for it. You will not allow yourself to love, or even receive love. Are you so selfish that you cannot see?" She stepped closer to him, the tiny pinpricks of lights beginning to glimmer under her skin.

Chaos launched himself at her. His strong arms wrapped around Aroha and clenched tightly, squeezing the life out of her. In the same instant the lights under her skin glowed so brightly that they blotted out everything else from sight. Matt groped for Claire and held on to her, closing his eyes tightly in the iridescent light. Claire threw up a hasty protection for them both as the two beings clashed with each other. From somewhere above, a great groan seemed to come from the Universe herself.

With a final roar of agony, Chaos fled, and the light dimmed. When Claire opened her eyes, she saw Aroha crouched beside Callum. The dark Being had gone. Finally able to move, she was at her son's side and looking up at her niece.

"Is he all right?" Claire asked, not yet wanting to go into Callum's mind.

"In a moment," Aroha said, as she gulped in a few good lungsful of air. She placed a hand on Callum's head and closed her eyes.

Matt was by his wife's side now, his arm around Claire as they watched and waited for Aroha to finish. Her eyes opened and she turned to them with a smile.

"Give him a minute. He's trying to compose himself," she said shyly and moved away.

Matt gently lifted his son, cradling him in a protective embrace and brushed the hair from his eyes. Claire held his hand and waited, willing him to wake, wanting to make sure he would be fine. Then Callum's eyes opened and met his mother's eyes, the same shade of blue.

"Callum!" Claire cried out and took both Matt and her son into her arms.

"Mum, Dad—" he started.

"Not yet, son. It can wait until later," Matt said, his voice catching with relief.

"We need to get him to the stones," Aroha said quietly, not meeting anyone's eye.

"I will take Matt if you could take Callum?" Claire asked her, releasing her hold on her family.

"If that is what you wish," she said and nodded.

Claire took Callum's hand and placed it carefully into Aroha's. Finally, Aroha looked at the blond boy she had known all her life and smiled at him. A bell tolled somewhere close by. Claire looked at Matt with another smile and transported her husband back to the stones that stood on the hill behind their home in Scotland.

Matt looked around for a moment and realised that Aroha and Callum were not with them. He looked at his wife; the question hung between them and all he got as an answer was a smile.

"You did it again," he said with a wry grin.

"I did nothing. Only that which the Universe wished me to do."

"That bell. I've heard it before," Matt said, placing his arms around her.

"That was the approval of the Universe. Our son will be fine. Here they come," she said and kissed him.

Aroha and Callum appeared in the centre of the circle, still holding hands and looking into each other's eyes. The love that had first stirred when they were fourteen was now given to them in full.

Callum fell to his knees and kissed the backs of Aroha's hands. Looking up into her face, he shook his head. "Please, do it quickly. Please. I want your face to be the last thing I see."

"Do what?" she asked, her brow knitted with confusion.

"Kill me. He has touched my soul and I am tainted with his darkness. While I am alive, he can reach out his hand to hurt you and those that I love." His eyes were pleading with her.

"I will not kill you. I did not save you just to kill you. Your life will go on and with my help and that of the Sentinels, we will banish the shadow from you. I have been blinded by my own thoughts, Callum. I sought to hide the feelings that I have long felt for you, because I thought that my role as The Ultimate One meant that I would not find love. But I have loved you for a very long time. I'm sorry it took me so long to understand and accept. I'm sorry to have put you through so much pain and uncertainty; it placed you in great danger."

Callum got to his feet and placed his arms around Aroha. "Do you mean it, really?" he whispered.

"I do mean it." She nodded and placed her hands on either side of his face. "Before we can do anything else, I need to see it banished and you protected from his force again." Aroha looked deeply into his eyes and he nodded to her.

"I'm ready," he told her.

In through the entrance to the stones came the Sentinels. Their points of light swirling gently and slowly as they circled the young couple in the centre. Claire joined the procession and behind her came Matt. As she stood with the host, he placed a hand gently on her shoulder, adding his own life force to hers in order to save their son.

Their voices started in chorus, their hands rising with the tone of their chanting. Around the large upright rocks sparks of light began to appear, at first small and insignificant, but soon rising in intensity. Aroha still held onto Callum's head and Claire felt Carling add her own will. The gold lights flared under her skin and Claire saw Aroha reach into Callum and wrestle with the mark that Chaos had left on her son's mind, heart, and spirit. He cried out into the darkness as it tried to cling to him, his knees buckled and once more he was down on the ground. Aroha refused to let go and worked hard and long with the aid of the Sentinels to rid the evil from the man she loved.

With one final cry from Callum's lips, it was wrenched from him, and his eyes rolled back into his head as he went limp and collapsed. But there was still work to do. Aroha held the darkness in her hands, now a tangible thing that they could all see and feel. It pulsated and tried to set itself free, but she held it fast. Encasing it with the rainbow hue from under her skin, she suffocated it, ridding the world of its taint. It flew apart with an audible growl and Aroha sank to the ground beside Callum.

Their part done, the Sentinels finished their chanting, lowered their arms and stepped back from the couple. Beside her, Callum's eyes fluttered open and he looked up into Aroha's face, the moon's first faltering rays touching her face.

"It is done," she said quietly with a smile. "You are free."

"No, I am not. I will never be free of your love ever again. I am yours, Aroha, forever I shall be yours," he pledged himself to her.

"And I will be yours. I love you." She nodded and bent to kiss him.

Again, the bell tolled in recognition of their vow.

"So, are we going back to collect James and Greg?" Matt asked as he pulled Claire closer to him in bed later that night. Her head was resting on his shoulder.

"No. They were not supposed to be with us in the first place. Tony told them to go home." She gave a little laugh as she indulged in Foresight, the Talent she had the least fondness for.

"What are you scheming now?" he asked, dropping a kiss onto her head.

"Nothing. I've just seen what's to come for James. I think he will like living in Italy." Matt did not need to see the smile spreading across her face to know it was there.

"What about Greg?" he asked her.

"Greg is another matter. I see him working in Tony's company for a very long time and rising high enough to run it one day. But I don't see a partner or children for him for some time yet. He is afraid he will be like his father and is holding back. I cannot help him until he is ready to be helped." She gave a sigh.

"Now, can you explain something to me?" he asked quietly.

"If I can, I will. What is it you wish to know?" She tilted her head to see him in the soft moon glow that came through the window.

"That bell. What is it?"

"The Universe accepting and acknowledging a vow or a pledge," she told him. "Why did you want to know?"

"Because I heard it the first time that we made love up at the stones." Claire could feel his blush and remembered that morning all those years ago.

"In a way, what we did was a vow. An acknowledgement of our love in its purest form. The Universe needs love of all kinds. Aroha found that out tonight. She had tried so hard and was so determined that she would not find love that she almost made the same mistake that Chaos did."

"Pardon?"

"That meeting tonight between Chaos and Aroha was a lesson. Aroha had to understand that she could no longer deny the love she felt for our son, because to do so would set her on the path to becoming just like Chaos. Did you not hear her words?"

"I heard, but they confused me a little," he admitted to her.

Claire raised herself up on an elbow so she could see Matt's face clearly. Her hair hung down in a curtain of soft gold in the moonlight and the points of light began to glow under her skin.

"By looking into the heart of Chaos she saw the deep-seated loneliness that he feels, but also his shriveled heart. The twisted and unfeeling heart that he does not allow to be set free to love and receive love in return. He feels only anger, pain, and suffering. He does not understand that if he let himself feel love, understanding, and compassion, he would receive it back twofold. He seeks domination over everyone and everything. To him it represents power and strength, and that is all he wants. Aroha learned tonight that love is the key to everything. With love our lives are enriched and happy. To cut oneself off from being able to give and receive it leads to pain and emptiness."

"Did you know that was what was happening?" He reached up and tucked her hair behind her ear.

"Not at first. It wasn't until we were back at the stones that I realised what had occurred and why it had to happen. Our son being in danger of being lost to her made her realise what could be her fate. She chose the right path and now the world is a little safer because of it."

"But still not safe enough. Chaos is still out there somewhere." He sighed and pulled her back down into the circle of his arms.

"He is and we need to do something about that. Jack's remains keep him anchored to this world and even if we could restrain him again, the strength that anchor gives him will allow Chaos to free himself again."

"So, we go back to the village?" Matt asked her.

"Yes, and regardless of what the Elders say, it must be done. I can burn his bones where they lay now, without digging him up, but the ashes will be contained in one spot. They need to be scattered to the winds, just like Marcus's were."

"A grim task, then. One that can wait until morning." He rolled over and kissed her gently, his hands moving over her body and the lights under her skin glowing once more.

Far away, in the deepest and darkest of cave systems in the lands now known as The United States of America, Chaos roared out his displeasure at being bested by Aroha. The tantrum he threw was monumental and great chunks of the earth were pulled up and crushed as he took out his frustration on the cave. His eyes burned bright red in the darkness and his muscles bunched with his anger as he stormed around the chamber, sending the earth above to quiver.

The Dark One's rage continued for hours, until it was spent, leaving him sitting on the floor panting, in amongst the destruction of his unrestrained emotion. That girl who had the audacity to face him would not beat him, and neither would Carling. Taking in a deep breath, he settled his mind and took stock of everything. For once he tried to think about what his next move should be, and not just a sudden reaction. He needed to be able to secure himself from any force the girl could bring to bear against him. He needed to defeat her attempts of banishing him. The plan, when it finally came, had him giggling with joy. Carling had overlooked a step.

Chaos reached out and found what it was that he was looking for, and quickly transported himself to it. Bright sunlight blared down around, and he squinted against it. Within his prison he had become used to the dazzling light. Now it no longer affected him as it once had. Still, he stalked to the dark shadows of a tree, where he felt more comfortable, waiting out the daylight hours.

As he sat in anticipation of his next act, Chaos became aware of a call. A soothing voice that held so much promise of hope and love. The call of home. Not for the first time did he harden his mind against it. Chaos knew who it was from, but also knew that it came with conditions, and he was not willing to abide by those. Pushing back against the call, he felt it fade and brooded over it.

The tall hills and mountains that surrounded that narrow valley cast their shadows long before the sun relinquished its hold to the night. Still, he waited impatiently until it was fully dark and those that were near were slumbering in their beds. Moving out into the walled enclosure, Chaos stepped over the grave markers and pushed others out of his way. Their bones were none of his concern and did not deserve his respect.

Chaos found the plot he needed. A large plaque confirmed for him the name of his creature. *"Jack Ryder, beloved son of Marcus Ryder and Mary Sheridan."* He scowled at the name of Marcus, his greatest of creatures, all his hopes he had placed into that soul, only to be disappointed in the final minutes. His bones were long gone from this world, Carling had seen to it, and he had felt the loss keenly when it happened. But here lay his son's, just under the surface, at rest and with rotting flesh still covering them. Ready and available for his use.

Standing at the head of the grave, Chaos bent his will to the task. The earth groaned and shifted. A large wedge of dirt and grass moved and hung suspended in the air. Underneath sat the top of the wooden coffin. The lid slowly moved and creaked as the rusted hinges gave way under the pressure of his word. He scoured the bones, stripping them of the remnants that clung to them and lifted the skeletal remains from the box. Under his command, they shrank to a small size—small enough to fit in a pouch produced from thin air, into which he deposited Jack's remains.

With a wave of his hand, the grave was carefully put back the way it was supposed to be, along with any other damage he had done that night. The thought of the humans digging up the body and finding it gone made him laugh out into the dark night. After making sure that not even a blade of grass was out of place, Chaos turned, and with a single step, was gone from the valley. His presence and passing unnoticed by the few residents that were asleep in their beds. But their nightmares that night were dark and fevered, unable to be broken until the first light of dawn.

Chapter Twelve

Since discovering the Ability to transport herself, Claire had found the process easy and extremely convenient. But the leap they made that morning was far greater than she had ever attempted before. When Bree and John had visited, she had discussed the Ability at length with her son-in-law and he had explained the limitations of it from his own experiences.

John recounted the story of how he had first discovered the Ability, when on one holiday to the States, Aroha had stumbled on the edge of a tall cliff and tumbled over. He instinctively threw himself after in an attempt to catch her and had somehow transported them both back to the top from midair. John had also related the experiments he had conducted, shuddering as he highlighted some of the near fatal falls and situations he had found himself in. The discoveries he had made were great and John had made sure to chronicle them all. There were limits to how far he could go, and he needed to know the area to which he was transporting himself. For instance, he could transport himself from one end of New Zealand to the other and had even attempted a jump to Australia, but he found it drained more of his energy.

The jump that Claire was now contemplating was from one side of the world to the other, and the thought daunted her, even though Aroha assured Claire that it was possible for her to make that distance. With Aroha's assistance, Claire thought about the house in the valley. The two-story house left to her by Great-Uncle Geoff. She imagined the back yard, with its old oak tree that gave wonderful shade in the summer months and was home to a chorus of birds that would sing just outside her old bedroom window.

Carefully, Claire's mind made the leap and thankfully her body followed, along with that of her husband. Their hands clasped tightly together; she could feel his trust in her Ability. When she opened her eyes, she found the world had moved and day had turned to night. The air was just as chilly as the beloved Scotland they had just left, and she looked up into Matt's face.

"Told you that you could do it," he said, grinning down at her.

Claire only shook her head and breathed deeply as she opened the back door. Inside the kitchen nothing had changed. It had been a very long time since they had visited, and the house had that closed up smell to it. She turned on lights and wandered through the home she loved, then she heard the voices of Aroha and Callum as they arrived and joined Matt back in the kitchen.

"Well, that was weird," Callum remarked, and Claire noticed he was gripping onto the bench to steady himself.

"What time is it?" Matt asked, looking at his watch.

"New Zealand is about twelve hours ahead of Scotland," Claire said as she stood in the doorway.

"We are going to have to wait until the morning to contact David, then. Can you see where Tony and Adam are?" he asked her, sitting at the table.

Claire concentrated a little and found them easily. "They're here in the village. It seems the rest of the family is here as well. Adam has brought Addy, and Bree and John are here as well. I wonder why they came?" she pondered.

"Knowing Bree, she wouldn't want to miss out on anything," Callum said, making his way shakily to the table and joining his father.

"Do you want to gather them tonight and get this done or do you want to wait?" Matt asked her.

"The morning will do. Let them enjoy a good sleep, there's no point all of us being tired. They have already called a meeting and I would prefer to get the permission of the Elders before digging up Jack's grave," Claire said, busying herself filling the kettle with water. "Who wants a cup of tea?"

"We only just had one back in Scotland," Matt laughed at her. "That seems very strange to say."

"It feels very strange. When will the earth stop rolling?" Callum asked, putting his head in his hands.

"You'll get used to it." Aroha reassured him as she laid a hand on his shoulder. "Well, you better get used to it. We will be doing it a lot more."

Callum could only groan at the thought.

With cup in hand and a blanket wrapped around her shoulders to keep out the early morning chill, Claire stepped onto the front porch and sat on the old bench seat. The clouds were shifting across the dawning sky, the sun kissing their underbellies with golden and orange hues as they lumbered their way over the hills into the surrounding valley. Birds swelled with their song to greet the new day, and taking to wing, went out in search of food. A fantail bobbed and weaved its way around the front garden, chasing the early rising insects. Having caught one, the small bird landed on the porch railing and made a chittering noise. The feathers on its tail spread out and it gave a small hop.

Changing her thinking and employing her little-used Whisperer Ability, Claire spoke to the flighty bird. "Good morning," Claire bade it.

"Morning, morning. Lots of bugs today. It is a good morning," the little bird chirped again.

"Enjoy your meal and may your nest in the spring be full of eggs." She smiled as the bird flew away.

Her eyes soon turned once more to the rising sun. The door opened and Matt joined her, a steaming cup in his own hands. Claire moved the blanket from one of her shoulders and wrapped it around his as he sat down, sharing the warmth she had already imparted to it.

"Did you sleep at all?" he asked quietly into the hush of the new morning.

"Not really. I think I dozed for a little, but the internal clock is all mixed up." She took a sip of her coffee and rested it on the arm of the seat.

Matt took her hand in his and raised it to his lips. "You'll be very tired later."

"I will sleep when this is all over. While he is out there, roaming free, I'll worry too much about what he's doing," she told him, leaning her head on his shoulder.

A loud rumbling could be heard coming down the street. Claire recognised it and waited for the beat-up old Ute to come to halt outside the gate. The door opened and a grey head appeared, and he stood as the door shut behind him.

"I should have known it would be you," David called out as he came around the car and in through the gate. "I got a phone call to say that there were lights seen on in the house."

"Good morning, Uncle David. Would you like a coffee?" Claire asked, standing to meet him.

"Yes, please. I left before Beth was up." He followed them into the house and sat at the table. "So, are you going to tell me why you're here?"

"Have Adam and Tony not spoken to you yet?" Claire asked as she sat down opposite him.

"No, they've called a meeting for today with the Elders, but they wouldn't say why. Some of them are still suspicious of Tony and his motives, and the fact that Adam is Marcus's son. They have very long memories," David said, accepting a cup of tea from Matt.

"I take it the knowledge that Tony is Marcus's grandson still hasn't been released?" Matt asked, sitting down beside his wife.

"No. That will go to the graves of everyone who knows. I have gotten to know him pretty well since… well, since that incident, and I know that Marcus never acknowledged him. Tony doesn't want it known and we should respect that," David said.

"It would only complicate matters," Claire agreed.

"But that still doesn't explain why the meeting has been called and why I find you two here," David said, an eyebrow now raised.

"Not just us, Callum and Aroha are here also," Matt told him.

"Are you going to put an old man out of his misery and let him know? Or are you going to wait and spring it on me with the rest of the old cronies who think they're in charge?" He gave them a lopsided grin.

"There have been some changes," Claire started.

Between the two of them, Claire and Matt brought David up to date, including why the meeting had been called. David sat back in his seat and stared at the pair of them.

"Life is never easy with you two, is it?" he asked, shaking his head.

"It's not, no," Matt replied.

"So, Chaos is loose, Callum helped him but is now safe, and Aroha and Callum are now together. Thank god for that, I never thought that was going to happen." He let out a sigh. "You are going to give a few of the old boys a heart attack or two, maybe an aneurysm. They're not going to believe this."

"They have to, Uncle David. I have never held anything back from them with my research and have kept them up to date with all I have found. They need to believe it. But regardless of their approval or not, I will be digging up Jack's bones to burn them. They cannot be left there," Claire said adamantly.

"Not without my help, you don't." David sat forward with his arms on the table. "I believe you, and so do many others on the council. But there are some that have lived apart from the Community for too long and don't know what happened when this all started for you. They are the ones you need to convince; they will not make a ruling until they are unanimous. I'll help you where I can," he told her firmly.

"Thank you, Uncle David," Claire said, reaching across the table to place her hand on his clasped ones.

The phone in David's pocket began to ring and he pulled it out, looking at the screen. "That is your Aunt wondering where I am." He answered it and quickly brought Beth up to date. When he hung up he looked at the pair. "Well seeing as you're here, Beth wants you to come to breakfast. You might as well go get the kids; she'll be furious if she doesn't get to fuss over them."

The morning was filled with family and idle chat after letting everyone know what was happening. Claire looked around the gathered group, taking in how much everyone had aged. Addy's hair was still ginger, but her roots were beginning to show. Tony was still strong and tall, but his dark hair was now shot through with white. Adam had lines around his eyes that deepened when he smiled, and a few tinges of grey at his temples.

Beth was still as fastidiously dressed as always. Her hair was neat and tidy, but not as severe as it used to be, and she had long since given up on dyeing it to keep the lustrous colour of her youth. She wore glasses now, but they only helped to enhance her natural beauty. Claire's heart melted to see Beth sitting by David and placing her hand on his.

She found herself in a strange mood, so she got up and left the large family room and headed outside. The swings showed signs of recent repair and the old tree still stood tall at the back of the house. Claire sat on the swing and gently rocked herself back and forth, looking out at the paddocks that stretched down to the river. The grass was growing quickly and turning green again after a long hot summer and the return of the rains. It moved in the gentle breeze that skated over the tops.

"When did you get here?" a deep voice asked, and Claire looked up.

"Hunter. How are you?" she asked her youngest cousin, amazed that he looked more like David every time she saw him.

"I'm good. So, when did you get here?" he asked again, coming to sit on the other swing beside her.

"Last night."

"Is this to do with why Adam is in the village?" he asked her, pushing off the ground and swinging freely, his long legs stretched out in front of him.

"Yep. It is. How's the farm going?"

"As it always has, producing well. It would be a lot better if Dad would just retire and leave it up to me."

"He loves this place; you have to allow him that."

"I do, and I have offered to build them a cottage nearby, but they aren't ready yet."

"It's their home, Hunter. A lot has happened to them here."

"Mum doesn't want to go until she's sure I can look after myself. God, I'm forty. When is she going to stop treating me like a child?" he said a little heatedly through a sound that was supposed to be a chuckle.

"When are you going to tell them that you've met your future wife?" Claire asked with a small smirk as she looked into her cousin's future.

"Don't do that, Claire." He shook his head at her as he came to a stop.

"I'm just surprised your mother hasn't looked."

"I told her not to. I didn't want to know my future."

"So, tell me about her?"

"She's too young for me."

"She is very pretty," Claire said, enjoying the blush that crept up his face.

"She is beautiful."

"What is her name?"

"Vanessa, but she's known as Nessa," Hunter said shyly.

Claire stared at her youngest cousin, peering into his soul, and she recognised him. The strength of the one she had known as Talorc shone from him.

"How did you meet?" she asked him.

"Through Jasper and Angela. She's the new teacher at the primary school and she is one of The Community. Nessa grew up in Auckland and would come here to visit with her parents. But as I said, she's too young for me."

"Nonsense. I think you might be surprised how she feels about you. And, you know, with you settled in wedded bliss, your mother may just convince your father to retire fully."

"Are you sure? I don't want to go and make a fool of myself."

"Hunter, take the chance. You and Nessa will be very happy together." Claire stood and left her cousin to think it over.

The noise of the chatter echoed off the wooden paneling of the walls in the community hall, which sat at the only crossroads in the village. The sun streamed in through the windows and the dust motes danced wildly as people moved around. Most of the gathered group were elderly but some still moved with surprising agility. Claire, Matt, Aroha, Adam, and Tony were standing at the back, waiting their turn to talk. With much shuffling and chair scraping, David called the meeting to order.

"Thank you all for coming at such short notice," he began, "but we have an urgent decision to make. You all know Claire, our niece and the Community Archivist, and you have all seen her latest findings." He indicated Claire and she nodded to several people she knew who all smiled in return. One or two scowled at her.

"It is to do with these new findings that she has come today with an urgent request, and to some, it may seem a bit abhorrent. But please, I ask you all to consider her words carefully, because what she has to tell us will impact our way of life and the people of our Community around the world. You all know me and my wife. You know we are honest people with the best interests of this village and our neighbors at heart. You know the stories of Claire when she was younger, and now you have been updated on what has happened since.

I am not a man prone to exaggeration, so please believe me when I say it is all true. Now I invite Claire to come and make her request. Claire." He looked at her with an encouraging smile and stood aside for her to take his place at the podium.

"Good afternoon," she said. "I am so pleased the whole of the Elders' Committee has come this afternoon to hear what I have to say. I hope you have read my latest report and understand the creation story I have learned. There is more. I have met the Guardians, the Sentinels who shaped our world. They are real, as real as you are sitting there. But they are not the reason that I come before you today. I come because the Being Chaos has broken free of his bonds and is now out in the world."

A general murmur of disbelief and astonishment rippled through the assembled group.

"Surely, this is just fairy tales?" one elderly man said, shaking his head.

"I can assure you it is not," she told him sharply. "I know sitting here in this idyllic valley it's hard to understand and accept, but this council gave me the role of archivist and historian. You all know of the extent of my Talents. As a Recaller I cannot tell a lie."

The background chattering continued for some time and Claire felt her confidence falter. She looked up at the small group gathered in the back of the hall and her eyes connected with Aroha. The girl nodded and Claire immediately knew what she had to do.

"Do you need a demonstration?" she challenged the man who had spoken up.

Silence fell on the group as their faces all turned to her. No one had spoken up and demanded evidence, but it was written all over their faces.

"Let me, Claire," Carling said, gently stepping forward in her mind and taking over. Her eyes closed and Claire could feel the energy building inside and then released. The constraints she had carefully been holding onto were shed aside and the lights burst under the skin of the woman most had known for some time.

They gasped and some even stood and stepped back, chairs crashing to the floor in their haste. Mouths hung open and one old woman fainted away, David rushing to her side to make sure she was all right. All the while the woman they thought of as Claire Drummond stood before them, with the golden lights swirling and glittering.

Carling added a little more drama to the visage by making their blonde hair gleam in a shaft of sunlight and glow just as much as the points of light. Then, adding another level of drama, she called out to the Southern Sentinels, and though weaker than their northern counterparts, they came to the small hall and stood behind Claire. Their own lights gleaming and shining brightly. They bowed to her.

"Welcome our Sister Sentinel, we hear your call for help," the Blue of the group spoke.

Carling nodded her acknowledgement to them. "I thank my Brother and Sister Sentinels for coming to our call."

When she turned back to the group, she found them staring at the gathered host. The man who had initially expressed doubt was now on his knees, holding on tightly to the chair at his side, with mouth agape and working, trying to say something. Carling walked to the man and held out a glittery hand to help him to his feet. Standing now before her he stared at her, still not trusting his own eyes.

"You are… one of them?" he asked, his words faltering. His face turned pale and he shook as he sat heavily back in his seat.

"I am," Carling replied softly. She turned back and stood once more before the Elders with head bowed. "It seems that my own story must now be told and explained. I had hoped that it would not be necessary."

She looked at each person in the room and then started her tale. Though the story was not long, to Claire it seemed to take an age for Carling to tell it. Then the questions started, and she answered them as best she could.

"So, who is the Ultimate One?" asked the woman who had fainted, and was now fanning her face with her hand.

"That would be me," Aroha said as she walked towards the front. Very gently and without as much show as Carling had used, her own lights began to spiral and swirl under her skin. Soft shades of many colours and dazzling to see.

"My mother was a Foresight," the old woman began. "When I was just a girl, she told me of a vision she had. I thought it was just a story to help me go to sleep, but now I see it for what it was. She told me that a glittering host would visit this village. That when they did, I must put aside childish disbeliefs and give my full attention and devotion to those that stood before me." She stood shakily. "What is it that you and this girl need?"

"I need your permission as Elders to dig up the grave of Jack Ryder," Carling said quietly. A sharp intake of breath echoed around the room.

"Why would you need to dig up and disturb his grave?" another asked.

"While his bones lie underground, he is the link that keeps Chaos on earth. It is only when he is without those ties that he can be banished forever," Carling told them.

"If this is true then you also need to find Marcus Ryder's bones," the original doubter spoke.

"His bones have already been scattered to the winds. I took care of that when he died." Claire looked up to the back and caught Tony's eye and saw him wince at the memory. Adam did not show any reaction.

"We need to discuss this matter. We thank you for your display, but it is necessary that you leave us so we may talk," the man said.

As Claire and Aroha left the front of the hall, the Sentinels each nodded to them and disappeared. They hid their own lights once more, and the room seemed darker. She approached the group and Tony herded them out the doors and back onto the street.

Outside the air seemed sweeter and less oppressive, the sun was shining, and a gentle wind blew through the streets. Across the road the café had its doors open and they headed there to sit and await the outcome. Claire started to eavesdrop on the meeting. Voices of exclaim and anger washed over her as she became aware.

"Some are still in doubt. They believe it was a hallucination of some sort," Claire told her family.

"How can they? They saw with their own eyes!" Matt said.

"Uncle David is there; he is talking now to them. There is nothing we can do until they get over the skepticism and accept it." As she started to withdraw her thoughts from the hall, another presence suddenly joined the Elders. She recognised Red's spirit as he materialised and began speaking.

"Interfering again," Carling said in her mind.

"But necessary, we think. We need their permission; we don't want to have to do it the other way," Claire said, standing at her side.

"No, that way is more dangerous." Carling smiled at the sight of Red.

"Carling, we are separate, aren't we?" Claire said, watching her other half carefully and taking her hand.

"We are like conjoined twins, if we want to think of it that way," Carling replied distractedly, still watching Red.

"Then that is why we have mixed feelings." Claire smiled a little.

Carling turned to her, a small smile appearing fleetingly on her own lips. "We don't know what we mean, Claire. We must go back now; the others are eager for news." As Carling released her hand, she felt herself being pushed back to reality and the small gathering around her.

"Have they agreed? Is that why you are smiling, Mum?" Callum asked quietly.

"No, it was something Carling said to me."

She studied her son for a moment. Since they had rescued him, he had been quiet and withdrawn, never far away from Aroha's side. She seemed to be still feeding him energy to keep his mind clear and protected. Her worry increased for her son; he was still not fully free of Chaos's influence.

"It is in hand, Aunty Claire," Aroha spoke softly as she took up Callum's hand once more. "He is in my care."

The words were spoken in Claire's mind and no one else heard. For that she was grateful, and she nodded to Aroha.

After a few cups of coffee, they noticed movement across the road as the elders began to leave, still talking and wandering away in ones and twos. Last to leave was David with Beth at his side and they turned to make their way to the café. They looked directly at Claire as they entered.

"While we try to keep these sorts of matters within the Community, there is some that fear the authorities will find out that a grave was exhumed. But thankfully the Elders have agreed. I am to act as their representative in the matter and some have asked that they also be present. They have agreed that it should take place as soon as possible, and they will meet you in the cemetery in an hour to begin," he told her without a smile and seeming to be agitated.

"I take it the discussion was a hard one?" Matt asked him.

"It was. And one I don't want to have again," David told them.

Chapter Thirteen

The wind was getting up, bending the tops of the trees surrounding the cemetery. Claire shivered, but more because of what they were about to do, rather than the chilly late-afternoon air. The sun which had been shining brightly all day was now hiding behind the increasing cloud cover.

News of what was happening had spread around the village like wildfire and a crowd was gathering on the other side of the low stone wall, unable to restrain their morbid curiosity. Claire ignored their murmurs as she stood beside her husband and waited until the Elders' delegation arrived. She shivered again and Matt placed an arm around her.

"Are you cold?" he asked, concerned.

"No. I just want to get this done, and without the crowd watching," she told him in a whisper.

"It won't be long now." Matt glanced at David, looking for a sign that they were all there.

Someone grumbled in the crowd. It was the old man who had spoken first at the meeting. He stumped up to David and looked at Claire.

"Well, get on with it. We're not happy about this, but if it needs to be done it should be done quickly," he told her, leaning on his walking stick.

Claire nodded and stepped forward. She had located the grave marker earlier. Her eyes closed as she concentrated and lifted her hands. She blocked out the noise around her as she worked at moving the dirt that lay on top of the casket. It was heavy and she pushed more of her energy into it, feeling it resist her and then let go as one. As she opened her eyes, she saw the block of dirt and grass lift up and she moved it to one side. The hole left behind was deep and she peered down.

Clumps of dirt still clung to the wooden surface of the casket and the brass plate that lay on top was tarnished and hard to read. But there was no doubt as to the name that was written there: Jack Ryder. The others all took a step closer to the gaping empty space and looked down into it. With another gesture from Claire the lid to the coffin opened and they collectively gasped and stared at what was inside. Stained and hardened cloth lay in tattered piles. Other material which she did not want to think about, was also spread around the once white interior.

But there were no bones.

In the reaches of her mind she heard an evil laugh from somewhere far away and she grasped it to her and turned from the scene. Holding on to it tightly, she sent out a search, and then turned back to the crowd who were all looking at her.

"He got here first. Chaos is finally thinking for himself," she said.

Carefully she shut the lid and replaced the dirt on the grave, making sure to make it look as if it hadn't been disturbed.

"So, what now?" the old man asked her.

"Now we track him," she told him.

"Could there be other bones? You said that he has had multiple vessels he used against you. What of those?"

"Yes, there are." She pondered the problem a moment, aware everyone was still looking at her. "I want to thank you and the Elders for your acceptance and agreement of this matter." Claire held her hand out to the old man.

"You don't remember me, do you?" he asked her as he took her hand in his to shake.

"No. Should I?"

"I worked with your father and Tony. I'm Oscar," he told her quietly.

"You always seemed so large a man." Claire smiled as she remembered him from the days when her father owned a garage in the city.

"You were a lot younger then, Claire." He turned then to Tony and shook his hand. "Good to see you, boy. You still keeping your hand in?"

"Every chance I get, Oscar," Tony told him.

"I knew you would never let her out of your sight." The old man chuckled and then started to move off. "Good luck, Claire. Come back and visit me when you are done. There are a few stories I can tell you about your dad and this one." He continued chuckling as he left them.

The crowd had come to see a spectacle; now they started to leave with shaking heads and disappointment. Soon it was only their own small party that was left standing in the cemetery.

"Okay, Claire. Now what?" Tony asked.

"Like I said, we track him. He was silly enough to leave me a calling card which I can follow. But first, Aroha and I have a little travelling to do," she said, turning to her niece.

"Right, so where are we going?" Matt asked her, taking her hand in his.

"Sweetheart, it is just Aroha and me. You can't come this time," she told him gently.

"But I have to go with you. I'm your protector, remember." His eyes narrowed as he began to protest.

"I can't take you back in time, my love. That is where we need to go. There were incidents where the agents of Chaos confronted Carling and they were left to lie where they fell. The fragments of their bones are now scattered and too small for us to find them all. We have to go back to the moment they died so we can deal with them then and there. Even just a small fragment is enough to help keep Chaos's link to this world."

"You can do that? Go back in time? I knew you could stop it, but…"

"We can even go forwards as well, Uncle Matt," Aroha told him.

"I can't do that, Aroha. Only you can." Claire smiled at her.

"I thought you had that Ability as well?"

"I can only act in the present or the past. I can't alter the future in anyway. Those are my limitations."

"So, when are you going?" Matt asked her, still holding her hand.

"We'll go now. I want to get this done and have no more possibilities for him to fall back on," Claire said.

"What happened to Jack's bones?" Adam asked, looking down at the headstone.

"Chaos has them. He took them so we couldn't burn them."

"I never really liked Jack, but he was still my brother. Get them back, Claire. Get them back and put his soul to rest." Adam came to her and kissed her cheek.

"I will." She then turned to Matt. "Keep an eye on Callum while we are gone. Keep him safe," she whispered low.

"With everything we have," Matt told her and leaned in to kiss his wife. Claire threw her arms around him and held him tight for a moment, then broke the hold to face her son. "Keep your defenses up, Callum. If you find yourself…"

"Mum, I'll be fine. I have Bree with me and there is Dad and Uncle Tony to turn to. Plus, you won't be long." He gave her a crooked smile and put up with her moving his hair from his face, then hugged his mother tightly, before turning to Aroha. Claire and the others moved away a little to give the young couple a moment together.

Aroha made her way hand in hand with Callum to the assembled group. She reluctantly let go of his hand and stood beside Claire.

"You know the times and places that we need to go, Aunty Claire. Lead the way," she said.

Claire took one last look at Matt before clasping Aroha's hand in hers and transporting them to the first time she had encountered Chaos's minions. The world slipped and it seemed to take an age to get to where they wanted to go. When the sensation calmed, they found themselves standing on top of a large ridge leading to a sudden drop into a loch valley. The water in the loch below was a flat steely grey, reflecting the clouds, while the sun, hidden behind them, gave only a muted light.

She looked down over the edge. There was evidence of subsidence. The escarpment used to be wider, and Claire judged that they were now standing where the fire was, the one Loc had made after finding her and dragging her back from the edge. The thought of her long-lost brother brought a sense of grief.

"We need to go down to the bottom. Before we go back in time. It was dark when it happened," she said.

With only a little effort they moved quickly to the edge of the loch where they could hear the waves lapping on the shore. They moved from the edge and headed up the slope, keeping their eyes on the edge.

"What happened?" Aroha asked her.

"Loc and I were heading to the Sentinels' home. We had been woken by Orange, who warned that there were men looking for us. We ran for two nights, trying to get away from them. They finally caught up with us and I made Loc hide; it was me they were after. I ran on until I met with the Sentinels." Claire stopped and looked back at the loch to judge how far they had come.

"They surrounded me and that is when I first learned that Chaos could use other people to get to me. There were words spoken between the Romans and the Sentinels and then I was off running again. Yellow had told me what to do. They took off after me, finally breaking through the Sentinels' efforts to hold them back and they caught up with me at the edge of the cliff up there." Claire looked back up and pointed.

"As they drew nearer, I used an Ability for the very first time. I could feel the heat and energy rising, filling me as I drew it from the area around me. I released the light into that dark night, sent it out to deliberately blind the men and their horses. They couldn't see the cliff, or the drop that would ultimately take their lives," Claire said sadly.

"It was necessary, Carling," Yellow said, appearing at her side.

"Mother," Claire wrapped her arms around the Sentinel and clung to her.

"Do you forgive me, Child, for giving you the knowledge of what you had to do?" Yellow asked her.

"I forgave you a long time ago, Mother. I am sorry I reacted the way I did."

"Your reaction was normal." Yellow smiled at her. "It was necessary to ask, to push you. We needed you to see your potential, so that you could accept that part of your life."

"I know what it was for. I understand."

"Then I will leave you to your work. You do not need our help for this task. Great One, we will be with you when your time comes and will give our strength and assistance to you then." Yellow bowed to Aroha.

"I appreciate that, Yellow, and will welcome it greatly. But please, no more bowing. I'm just Aroha," she said shyly.

"It will be as you wish. I will say my farewells. We are always here when you need us." Yellow stepped away and was gone.

"Can I ask you something, Aroha?" Claire started hesitantly as they moved along up the slope.

"If I can help then go ahead. But, Aunty Claire, I am still me," Aroha laughed.

"I know you are. It's just that in the last few days you have been exuding a sense of great power and we are all reacting to it." Claire smiled at her.

"I will try to curtail it then." The two women laughed together for a moment. "What is it you want to know?"

"You know about the separate spirit of Carling inside me?"

"Yes, of course I do. I have met her." Aroha stopped and looked at Claire.

"The Sentinels don't know that we are separate, that we are twins, but are like one?"

"No, they don't know and there is a purpose for that, except I think Red suspects. I don't think they need to know just yet. I have seen something that I think you already know, and it will give them all pleasure when it comes to pass," Aroha told her cryptically.

"I was just making sure." Claire smiled again and they resumed the climb once more.

The trees that grew around the area were scrubby and hardy. They anchored themselves deep into the loose stones and dirt from the numerous slips over the centuries that had come from above. Finally, the two women broke through the trees. The clouds had parted, and the sun was now shining down on them. They could feel its warmth between the gusts of cool wind that circled around the cliff face.

"This should do," Claire said puffing slightly.

"When you're ready, then." Aroha stood beside her.

Claire felt the years passing as she pushed through the barrier. The weight of events in the area was not as heavy as some places, being so remote and not regularly visited. She felt the sparks of life of the creatures that had roamed the slope and the occasional human who had wandered into the area, and then she pushed back further and further into time.

Carling's memory of that night helped to guide Claire. She slowed down the passage of time as it approached the exact time she needed with some reluctance. She didn't really want to face the screams of the men and horses that died that night as they fell from the cliff edge. Finally, she found the night and restarted time an hour before the dreaded moment.

From out of the bushes a bear burst through and lumbered its way towards them, its shaggy fur rippling as it moved. The two women stood stock still as they watched it, ready to react to any act of aggression it may have towards them. It stopped and sat down on its haunches and stared at them. Claire sent out a search to its mind and recognised it: the bear to whom she had been bonded in her second life.

"How is it with you, my friend Bear?" she asked the animal.

"All is well in my life. I sense my ancient one around you," the large shaggy animal replied politely.

"Yes, she is my ultimate mother. And one day in another of your lives we will be bonded," Claire told him.

"That is why my spirit was created. It will be good to know you then and I look forward to helping you in that life. But I sense danger around tonight. You will need to be on your guard," he told her.

"Thank you for your warning. We will make sure we take extra care."

"I will leave you now. I have done what was needed of me and wish you well." The bear got back onto its four paws.

"Until we meet again, Bear, may your hunting and fishing be mighty, and may you have many offspring," Claire bade him.

"I wish you luck also in your endeavors. The fate of the world rests so heavily on your shoulders. Stay strong and until we meet again." He lumbered off back into the scrubby trees and was soon out of sight.

"Amazing," Aroha said quietly.

"Yes, it seems that I keep coming across those with the same spirits a lot lately. Somehow it has been rather comforting," Claire said.

The moments ticked by in the hush of the night, while the two women sat quietly, neither needing to talk in the darkness. The wind stirred in the trees, leaving behind a soothing sighing sound as the night animals came out to feed in the underbrush. Out in the darkness somewhere an owl called out.

A bright flash of light lit up the sky above them, silhouetting the edge of the cliff for a moment. Then all went dark. The screams, when they came, turned her blood cold and the sound of flesh and bone hitting the rocks made her shudder. It was a sound she had heard many years before, when Tony had dropped Jack off the side of the hill.

The crashing stopped and only the occasional noise of a tumbling rock continued. Claire stood from her seat on the rock and started to head further up the hill. Without any hesitation she found the discarded bodies. Claire started to transport them all together, piling each battered and broken body on top of each other. With a wave of her hand she stopped time.

"Why did you do that?" Aroha asked her curiously.

"Because Loc never mentioned a great bonfire at the bottom of the cliff. I want to do this while time is suspended, then their bodies will be gone and no trace will be left behind in the morning, for when my other self looks down the cliff," Claire told her.

The spark of light she created in her right hand sat sizzling away, eager to do its job. Gently she blew on it, sending it on its way to the pile of flesh. The spark caught and grew into flames, hotter and hotter, burning bright in the night. The flames spread, golden white as the intensity increased, until it was too bright to look at. High into the sky the flames leapt, the heat immense. Still she urged it on to burn, watching until it had consumed everything.

Once the fire had gone out, it left behind a mound of ash. Strangely, none of the grass or vegetation had been scorched. Claire drew in the air around her and the wind blew the ashes out into the world.

"Interesting." A harsh voice spoke behind them.

"Chaos. You came for the final showdown?" Claire called out as she turned to face him.

"Carling, you should know me better and you should also know we cannot meet here while time has been stopped," he laughed a little.

"Where are Jack's bones?" she called out to him.

"Somewhere safe where you cannot get your little sparks to reach," he grinned at her.

"Are you enjoying your cave? It goes deeply into the earth I feel. Is it dark enough down there for you?" Claire watched him carefully and enjoyed the momentary flicker of annoyance her question had caused him. "I would have thought that you had spent enough time in caves and would want to move about in the world."

"When you and that girl there have been dealt with, then I will enjoy the surface. For now, the cave suits my needs." He stood facing them and folded his arms across his chest.

"It is not us who will be dealt with, Chaos. You do not decide the outcome of our next meeting. We do what the Universe, your mother, requires of us. Your sister shall overcome you and you will no longer be able to defile this world," she said.

Claire started to move down the slope towards Chaos with the steps of a much younger woman and a confidence that shone from her, watching him closely and carefully. With Carling's help she sought out his intentions and could feel the animal desire he still had for her. She felt his need to take her into his arms and possess her, the need to own her fully as he had always done. Then she stopped.

"Are you afraid to get closer to me, Carling? Afraid of becoming attracted to me?" he smiled at her.

"No, Chaos. I have never and will never be attracted to you. I have told you that before."

"Then why do you move as if you are?" Chaos asked her, the grin now spreading wider over his features.

A crashing came from behind him and he turned slowly to see what it was. The large brown shaggy bear roared out as it charged at Chaos, his jaws gaping to reveal long, sharp teeth. Chaos brought up his hand in anger that this creature would dare attack him, but it disappeared just as quickly as it had charged.

"I only get closer to protect those that think I need protecting," Claire said quietly. "Go back to your hole, Chaos. Even nature is against you."

"Why should we wait to decide this, Carling? We can do it now. Just wave your hand and start time again."

"Because there is something I need to do first, to ensure you do not come back," she told him.

"But you will never find them, and there is one more out there, too, that I think you will have difficulty with," he laughed.

"I found these. That one is not so difficult. Tell me something, Chaos. When they died, and you were still fighting to make their broken bodies work, did you feel their pain? Did it affect you at all?"

"I am not so weak as to indulge in feeling the likes of remorse and pity. I will leave that up to you and your kind. It only makes you weaker."

"So, you did not grieve for the loss of your empire and the Romans? Not even a little?" she cocked her head to one side as she studied him.

"No. I told you, I do not waste my time on such emotions. The Romans were only useful up to a certain point."

"But love is stronger than hate," she told him. "You can achieve so much more in the name of love than you can of hate. That is something you have never understood. The people you wish to rule are human, and all humans love and crave love, in one form or another. They will not love you back and give you the worship you think you deserve. They will demand that you love and care for them. It is what is expected of a higher being. You will not win their hearts. They will reject you. And then, what? Will you crush this world like the last one? Will you obliterate everything in this world out of petulance for not getting your way? You are nothing but a child, Chaos. You stamp your feet and wail when you do not get your way, just as a two-year-old would. I had ways of dealing with my children when they were like that, and I think that they may work for you now. Go back to your cave and think about what you have already done and how you can do better. Go now." With a curt gesture she flung him from her.

"Aunty Claire, was that wise?" Aroha said, trying to stifle a laugh.

"All children need discipline. Chaos is a child. He thinks of this world as a plaything. If he wants to act like a child, then I will treat him as such." With another wave she restarted time and then took her niece's hand.

When Claire opened her eyes they were on the floor of a wide valley. Steep, tall hills surrounded each side and stretched out far and wide, with bare rock poking out from the grass and heather that covered them. Looking around, Claire spied the berry bushes that she was looking for and found only a couple, not the great clump she was expecting.

"We are in the wrong time," Claire muttered, frustrated that the encounter with Chaos had affected her concentration. Soon the years were slipping away fast. This time she did not shut her eyes but watched in fascination as the landscape around them changed. The bushes grew and multiplied, spreading out before them, rapidly blooming and then quickly followed by fruit. The animals and birds that foraged in amongst the juicy and succulent red berries, appeared as blurry, fast-moving shapes.

The day Claire wanted came and she stopped as the night was falling. It was dark and the only light available to the two women was the dim glow of the fire that Loc had made for himself and his sister that night.

"This was the night when Order visited and showed me the lights that shine under my skin," Claire said quietly to Aroha. She looked down at her hands and caught the dim light that swirled there, shining brightly in the darkness that surrounded them.

"The lights have always shone in you, Aunty Claire," Aroha said placing her own sparkling hands over the top of Claire's and smiling at her.

"The part that we need happens the next morning. One of the Roman soldiers that Chaos sent did not go over the cliff and managed to catch up to us here. By the time he had reached us there was only a small flicker of life in him when he attacked me, Chaos had kept him moving." Claire told her.

Claire sped up the scene around them and the night passed within a matter of minutes rather than hours. The light of the new dawn was soon evident on the eastern horizon, and she let it play out at normal speed from there.

Soft padded footsteps made the two women turn and a large wolf stepped into the small clearing where they were standing. Its tongue was hanging out and she sniffed gently the scent of the two humans before her.

"Well met, pack-mate. It is a strange thing you can do to be in two places at once," the wolf said, grinning at the women.

"I hope all is well with you, pack-mate. It is so good to see you once more and be able to talk to you," Claire said formally.

"And I you. You have changed much; we can see you have reached your full potential." Her tawny-coloured eyes turned to Aroha and she seemed to bend her head. "Our greetings to you, honoured one."

"Greetings, sister wolf," Aroha replied in acknowledgment.

"We must hide soon, so the Carling of this life does not discover us. We would be most grateful, pack-mate, if you could not say you have seen us," Claire asked her.

"I will not mention that which should be kept secret. May your hunt be successful and may your life be long, pack-mate." The she-wolf stepped forward and licked Claire's hand. Soon

Claire's arms were around the neck of the wolf and her face buried deep in the dark fur.

"Thank you, pack-mate, and may your life be long and your hunt successful," Claire said in return. She pulled away and the wolf licked the side of her face, then turned and departed through the thicket of bushes.

"Aunty Claire," Aroha reached out a hand and laid it on her aunt's arm and Claire could feel her working to make them both invisible.

With quiet fascination she watched a younger version of herself step into the clearing and pluck the succulent fruit from the thorny branches of the bushes. A man shambled up behind her and clamped his arms around her small frame. The struggle she remembered so vividly was now occurring right before her eyes. She could once more smell the rotting flesh on the half dead man who was trying to kill her in that life.

Her screams split the quiet of the early morning. The sun shone down on her at that moment, a detail she had not remembered. Her amazement was interrupted with the crashing sound of footfall. Loc burst onto the scene and went to Carling's aid.

As she watched what happened, Claire shivered when she heard the voice that emanated from the dying man. His whispers were almost lost in his dying breaths and overshadowed by Carling's reply.

"You will not defeat me, Chaos," the younger woman cried out into the morning air as loudly as she could. "You will not defeat me."

Birds burst from their cover, disturbed by her call, taking to wing and crying out into the stillness.

The man's broken and beaten body was left to the scavengers as Loc and Carling left the clearing. Claire watched them as they left, drinking in the image of Loc's face one last time. Aroha held her hand, keeping them both invisible to the world around them until she was sure that they had left the area.

Claire sighed as Aroha let her go and released the Hide Ability from them. "I will never have the chance again to speak to my brother," she said sadly.

"In another time you will. You know that Loc and Wolf have been reborn many times," Aroha told her.

"No, I did not know. I have not seen them in amongst any of my family," Claire said quickly.

"That is because they are still wolves. There is small pack in the highlands, in a sanctuary and they are in amongst them."

"When this is all over, I think I would very much like to go see them," Claire said with a smile. "But first…"

As she stood at the side of the dead Roman soldier, Claire produced a light and sent it to catch the body alight. It burned brightly and hotly, and it was over once more. The ashes which were still warm immediately began to scatter on the increasing wind and were soon gone.

"Time to go back and make some decisions about what is to be done about Chaos," Claire said grimly.

Chapter Fourteen

The farmhouse and surrounding land materialised around them and Claire looked up at the old building. Lights shone brilliantly out of the windows. The house had just been repainted and was sparkling in the dying evening light, the sun having only just dipped to the west. The gardens were neatly trimmed and planted. Somewhere in the distance a cow made a mournful call and Claire sighed.

"Are you coming in, Aunty Claire?" Aroha asked, heading towards the steps of the porch.

"No, not yet. I need a moment. Tell them I'll be in shortly," she said, waiting until Aroha had closed the door behind her.

She went behind the house and took the path down to the river. The closer she got, the louder it sounded, dancing over the stones and boulders. The hedges that separated the fields were darkening as the light faded, while the birds made their final calls before settling in for the night. The path led her to the river and under a large willow tree.

Being by the tree brought back such wonderful memories it made her smile. Summers leaping into the deep pool under its branches and lying on a blanket with Adam while she supervised her younger cousins. That first summer they were together, their lives had stretched out before them, so full of possibilities. Neither could ever have dreamed how things had turned out since then.

The remaining leaves trailed in the water and she sat at the base of the trunk watching the waters pass by. She leaned her head back against the rough bark, becoming aware of someone close even before he made his presence known.

"Join me, Tony." She smiled and looked up at him coming through the curtain of leaves and twigs.

"Are you okay?" he asked, sitting down beside her.

"I'm fine. Just memories. Old as well as new," she said with another great sigh.

"Don't go burning yourself out, Claire. You still need to get through this, you know." Tony let out a little moan as he sank down to sit beside her.

"You getting old there, Tony?" Claire teased.

"Sixty-six is not old, I'll have you know," he laughed, then picked up her hand. "Now, why are you avoiding the house?"

"I'm not avoiding it; I just needed some peace. I saw some people today who my collective spirit had not seen for a long time." Claire paused for a moment, squeezed Tony's, and then started to explain. "In my first life I had a brother called Loc who was a Whisperer. He was partnered with a she-wolf and she became dear to me, just as a sister would. I helped Loc become his true form: a wolf. I found out earlier that their spirits have returned to this world as wolves in the Highlands of Scotland. He was so kind and gentle, and his love for Wolf was so encompassing. I just miss him, I guess, and it caught me unawares."

"When you say you changed him, do you mean physically?" Tony asked her.

"Yes. I can do so much that I was unaware of, and your daughter can do so much more."

"But, what I mean is, you changed him from a man to a wolf?" Tony was still stuck on the idea and Claire smiled at him.

"He was already mostly wolf. As he told me back then, he was born in the wrong body."

"But how?" He looked at her and she could see that he would not be satisfied until she had told him the whole story.

"Wolf was aging, and she needed to have a litter of pups, to ensure there was another wolf in another life descended from her. But she would not go and find another mate. To her, Loc was already her mate. Loc was so in love with Wolf's spirit that he didn't want to let her go, nor could he. Their love was so complete, but they could never truly be as one. So, with the help of the Sentinels, I changed him physically into the form of a wolf. From that moment he was truly and wholly a wolf. They lived, with the extra time I was able to give them, for many, many years and had many litters. And the wolf that came was necessary and just as loved by my spirit."

"That is incredible. What else can you do?" he asked her eagerly.

"Tony, I cannot and will not do what you are thinking."

"And what do you think I am thinking?" Tony looked down at the woman he had come to look at as a sister.

"I cannot look through the veil of death and seek out the souls you wish to talk to. I won't do it."

"But you could if you wanted to?"

"Yes, I could. But I won't. And anyway, they may already have been reborn."

"They left me too early, Claire. I miss them both," he said quietly.

"I know. It wasn't fair on you. To love so completely with both your wives, to have been so doubly blessed, you were lucky. Tia would not want you to try and contact her. Remember her vehemently denying the actual existence of the spirit world. She didn't even believe in her own people's traditions and spiritualism; there was no way she would embrace her own Abilities."

"No, she didn't." Tony chuckled slightly at the arguments they had had. "Could you see then if they have been reborn? I would like to know that at least Maddison has had another chance at life."

"You set her free when you went back, I remember you telling me." Claire gave his hand another little squeeze and then sent out her thoughts, searching for the spirit of the woman she had never met, only seen through images in Tony's memories.

The search was hard, and she almost gave up until she found a hint in the form of a blazing green beacon. Claire followed it in her mind and halted beside the image of a sleeping small child. Her curly strawberry blond hair was spread over her face, and she turned over in her sleep under the influence of a bad dream. Placing a gentle hand on her forehead, Claire soothed the little girl's dream and replaced it with a happy one and smiled at her.

"Maddison has been reborn, Tony. She is already three years old and very pretty."

"Where is she?" he asked her.

"Why do you want to know?"

"Claire, I treated her so badly. I never appreciated what she offered me while she was alive. I know her new life will not remember her old, but If I could somehow make it up to her…" He trailed away, his voice catching on his words as his emotions came bubbling up to the surface once more.

"Tony." Claire gathered him to her and held him as he wept.

"Will I always be alone? I started my life alone. I have lost so many people, Claire. My own parents, my adoptive parents, yours, my wives. I just want you to stay safe and…" His voice broke and he sobbed into her hair.

"I am not going anywhere. I promise," she said, trying to reassure him.

They stayed that way for some time and it was dark when they finally released each other. Claire wiped her own eyes and then produced a light, releasing it to the canopy of the tree. Tony followed her lead and soon the willow was twinkling and lit up with hundreds of small lights of varying sizes and colours. It was like they had been visited by an entire city of fairies.

Tony looked up into the glittering display and smiled. "I remember the first time I used the Light. It was for you," he told her, staring up in wonder at the illuminated tree.

"For me? When was that?" Claire asked, tearing her eyes away from the lights.

"You were young, about five or six. Your mum had an appointment and your dad had picked you up from school and brought you back to the shop. There was a thunderstorm, and you were scared; the power went out and it all went dark. I was looking for a torch and then it just happened. I didn't even know I could do it until then," he told her, still looking at the lights.

"I can't remember. I can't even really remember you from that time," she said quietly.

Tony turned and looked at her. Taking her hand, he gently raised it to his temple and held it there. "Let me show you," he told her with a whisper, and he pulled her into his memory space.

The images flickered on a large screen and they both took a seat to watch them. A gangly teenage boy with dark hair covering his face was sitting in a hospital room. Claire's mother was on the bed and her father was handing the boy

Tony a bundle, wrapped up in blankets. He held her so gently and tentatively, and Claire could see he was scared of dropping her. The memory changed and she could hear a baby, not just crying but screaming. Tony rushed to her side and lifted her from the crib and raised her to his shoulder. He was shushing her and rubbing her back and her crying stopped.

Watching, a tear slid from her eye as she saw him reading to her, playing and comforting. She saw him make her laugh while in a fit of tears and then she saw him pull away. Claire reached for Tony's hand and held it as it became hard for him to keep watching. The times after when she would visit the old workshop she could see were special for him.

"Thank you for showing me," she said as it came to an end.

"But it isn't finished yet," he told her, and the memories kept going.

In his memories of her parents' funeral and watching ten-year-old Claire being led away by her Uncle Geoff, she could see how wrenched his heart was that he could not do more for her. Claire heard him make the vow he had made to her parents to protect and watch over her. The images continued as she grew before her eyes. Vision of Tony watching her in free running competitions and even in the city while she mucked around with Adam in their free time and their eventual break-up. Claire's first trip to Scotland, where she met Matt and then all the little moments Tony and Claire had shared. She laughed when she tipped the glass of lemonade over his head and gasped when his arms went around her the next morning.

Claire witnessed his pain of losing her, the longing he had for her, which soon turned to anger after his son was kidnapped and his wife murdered.

"I don't blame you anymore," he whispered to her.

"I know," she replied.

The images were now happier as they shared their new-found relationship as brother and sister. The final image was the pair of them holding hands as they stood by the spring by the standing stones, the sun setting and the feeling of closeness between them.

"I had no idea. I knew that you had followed me, had looked out for me, but not to that extent," she whispered. "I love you."

"Love you, too, Claire. Sometimes I don't think I could have gotten through some of the things I have been through if it weren't for you. For you to accept me and call me brother was so enormous for me. You saved me, Claire."

"No, I did not. You saved yourself. Your life has been hard, yes, but it was you who never gave up and kept going. You stuck to what you believed in and not just following what was expected of you. I am so proud of you, Tony."

"But I still want to do something for the spirit of Maddison," he said quietly.

"As you said, in this life she will not remember anything."

"What can I do? I have to do something, Claire."

"Where was her favourite spot, her favourite place she liked to just be at peace?" Claire asked him, an idea forming.

"Near the river where she grew up. When we were first together she would take me there and we would make love," he blushed.

"Can you imagine it for me?" she asked him, their minds still connected. "The place, not the act, Tony," Claire laughed as she saw him blush deeper.

Holding on tight, she transported them both to the spot that grew in his mind. She held onto him while he got his feet back underneath him and recovered from the dizziness. The sun was up, and it was still early in the morning. He spun around and looked at the area.

"This is it," Tony said, stunned.

"What was Maddison's favourite tree?" she asked him.

"What? Oh, I don't know," he said turning back to her.

"Okay. I want you to think of Maddison and then imagine her leaning up against a large tree. What type of tree is it?" Claire asked gently.

"I have no idea. I don't really know what tree is what," he said shaking his head hopelessly at her.

"Just imagine it then," she told him and sorted out the image he had held in is mind.

Stepping away from him, Claire went to a spot a few paces away. Holding out her hand she concentrated, and a seed appeared in the centre of her palm. Bending down, she placed the seed just under the surface of the damp soil, in amongst the long grass and then went back to Tony's side.

"I am going to need your help, Tony. Can you lend me some energy?" she asked him, taking his hand once more.

"You have it, you never need ask, Claire," he told her.

"There may come a time when you will want to keep your energy to yourself," she told him as she felt the transfer begin.

Using the image, Claire began to encourage the seed to germinate. She could feel the first hesitant shoot as it burst through the husk and sought out the moisture and minerals in the rich soil. A small stem pushed through the ground and sought out sky, with leaves beginning to form as the stalk became thicker and thicker. Again, Claire gathered energy from Tony, feeding it into the sapling, and then she pulled something else from Tony.

"Don't fight me, Tony," Claire said through clenched teeth, as she began to draw out the love he still felt for his first wife, the memories of her were added to that love and she fed it into the tree.

Before their eyes it grew taller, the branches spreading wide and covering a large area of the meadow they were standing in. The leaves developed and pushed through the buds on the branches, large green leaves with brown on the underside. Mixed now in the foliage white flowers burst forth and brought with them a heavy perfume that hung in the air. Still the tree grew. The trunk wide and strong, the roots going deep to hold it in place. Claire, now satisfied that it fitted the image in Tony's mind, pulled away from the tree.

"That's it!" Tony was in awe of her Ability.

"Good." Claire stumbled a little and sunk to the damp grass.

"Are you all right?" he asked, concerned she may have used too much of her energy.

"I'll be fine in a minute." Claire waved away his solicitous hands and took in a deep breath, telling him, "Go, visit with your tree."

Tony left her side and wandered over to the large magnolia tree. He placed a hand on the thick trunk and a tear escaped his eye as he pictured Maddison sitting in amongst its twisted roots. Sitting where he imagined her to be he saw a small plaque and read what was there.

"In memory of Maddison Benning. Beloved wife and mother."

He leaned over and placed a hand on the cool brass.

"It will never tarnish, but will remain here for all time," Claire said quietly behind him.

"Thank you, Claire. It's perfect." He stood and looked up into the branches.

"Where have you two been?" Matt asked as Claire and Tony walked back into the farmhouse.

"We were taking care of a little unfinished business," Claire told him as she sat down at his side then whispered, "I'll explain later."

The evening passed with lots of laughter and no one asked the two women what had happened. Claire watched her family carefully and did not realise that she had been studying their faces. Matt noticed that she was quiet and gently placed an arm around her shoulders, drawing her into him.

The door opened some hours later and Bree came in closely followed by John. They were greeted warmly, and Beth fussed over Bree making sure she was well fed and comfortable. Bree allowed herself to enjoy her attention.

Later that night in the quiet of their bedroom back in what was once her Great Uncle Geoff's house, Claire lay in the circle of Matt's strong and caring arms.

"It's 'later' now," Matt said softly.

"It is." Claire paused for a moment. "I helped Tony finally put his past to rest. He was still clinging onto guilt over Maddison's murder. And we talked a little."

"You know it has been a very long time since I worried about Tony and you."

"And there is nothing to worry about now, either." She slapped him playfully on his chest.

"I know. I'm only teasing. Anyway, all that was resolved between us a long time ago. Did you know he even invited me into his mind to reassure me?" Matt laughed with her.

"No, I did not. When was this?"

"Oh, years ago now. He told me he was getting sick me sending bad energy his way, so wanted to finally put to rest." Matt pulled her closer and kissed her shoulder. "There was something else tonight. You are never that quiet without cause and you were studying everyone. Is there something you're not telling me?"

At his question, dim lights appeared under her skin, just visible in the darkness of the room. Claire felt the shift as Carling took over her speech.

"It was nothing, just going back and removing the lost bones put me in a sombre and reflective mood, I suppose," Carling said quietly.

"I hope that was all and you've not had a vision," he said quietly.

"No. No vision, my love. You know I don't like using that. Now, go to sleep. It's going to be a busy couple of days," Carling told him and pulled away and let Claire have charge once more.

When Claire was sure Matt was asleep, she crept from the bed and headed downstairs. She made herself a cup of tea and took it to the table, sitting across from the empty chair where her uncle used to sit. She could almost see him in the shadow.

"A penny for them," his voice whispered in the air, and she smiled.

"You're still here, then, Uncle Geoff? I did wonder." Claire closed her eyes. She drew in the energy from the valley to feed the spirit in the room, before slowly opening them.

Leaning back in the chair, his fingers laced together, sat the image of her beloved uncle. The man who had raised her from the age of ten, who had come to mean as much as her own father. He smiled back at her, his brown eyes twinkling as they always had. The last image she had of him was of a body ravaged by illness. But the vision that was before here was how she preferred to remember him: healthy, hearty, and strong.

"So, a penny for your thoughts, Claire. I can see something has you worried and it's enough to have you up at all hours of the night." He sat forward and placed his hands on the table.

"There is so much at stake, Uncle Geoff. What if I can't pull this off? What if I can't help Aroha? I'm scared," she told him with a sigh.

"You can only do your best, Claire."

"What if it isn't enough? The world would then come under the domain of Chaos."

"Since I have passed, I have learned so much about you, daughter of my heart." He gave her a lopsided grin. "You are not alone in that head of yours, are you?"

"How did you find out about Carling?" Claire asked him, surprised.

"I have had instruction from Red. I like him. He gets to the point."

"Why am I not surprised?" Claire shook her head and smiled. "But, like me, she doesn't like to use foresight. She does not know what is to come either."

"That is not what I was referring to. You must work together to defeat this Being."

"What is it like, the other side?" Claire asked him, wanting to change the subject and push away the forthcoming confrontation.

"It's peaceful and quiet. And I cannot abide it," he laughed jokingly. "I have no one to argue with. But it doesn't stop me from looking in on you once in a while. And also, to see the error of my ways. There is so much I regret doing when I took you in, Claire. So many things should have happened, but I was so arrogant, and thought I was protecting you."

"I don't understand."

"As soon as your parents died, I should have brought you here to the village. I should have taken Tony with us and set up here. It would have given you a better grounding in your talents."

"What do you mean, 'Tony?'" Claire asked quickly.

"Your father's business was left to both you and Tony. He could have helped protect you here. I am happy that you two have found each other once more and become friends. I knew that he loved you and cared for you, that when you were younger you had a very special bond with him. But I was hurting, I had lost more of my family and all I could see was his unstable parentage. I could see the grasp Marcus already had on him. I'm ashamed to say that I used him. I pushed him into his grandfather's service and got information from him. He always asked after you. When he rang me and told me he was getting out of Marcus's organization, and going out on his own, I was only too happy to buy his share of the business off him, on your behalf. I wanted him well and truly out of your life, no connection whatsoever between you. But life has a funny way of turning in on itself. I am so sorry, Claire."

"You weren't to know what was to come. I want to thank you for being so protective. Uncle Geoff, I can remember all my past lives and you have always been there to protect me. Always an uncle who has cared in one way or another for me. Are you able to see your past lives?"

"No, I can't. I didn't even know I had them."

"Would you like to see?" Claire asked him tentatively.

"I would, very much," Geoff said eagerly.

"Take my hand." Claire reached across the table and felt his cold hand touch hers.

Within moments, she shared with him the time she had met him in her first life. A large man on the back of a small horse entering the valley, with Galen at her side. Uncle Gart, her foster-father's elder brother, with his large dark beard and tattooed arms and face. The images shifted to his second life, as her Uncle Longas, on the banks of Loch Tay as he emerged from the crannog. This time his beard and hair a bright ginger, filling up the small frame of the doorway with his wife at the time, Bron, standing closely behind him. Geoff gasped and peered closely at the woman stood next to him.

"What is it, Uncle Geoff?" Claire asked suddenly concerned.

"She does not look like her, but that woman… That woman is my Katherine. I would recognise her anywhere," he said, his words catching in his throat.

"Uncle Geoff, is she with you? Have you been reunited with her?" Claire asked quickly.

"No, I have not seen her since she passed." Regret seeped from him, and Geoff continued to stare at Bron's image.

Claire knew immediately what she had to do. It was easy to transport Geoff's ghost from the house to the other side of the world. Her eyes opened and they stood within the stone circle; Geoff was at her side, still holding her hand.

"Sentinels, please help me. I have an important request to make of you," she called out into the sunshine of the new afternoon.

It was only a short time until the Sentinels joined them in all their colourful and glittering brightness. They arranged themselves around the stone.

"We have come at the call of the Guardian of the Stones. What is it that you need, Carling, One True Child?" Red spoke formally.

"I would request that my Uncle, and the father of my heart, be reunited with his beloved Katherine. I have discovered this day that they have known each other and loved one another for longer than my spirit has been on this earth."

Geoff stared at the gathered host and turned on the spot so he could see them all. He gawped at Claire in shock.

"It is within our Abilities to grant this request. The spirit you speak of is a child of mine, Carling," Green spoke up and stepped forward and bowed his head.

Beside him a woman in her middle years appeared. Her brown hair was pulled back off her face into a ponytail and she was dressed impeccably. As the awareness of her spirit grew in her brown eyes, she smiled at the ghost of Geoff.

"Katy!" he exclaimed and went to her side. Their hands joined and he looked down into her face, drinking in her beauty once more.

"What have you been up to, Geoff, and why did it take you so long to find me?" Her voice was rich with a teasing laugh.

"I don't know." He looked at Green and asked. "We can be together now?"

"You can be together now," Green smiled at the pair.

Geoff turned and walked with Katherine to his great-niece and introduced them.

"So, you are the reason he could not come to me sooner," Katherine teased her. "I wish that we could have known each other in the mortal world, Claire."

"So do I, Aunt Katherine," Claire smiled at her.

"Carling, you must now send them to the spirit world, and we will watch over them as they abide with us," Red spoke to her, prompting her gently.

Claire nodded and turned back to her uncle and aunt.

"Before you do, Claire, I know you," Geoff said. "I have watched you grow, and I have seen the great woman you have become. You will know what to do when the time comes, and you will do it to the best of your ability. Have faith in yourself and those around you. Not just the living, but those of us who have passed. We love you and we will be with you when you face your final task." He enfolded her in his arms, dropping a kiss on her forehead as he had done so many times when he was alive.

"Thank you, Uncle Geoff. I miss you so much. I love you," she said, a tear forming in her eye.

He nodded then stepped back to take Katherine in his arms. Claire raised her hands before them.

"Go in peace, Father of my heart. Sentinels, hear my plea, guide the spirits of Geoffrey and his beloved wife, Katherine. Let them be together so they may be with each other, for all time," Claire cried out into the stillness.

"It shall be as you have asked, Guardian," both Red and Green spoke together.

"Thank you, Claire," Katherine spoke quietly as both she and Geoff faded from her sight.

As they left, she crumpled to the ground and let out a long cry to the stones at the loss of her uncle once more. Tears raced down her cheeks and dripped off her chin and soon she was bundled up into caring arms.

"It was yet another necessary act," Yellow said, trying to comfort Claire.

"I know, Mother. But it still hurts to lose him again," she cried into Yellow's shoulder.

"As it should." Yellow smoothed her hair and looked down at her spiritual daughter.

"It only hurts because you love so deeply those that are around you. And we love you in our turn, Sister," Indigo said, coming to join them.

"Use that love to shield you in your coming task, Carling. We shall be with you," Orange spoke.

"You are never alone, Carling. We are with you in your heart," Blue told her, joining Yellow and Claire on the ground and placing his arms around them both.

"You are our beloved," Red told her simply and Claire looked at him carefully over the shoulder of Yellow and nodded.

Pulling herself out of their embrace, Claire stood in the middle of the gathered Sentinels and felt their love, given freely. She pulled it from them and filled her heart with it, along with the energy from the stones. The lights under her skin flared and shone brightly. More intense and brighter than the gathered host around her.

Chapter Fifteen

The kitchen was a hive of activity when Claire came downstairs the following morning. She stood outside the door, listening to her two children bantering back and forth. Callum seemed to be back to his normal self as he reacted loudly to his older sisters' sarcastic wit, all the while Matt was telling the pair to be quiet to avoid waking their mother. She smiled.

When she had made it to bed the previous night it had been in the very early hours. Matt had woken when she got under the covers and pulled her to him. They made love with more intensity than they had done for years, reminding Claire of when they had first met, and their first time by the stones. She wondered how the stones could affect her in such a way.

Laughter from the kitchen brought her back to the present. She tucked the events of the night to the back of her mind and went in. The smells of coffee, bacon, and eggs washed over her.

"Morning, Mum. How did you sleep?" Bree asked, a large breakfast before her at the table.

"I slept," she said cryptically.

"Sit down, my love. Your breakfast will be ready soon," Matt told her with a smile and a wink from the stove where he was busy cracking an egg into the pan.

John got up and went to pour Claire a cup of coffee.

"Thank you, John. Are you two starting to get ready for the baby?" Claire asked the young couple sitting opposite her.

"Slowly," John said with a smile. There were times when he still did not say much, even after all the years that they had known him. The treatment at the hands of his great-grandfather Marcus, as a boy, had left scars that still affected him.

"We have cleared out the spare room," Bree said. "And now we just have to choose a colour to put on the walls."

"Just don't choose a gender specific colour," Matt called as he plated up a helping of breakfast and brought it to Claire.

"Thank you, sweetheart," she said.

"Unless of course you know the gender of the baby?" Callum asked as he mopped up the last of his meal with a piece of toast.

"We don't want to know," John told him. Claire caught the brief look of guilt that flashed across Bree's face as she moved a little uncomfortably in her seat, and winked at her daughter.

"No. It will be something neutral. A nice soft green or maybe a yellow," Bree said, trying to keep a straight face.

As Claire finished cleaning up the kitchen with Bree's help, her daughter took the cloth out of her mother's hands and took her hand, leading her out the back door to the seat under the large old tree at the back.

"We need to have a little chat, Mum," she said, taking a seat beside Claire.

"What about? Are you all right, there's nothing wrong with the baby?" she asked concerned.

"No, everything is fine with her. She's asleep at the moment." Bree smiled and placed a hand on her slight bump which had only just made itself known. "That is not what I wanted to talk about." Bree paused for a moment as if she were struggling to find the right words. "Granddad is gone. I can't feel his spirit anymore."

"I know. I helped him cross over last night and reunited him with his wife," Claire smiled.

"Oh, thank god. I was worried that something had happened to him. I've been telling him for years that it was time for him to go. But he would just laugh at me."

"You've seen his spirit before?" Claire asked her.

"Of course. From the moment he died. Couldn't you?" she asked, surprised by this piece of news.

"No. I only saw him again last night. He knew something was bothering me and came to help."

Bree took her mother's hand again and gave it a squeeze. "He has been watching over us, making sure that we're all right."

"That wasn't the only thing that made you bring me out here. What is it, Bree?" Claire asked and could see the hesitancy in her daughter.

"I looked into the future for our daughter. I wanted to see and make sure that she will be… Well, that she would be…"

"If she would be like you or not have Abilities at all?" Claire finished for her.

"Yes. But I should have known better and realised that coming from the line she does, that the Talents would be strong in her as well. But it was something else I saw that has me concerned. In all the visions I had, I couldn't see you, Mum. I'm frightened of what is to come, this meeting that you must have with Chaos."

"Yes, she must have it soon, Breena." Blue materialised before them and lowered himself to sit cross legged on the grass before the two women, giving them both a smile. "Your Mother's future has always been hard for anyone to see. We see glimpses of what must happen, but it's often not coherent. It was the same in her first life before she confronted Chaos. You must not let it worry you."

"Can I help, then? I want to make sure that my mother comes back to us, that she is here to see her granddaughter grow. I helped last time," Bree asked him.

"Bree, this is different. This time I am facing Chaos himself, not just one of his men," Claire interjected.

"But Mum—"

"Breena, it is not your fight," Blue said as gently as possible. "Your task has been completed. The only thing you need to worry about is the child that grows inside you. You need to be here for her. If you go off trying to help your mother, then you and the child would be hurt."

"Mum?" Bree turned imploring eyes to Claire.

"Please, Bree. He's right. I need you to be kept safe." She pulled her daughter into an embrace and held her close.

"Is there any way I can help?" Bree clung to her mother.

"Yes, there is. As always, gather and send her your love to keep her strong." Blue got to his feet and stood over the pair of them. "The child shall be blessed and the line that comes from you will be strong, Breena."

"Thank you, Blue," Bree said. She was not happy, Claire could see that, but she would do as she was told and stay out of it.

"I need a word with your mother, Breena. Can you leave us, please? I promise I won't keep her long," Blue asked.

"Of course." Bree sniffed back the tears that had started to form. "I'll see you inside, Mum. And Blue, please make sure she comes back to us."

"We will do all in our power to do so, I promise," he said solemnly and watched as Bree headed into the house. He sat next to Claire and turned his gaze to her.

"Father, what is it you wish to speak of?" she asked, as Carling took over her mind.

"All this meddling with your family, making sure things are put right and are in place is not necessary, you know. You are only making yourself anxious about the forthcoming meeting and that will not help you," he said quietly.

"I have this feeling that I am not going to make it out alive, that both Claire's and my life will be sacrificed, so that the world will be made safe. Is that what we were born for? To die so that others may live, so that Aroha can conquer and heal this world?"

"That has not been seen, Daughter. You know this. There is no way we can tell if you will succeed. Again, it will be down to chance. Even though we can see the future of what the world would be like after this event, it is not yet written in the Book of Destiny. Nothing is written for anyone. You have read the book and seen for yourself." He took up her hand and held it gently.

"Why are you here, then? Just to tell me to stop trying to make my family happy?"

"Yes. We can feel your anguish over what will happen to them keenly. As always, your emotions are heightened and being sent out to the world. You must keep them in check, keep them close to you. It is time to head out and prepare. There is nothing more here that you can do for them. They love you and know that the time is coming. When you leave, you should take Galen and Anthony with you. They are the only ones who can help, and they are the ones who love you the most and can work together to truly support you. It was the two of them that crafted the rose that sits around your heart, that you hold so dear. You will need their skills."

"What of Callum? I cannot leave him behind. He is still vulnerable to Chaos's will."

"If you take him, he will be in more danger. Leave him here in this valley with Breena and John. The Sentinels shall protect them, I will make sure of it." Blue reached out a hand and placed it on the side of Claire's face. "Our Daughter, we will be with you. Our love goes with you. You must leave today."

"But where, I have no idea where he could be?" Carling said desperately.

"You will know where. You will find him. Take care, Daughter. Come back to us. We love you," he whispered. As the last word died on his lips he faded from sight, the feeling of his hand still on the side of her face.

Claire sighed deeply and looked about the backyard. Birds were chirping in the tree above her, the sun was shining down on the green grass and the air was still and quiet.

"It is a good day to start," she said getting to her feet.

The owl sat on the highest branch of the tree beside the road, its beak carefully preening its snowy white feathers. A noise in the long grass in the field beside the lofty perch broke its concentration and it turned its eyes towards the darkness. Slowly it found the prey, a scurrying creature trying to get to cover to eat the seeds it was carrying in its mouth. The owl launched itself on silent wings and swooped down, stretching out its talons and clamping down on the furry creature, taking it back to its high perch to consume it.

A laugh under the tree scared the owl and it dropped its half-eaten meal as it took off, fleeing from the evil sound, flapping away into the dark of night.

"Flee, silent creature of the night. I will not harm you." Chaos laughed as he watched it take flight.

Down the dark strip of road, two circles of light pierced the darkness, illuminating the road ahead. Chaos waited for the vehicle and the man he had guided to help him. Carling's son was wrested from his grasp, but this one, who he had guarded and protected from her sight, would be able to carry out his deeds. It was time the boy joined him and be one with the darkness. His boy, the child he had spawned.

She had thought he was safe, was one of them, but little did Carling know that his son had already done some of the work. He had hidden him well, kept him until he was required and now that time was coming fast. This man would do his bidding, would carry out his wishes and he would have them both, Carling and the girl. The girl he could not name, the word a curse on his lips; he would have to find a more suitable name for her. She would be his bride and Carling their slave. He would use them both, their powers would be his to control and he could finally bring this world under his domain.

It was almost time. For decades, the world had been tearing itself apart under his influence as his restraints had weakened. Countries were at war and others on the brink. It had happened a few times already, but not to its fullest extent as he had been thwarted by the Sentinels and their humans. It had enraged him and had depleted his energy, but each time he recovered quicker as Order waned in strength and he smiled.

The car pulled up at the side of the road. The door opened and a young man stepped out. His power of flight was strong and so was his will. The man stood before Chaos and knelt before him.

"My Master." He bowed his head to Chaos.

"Welcome back. It pleases me that you have returned at my call. When my plan has come to fruition you shall be well rewarded for your faithful service. You shall be the highest of all who serve me, and you shall want for nothing."

"I thank you, my Master. I am here to do your bidding."

"And you shall. I have plans for you, my son." Chaos

grinned down at him as he felt Carling starting to search for him.

"This is useless. I can't get a hold on where he might be," Claire cried out in frustration and paced the room.

"Claire, you are doing fine. You need to calm yourself and centre your thoughts," Tony told her from where he sat at the kitchen table.

Matt and Aroha looked at her and Claire came to sit back down. "Help me, Aroha. Please."

"I cannot help you search for him. I am not supposed to open myself up just yet. I can feel your frustration, but you are doing really well, Aunty Claire." Aroha reached across the table and took Claire's hands in her own. "Reach down deep, down into the depths of your memories and all your dealings with Chaos. Use them. They will guide you and help you find him."

Claire nodded once more. The two men each placed their own hands over Claire's to add their energy to hers. Matt gave her an encouraging smile. "You are a warrior, and a warrior never gives up," he told her with a smile.

Once more Claire collected her thoughts and concentrated. The energy that was being fed into her calmed her mind and Carling joined her. Linking hands in her mind, the pair sent out the thought to search for Chaos. Claire began to shake with the effort she was putting in and Carling supported her.

The threads spread out across the world, knotting and creating a net, trying to pick up even the slightest hint of where he could be at that moment. The golden threads, which she could see in her mind, snaked their way over water and land alike to converge on the other side of the world. The odd tug sent her searching in that area it had originated from again and again as she danced around the world trying to pick up the hints. Then she stopped.

The hints were just that, hints. Made to make her expend her energy and use up her resources. Stopping where she was, Claire closed her eyes and breathed in deeply. The stillness only enhanced these false threads and she discarded them to focus on the true one. Chaos was trying to hide from her, trying to keep her on her toes. But she narrowed it down. She had found him. And he was alone.

Carefully she marked him so she could find him easily the next time she needed to and withdrew her thoughts. When she came back to Carling she was panting and almost collapsed into her twin's arms. Carling gently lowered her to the ground and held her, feeding her desperately needed energy to bring her back.

"We have him," Claire said quietly to Carling through panting breaths.

"Good. Now we must find where he has put Jack's bones. That is the first part of this task. We must destroy all trace of him," Carling said.

"That is going to be hard. I have no idea where to look first." Claire sat up and disentangled herself from Carling to get to her feet.

"Where is Chaos now? He will not let those bones out of his sight. My guess is that he will be carrying them with him."

"He is in a cave. It is typical of him to find the darkest of places to reside."

"Can you see him? Can you see what is on him or around him?" Carling asked.

Finding him was easy now and she shuddered when his person appeared before the two women. He was as he always had been. Chaos never changed. A large muscular man, with dark hair and eyes. At that moment it struck Claire how much like Marcus he looked, and then decided that it was not so unusual. Marcus had been Chaos's creature. He had been molded and carefully crafted by Chaos to do his bidding. While she was certain that the dark being would not intentionally make his men in his likeness, his influence over their souls would change them and mark them as part of him.

Carling pointed. "There, on his belt."

A small dark leather bag hung from his belt; the top was tied with a drawstring. Claire carefully stepped towards the vision and studied it. She reached out to try and touch the pouch when the vision moved and snarled at her. With a lightning reaction, Carling pulled her back and stood between her twin and Chaos.

"That confirms it," Claire said as she dismissed the vision. "Now we just have to get it off him and deal with the remains."

"I think I know how to do that, and that will be my job when we confront him," Carling said, letting her go. "It is time to go back. They are waiting to hear what you have found."

"Carling, you will have to be careful when you do. I sensed some protection on the bag, he will not let it go easily."

"No, he won't, and with you and Aroha distracting him, I'll be able to slip in. Don't worry about it now. We still need to travel to find him." Carling moved away a bit then turned back to Claire. "There are going to be things that I need to do when we face him that you will not be expecting. Claire, I need you to understand that I will never put you in danger deliberately, but you are going to have to react a certain way. Chaos cannot know that we are actually two, and not one. It is the only way we can defeat him."

"A little warning before you act would be helpful, but if that is the only way we can deal with him then I understand and will try to help all I can."

"No, you cannot help when I start. This will be my part in the task. I think this is why we were separated. To confuse him."

Claire understood that Carling was just as much afraid as she was, and she ran to her twin, holding her close.

"We will beat him. We are the Staff and Sword of Order, we are The Great Light's champions and this is why we were born. We are not alone. We are together, and together we will prevail. We are one," Claire said.

"We are one," Carling agreed, nodding and standing straighter in her twin's arms. "Now, let's go back to our husband and brother. They are worried about you."

Carling released Claire and gently pushed her back to the world outside their shared mind. She sighed, knowing what was to come and the pain it would cause. With silent footsteps Carling made her way to the primeval part of the mind and once more pushed her way into the dark depths.

"Mother Universe, must it be so?" she cried out.

"It must, child of mine. But the rewards will be great. Rest now and restore your thoughts and energy. We will take care of you."

The lounge in the terraced house in Glasgow suddenly went from empty to full. Tony groaned as the world shifted and he clung to his daughter. Aroha guided her father to a seat, and he placed his head in his hands to overcome the dizziness.

"God, John never said this was going to happen," he complained, his face going white as he started to tremble.

"That is because John can only move a short distance and he has not experienced this kind of jump," Aroha said quietly to her father.

"Would you like some water, Tony?" Claire asked, concerned about his reaction.

"No. I'll be fine soon." He waved them away with a limp hand and leaned back in the seat and rested his head on the back, closing his eyes to the world.

"I hope you aren't going to be like this every time we move around," Matt said, sitting opposite him.

Tony opened one eye and looked at the younger man. "You are not getting rid of me that easy. Claire said the Sentinel told her I have to be here."

"Wouldn't dream of getting rid of you, Tony. Just be aware that we might need your skills and Abilities in a hurry when we get to wherever we are going."

"I'll be fine once I get used to the movement," he told them.

"Okay, so where to from here?" Matt asked Claire.

"That cave is on the east coast. I have a book upstairs that might help narrow it down." She ran up the stairs and headed to the small office, then ran her eyes over the shelves.

"Claire?" Matt said from the doorway.

"What?"

"You already know where the cave is, so why do you need the book? And knowing you, you know where the book is and what the contents are. What are you doing?" He stepped into the room and placed his arms around her.

"Nothing, just research. It is what I do best, remember?" She tried to pry his hands apart and take his arms from around her.

"Stop, Claire. You are not going off by yourself. That is what you were going to do, isn't it? Run off after Chaos and leave Tony, Aroha and I here worrying about what was happening to you."

"Matt, no. That's not what I was doing." Matt turned her in his arms and stared at her hard.

"Don't lie to me! You can't face him alone. You were told specifically to take us with you, to help. I won't let you go. I can't let you go," he told her quietly.

"I'm not happy about it. What if you or Tony get hurt? What then? It would only distract me. I would be too concerned about how you are to help Aroha properly."

"And the reason you would be leaving Aroha with us, is…" he prompted her.

"I can't risk her life. I can't risk her mind. If Chaos takes her mind it would be disastrous for the world."

"And if he took yours because Aroha was not there, what then?"

"I have to do this, Matt. I have to face him. The more I've been thinking about it, the more I have come to realise that I'm the one who should banish him."

"You were told that you're not, that Aroha was the one created by the universe to do this task. Claire, you cannot take this task on by yourself. For a start, you would falter without our love to support you, remember? Our love, our devotion to you. As much as I still don't like the idea of Tony loving you, he is an important part of your life, and has been since the moment you were born. You told me yourself about his memories of you. It is our love, our care that will protect you and be the resources that you will need to draw on." Matt cupped her face in his hands and bent to kiss her.

"I'm scared, Matt. When will I stop being scared? Every time we have one of these confrontations all I can feel is fear."

"You conquered that fear when you confronted Chaos with me at your side. Then again in the form of the first Marcus. You had no fear then."

"I still see all the possibilities if things go wrong."

"Red, I need you," Matt suddenly called out to the room and Claire looked confused at him.

"What are you doing now?" she asked him.

"Just wait," he told her patiently and then called again. "My Ancestor, please join us, we need your counsel. Red, I call to you to help us."

"Greetings to the Protector of the One True Child and my son." Red stood before them and bowed his head slightly to the pair.

"What is going on here?" Claire asked them both.

"Well, Sister and Most Beloved, Galen called to me a little while ago. He had a suspicion that you would attempt to leave your companions and try to face Chaos on your own. I told him that if that day should come, he should call me to help reinforce to you that that must not happen." He had a crooked grin as he spoke.

"You did that?" Claire turned to her husband.

"Yes, I did. I was worried. I had been examining all my memories and I found all those times that you ran or tried to keep me away and safe. I needed help, so I went up to the stones and called Red. I asked him for his assistance if you should try to leave us behind. And he agreed."

"Carling, if you try to leave behind my sons and the Ultimate One, then I would have no choice but to find you and deliver them to you." He stepped closer to her, placing his hand placed on the side of her face. "You must be protected. You must have their love to get through this."

Claire could feel him trying to lay down a suggestion and she rebuffed it, pushing it away as if shooing a fly. Red looked down on her with surprise.

"Regardless, Carling, you must still take them with you," he told her firmly.

"Why are you ganging up on me?" Claire buried her head into Matt's shoulder.

"Because we all love you, and want to be there to support you, sweetheart," Matt told her.

"We, the Sentinels, will also be with you, Carling. We will add our light and love to those that are closest to you," Red said. "The time is coming. You must accept their help, Carling. I will leave you now with your husband," Red looked up at Matt and nodded.

"Thank you, Ancestor."

"Go with my blessings, both of you."

With his final word, he faded out of the room.

Chapter Sixteen

With her plans now scuttled by both Matt and Red, Claire retuned to the living room and began telling the small group about the cave she had located Chaos in. It was one she had found when researching something else and its tale was a grim one, which of course would suit the dark one perfectly. In the 1500s, the caverns had been the home of a family who would capture travelers on the road and take them back to their home to meet their deaths and their bodies disposed of in the most gruesome way. The souls of over a thousand victims were said to still haunt the place. Claire called forth the books from the shelves upstairs so they could see exactly where it lay and more information about the case.

It was as they were discussing the story over the dinner Matt had cooked, when a loud, heavy knock came from the front door. Matt stood and went to answer it. On the other side of the door was a young man, someone they knew.

"Finn, what are you doing here?" Matt asked him, still holding onto the door and barring the way into the house.

"Mr. Drummond. I was looking for Callum. No one has seen him for a few days and his professors are asking questions. Have you seen him? Has he called you?" He took a step forward and Matt opened the door for him to step in.

"Yes, we have, Finn. He's been very sick for a few days and is recovering. He'll be back hopefully soon," Matt told him.

"Sorry, I didn't know you had guests," Finn said looking about the room and his eyes resting on Aroha, seemingly ashamed for barging in.

"It's all right, you've already met before. You remember my brother, Tony, and his daughter, Aroha?" Claire said.

"Yes, we met at the house in the hills. It's nice to see you again," Tony said, shaking the young man's hand, also breaking Finn's stare at Aroha.

"It was nice of you to go looking for Callum. Would you like a drink or something to eat?" Claire asked, as she bundled up the books and placed them on a shelf behind her.

"No, no. Thank you. I was just wondering where he could be. But if he is fine then I will leave you. I was just passing and saw the light on, so I thought I would ask."

"What brings you to Glasgow, Finn?" Matt asked him.

"Nothing much. A few friends were coming for a pub crawl. I thought I would tag along and keep an eye out for Callum," he told them and then looked to Aroha again. "Would you like to join us?"

"No. I don't think I will, thank you," Aroha replied. "I don't drink that much."

"Oh, you don't have to drink. I won't be. I've been roped in to being the designated driver. You could keep me company against their drunken antics," he smiled at her.

"No, thank you. I have things I need to do with my family for the next few days," she told him, looking around at her father, uncle, and aunt.

"Okay then." Finn looked uncomfortable under their scrutiny and blushed slightly. "Well, if you are talking to Callum, tell him I hope he gets better soon, and I'll say goodnight." Finn turned to the door and Matt opened it for him.

"Thank you for stopping by. We should get together soon, so we can give you some instruction about The People," Claire said as she walked after him.

"That would be great, Mrs. Drummond. I would appreciate that. Good night." He turned and headed down the steps as Matt closed the door behind him.

"That was a little strange," Tony said as he resumed his seat.

"Not really, he was just thinking of Callum," Claire said as she started to clear the table. Quietly she was watching Aroha, who seemed a little tense at the conversation she had just had with Finn. "You okay, Aroha?"

"I'm fine, Aunty Claire. Here let me do that for you." She took the plates from Claire's hands and headed to the kitchen. As Claire came into the small space behind her, she watched in fascination as Aroha almost absentmindedly wiped her hand over the plate and it was suddenly clean.

"That's one way to do the dishes. When did you start doing that?" Claire asked, leaning against the bench.

"What? Oh, that. It was after Mum died. I found that the dishes had a nasty way of piling up when we weren't watching and I sort of cheated," she blushed a little.

"There's no harm in using a little of our Abilities in doing a repetitive and boring chore. I like your way of doing them, though I don't think I could do it." Claire reached over and put the pots down in front of her with a small smile.

"Aunty Claire, can I ask you something?" Aroha waved a hand over the pot on the bench, then again when a stubborn bit was not removed the first time.

"Of course, you can."

"Finn. Does he strike you as a bit closed off? I mean, I can feel when people have Abilities and they don't know they have them; or if they do, and they use them without noticing. But in

Finn there is something else. I noticed it the first time I met him up at the cottage. I was trying to see what it was but something else always distracted me."

"Do you distrust him?" Claire asked curiously.

"I'm not sure. I'm wary of him. I can't clearly see what his motives are, or what he is expecting like I normally can."

"Stick to your gut instinct, then. Keep him at bay and watch. I don't think it likely that you will meet him again, though."

The dishes now done and put away, the two women headed back into the lounge to join Tony and Matt.

The car hurtled through the night along the narrow country roads, the headlamp beams piercing the darkness. Occasionally the squeal of a tire screamed out as the driver took an unseen corner too fast. The drive was urgent and necessary, and the driver was focused on what he needed to do.

Hours later the car pulled up on a deserted road near a beach. Dark, thick clouds hid the moon from view. There was a hint of a chill and the smell of squally rain driven in by the wind. The driver stepped out and carefully shut the door behind him, then headed towards the waves crashing onto the shore.

Finding the path wasn't hard in the darkness, as the man enabled the night sight which came with the Stealth Ability. He passed through the small gap between two dunes and headed onto the beach. The destination was only a short walk away, and with the combination of the dark night, stormy conditions, and the high dunes, his presence would go unnoticed on the sandy shore.

A large stone wall loomed out of the darkness. Carefully he mounted the worn and craggy steps, crouching at the top to look around, sending out a search to see if anyone was there—a fisherman coming back in late or someone out fishing off the wharf. He could see two small boats tied to the wharf, bobbing up and down with the waves. He started out, his dark clothing cloaking him in the darkness, but even if anyone had seen him, they would have not taken any notice. He tightened his invisibility with Hide, making sure he was undetectable.

He stood now at the front of the boat tied up on the left-hand side of the wharf. It had a high prow, and he searched the side for the name, grinning when he saw it. The gold paint looked like it had recently been touched up. *Little Champion*. He laughed at its veiled connotation. With great dexterity in the worsening weather, he climbed on board and headed to the hatch within the wheelhouse. The latches were soon undone, and it opened without protest. He stood staring down into the inky blackness below before descending down the steep ladder.

The darkness was of no matter for the man as he searched through the maze of machinery and quickly went to work. A little snip there, a change of wiring here and his work was done. He sneered at the boat and remembered what she had been like while she was on it last. He left the boat carefully, making sure there were no tell-tale signs that anyone had been on board, and headed back to the shoreline to find the perfect vantage point.

Over the mountains the sun was slowly making its presence known as it climbed towards the horizon. Movement near the dock caught his attention and he watched as a man about his own age parked his car and headed down to the wharf then climbed aboard *Little Champion*. The man moved about the deck, making sure things were stowed properly and everything was ready to head out to the harbour and sea beyond. A great plume of diesel exhaust chugged out into the morning air and was quickly taken away on the wind that was now howling. Slowly the man untethered the boat and cast off, quickly heading to the wheelhouse to manoeuvre the boat out into the harbour. It was slow to begin with as the engines began to work the propeller and move it forward. The prow rose and fell with the smaller waves that had been dampened by the sea walls, and soon it was up to speed.

Just as the boat reached the head of the harbour, a great explosion erupted. A giant ball of flame billowed up out of the boat, sending splinters of wood and glass out into the water that surrounded it. The flash of the initial explosion was replaced with thick black smoke that rolled from the wreckage, and orange fingers of flame could be seen consuming what was left, still floating on the waves.

The man stood with a smile on his face and headed back to his car to wait out the rest of the day, his anticipation of what was to happen was heightened and he knew he could not sleep even if he wanted to.

Claire sat up in bed, suddenly awake and gasping for breath. The sudden movement woke Matt. He reached out, touching her shoulder, and it made her jump and look around, eyes wide with fright and horror.

"What is it, Claire?" he asked.

"Chaos. Oh my God, Matt. He's near Lucan and his family. I kept up the link to see if he would move. Matt, I got a sudden feeling of delight from him. He's hurt someone. We have to go to Lucan. Something is wrong," she blurted out while fighting with the bed covers as she attempted to climb out of bed.

"Are you sure?" he asked her.

"Yes, I'm sure. Something has happened. Something really bad." Picking up her dressing gown she threw it around her shoulders as she raced out of the room.

"Claire!" he called out, but she was already heading downstairs. Finally, he threw off the covers and headed out himself. He found her in the kitchen filling the kettle. "So, you want to go and find out?"

"Yes, as soon as possible. We'll get dressed and have a quick cup, then you and I will go investigate," she said, looking at the figure curled up on the couch beyond the kitchen. "I don't think we should take Aroha or Tony. I want to find out before involving them."

"Could you just be overreacting to the change in location?" he asked pulling her close to him.

"No," Claire shook her head emphasizing her answer. "The delight he had he only feels that way when someone is in great pain or dies. I'm afraid he may have deliberately hurt Lucan or one of his family to draw me to him. He knows that it must be soon. He can't carry out his further plans for the world with Aroha here. It would confuse everything."

The kettle pinged and Claire turned to start making tea. Matt stood back and waited while she moved around the small kitchen, until the cup was prepared and handed to him. Silently they headed upstairs to get dressed.

Five minutes later, Claire took Matt's hand and slowly the world slipped around them. The warm terraced house was replaced with the wild wind coming in from the sea. She steadied Matt as he found his feet and looked around her. Her eyes came to rest on a large plume of black, oily smoke which boiled up into the fresh morning air, along with large bright orange flames out in the harbour. Her grasp suddenly tightened on Matt, and he followed her gaze.

"You don't think…?" he let the question hang between them.

"I do. Oh, Matt. He killed an innocent man," she gasped in a breath and pushed down the sadness that threatened to swamp her. Instead, she chose anger, pulling it forward from where it sat waiting to follow the sadness, and took it on.

Cars started to turn up and park at the head of the wharf. People were rushing out to witness the raging fire that still burned out on the water. She recognised one with his walking stick, making his way slower than the rest. Claire let go of Matt and rushed to his side.

"Lucan," she greeted him.

"Carling? What are you doing here?" he asked her, surprised and shocked, his eyes going from her to the vessel. His comprehension dawned on him that it was his grandson's boat. "No, it can't be Niall," he said, his hand reaching out for her to support him as he stumbled.

Claire held onto him. Matt was holding his other arm and they found a place nearby to sit him down. She sat at his side and a tear trickled down her cheek unchecked.

"I'm afraid it is. I am so sorry, Lucan. This was never meant to happen. I did not see this," she told him quietly.

"Granda," a voice called out and the bright, red-haired Keelie came running up to them.

"Oh, my girl," Lucan reached out his free hand and caught up his granddaughter's, then told her simply, "It's your brother."

Keelie's eyes went wide as she looked out to the head of the harbour and the plumes of smoke rising from it. Slowly her head shook. "No, no, it can't be. How? Are you sure?"

"*Little Champion* is not tied to the dock. It's the only vessel it can be," Lucan said as he began to stand.

"But how? That boat was fully serviced. He was so proud of how he kept her running. It never had a breakdown, never had problems. Niall was so careful."

"It was nothing that Niall did. It was not his fault at all. I am so sorry, Keelie and Lucan. But it was Chaos," Claire said, looking up at her.

"Chaos? Why would he target our Niall? Why would he do that?" she demanded through her tears.

"I am so sorry," Claire apologised again. "It's entirely my fault. He's trying to goad us into action. He knows I can feel where he is, knows I can track him."

"So, he killed to make you come here?" Keelie turned to Claire, her eyes now flashing angrily. "God, I wish you had never stepped foot in this place."

"Keelie, Carling had no way of knowing this was going to happen," Lucan said gently.

"Yes, she did. She is part Sentinel. She should have used her Foresight," the young woman flung at him.

"Keelie, she had no reason to," Lucan said, standing and taking her into her arms as she started to sob.

Keelie glared at Claire. "This is your fault." She wasn't going to back down.

"It is. And I accept it on my shoulders to bear. I can't..." She had been about to say that she could not change what had happened, but realised that that was not entirely true.

"You can't what?" Keelie demanded.

"Can we go back to the hotel? I need to think and call on the Sentinels, and especially Order." Claire turned quickly. The other three stood there watching her walk away.

"Claire, wait!" Matt cried out. "Claire what are you thinking?"

"I can stop time and I can move around in the frozen moment. And I can also go back in time. What if Aroha and I go back so we can fix whatever happened here?" She carried on walking up the road.

"Stop right there." Matt caught up to her and held onto her arm. "Are you sure you can do this?"

"We have just done it with the bones. Matt, Keelie was right. My own stubbornness for not using Foresight is the reason this happened. I dabble with it and use it when it pleases me, but not for the important things. It is time I stopped being so precious with my gift and started using it." She took a couple of deep breaths and looked up into his eyes. "I must do this. I have to try and fix this. Otherwise, I will feel guilty for the rest of my life."

"Okay." He nodded then looked up at Keelie and Lucan as they approached the couple. "We need to get Aroha here. Tony will want to come too. When we get to the hotel, I'll call them while you talk to the Sentinels."

"Can you really do this, Carling? Are you really that strong in the Abilities?" Lucan looked almost in awe of her.

"With Aroha's help I think I can."

The trip to the hotel took only a few minutes in Lucan's car, with Keelie following in her own. Once inside, she led them to large unused dining room and made sure the doors were well and truly locked behind them. Claire sent out the call.

"Sentinels, Order, my family, I need your assistance once more. Please come to my aid," she asked softly into the room.

Off to one side, Matt was sending out his own call to Aroha and then jumped when Tony and his daughter suddenly appeared at his side. Tony once more reacted to the sudden jump in space, but only slightly this time. He sat down heavily on the nearest chair and waited for the world to stop spinning.

Slowly, on the other side of the table, a dazzling array materialised before the group, their lights swirling under their skin and the colours of their robes denoting their names. Another light soon joined them, that of a beautiful pure white. Order.

"Our Child, what is it you wish of us?" Order asked.

"I need to know if what has just happened is set in stone. Is it Niall's destiny to pass on the way he has, or is there an opportunity to put right this whole mess?"

"Is that the only reason you wish to do this, our daughter?" Blue asked her.

"No, it is not. I feel the guilt of this man's death heavily in my heart, just as if I were directly responsible. I should have seen it and prevented it from occurring," she told them.

"Deaths occur each and every day that are accidental and have not been seen. Your sister Breena was one who was taken too soon. These things happen, Carling," Green told her.

"Yes, dear Brother, but they are that, accidents. This was a direct cause of intention. Can I do it? Am I allowed to go back in time and fix this?" she pleaded with them.

"You already know that both you and Aroha can indeed turn back time. You have already meddled in the past by destroying the bones that remained of Chaos's agents," Order said. The Great Light walked around the table and took up Claire's hands. "This was not a predestined passing. You must look to your heart and see if this is right. You are the only one to see if it would make such a great difference that this man does not die."

Claire nodded slowly and turned to Aroha. She joined Claire and Order and took each of their hands in hers.

"Will you … can you help me, Ultimate One?" Claire asked her.

"It will be as you wish, Carling. I can see that this matters a great deal to you and that you will not rest easy with it on your mind. I will assist you with your plan."

"How did the accident happen?" Tony asked from the other end of the table.

"There was an explosion. The boat blew up," Lucan offered him.

"Then you will need my help. If it is something mechanical, I can fix it," he stood and leaned heavily on the table.

"My son, you are having trouble with the shifting of space. You will feel the shift of time a great deal more. Green, may I ask you to help my son? I feel that there may be something wrong," Red spoke up as he walked towards Tony.

"It could be an inner ear problem." Green looked thoughtfully and stepped up behind Tony, laying a hand on either side of his head. "Ah yes, as I suspected. Anthony, will you allow me to enter and make the necessary change to help you with this problem," he asked formally.

"Ancestor, I do so give you permission, if it helps to stop me feeling like I am going to be sick." He gave the Sentinel a weak smile.

Green concentrated for a moment and then pulled his hands away. "There, that should do it. You will have no problems now. You had a slight infection which was throwing you off balance, but it is now clear."

"Thank you, Ancestor. I feel better already."

The darkness surrounded the four people and Claire shielded them from both physical sight and that of any search that might come their way. That search came just moments after they had arrived on the wharf, but the search was designed in such a way that it could not be followed back to the person who made it. And that frustrated her. Trying to see exactly who this clandestine person was proved impossible also, as they had hidden themselves away with the Hide Ability.

They made their way to the boat, and just as she was about to board, faint noises from between the gusts of wind blowing in from the sea alerted the group to this person's presence. They waited until the noises stopped and they could hear the cover to the engine room going back into place. Although the person had masked himself, he had not masked his footsteps. Ghost-like they gave away his position as he climbed back onto the wharf and casually walked back down towards shore.

As quickly as they could, they climbed aboard and headed straight to the engine room. Matt and Tony headed down the narrow stairs as Claire produced a light for Tony to see what was what. He ran a critical eye over the large engine, following lines and wires, his mind easily remembering the skills he had from so long ago and congratulating himself in keeping his hand in by maintaining his own cars and boats.

Something caught his eye and he traced it back, which revealed the way the saboteur had changed the engine and what the effect would be. Tony shook his head and started to get to work.

"What he has done is put another line into the tank and changed some of the wiring around. It would overheat and then cause a small fire, which would have fed straight into the tank causing it to erupt. It was clever, but clumsy. I can think of about two or three other ways he could have done it more effectively and wouldn't be traceable. This was done by someone who doesn't know engines very well. Hand me that screwdriver will you, Matt?" he asked as he worked.

Putting it all back to the way it should have been took a little time, but once it was done and Tony was wiping his hands on a rag he found in the small cramped space, he nodded. Satisfied that the engine would work perfectly now, he was impressed and approved of how the owner had kept up the maintenance on the machine. They left quickly and headed back to the dunes to wait, Claire all the while shielding them and trying to find the trace on Chaos. So far, the sense of him was still in that cave up north and it didn't seem to be moving at all.

Around first light, the hint that he had changed position came to her and she suddenly became alert. Searching in a panic, she felt the calm and reassuring hand of Aroha on her arm. Methodically she made the search again, this time quietly and with great pains not to miss any position. For a moment it flared brightly on the other side of the wharf. Almost without thinking she started to move towards it.

"No Carling. Not yet, it is not time," Aroha spoke softly to her.

On the other side of the wharf the man stood with great anticipation. The signal he now sent out was that of his father. This was the greatest part of the plan. He knew Carling would be searching for any change of location of Chaos and this is what they wanted. They needed her to rush around the country to find where he was, he wanted her to be so tired and frustrated that she would make a mistake when she finally met his father.

He stood in the cold, almost jumping out of his skin in anticipation. He was his father's creature and the destruction and death that would occur also fed part of his own soul. The sun was just about up over the mountains when a car pulled up and a young man of about the same age as he was, climbed out and headed towards the boat named *Little Champion*.

Watching him going about his tasks before he cast off was taking an age. He willed him to work faster and was pleased with the great black plume of diesel exhaust fumes which belched into the air as the engine started. The lines were cast off and he maneuvered the boat away from the dock and headed out to the harbour mouth. He watched, willing his work to ignite, knowing that it could not be long now until it did. The boat moved up and down against the waves that came through the narrow gap that protected the harbour from the worst of the weather. It gained speed and passed through the embracing arms and heading out into the straight beyond for a day's fishing out in the sea beyond the Isle of Mull.

There was no explosion. There was no sudden and agonizing death on which to feed. The man stood watching, perplexed. He turned on the spot and looked around. There was no reason for his plan not to have worked, no reason for him to fail. He had followed the instructions to the letter. The boat should have exploded by now into a thousand pieces.

"You have failed, my son. What has happened?" Chaos demanded beside him, before materializing.

"I don't understand, Father. It should have worked, and I checked it twice before I left. That boat should be no more right now," he said, not backing down or even showing the hint of being afraid of Chaos.

"Something went wrong." His father looked out at the fast-disappearing boat and nodded. "I sense the work of that girl and Carling. They will be punished for this. Go. You have a long way to go to get to the next part of our plan. This time make sure you do not make any mistakes. I did not create you to be disappointed," Chaos told him curtly and disappeared.

"Yes, Father," the man said and headed away to make the long walk back to his car.

Chapter Seventeen

Claire woke to the sound of the alarm. She could hear rain pelting down and cars rushing through the puddles. She lay back down on her pillows thinking about Niall and sent a search out to find him. She breathed a sigh of relief when she found him out over the water, working hard. Snuggling deeper into her bed, she tried to close her eyes again, but Matt was already stirring beside her.

"Did it work?" he mumbled sleepily.

"It did. Niall is safe and very much still alive."

"Well done us." He reached out an arm and pulled her closer to him. "Good morning, my love," Matt whispered in her ear.

"Good morning, my sweet husband. And thank you."

"For what?" His blue eyes opened and looked at her, now nestled against him with her head on his shoulder.

"For believing in me."

"I keep telling you, that is why I was created. To be your love, your cheer squad and support. You have it for all time," he told her, dropping a kiss on her head.

"It's still nice to hear though, isn't it?" she grinned at him.

"Yes, it is. So now that we have averted that crisis, what are we going to do next?"

"I don't know, to be honest. It still doesn't feel quite right for the meeting. I have a feeling that Chaos will try to delay it again. I'm going to have to keep a close eye on everyone that we know that has helped us in the past. Anyone could be vulnerable."

"Just as well most of them are in one place. I remember a protection you placed on the valley. Could you do something similar to the village back in New Zealand?"

"I could. The cottage was only a small space. I think I'll need Aroha's help for the village. The family are all still there."

"When we get up, you'd better talk to her. I know I'll feel happier if it's in one place. I don't feel like slipping around the world every five minutes to save someone over there."

"In the meantime, we don't have to get up just yet…"

Over breakfast, Aroha and Claire talked in depth about what would be required to place the protection on the village in New Zealand and the people that they loved. But to Claire's surprise this feat did not need their actual presence to accomplish. In fact, Claire did not need to help her niece at all. Aroha held her cup in her hands, steam rising off her tea, her eyes peering into the distance. When she came back to them, she was smiling and looked pleased with herself.

"Done," she said, blushing slightly and taking a sip of tea.

"Right, so that's done, is there anything or anyone else you can think of that could be vulnerable?" Tony asked them

"None that I can think of. I thought today I would go and scout out that cave," Claire told the people gathered at the table.

"Not without us, you don't," Tony and Matt said together.

"I wouldn't dream of it, gentlemen," she said, slightly annoyed.

Claire quietly fumed over the fact that they were being overprotective. She was certain that there was nothing that either she or Aroha couldn't deal with. Then Carling spoke.

"Don't be so silly, Claire. You know they have to be there. This is not the time for petulance. You must be fully aware of your surroundings. There will be danger there; you can be sure of that. Remember who we are dealing with. Aroha cannot take direct action against Chaos until the appropriate time." Her tone was scolding, and Claire felt ashamed of herself.

"You are right, of course, Sister." She felt dutifully admonished.

"Sister?" Carling enquired.

"Yes, that is what we are, after all. Like twins, but not. Doesn't that mean we're sisters?"

"I believe you are right then, Sister."

Claire grinned and then said, "And you can take part responsibility for our brother Tony and your brother-in-law, Galen."

The laugh that rang out was long and full of mirth. Carling shook her head. "I guess it does, but I have you there on your logic, Claire. I have my own duties and tasks to perform, and I can't keep my eyes on them all the time. You're going to have to look after them for just a little while longer."

"That is so not fair," Claire joined in her laughter.

"Go get ready for our next journey. And please be careful," Carling said as she bundled Claire up in a hug.

The rain had set in for the day across the country. On the coast the wind whipped up the waves, creating great white caps that barreled their way to shore, crashing onto the rocky cliff face and sending up a great spray of water that carried further on the gusts and making the ground tremble with their force. The heavily laden clouds dumped their load on sea and land indiscriminately in sheets of water.

The travelers stood huddled on the cliff above the cave. Around them the rain made no inroads into their clothing and the wind did not disturb a hair on their heads. Aroha had surrounded them with a protection aura to keep them from the elements and the air inside was warm.

"I don't think this is a good idea." Matt had to raise his voice over the noise of the wind.

"I agree." Tony looked at Claire and Aroha. "Do you really need to go into the cave? Can't you just send your thoughts out and see if he is in there?"

"I already can sense him there," said Claire, "but I don't know if it is just something he has placed there to keep me off his track or it really is him. I have never actively sought him out for one of our confrontations. He has always come to me." She was nervous, now she had arrived. The place felt evil.

The space below them sent out an impression of danger, horror, and death. The acts that had been performed there still lingered in the rock.

"He is not there, Aunty Claire. I saw into his mind when we rescued Callum, and the feeling I am getting from below is just an empty shell. It holds no person, human or celestial. It is just a cave," Aroha told her, feeding energy into her aunt, supporting her as she felt the self-doubt and fears creeping in.

"I'm sorry this has been a waste of time," Claire told them taking a deep breath.

"No, it had to be crossed off the list. You can feel the signal that is being sent out and it is a false trail. You need to find the true energy of him. It is much darker in his soul; no light could ever penetrate it."

Claire nodded as she remembered how Chaos's presence had felt in person. She sent out another search, teasing through the false signals until she touched upon the true one. He was not far—further north in another cave. Her mind searched for the information of where he was.

"North, near Wick." She turned her eyes to Matt.

"Tinker's Cave, but there was no murder there," he responded.

"Not that we know of, no, but there was suffering. The human degradation and the mental illness that was rife in that cave. You remember reading the reports."

"I do, Claire, but if you want to check every site where there have been violent deaths, we'll be running around the country forever," he argued.

"Are you sure of the signal?" Tony asked her.

"I'm sure." She turned to him.

"Then I suggest that we go back to your place, and you keep an eye on it. You keep your senses tuned to him, so you know the moment he moves. Otherwise. all we would be achieving is running around after ghost stories. Are you even sure that the confrontation will take place here in Scotland? I seem to remember you banishing his spirit from the sacred lands when you faced off with Jack."

"I don't know." She seemed to crumple a little and Matt held her up.

"That's it. Aroha can you please take us home to the valley." Then when Claire started to protest, he told her firmly, "No. You are weakening. You need to be near the stones right now. No arguments, Claire."

Claire nodded feebly and leaned against him, seeking comfort and love. Matt nodded to Aroha over her head and within a moment they were standing outside the cottage that was their permanent home. Matt picked Claire up in his arms to head to the stones, placing her down against the large entrance stone.

Immediately there was a change. Energy seeped into her, and she sucked it up greedily, wanting to bolster her reserves.

"You silly woman, why didn't you tell me you were getting low?" Matt asked her, sitting down beside her and holding her hand.

"I just want this over with, Matt. I need to finish this soon."

"I'm going to repeat Tony's question: are you sure it'll be here in Scotland?"

"It feels right. He still thinks of these lands as the most sacred to the Sentinels and Order. He is like a child."

"Okay then, how about we think like a child? He has had his favourite toy taken from him. He has thrown multiple tantrums to get it back, but that didn't work. He confronted you and tried to get you on his side, and that didn't work. Could he be learning from his mistakes?"

"This masking and sending out false trails is a new thing for him. He knows we can't properly banish him without Jack's bones being dispersed. He has learned that. I still think that it will be here. But I don't think that he is through with hurting those that I care about. I am almost certain that he knows about my meddling in the past and changing the future. If it happens again, I think he may lay a trap for me."

"I know you hate to use it, Claire, but I think you might have to. Look to the future and see what is to come."

"I will. It has to be done. I can't keep groping blindly around trying to figure out what to do next, where to go." Feeling stronger than she had in the last few days, Claire stood and turned, then stepped into the circle heading to the centre.

Kneeling on the grass she placed her hands on her thighs and bent her head. She went to the part of her mind she usually kept closed off and opened the metaphorical door. Images began to swamp her, pieces she knew of her family's futures, their faces changing as they got older, and the events that would surround them. She watched with fascination at the number of children Bree and John would have, and more curiously the children that were to come for Callum and Aroha. She watched as she saw herself and Matt together. But there was something different about herself. She seemed lesser than now but couldn't figure out why.

Pushing that to one side, she searched for those in her wider family circle. The possibilities of their lives and loves, their happiness and heartaches, were all normal. Now in the circle of friends, she dismissed each and every one as they came to mind. There was nothing out of the ordinary. Until she came to two specific people.

A red hue surrounded these two, the colour of blood and danger; almost like an alarm ringing out, it flashed about them. They seemed so happy on the hillside, looking out over orchards and vineyards. Their arms around each other, the love that was long felt and now just being explored. She saw the holes that suddenly appeared in their chests. The blood soaking through their clothing as they fell together.

Claire gasped loudly and her head came up. Her eyes still closed she searched for clues of the images again as they were presented to her. Trying to figure out who and where the shooter was, and most importantly, when. They were vague but there. She saw and her eyes flew open.

"We need to go back to Italy. James and Gemma are in danger."

The ground was damp, and it was starting to seep into the man's clothing as he lay hidden. It was finally getting light, although he still had another twelve hours to wait for his prey. Ignoring the increasing insect activity, he rested his head on his arms and promptly fell asleep. The flight had been hurried and he was still fuming over the lack of success in his last job. His father's anger was still weighing heavily on his mind.

His true parentage had been a great revelation to him, but not an unwelcome one. All his life he had felt different from other children, even his younger half-brothers and sister. He knew his emotions were not what they should have been. He had never been able to understand empathy and pity, or any of the other "soft" emotions, as he had come to think of them, that others clearly could. His mother had treated him differently, had favoured him a little more than the others, and when he finally met his true father it all fell into place.

Chaos was not a kind father; he was not pandering, nor did he give praise when it was deserved. No, he was the opposite—hard, cruel, and exacting. The man was not put off by that, but instead felt like he belonged to him. He was sick of acting as if he were like every other person, weak and willing to accept their lot in the world. He had always wanted more—more money, more power over people—and now he was on the cusp of getting it. He could taste and feel it just out of reach.

His father was expecting him to succeed this time and he was determined to do just that. This time he had a backup. Not only did he have his firearm at his side, with its high-tech scope, but he had also placed a few explosives around the house. If for some unknown reason he had missed the mark on his prey, he would be able to detonate the building around them.

That had been an exercise during the night. There was one moment when he thought that he would be found, knife in hand and ready to attack, but it was only a cat. He felt disappointed then. The rush of adrenaline had been intoxicating. He was ready to kill again.

Now he had all this time on his hands to wait for the perfect moment when he could have that release. The moment when he could see the lifeforce seep from their bodies and feed off their pain, but only from a distance this time. He would have to be satisfied with the ultimate kill that was coming his way. Chaos had promised him that he would be allowed to take her life, but only after convincing him. That had taken a lot of fast talking and flattery to make him see the sense in getting rid of Claire. His father was not happy at first. He had wanted to keep her and use her powers.

To him the release of her soul was an opportunity too precious to waste on keeping her alive. He wanted to use it. He had his own plans that did not involve Chaos. He had understood his father the moment he met him. He was a child inside. His petty desires and needs, were that of a two-year-old throwing a tantrum. That disgusted him. There was so much more he could do, so much more pain he could inflict and thrive on. He was not his father's son for nothing, but he did realise that he was more intelligent than Chaos.

The day slipped away as he slept. He ignored the insects trying to bite, the rising heat as the sun climbed higher, and the hunger in his stomach. There would be time enough to indulge in human foibles. The afternoon dragged and he stirred restlessly on the top of the hill.

Finally, the sun dipped towards the mountains in the distance. He pulled his firearm closer and lined up his sight on the house across the valley, nestled in among the old olive and fruit trees. Then he saw movement.

They walked out into the last of the light from the setting sun, hand in hand with a glass of wine each. He watched them and saw them talking and laughing. Her pale blonde hair, tinged with golden light, flowed down her back and was picked up by an errant wind. They took a seat on a bench and he placed his arm around her shoulders, pulling her closer and they kissed.

Carefully he calculated the wind and the distance between the end of his barrel and where they sat. His finger moved carefully and placed lightly on the trigger. His thumb shifted the safety to the live position. He took a deep breath and let it out slowly. The time had come. This was it. He had wanted this moment just a day before and was denied it. Now here it was again. Another breath, he held it this time, until he could hear his heart beating in his ears. His finger began to press the trigger, while the sight remained firmly in place on the woman.

He felt it move under his pressure, felt the cold metal slowly and surely press the release. A loud bang reverberated from the weapon, sending its little sting to its target. Just as quickly as it released, he stirred to make his second shot.

When he searched for the next target, he moved his eye from the view finder and then back again. There was no one there. The couple were nowhere to be seen. Scrambling now he searched for the detonator and smashed the button down, standing as he did so he could see the explosion.

He was not disappointed. A ball of fire exploded out of the roof and windows of the old building. Bits of masonry flew great distances even before the sound reached him across the valley. An almighty boom shook and rattled him. He searched out with his senses, looking for the pain that should be coming from their deaths. There was nothing. Nothing at all came from the building.

"No!" he shouted out in frustration.

She had done it again. He knew it had to be her. He picked up his weapon, crushed it in his hands and threw it down the cliff.

His father's presence was drawing near, and he didn't want to be there when Chaos reached him. Carefully he selected a destination and transported himself. As soon as he reached the confines of the abandoned building, he set up his walls and defenses against his father.

Claire looked at Aroha. She felt her nerves racing. This was going to be a very close thing and they would need to appear and stop time within less than a second to make sure that both James and Gemma would be safe. It was with great relief when she found out that Greg had already left the villa to return to New Zealand. This would have been harder to achieve if he had still been there.

Carefully she took in a deep breath and held it. Claire gave Aroha a nod and the pair disappeared from the living room of the little terraced house in Glasgow and reappeared behind the couple as they sat on the bench. All at once she had frozen time and Aroha went to study the bullet that was suspended in mid-air.

"I still find it fascinating watching it hang there," she said as she moved around James and Gemma to look at it closer.

"Yes," Claire said absently as she searched for the shooter and then her eyes narrowed as she found him. The sense she got back from him was immense. His powers were a match for hers and she could feel his anticipation in the kill he was trying to make. He was dark. So very dark. The only other being to have emitted that same sense was Chaos himself. When she looked for people like this, she always saw colours, the colours of the rainbow, like Matt's beautiful blue beacon which was the same colour as his eyes. But this man she now sought only showed black, totally devoid of any colour or warmth.

Slowly she tried to enter his mind, but found her way blocked, not just with the normal defenses she was used to, but by an almost physical barrier. He did not want to be disturbed by anyone, including Chaos. Claire pulled back from him, trying to solve the puzzle. A slight tug, a hint of who he was snaked its way closer to her and she tried to reach out for it.

"Aunty Claire?" Aroha broke through her thoughts. "Don't you think we should be going? As much as I find it fascinating watching this little lump of metal hang in the air, I believe we need to get these two to safety."

Claire looked up suddenly. "Yes, of course we should." She moved back around the bench seat and placed a hand on James's shoulder, while Aroha touched Gemma and then restarted time while they disappeared back into the same living room.

To Matt and Tony, it seemed as if the couple suddenly materialised on the couch before them, not even a drop of wine from their goblets had spilled. To them, Aroha and Claire had remained where they were. The couple looked startled and shocked as they looked around them.

"Just keep calm," Claire said as she kept her hand on James's shoulder, holding him in place.

"What the hell?" James exploded, finally finding his voice, trying to move out from under the pressure of her touch. Beside him, Gemma was making a strangling noise.

"It's going to be fine, James," Tony said sitting forward. "Just give yourself time to adjust to the movement."

"What's going on, Tony?" James demanded, still clutching the glass of wine and his arm still around Gemma, protectively now.

"We had to get you out of harm's way," Claire said, now releasing him and moving around the couch to sit on the arm beside her husband. "You were targeted."

"Targeted by who?" he demanded, his eyes still a little wild looking.

"I don't know who, but he's strong. He's trying to hide from Chaos, but I got the feeling that he's connected to him.

His soul was so black." Her thoughts were returning back to try and unravel the mystery of the man.

"What do you mean 'strong?'" Matt asked her.

"Strong in every way, with all Abilities, just like me. But I don't think they were bestowed on him like you and Tony were given yours. No, this man was born with them. I don't know where he came from or who he is."

"If the danger has passed, can we go back now?" Gemma spoke up for the first time since arriving.

"No, you can't, there's nothing left of the villa. It's been destroyed. I'm sorry, Gemma," Aroha said from where she sat by her father.

"Gone?" she said dumbfounded.

"Yes. It exploded shortly after we got you here. There is nothing left."

"You will be compensated, Gemma, I promise," Tony tried to reassure her.

"It was my nonna's house." She shook her head in disbelief. She raised her glass of wine and downed the deep red liquid down in one gulp then very carefully and gently placed the glass on the coffee table before her.

"What happens now, then?" James asked.

Claire looked around the room before she spoke. "What happens now is that we find you two somewhere safe to stay. My suggestion is our cottage in the valley, and then we four confront Chaos and banish him for good."

"You've got to let me help you," James said eagerly.

"No, you can't. There must be only the four of us when we do. You need to look after Gemma. Your debt is paid in full, remember." She smiled at him.

"I do. But surely the more people you have with you—"

"No. It must be just us four. And I think we should move to the cottage tonight. I get the feeling this is the first place either Chaos or his man will come looking. There was something about him. I almost had it before we came back." Claire's brow creased in thought.

"I can take Dad and Uncle Matt if you can take James and Gemma. It is only a short leap so it shouldn't drain your resources much." Aroha once more broke through her thoughts.

"Yes, of course."

Chapter Eighteen

Claire stood at the bench sipping her coffee the next morning, just has she had done on so many other mornings. She stared up at the spot where the two hills met behind the house, to where the large rock protruded from the ground, protecting the sacred ring of stones. The stones where her spirit was born, so many centuries ago. She followed the ribbon of water as it tumbled from the spring and out into the valley where she now stood.

It was up there that she had last come face to face with Chaos in battle. In her first life she had imprisoned him deep within the Sentinels' island home. It was where she had battled Jack; now she realised it was Chaos who was acting through him. It had been hard, and she still shuddered when the memory surfaced.

Now Claire was facing another battle. Somewhere off in the distance she could feel the Dark One raging at his agent's latest failure. She could feel him trying to search for the man. Claire gave a self-satisfied smirk at the fact that she knew where he was. She had seen him go there. He was in an abandoned building in Edinburgh, deep in the basement that predated the building. He was still there now, desperately trying to keep his defenses up.

The idea, when it came to her, took hold very slowly in her mind and she wondered why she hadn't thought of it earlier:

a bait to lure Chaos into the final meeting against his will. It would be perfect. Between the four of them they should be able to control his Abilities. A quick snatch and grab, just as they had done with James and Gemma the previous night. She took another sip of her coffee and thought about it some more. There would be dangers and pitfalls, but it could be done. It would require a little talk with Matt and especially Tony, as it would be his original talent that they would have to use to subdue Chaos' agent.

Claire's thoughts then turned to the man himself. She had felt that first hint of recognition when they rescued James and Gemma. She had felt there was something about him, that they had met before, but it would not come.

"Where are you going?" Matt asked gently, almost as if he were talking to someone who was sleepwalking.

"Up to the stones," she replied, as if he had asked the most ridiculous question in the world. Her hand was on the door handle to the back door.

"Dressed like that?" Matt stepped closer to his wife. "Are you all right, Claire?"

"I'm fine," she said, and looked down at herself. She still wore her pajamas and dressing gown. She laughed. "I guess I'd better get dressed first."

"Why were you going up there anyway?" Matt said as they headed upstairs, his voice low to avoid disturbing the others.

"I was hoping that the stones could help me focus on a Recall I want to do. There is something about our opponent's man that just seems so familiar," she said, already shedding the robe as she entered their bedroom.

Matt closed the door behind them and stood watching as his wife began to lift the singlet top she had on over her head. He took in her still firm and slim body and other feelings started to intrude on his mind. Slowly he made his way towards her, his arms going around her waist and pulling her into him. His lips found the space between her neck and shoulder and began to kiss and nuzzle it, knowing that it would arouse her. Claire turned in his arms and kissed him back, pressing herself against him. Slowly he picked her up in is arms and placed her on the bed.

It was some hours later when Claire finally made it up to the stones, entering the circle through the two largest ones. Her hands rested on both before she stepped in and felt their energy race into her. Her feet found the centre and she knelt on the grass. Closing her eyes, she pulled in all the energy she could as she searched for any recognition of the man that had become an enigma. She searched through all her work, friends, acquaintances, and even people she had only bumped into. As she worked out of her circle, she started with people she had met through others, but still no hint of who he could be. She opened her eyes and calmed her mind once more, pushing down the mounting frustration. Then she found him.

Her eyes opened a little wider as she remembered the times that she had been in his presence. Not once had there been any hint that this man was hiding so much of himself. It had to have taken great skill to craft another persona completely to show the world around him that he fitted in, when in fact he was the complete opposite. Claire was going to have to treat him with great care. She was uncertain what he would do when they confronted him.

Getting to her feet she made her usual circuit of the stones before she left. When she reached the entrance once more, she stepped back inside.

"Red, I need you," she said softly. There was no demand or urgency to the call. It was not even said in her own voice, but that of Carling's, who had taken over once more.

"I am here at your command, Carling." He bowed to her with a great flourish of his arms and a cheeky smile on his lips.

"Yes, thank you for coming," Carling said, distracted.

"Carling?" He stepped closer to her, concerned that she had not responded in the usual way.

"I need you to do something for me, Red, something very important." She turned her blue eyes to him.

"Anything for you, dear one."

"There is a man I need you to find. I can give you his description and I can show you where he is at the moment. I need you to watch him for me, let me know if he leaves his current location."

"Who is he?"

"Chaos's latest minion," she said derisively. "But be careful, he is as blessed with the Abilities as I am."

"How can that be? We are the only ones who can bestow such Abilities and you only have yours due to your original parentage."

"Yes, and I believe I am the inspiration for this man. I believe that Chaos may have tampered with things while he was imprisoned on that island. I get the feeling that for the last few decades he has only been biding his time. I believe he did not need anyone's help to escape."

"You don't mean that he has been coming and going from that island? We would have felt him out and about." He seemed alarmed at the idea.

"I do mean that. I also believe that this man is not just a human agent for him to act through, like he used with Marcus. But that he is actually his son. It fits so well, the things that he has been able to do."

"Will you promise me that you will be careful, Carling? I know both you and Claire can be rash and rush headlong into things. Think it through first, talk with Aroha and the others before you act. Please, promise me," he said, taking her hands in his and holding them tightly.

"I will, Red. I promise. It is not just my life that is in danger, but everyone in the world." As quickly as she could, and without giving any more of her plan away, Carling transferred the information on the man to Red and then pulled her hands from his.

"I'll go now," he told her a little sadly.

"Go with my blessings and my love, Red," Carling told him and watched as he faded slowly from sight.

Carling walked to the entrance of the stones, and as she passed through, she relinquished control back to Claire. Taking in a deep breath of the sweet, clear air that surrounded her, she walked to the track and slowly made her way down the hill, taking in the beauty of the hidden valley that lay before her, seeing once more the history and age of the place. As she reached the base of the hill, she looked at the cottage. Superimposed on it now were multiple buildings, going right back to the original round house. Again, she saw her first family: Tarl'a and Mailcon, her parents down the ages, she saw them as Breena and Cavorst and finally as Jess and John; her brother Ru, who now inhabited the form of Tony; her brother Uven, who she now recognised as Jasper; finally, her brother Loc, who she saw only as a silver wolf. She saw Galen. Although his face had changed, his eyes had not.

Opening the back door, she entered the kitchen and placed the kettle on to boil then set to making herself a cup of tea. As it began to whistle, and she poured the boiling water into the cup, the others slowly joined her one by on and they sat at the table.

"I have a plan," Claire started.

Reaching out over the distance Claire kept her thoughts small, hoping to conceal their conversation and warning to

Red as quiet and hidden as possible. She called out to him softly, with the help of Carling. Claire observed the tone with which her twin used, and smiled to herself. She felt him return her call and she established the link in their minds.

"He is still where you sent me," he told her, his voice like a soft breeze on a hot still day.

"We will be there soon. Can you be ready in case we should need your help?" Claire asked him.

"Of course, Claire. I will be ready." He broke the connection.

Claire noted that he had used her name rather than her twin's, and that amused her even more. He could sense when it was either herself or Carling talking to him now.

"Red is in position. Tony, as soon as we get there you are to suppress him, and we will do the rest and be there if we are needed.

"Are you sure this will work? I mean, if he is like you—"

"I am hoping that he is not quite like me. That Chaos would have inhibited him in some way, so that he is not as powerful as himself. We have to try. I need him not only to lure Chaos out into the open, but also to put a stop to him. Left to himself after Chaos has been banished, he will be a force of evil, and I'm sorry, but I will not leave that kind of person behind for Aroha to deal with." Claire reached out and took her niece's hand.

"He will be dealt with then, with justice and fairness," Aroha told her.

"Okay, let's do this then." Tony nodded and took his daughter's hand, preparing himself to be transported.

"Good luck. I'll be here when you get back." Matt kissed Claire and hugged her close for a minute then moved away to give them room to return with their one extra.

Building up the image of the dim interior of the deep basement, Claire slowly felt the world shift under her. This was not the time to suddenly appear. The room started to emerge, a lone lamp burning on a stool that sat beside the dingy bed where the sole occupant was lying face up, his hands behind his head and snoring softly. Even before the world was settled under their feet, Tony was reaching out to the man. His large hand clasped about his neck, surprising their target awake. He desperately grasped at Tony's forearm and hand, fighting to get free. With the strength of a man half his age, Tony pulled him up off the bed and free of the covers. The strangling noises became louder as he was lifted up and held just off the dusty old flagstone floor.

"What the fuck?" the man managed to get out, his toes scraping on the floor frantically. Tony lowered him down, so his feet finally came to rest, but did not ease off the pressure on his throat.

"Hello, Finn," Claire greeted him casually.

"Mrs. Drummond!" Finn's eyes were wide as he took in who his assailants were. "Thank god, someone found me. Quick! We have to get out of here before he comes back," he blurted out without missing a beat, still trying to remove Tony's hand.

"You had me fooled and played me for the fool too, Finn. But now I see you for who you are, who you truly are," she said, still watching him closely.

He straightened himself, his arms now hanging at his side instead of clawing at Tony's grip. His face lost its look of desperation and turned instead to a self-satisfied sneer. His true personality was now shining brightly.

"I can better you any day, Claire. It will not end well for you should you insist on this meeting with my father," he spat.

"But Finn, it will happen. You should know that by now. Once something is written in the Book of Destiny it cannot be unwritten." Claire could feel him trying to use his Abilities. Tony's Strength was once more working well and she remembered when he had cancelled out her own all those years ago.

"That book is a farce. A book can be destroyed, can be erased and rewritten. It is what is not written that fascinates me. And that book is just an excuse for Order to get people to do what she wants."

"I did not come here to discuss the book. Are you ready, Aroha?" Claire asked the younger woman.

"I am, Carling," she replied, her eyes still on Finn.

"Let's go home, then." She reached out and placed a hand on Tony's shoulder, while Aroha gripped Finn.

The world changed from dank darkness to a room bathed in sunlight—the room that once held Leanna's studio and had become Gran's bedroom until she died. As soon as they were aware of the change, Tony pushed Finn into the chair and Matt was at his side, aiding in the restraint. Together they joined forces. This was something that neither man had ever tried to do before, but both were reassured that they could do what they were attempting. Producing a strong light each, they pushed them together, merging it into a larger ball that they passed onto Claire. Then, drawing down deep from their resources of Strength they began to imbibe the ball with the restraining properties of the Ability they shared. As they did so, it grew on the palm of Claire's hand, and she stopped them before they could drain their Ability completely.

Claire passed the ball of light carefully onto Aroha who raised it to her mouth and began to whisper to it softly. Her lips hardly moved while the words were completely indistinct. As soon she was finished, Aroha raised her hand, she let it go to slowly fall onto Finn's head, as he was looking up at the light, fascinated. It expanded as it neared him and flared out slipping over his head and around his body. Both Tony and Matt released him as it held him fast in the chair on which he sat. Finn tried to escape but found that it was completely useless to try to break physically. He tried to use his Abilities but found them blocked for the first time.

"Argh!" he cried, infuriated. "You will not get away with this. My father will find me."

"That is what we are hoping for, Finn. And by the way, I have a lot of experience with little boys who keep referring to their fathers in such a way, so threatening me with Chaos won't work," Claire told him calmly and left the room, with Aroha and Matt following. Tony stayed to keep an eye on Finn.

The moment Chaos had located Finn, Claire felt his exaltation, which was quickly followed by annoyance and aggravation when he realised exactly where he was. Claire warned the others that he was aware, and they moved Finn up to the circle. For the fun of it, Claire insisted that they place Finn in the centre of the circle.

The Sentinels came shortly after, walking in single file through the entrance and arranging themselves around the circle as their lights flared brighter. The swirls of lights that Claire had worked hard on keeping hidden under her skin were now bursting forth in a dazzling display. Matt and Tony each stood on either side of Finn and Aroha stood behind him.

"Carling, surely we can now release his bonds? He does not need to be tied up so here in the circle. After all, we are not like him," Aroha spoke quietly.

Claire looked over at the young man, the same age as her son, who had tried to dupe them all into believing he was one of them. She nodded.

"No, we are not like him. I think you're right, Aroha, we should release him," she told her niece.

"We shall hold him here, he will not be able to leave the circle," Red told the small group in the centre.

"Thank you, Red."

With a wave of Aroha's hand, the glowing bonds dissipated on the wind and floated away. Finn immediately stood and they watched him try to step out of the circle, but a barrier prevented him, pushing him back. He tried again with more force and this time, he flew through the air, landing on his feet.

"You will not win, you cannot win against us," he shouted at them, pacing like a caged animal. He stopped, then and looked up. "Father."

"You disappoint me, son," Chaos growled from the other side. "Not only did you fail yet again, but you managed to get yourself caught." His eyes turned to Claire. "I am here, Carling, let us get this over with. The sooner we fight the sooner you shall be my servant and the girl my bride."

"I don't think that will happen, Chaos. But yes, it is time we put this matter to rest."

Claire moved to the entrance and passed through easily where Finn could not. Following close behind were Matt and Tony. Aroha remained where she was in the centre of the stones.

"Galen, my son," Red called out to Matt. "You will need your weapons." In his outstretched hands, two large highly polished and honed swords.

"Thank you, my Ancestor." Matt stepped up to the Sentinel and took them. It was like he had wielded them all his life. The muscle memory reached down from the first Galen, as they hissed through the air around him. He bowed slowly to his Ancestor and then went to join Claire and Tony.

The lights were now rushing over Claire's body, heading to her outstretched hands, pooling into her fingers and then coalescing into her own gleaming golden weapons. A staff in her left and a sword in her right. She felt the balance of them and the weight, an extension of herself as she swung them through the air

"It is time," Claire said to no one in particular, and headed to the flat area around the other side of the stones. She stood almost exactly where she had when she faced off with Jack and found Chaos in the same spot he had held the last time they met. He eyed up the weapons that had caused him pain in the past.

"Well then, Carling, shall we get on with it?"

From nothing, darkness formed in his hands, like a shadowy and menacing fog, materializing into his own weapons. Wicked and evil looking things, a cross between a sword and an axe.

Matt and Tony spread out, one on each side of her. In his hands Tony created a burning light. It was bright and piercing to look at, the flames dancing in the breeze. He juggled it casually between his hands, eager to let it go.

All at once Chaos lunged at Claire, his dark sword coming down close as she stepped out of its way, remembering the sting from its sharp edge and the wound it had left behind.

"Don't let that blade hit you," she warned her husband and brother.

Her staff came up and deflected the next blow from her body and she spun around to deliver her own cutting slash at his unprotected side. Her golden blade bit deeply into his ribs and black blood came pouring from the wound, splashing onto the ground at his feet and burning the grass. As he tried to recover, Tony fired his ball of flame, hitting him on the back, spreading out like a sticky gel, searing his skin underneath, making it bubble and sizzle, burning down to the bone.

Chaos roared and tried to heal his wounds, pulling back to do so. He did not see Matt coming up behind him, slashing out with both swords, using them like scissors on the back of his thigh, severing the tendons and bringing him to his knees. Matt soon danced out of the way of the dark axe and stepped back into his original position.

"You cannot keep this up, Chaos. We will keep coming for you," Claire shot at him. In her mind she could feel Carling working on something and tried to keep that part separate to the job a hand.

"I can heal myself easily, over and over. Can you keep up the pressure before your energy wanes, Carling?" he roared, getting back to his feet.

Once more Tony shot a fireball at him. It splattered at Chaos's feet, the flames creeping up his legs. While he was distracted Claire lunged forward and struck him on the side of the head with her staff, before swinging it around and hitting him in the throat. For a moment he choked on the blow, trying to take a deep breath, before his collapsed windpipe righted itself. The deep breath in came out as a roar as he rushed at her, one sword high in the air and the other coming from the side.

With a roll that even a younger woman would be proud of, she moved out of the way, and as she came upright, Claire lashed out with her staff, tripping him up and laying him flat on the ground. Matt rushed in and again attacked his legs, hacking at the hamstrings, before moving clear of the dark one's reach.

He leapt to his feet once more. As he turned slowly to face them again, Carling called out to Claire.

"When he is injured again, I will be transporting us and him into the centre of the circle. He will be weaker there. Do not do anything when we get there." Then she was gone. Claire relayed the message quickly to Matt and Tony in the same way.

Again, Chaos came on, his focus fully on Claire and ignoring both Matt and Tony, to his detriment. Tony flung out another burning light, only this time using it like a whip, catching it around Chaos' ankles and holding them tight. He wobbled a little before trying to slash down and release himself with his own sword.

Matt used the distraction to his advantage, once more running in, cutting at Chaos' exposed back, trying to get to his unprotected spine. At the same time Claire stepped forward and with a great hissing sound slashed out with her sword in a broad arc, while waiting for his own counterblow. The edge of the sword sliced through the thin skin and flesh on his neck, leaving a great gaping gash that spurted blood. Quickly she spun out of the way of its flow, but heard it sizzle on the ground behind her.

Chaos gurgled as he dropped his weapons and his hands clutched at his throat, desperately trying to stem the flow of black blood that now seeped between his fingers. All the while trying to knit the flesh back together, creating a ragged scar that ran around his neck.

Now that he was disarmed, Carling took control and reached out with her staff. The tip touched Chaos and he disappeared along with herself. When Claire looked out of her eyes once more, she was in the circle with Aroha at her side. Matt and Tony came running and joined them. As soon as they stepped through the entrance, a light was sent up and around the large stones. A rainbow of colours, racing around the circle to make sure that Chaos stayed where he was.

"Your lights do not hurt me anymore, you fools. I have spent all that time in the cave with your precious Order, and I have grown quite used to the brightness. I became stronger because of it," Chaos called out to them.

"I am with you, Father," Finn cried out as he came to his side.

"He cannot love you as a father, Finn. He is incapable of love," Carling called out.

"I know that, and I can well live without his love. I have no love for him," Finn spat at her.

Claire could have sworn she saw a flicker of disappointment cross Chaos's face. It was gone just as quickly, but she knew he had felt something for the son he created.

"With his backing, I will be his second and rule the world," Finn continued, and Claire turned her attention back to Finn and recognised the madness that shone out from his eyes, a madness she had seen in Marcus and Jack. A madness that only Chaos could inspire.

"You truly are his son, then. Tell me, Finn, are you prepared to die for him? For he will not mourn you when I kill you," Carling goaded him, hefting the sword in her hand.

"No!" Matt called out. "You will not be killing this piece of shit. I will not let you waste your energy fighting him." He stepped up to Carling's side, his own swords clenched in his hands.

"My father will lend me his strength. You will not survive much longer," Finn turned to him.

"Then, what are we waiting for?" Matt put out an arm and pushed his wife back behind him, moving into a fighting stance, his swords ready to strike.

"Father lend me your swords," Finn pleaded with Chaos.

"No, you cannot have them. They are mine. Find another way," Chaos said cruelly.

"I will not fight an unarmed man. Here, take one of mine," Matt offered and tossed the sword in his left hand, landing point down at Finn's feet.

Finn pulled it from the soil. It was obvious he had never held a sword before. He gripped it in both hands and raised it above his head, coming on towards Matt, swinging it towards his head. Matt stepped to the left and flicked out with the tip of his own sword, creating a cut on Finn's shoulder. Again, Finn advanced, swinging wildly, only to be brought up short by another slight cut from his opponent. They carried on this way, with the others watching on, for some time.

Matt finally tired of playing with him. The next time Finn approached he was breathing deeply with the exertion, and it was a weak side swing. Once more stepping out of his way he used the movement to bring the point of his sword up to push into Finn's chest.

Looking down at the sudden halt in his advance, Finn was confused by the metal object protruding from his chest. Blood dripped down the sword, the strength leaving him, and his borrowed weapon dropped to the ground with a clang. Slowly Matt pulled the sword from him and Finn clutched at the wound that had gone deep, falling to his knees in shock. He looked up desperately at Chaos who turned his back on his son.

"It is time, Chaos. Accept your fate," Carling called out to him over Finn's dying breaths.

"You will never get rid of me, Carling." He started to bring his energy and will to bear and was focusing solely on Carling.

"No. This shall not be." Aroha called out into the circle, her voice loud and penetrating. "Order, it is time."

As her words slowly echoed away a bright light appeared beside her. The Great Light stood shining brightly and went to stand beside his brother who was now immobile at Aroha's command.

Aroha walked towards Chaos and tugged at the small pouch hanging from his belt. He tried to stop her, to keep his only talisman to the world, but he could not move a muscle. She moved back into the centre, held the bag in her hand, and it began to smolder. Wisps of smoke curled up from the leather and it caught fire. It burned brightly in the palm of her hand and when it died down the ashes were like dust, falling from her fingers.

"Do you accept your fate, Order, first of this world?" Aroha asked the Great Light gently.

"My Sister, I do accept my fate. I go to our Mother and will be comforted by her," Order called back to her.

"Do you accept your fate, Chaos, the destroyer?" She turned her gaze to her other brother.

"I cannot and will not accept this," he roared back at her.

"Be that as it may, our Mother has called you and you must obey. Her will is absolute. There is no going against your destiny," she said, shaking her head sadly at him. Taking a great breath and raising her hands, Aroha pointed to each of them. "It gives me great sorrow to do this, but our Mother has asked it of me, and I will obey her. Go now and never more step foot on this world. Go to our Mother and seek her comfort, my sister. Go to our Mother and accept your fate, my brother. I now banish both of you, Chaos and Order, for the world cannot have one without the other. I now assume your places and will take up the care of this world. I will be fair. I will be just. I take on the mantle as the First of the World. Goodbye, my sister, my brother."

A great bell pealed around them. It was a sound that Claire had heard before and it rang clear and true. The Universe had heard the pledges, had heard the request and had accepted.

The lights under the skin of Order grew bright and sped faster. In contrast dark points moved under the skin of Chaos. He looked down at them and raised his arms to the sky. His mouth opened to deny what was happening, but no sound passed his lips. The points in both beings grew faster and faster until it seemed that that was what they were solely made of. As they increased speed, they became free of the bodies that held them, flinging themselves out of the husks and heading skywards. Up and up they climbed, now merging into one as they disappeared into the atmosphere.

Chapter Nineteen

The area around them was quiet. The Sentinels bowed their heads and mourned the loss of their creator, Order. Aroha turned to face Claire, her mouth opening to bring her blessings on her aunt, instead they turned to a cry of warning.

"Claire!"

Aroha's cry was too late. With bloodied hands and a deathly pallor, Finn rose to his feet with the discarded sword in his hand. He pushed the tip into Claire's back, the blade emerging from her front and running red with blood. Claire gasped and clung onto the metal as she fell to the ground.

Tony picked up Matt's other discarded sword, slashing it through the air, its glinting edge slicing Finn's head cleanly off until it rolled away, blood spraying onto the grass.

Matt was at her side immediately, holding her, trying not to make the wound worse by moving her.

"Help!" he cried out desperately to Aroha. "Help her!" he demanded of the Sentinels.

Aroha placed a hand on the forehead of her aunt.

"You know now what must be done, Aroha," Carling said weakly to her through Claire's lips.

"I do, Carling. Are you sure?"

"It must be done. It is now written in the Book and so it should be carried out," Carling told her.

"It will be done, then," Aroha agreed. She looked up at Red. "It's time for you to step forward, Red. You must help them."

"I am not sure that I can. It will bring pain and possibly death to Claire."

"You have the necessary skills," Aroha insisted.

"What are you going to do?" Matt looked up, suddenly scared.

"Whatever can be done so that Claire and Carling both survive. While they remain in this state either one or both will die. Please trust me, my son. I will not harm either one. Help me to help them," Red said calmly.

"I trust you, Ancestor," Matt relinquished his dying wife to Red.

"Take the sword and pull it from her body, Galen," Red instructed.

"It will kill her."

"No, it will not. I promise you."

With hesitation, Matt gripped the hilt and looked down at his wife. Slowly he began to pull. It would not give straight away and he had to tug harder. As it moved, it slipped from her body, more blood flowing in its wake.

"Place your hand on her back," Red told him quickly while covering the same in the front, then looked up at Aroha. "We are ready."

Aroha placed her hands on Claire's temples and closed her eyes. As she entered Claire's mind, she could feel both Matt and Red working on closing and repairing the wound. It was important that it be these two, the love that they shared for the twins was important to her own task.

She found the twins standing together, their hands clasped and very weak. Aroha took their free hands and turned first to Claire.

"To save you we must take one from the other. You must be separated." Her words were gentle and Claire understood immediately.

"Take me. Let me die and let Carling take over my body. It is only right that the Sentinel side of us lives to carry on," Claire said bravely.

"No, it must be me who goes. I must go and finally be with my brothers and sisters. You do not have to sacrifice yourself, Sister," Carling told her.

"You knew this was coming?" Claire asked her.

"Yes, I did. I could not tell you because it would worry you and I needed your mind focused on what we had to do." Carling drew her in for a hug and held her close.

"But what will happen to you?" Desperation clung to each word as Claire began to cry.

"I will be going where I need to be, Claire, where I should be. I will miss you, Sister."

"But I..."

"Time is running out, Claire, I need to do this now," Aroha said desperately.

"All right then. Are we ready, Carling?"

"We are ready, Claire."

The two women stood looking at Aroha, their hands clasped together, and their minds still linked. Aroha closed her eyes and bowed her head.

"Mother, work through me to do this task you have lain at my feet. Use my skills and my mind to sever the link between these two sisters. Set them apart, make them whole and give them their own lives. The twins have done your work, have performed their tasks throughout their lives with honour and always to the best and more of their Abilities. Grant them life. Grant them love."

The bell rang in Claire's mind and a light descended around them, glowing brightly with warmth and love. It shone both around and through them.

"I love you, my Sister, and I shall watch over you," Carling called finally as Claire felt her hand slip from her own.

"Carling!" Claire called out. "I love you, too."

Then there was silence. As her eyes adjusted once more to the interior of her mind, she found she was standing alone with only Aroha holding her hand. Claire felt Carling's loss and it was strange. She was so used to having someone inside her mind that this made her feel profoundly alone and adrift.

"She has not truly gone from your life, Claire," Aroha tried to reassure her.

"But she is not here," Claire said sadly.

"Take your time. They are working on you now, to heal your wound. Don't fight them." Aroha embraced her close. "Wake when you are ready, my dear aunt."

Releasing her, Aroha left her mind. Claire could feel the emptiness close in around her, and she cried.

Clutched tightly in Red's hands was a tiny golden spark. He held it close as he pulled away from Claire's body, his place taken by Tony at Aroha's insistence. The two men now worked on the sister of his beloved, healing her pierced flesh, knitting together the muscles and expelling any foreign material they found. Red cradled that spark gently, keeping it close to his body to protect it.

"It is time now, Red, to go to the Sentinels' home on the island," Aroha told him gently. Red nodded and one by one the celestial Sentinels left the humans to their work and returned to their island.

The room appeared around him, the ancient room that they barely used. As his brothers and sisters arrived, they moved the table and chairs to one side then stood back, leaving Red in the centre. Raising their arms, they began to chant. It was a whisper that passed each set of lips. Love radiated from them to their brother and the precious spark in his hands grew stronger and stronger.

Red added his own to that of the rest of the host. He poured his love that had been there since the moment the spirit had been brought forth into the world. Each and every precious memory he had of her Red called forward, as he tried to help his beloved. Each time she had smiled at him, each time she had laughed with him. Each moment they had shared together. The last being the only kiss they had shared, just before he had retreated into the oak tree.

The spark grew in his hands, fed by the love of them all and by the one who held it. It began to swell and golden sparks flew off, crackling with energy. The intensity of light flared into the room, pulsating now and stretching. Red placed it down on the ground and continued to feed it his love. Pushing at it, willing it to grow and become what it should be.

The light was so bright it stung his eyes, but he still continued to watch it, now almost as tall as he was. Not once did he step away from the intensity, or flinch from the dazzling display of light and sparks. He held firm and believed in her, in the love he felt for her. Then she was there.

As light faded ever so slightly, standing before him, was Carling. Her lights bright and swirling under her skin, her eyes closed, and head bowed. She lifted her head and took in a deep breath of air into her lungs and opened her eyes and they widened more as she took in the first being she saw. Red.

"My love." Carling smiled as she said the words and was soon caught up in his embrace.

There were murmuring voices around her. Softly they spoke, about how her wound was closed and healed, about how long she had been asleep. Claire's eyes fluttered for a moment before they opened. The sky overhead was blue with white clouds moving lazily under it. The sound of the spring bubbling forth its sweet fresh water to tumble down the hill, was like music. And then the face of Matt came into sight.

"Claire, don't move just yet," Matt cautioned her. "How do you feel?"

"Sad."

"Aroha explained what happened," he whispered.

Claire tried to sit, but her insides hurt where the sword had penetrated. Matt gently helped her to sit comfortably, and Claire looked around. The stone circle was empty apart from Aroha, Tony, and Matt. The Sentinels had gone.

"They will be back soon, Aunty Claire, they had their own task to do," Aroha said.

The other noticeable difference was the lack of a body that had been Finn. There were also no blood splatters and no burnt grass from the dark and poisonous blood of Chaos. All marks of the fight they had just endured were erased from the area. All signs of battle on their skins and clothing gone.

Claire wobbled a bit on shaky legs as she tried to stand, and Matt held her up with one arm around her waist and the other holding her arm. Stumbling over to the stones she placed her hands on the largest at the entrance and drew on the energy that lay there. It fed her, but it could not fill the hole inside where Carling should have been. She leaned forward and placed her forehead on the cold stone.

They had been working toward this for so long, but she could not celebrate the banishment of Chaos. The world had also lost Order, the gentlest of beings, the kindest and most caring. They had also lost Carling. Her knees buckled at that point and she fell to the ground as tears crept from under her lashes and snaked down her face.

"Be well, our dear Claire," a soft voice spoke beside her, and she raised her head to see who it was.

Yellow was now at her side along with Blue. Behind them entering the stones were the rest of the Sentinels, Green, Indigo, Orange, Violet, and Red. But he was not the last and Claire looked past him to see a golden woman walk through the entrance.

Claire scrambled to her feet and rushed to her. The smile on her twin's face was as broad as her own and they clung to each other.

"All is well now, Sister," Carling said, clinging to her. "I am here."

"But how? I thought you had died."

"I cannot truly die. I am a Sentinel, remember."

"Carling and Claire, will you join me in the centre for a moment," Aroha asked the pair.

Hand in hand once more, they stood before the Ultimate One. The Child of Love raised her hand.

"Claire, my blessings are on you, the blessings of my Mother, the Universe, are on you. A long and happy life is now granted to you for your faithful service to the Sentinels, Order, and the Universe. You have completed all your tasks and there shall be no more. You can lay aside your weapons Staff and Sword of Order. I now take on the mantle, the care of this world. But you shall remain Guardian of the Stones for as long as you shall live." Her hand came to rest gently on the top of Claire's head and once more the bell tolled.

"Carling, my blessings are on you, the blessings of my Mother, the Universe, are on you. You are now who you should be, Gold. Your light is a symbol of the love that surrounds you. The love of your parents, brothers, sisters, aunts, uncles and the love of your intended. You shall have what has been denied you; you shall now be fully Sentinel. The tasks of the Sentinels on this world are now done. This land no longer needs protection from Chaos. Go with your kind onto the next set of tasks the Universe shall place upon you. Go and be happy with your beloved." Aroha placed her hand on the golden head of Carling and smiled at her.

Each woman, alike as each other, turned then into the arms of the men that loved them. Claire rested her head on Matt's shoulder and watched as Carling was taken into the arms of Red.

"I understand so much now. It was not you he was in love with, but her. You were both so tightly wound together I could not see the differences, but I do now," Matt said, kissing the top of her head.

"I could not see the difference in us. I wish I had been aware of her a lot sooner. I wish that we could have had more time together," Claire said sadly.

Slowly Claire, Matt, Tony, and Aroha began to leave the circle and the group of Sentinels as they joined Carling and Red in their celebration. As they stood on the outside looking in, the group inside changed. Once more they were standing in their accustomed spots, in between each stone, with Carling in the centre.

The earth at their feet began to tremble slightly, a noise from deep underground rose up and at the very focal point and centre of the ring the soil began to move. Pushing up and aside the dark rich earth and the green grass that clung to it, a stone sought out the light that stood beside it. It rose into the air, higher and higher, seeking its rightful place. The large dark rock, the same rock that made up the island home of the Sentinels, gleamed in the sunshine. It stood proudly in the centre, the energy crackling with golden sparks through it. Carling reached out her hand and placed it on the flat surface of the stone and closed her eyes for a moment as she communed with the earth on which they stood.

Carling then reached out for Red, who came to her side taking up her offered hand. In pairs they stood, followed by Yellow and Blue, Green and Violet, and lastly Orange and Indigo. The Sentinels beckoned the small group standing by the rocks that protected the stones, and they re-entered the circle.

"This is goodbye, Claire. It is time for us to go," Carling told her.

"We have another world that we have to shape. Blue and Yellow spoke of it once with you," Red said to her.

"They did," Claire remembered.

"Be well, Aroha, our blessings and our love go with you. If you should have need of us, we are but a call away," Blue spoke now.

"Go with my blessings and my love. May your next task be a gentler one than this," she bade them.

The Sentinels arranged themselves now around the new central stone, their hands clasped and faces looking up into the sky. At that moment Carling looked one last time on the face of her twin, a look between the pair that expressed all the love each felt for the other. Her head turned back and the lights under their skins grew until their bodies were lost in their colours. A great arc of light shot up from the places where they stood. A large and brilliant rainbow in the sky merging into the deep blue above them. The trail was a long one and Claire watched until it disappeared from view.

A large, single tear dropped slowly from her cheek, stopping at her jaw to drip unnoticed into the circle. Leaving the supportive and comforting arms of her husband she walked to the central stone and placed a hand on it.

"I will always be with you," Carling's voice came to her, and she smiled.

Epilogue

On shaky legs Claire began the long climb up the path to the Stones. They were calling her once more. It was a call she had not felt in so many years, not since the Sentinels had left them. She stopped every so often to catch her breath and cursed herself for being so old. She was ninety-six years old and life in the valley since the last and final task had been completed had been beautiful, peaceful, and full of love.

She and Matt had semi-retired to the valley, still keeping their hand in archaeology, and were credited with finding the large town on the coast where Lucan had come from. They had been celebrated and awarded many accolades, but it did nothing to compare with the other of her greatest achievements, she thought. And it had to do with the valley itself.

At the entrance, where the brook met the river that cut the valley off from the rest of the world, Claire had planted a forest. She had taken care to choose the trees carefully and had consulted several experts on the native flora of the area as to which ones she should plant. Now, almost forty years on, the trees stood magnificently at the end of the valley. Their deep green foliage swayed in the breeze as she looked at it from where she stood on the path. She sighed and carried on.

Her children were happy. Bree and John had had three children. After their first, Jessica, was born, she was quickly followed by Thomas and Anthony. Their business was a success and they lived happily in New Zealand.

Callum and Aroha travelled the world. When Claire stopped again, she used her Foresight to check on their futures and smiled. Aroha and Callum would live a very long time. Forever in fact. They had had only two children thus far, and Claire had seen so many more to come later on, but for now little Galen and Tia were healthy and growing fast.

Carrying on, she made it to the top and stopped by the spring that still bubbled up from the earth and hurtled its way down the side of the hill. The hand that was free of arthritis cupped some of the water for her to drink. It was cool and refreshing as it slipped down her parched throat.

Around the rocks she went to the ancient stones. They stood tall and straight as ever, anchored to the centre of the earth; nothing could ever knock them down. Her hand touched the flat surface of the larger of the entrance stones and slowly she made her way around the outside of the ring. Each one sung to her, welcomed her to them, giving her the energy stored inside them.

Making it back to the entrance she placed a hand on either side. Before she stepped in, her mind went on looking at her life. Her husband Matt had been taken from her twenty years previously and that had brought her anger. She had thought that he would be with her until the end and that they would go to the afterlife together. But it was not to be.

She had struggled for a long time with the loss of her soulmate and her brother Tony had moved in with her to keep her company. For another twenty years they muddled along together. Tony was one hundred and eleven when he finally passed quietly in his sleep. Aroha had appeared early one morning and helped her through another loss.

It was hard to watch those that meant so much to her leave her behind to keep going, but now there was a bright flame in the form of her great-granddaughter who had come to live with her. Breena.

Yet another bright child with incredible talents to be named in that long line. And just like her mother Jessica, and grandmother Bree, she had the long curly dark hair and brilliant blue eyes of her husband's sister. But then, they all had the same look, all the family who had lived in the valley. There was always one there, and now another had come. As soon as the younger Breena had landed on her doorstep Claire knew why she was there. She was to be her successor. The next Guardian of the Stones.

Claire smiled as she stepped into the circle and headed to the central stone. The newest stone or, as she like to think of it, her sister's stone. She laid a hand on it now and pulled away quickly. It was warm under her touch.

"Gran?" Breena asked as she stood in the entrance watching her carefully. "Why are you up here, I thought you were asleep."

"I was, but I had to come. They called to me, Breena. Step in my girl, come and join me in the centre." She reached out a hand to her great-granddaughter and Breena took it.

"I don't understand."

"Do you like it here, Breena?" Claire asked her seriously.

"Yes, I love it. I've always loved the valley."

"Do you love it enough to live here for the rest of your life?"

Breena looked at the old woman before her. She had heard all the stories of her Gran's life, of the things she had seen and achieved. Growing up she had not really believed any of them, but now in the stone circle in which she had loved to play when she was a child, they came crashing down onto her. With sudden insight they rose before her eyes, and she believed with every fiber in her being that they had happened.

"Breena?" Claire prompted gently.

"I believe that it is a place I can work and live quite comfortably, Gran. There are stories here that are crying out to be told and given to the world, yours included, now that you have let me write them," she said shyly.

"I agree that the stories should be given to the world. Whether they are believed or not is another matter. And yes, you have my permission to tell my story. It has been a long one." She smiled and her eyes crinkled at the corners.

Claire closed her eyes while she still held onto the young hands of Breena and she passed on the memories both her own and Carling's, far more than they had spoken about previously. Gifting them to Breena to write down and let the world know the secrets of not only her life but also the valley below.

"So much material. I am going to be busy," Breena said with a smile. "But you didn't explain why you made the hard slog up the hill, Gran."

"I was drawn to the stones, especially this one." She reached out her hand again and placed it on the central stone. "My sister's stone."

The hard, dark rock under her hand was warm to her touch and it vibrated. Aroha came to mind and within a moment the woman was standing at her side. She had not changed much in the last forty years. She was still youthful looking, and still had the strength about her that Claire had first felt when she was just a baby.

"Aunty Claire," Aroha embraced her warmly and gently. "Call and she will come."

"You know why?" Claire looked at her.

"Of course I do. Why do you think I came so quickly? Do you wish me to bring the others to be with you?"

"After, when I have finished with her," Claire said quietly.

"Call. She's waiting. I have already reached out to her." Aroha stepped back to the edge of the circle, taking Breena with her.

Claire placed both hands on the stone now. She bowed her head and called out to the space around her the name she had not spoken for so long.

"Carling."

"Claire," came the response and she was there before her, unchanged and the lights still swirling under her skin.

They fell into each other's arms, both with tears in their eyes as they once more sought comfort from each other. The breath caught in Claire's throat, and she collapsed onto the ground.

"Gran!" Breena called, trying to release herself from Aroha's arms.

"Wait," Aroha commanded, and lifted her eyes to the sky.

Around the stones they came. Claire's children, now old themselves, but Callum looking as if he had never aged, holding a hand each of his two young children. Bree and John were joined by their sons and Jessica, while her cousins Jasper, Hunter, Owen, and Oliver, all very old men themselves now, came up from behind. The call had been placed and answered by them to be with her.

Claire reached out for Breena. Aroha released her and the young woman came to kneel beside her.

"I, Claire Drummond, twin to Carling, the One True Child, do relinquish my role as Guardian of the Stones. I pass it on to my great-granddaughter Breena, if she would take up the mantle and protect the stones and guide those that seek it out,"

Claire said quietly, though her words carried to all that were gathered there.

Breena looked stunned but nodded. "I, Breena, great-granddaughter to Claire, do take up the role of Guardian of the Stones, and dedicate my life to them and to the valley below. I will keep the old lore and help those to come, understand The People," she vowed, then bent down to kiss her Gran's cheek.

Breena stood and went to stand by the stones. One by one the gathered group went to her side to say their goodbyes—a kiss, a hug, and tears in their eyes. She was the elder now. The eldest of the older ones and she began to feel it as her breathing began to shallow. She looked into each face that presented itself to her, seeing into their souls and the past lives that had been with her all along her long journey.

Carling cradled the aged Claire in her arms by the central stone as the family joined hands together around them, their love pouring out to her.

"Go be with Galen, Claire. He's waiting for you," Carling told her softly.

"Are you happy, Carling? I have to know before I go. Was it worth it?" Claire asked her breathlessly and whispered.

"Yes, so happy, and it was all worth it, Claire. All the heartache and pain, all the laughter and joy." Carling smiled down at her. "Now sleep. Rest. Your work is done."

Claire's eyes closed slowly, her last look was the blue sky above her, the same blue as her own love's eyes. She sighed deeply for the last time and the breath left her slowly. Her heart was searching now and he came. Galen.

He stood before her as he had been when he was young, so tall and strong, his eyes twinkling, full of mischief and love. She stood from the ground and found her body had changed. The wrinkles had gone, her hair was long and golden once more, not a trace of white in amongst its locks, and her body once more moving as she had remembered.

"My Claire," Galen spoke to her, the smile that played on his lips full of warmth and longing.

"Galen!" She ran into his arms and held him close.

The End

Loraine Conn grew up on the outskirts of Upper Hutt, New Zealand. Her backyard encompassed the surrounding farmland, river, hills, and mountains which she wandered with her brothers and fed her imagination. After discovering a love for writing in English class at the age of eight, she continued to write in secret. It was not until much later in life that Loraine turned what she thought was a hobby, and something fun to do, into her first completed novel. Now married, Loraine moved from New Zealand to Perth, Western Australia in 2008, and became a stay-at-home mum. While caring for her family and after battling breast cancer, a series was born from a kernel of a dream. Loraine has now published the seven book fantasy series, The One True Child Series, and Realm of Dragons, Fight for the Crown. Both the series and book have been released with the American based indie publishing company Between the Lines Publishing, under their Liminal Books branch, using the pen name L.C. Conn. She continues her career with many more stories waiting in the wings to be released, and even more ideas to be written.

CONNECT WITH L.C. CONN

Email: raindropc1970@gmail.com
Facebook: http://www.facebook.com/LCConn
Twitter: https://twitter.com/ConnLoraine
Instagram: https//www.instagram.com/l.c.conn
Web Page: https//lcconnwriter.wordpress.com/